The Inspirational Fiction of Eugenia Price

Can a novel, in this day and age, be both wholesome and exciting?

Can it deal with America's romantic past and still maintain the vigor, honesty and passion of contemporary fiction?

With a reverence for the beauty and simplicity of a bygone era, with a meticulous eye for historical detail and accuracy, here is a novel that, in any age, stands as an enthralling good story and a joyous, unforgettable "good read" . . .

LIGHTHOUSE

Eugenia Price's stirring novel of love and faith in the golden days of America's youth.

Bantam Books by Eugenia Price

LIGHTHOUSE
NEW MOON RISING

Lighthouse

Eugenia Price

BANTAM BOOKS
TORONTO • NEW YORK • LONDON

This low-priced Bantam Book has been completely reset in a type face designed for easy reading, and was printed from new plates. It contains the complete text of the original hard-cover edition.
NOT ONE WORD HAS BEEN OMITTED.

LIGHTHOUSE

A Bantam Book / published by arrangement with J. B. Lippincott Company

PRINTING HISTORY

Lippincott edition published October 1971

2nd printing	*.... October 1971*	*3rd printing*	*.... October 1971*

Bantam edition / October 1972

2nd printing	*.. November 1972*	*6th printing*	*........... May 1977*
3rd printing	*.......... April 1973*	*7th printing*	*.. September 1977*
4th printing	*.... February 1974*	*8th printing*	*.. December 1978*
5th printing	*........... July 1975*	*9th printing*	*........... May 1980*

ISBN 0-553-14195-3

Published simultaneously in the United States and Canada

Bantam Books are published by Bantam Books, Inc. Its trademark, consisting of the words "Bantam Books" and the portrayal of a bantam, is Registered in U.S. Patent and Trademark Office and in other countries. Marca Registrada. Bantam Books, Inc., 666 Fifth Avenue, New York, New York 10019.

PRINTED IN THE UNITED STATES OF AMERICA

18 17 16 15 14 13 12 11 10 9

To Walter Charlton Hartridge

Part One

Chapter 1

James Gould's eyes stung from the heat of the fire he had tended through two days and nights in the strange house at Petersham; his blistered hands stung too, and for the first time in his almost twenty years, he didn't know what to do.

He leaned into the big fireplace to wring another towel from a kettle of scalding water, then knelt beside the pallet where his best friend, Timothy Stiles, lay unconscious, packed the hot compress around the swollen, red-streaked foot, and waited for Tim to cry out.

The room was cold away from the fire, but James walked to the window to press his raw hands against the frosted pane. Would Tim do for me what I'm doing for him? he wondered. Except for his sister, Mary, Tim had been his one loyal friend since the year the fight for independence began, when all the boys in Granville, Massachusetts, had worked together like men because the men were gone. Had the hard, demanding tasks always fallen to James? He had not thought much of this before, but now he did.

His brain felt heavy, his arms and legs stiff with fatigue after the thirty-mile march through a knifing northwest wind—so cold that ice matted around his nostrils until breathing became a conscious effort. On the wind had come a blizzard, the sky dumping snow down on them, the ground turning white as the wet blasts swept through the gulleys and hollows, piling peaked ridges on fallen trees and clumps of stiff weeds. Toward dawn, when the blizzard had stopped, the tall pines and hemlocks stood gaunt and isolated in the silence.

For the last five miles to Petersham, James had dragged most of Tim's weight. Attempting to help an older man drive the artillery cart, Tim had slipped on an icy rock—and an iron-tired wheel had rolled over his foot. "If he doesn't die from blood poisoning," the Petersham doctor had warned, "I'll have to chop off that foot—unless you save it with hot towels."

Staring out into the empty, drifted street through the clear places his hands made, James shuddered. He had always hated the cold, which never seemed to leave his bones from November to May, even inside a warm house. Not once could he remember sharing the exhilaration of his friends when a heavy snowfall brought out sleds and spawned flying snowballs. He took sides in snowball fights, but hated them—not because he was afraid of the bruising blows; he could stand pain as well as any of the others. What he hated was the cold.

In the big geography book at Miss Elizabeth Babbit's school, he had devoured the pages which told about southern lands where no snow ever fell and where something bloomed all year long. In that magic climate people visited their neighbors in winter as easily as in summer. The book described a neighborhood barbecue on Christmas Day! It was true that he disliked gatherings of people and their talk, but it would be nice to know you weren't caged in all winter, just in case there was something you wanted to do like following deer trails until you came upon a herd grazing, flipping their white tails, unaware that you were there because you had been careful and quiet.

He had stood at the window so long the clouds looked to be lifting a little, and only fine needles of snow scratched at the glass. If the sky cleared, the full moon would come out. Tonight he dreaded the dark, because of the fear that was in him. He had tackled a man's problems from the age of ten and had almost always found a way through, but the fear spread now unchecked because there was nothing he could do to end this trouble. Nothing.

If he could just shut out the snores and groans and coughs of the other men sleeping on the floors in adjoining rooms. He had come to loathe most of the ragged band of Shays' Regulators with whom he had marched, burning, demolishing everything before them during the past three months—the winter of 1787. The men who had been friendly, full of cheer and sympathy for each other when they began the march toward Springfield to blow up the Government arsenal, had changed. What good instincts they once shared were gone. No one had even offered to help him nurse Tim. Wretched in their filth and rags and lice, the few who had surrendered with him and Timothy to Captain Park Holland's ailing wife two days ago now filled James with revulsion. One or two still wore sprigs of drying hemlock in their cocked hats, imitating Captain Daniel Shays, still proud to be known as his followers. During the agonizing march to Petersham, James had ripped the hemlock from his hat and Tim's. "Not that I don't believe Daniel Shays meant to be doing right all along," he had told Tim. "Those corrupt Massachusetts courts had to be shut down. You know that, if anybody does. Hill farmers like us can't pay the same taxes those rich Boston merchants pay."

He and Tim and the others had left their farms and sawmills and shops believing that if they armed themselves and marched on courthouses in great enough numbers, they could change the rotten system. In the beginning, they had felt encouraged. At North Hampton, in James' own county of Hampshire, and at Worcester, Shays' rebels had broken windows, set fires and at gun point had kept out the sheriff, the members of the court—even the judge himself. Maybe he could laugh again some day at the sight of Tim prodding the short, dumpy Worcester judge with his musket to make sure he hopped all the way out the courthouse door. That was in the beginning. Now there was only anger and humiliation and fear. Not because he and Tim had gone with Shays but because their rebellion had failed. James felt cheated. Duped. He had obeyed Shays' erratic, sometimes insane orders, had marched for miles over and around the Berkshire Hills through the worst part of the winter, had slept in barns and on the cold floors of houses commandeered by Shays. He had known real hunger. He had done nothing of which he was ashamed except that, along with the others, he had failed. As a schoolboy, his were always the highest marks in his class. In the fields, James Gould expected to finish hoeing first, to gather more hands of wheat than the other boys. His pride in being able to plow a straighter row than his brother, Horace, carve a more shapely trencher for mother's table, chop a neater stack of cordwood had come to be a part of his very being. Why not? There was certainly nothing admirable in Horace's clumsy fingers, even if he had always been able to talk rings around James to win their mother's attention and approval.

By now, the other men seemed to care only about giving up. Exhausted and homesick, they cursed Daniel Shays along with the courts. Their surly silence, even as they bolted down the good food supplied them by Mrs. Holland, seemed to shout: "The country be damned!"

Why do I go on caring? James had asked himself that question before. I still think something has to be done. What good will it do for these men to run back to their own woodpiles and fields when the same injustice in the courts will go right on? Yet, as if his plow had hit a rock, he was stopped dead each time he tried to explain to himself how he had ever felt kinship with these ignorant, opinionated hotheads.

For Tim's sake, he must stay awake. If only he could stop thinking . . . it shamed him that tears again stung his eyelids. There had never been time or freedom to cry. Not since his tenth birthday when his father and William had gone to fight for liberty. What had happened to that liberty everyone shouted and sang about when Cornwallis surrendered at Yorktown?

Dropping onto a settle by the fire, he buried his face in his hands. Captain Park Holland was undoubtedly headed for Petersham right now, leading the Petersham recruits—part of the forty-four hundred Government men ordered to hunt down Shays' Regulators. He tried to imagine what would happen to them once they fell into Holland's hands.

Captain Park Holland. For years James had

thought of this man with awe and reverence. At the battle of Bemis Heights in 1777, Holland had saved James' father's life. As though he had read it yesterday, he remembered the flowing script in the long, careful letter Holland had written to his mother, describing his father's serious wound, but promising her that he would be home for Christmas. Sure enough, three days before Christmas, a big, gentle, black Continental soldier had managed to reach Granville, and in a makeshift sleigh, under a torn piece of canvas, lay a bearded, emaciated stranger. Only the proud Gould nose looked familiar. Papa had not recognized any of them.

James wrung another of Mrs. Holland's linen towels from the steaming water and packed it around Tim's foot. Inexplicably, Tim's cry made him think of his brother, William.

Where was William?

For nearly ten years that question had been a habit of mind. He remembered his mother's tear-thickened voice trying to comfort him on that black August day when he had run all the way home to tell her that William's name was on the list nailed to the Meeting House door. "William is in heaven," his mother had said. "God took him." James had not been comforted. Her words had only made him afraid of God. He was still not comforted. His mother's God had a strange, cruel way of showing His love.

He had never stopped missing William.

How could I? How could I when William taught me almost everything I know? When it was always William with me at night in our attic, where we could talk by ourselves about Indian ghosts and trapping and fishing and how some day when I was a man I would build fine houses. How would my life have been the same without William to tickle me awake in the dark every morning when it was time for us both to do chores? Without William to slip up ahead of me at night to put a hot brick in that old feather bed?

If William were alive, James was sure they would

have both gone with Shays to help put down the courts.

He sighed. Horace makes Mama and the girls laugh, but he does it with teasing and jokes. William made us all happy by just being William. Now and then James almost admitted to himself that perhaps his growing annoyance with Horace stemmed only from the fact that Horace was not William. That was silly. He didn't think he resented that Horace was his mother's favorite, could charm a limb off a tree. He had never resented it about William. But then, he had depended on William.

What kind of God would take William and leave his father?

His helpless father, who had to be carried to his chair every day—the stomach wound scarred over at last but his once quick mind ruined by a fragment of grapeshot which had entered his brain that day at Bemis Heights. Mama would have been better off as a widow. The shock of death would have been clean and one day finished. As it was, she nursed a thin gray form sitting in a chair, unable to do anything for himself, staring into space. Whether anyone listened or not, Papa talked on for hours about his boyhood in York, England, or retold in that soft fuzzy voice how his son William died. "I didn't even know my boy was fighting with us at Bennington. I was there, too, you know, but I didn't know William fought at Bennington. Found him myself—on his back over a big, fallen sycamore—one side of his fine young head blown clean away. So, you see, William not only turned the tide at Bennington, he didn't suffer *one smidgeon*. Died, William did, with glory all around him!"

James remembered all the pillow-pounding prayers he used to send up to God begging for just one visit from William's ghost. It had been a long time since he had even thought of his brother's ghost, but he knew they would all be grateful now if Papa would let William's ghost sleep.

His sisters, Mary and Rachel, he was sure had given up their long-planned visit to their aunt in Old

Fort Schuyler, New York. They had been packing their valises the night he left to follow Shays, but his mother couldn't possibly handle the work and care for their father with only sixteen-year-old Horace to help. The thought of his sisters' disappointment and his overworked mother brought fresh shame, but he quickly blamed it on the corrupt Government. What he had meant to accomplish with Shays was far more important than a visit to New York. Mary would never hold his going against him. Once he had a chance to explain, Mary would understand.

Knowing Mary would be there was the only good thing about returning home. She had never made him feel tongue-tied or awkward because he didn't talk much. He had never wondered if Mary cared about him, any more than he had wondered if William did. What he had worked all his life to gain was the assurance of his mother's love. Kate Gould didn't waste words, and he was never sure what she was thinking. For as long as he could remember, she had been too tired for hugs and kisses and pats—except from Horace, who had always gone charging right up to throw his arms around her. Typical of Horace, not caring how tired anyone was if he wanted to do something. Horace's tall tales and laughter at the table, his way of trimming her old hats with new ribbons and helping her spruce up, did not nail down the loose clapboards or keep wood stacked by the fireplace, did not make good goldenrod or willow-bark dye, did not shear sheep or clear paths or mend fences, or operate Papa's sawmill to bring in extra money.

Maybe I've worked too well, he thought, stretching his cramped legs toward the fire. Maybe Mama is too used to me. Maybe now that I've been gone a while, she'll be different.

He wanted to go home. The thought of being able to walk into his mother's keeping room again seemed the most important thing on earth. He bent over Tim, half expecting his friend to know that as of this minute, for a reason he didn't yet understand himself, the best thing would be for them to go back to

Granville. The burned-out courthouses would be rebuilt. The crooked judges and the sheriffs would return.

The prospect of years in prison for what he had done suddenly became real—terrifying. He, James Gould, would be sentenced by the General under whom his father had served! When Captain Holland turned them over to General Benjamin Lincoln, they would be sent to jail. His mother's dependable son would be a man with a prison record for treason against the government for which William had died.

He paced the room, struggling to put out of his mind the picture of his mother's wide plain face studying him, puzzled at how a boy always so responsible and obedient could have gone off on such a wild-goose chase. He remembered the desperation in his own voice the night they had faced each other across the chasm that his decision to follow Shays had opened between them.

She had stood like granite, refusing to understand. "You were there at the town meeting tonight, Mama! You heard them vote down my bridge. You heard them, Mama!" That had been all he could say, but she should have known how unfair it was to a young man to be treated as the Town Council had treated him—as though he didn't matter. As though his future and his feelings were not even to be considered.

Eight months before, they had chosen him to design and build the new bridge over the Hubbard River, and then his mother had heard the bridge voted down because people didn't have enough money for either their taxes or their debts, let alone for a new bridge. She had seen Captain Daniel Shays in his old blue-and-buff Continental Army uniform burst into the Meeting House while all the wrangling and shouting were still going on; she had seen him leap onto the platform and promise that if the men of Granville would join up with him, they could be sure the tyranny of the rich man's system would be changed—that debts would be canceled and taxes cut in half so that the citizens of Granville could build an even bigger bridge.

He knew his mother had been pleased when he got the appointment to build the bridge. She knew he had worked night after night in the attic, over drawing after drawing, so that his would be the strongest and best-built bridge in western Massachusetts. She must have known that the bridge would have been the first step toward his dream of building something really fine one day. Certainly she knew that he would never be satisfied with the kind of slavish work that barely kept food on their table and a patched roof over their heads. With even one good bridge to his credit, he would have the courage to leave Granville to find more important jobs—houses for the wealthy, store buildings, churches—and, although he had never seen the ocean, some day he meant to build a lighthouse. He had never mentioned these dreams to his mother, but surely she guessed. Why had she begged him not to follow Shays? She couldn't have known then that the rebellion would fail.

He collapsed on the settle again, his head against the hard pine back. If his tutor and minister, Lemuel Haynes, had still been in Granville, James would not have lost the bridge. At the town meeting that night Deacon Rose had tried to persuade the angry citizens to postpone their vote, but he had failed. Only Lemuel Haynes could have done that. But he was gone.

From somewhere in the house a clock struck eleven. Not much longer to wait. Mrs. Holland expected her husband tomorrow, at the latest, bringing his captives back to General Lincoln. No one knew where Daniel Shays was hiding, but with over four thousand militiamen searching the countryside, he had no chance to escape either.

By midnight, Tim was tossing less, sleeping more quietly. James laid another steaming towel on the injury, and this time Tim swore at the pain. A good sign. Tim looked better somehow, as though he might sleep naturally through the night.

In the quiet, James became aware of creaks through the Holland house—nails popping loose in the clapboards from the cold, mice scampering in the walls. The long lonely night was settling in.

The sky had cleared. The moon was so big it filled the window, and there was more light outside reflecting off the snow than in the firelit room.

He was trying not to think what it would be like to spend every night in jail when he heard hoofbeats muffled by packed snow and saw a man rein in his horse at the Holland gate and sit for a moment looking up toward a second-floor window. Then James saw him wave and turn toward the barn.

Fear crept over James—as sluggish and as black as an ice-rimmed mountain stream.

He flattened himself against the wall to watch a tall, heavy-shouldered man return from the barn on foot, flip the gate latch as though he knew it well, and run up the path to the house. James listened to the click of the front-door lock, the quick footsteps mounting the stair, heard another door close—and for the remainder of the night, there was only silence.

Chapter 2

A little after dawn, James crouched by the front window and described to Timothy what was happening outside. "They're all lined up single file," he whispered. "They've got their packs, but no guns."

"Do they look scared, James?"

"Sure they look scared. Wouldn't you?"

"Wonder why old Holland left us behind?"

"You can't walk."

"But he left you too. Why would he do that?"

"How do I know? The great Captain Holland must not be expecting trouble—marching our men off in front of him all by himself."

"I guess he didn't know we were here or he'd have brought a gang of officers with him last night."

"There they go—a pack of whipped pups." James turned from the window. "Does your foot hurt much today?"

"Sure. But I know it's better. I don't care what old Doc Taylor says when he comes, you've saved my foot. My life, too, I bet."

"At least you can talk to me now."

"How long we been here?"

"This is the third day."

"I don't remember much."

"I wish I didn't."

"Will they throw those men in jail?"

James nodded. "Us too."

"Do you think we deserve it?"

"Stop talking and get some rest while I scrape up breakfast. When they come for us, you're gonna need every bit of strength you can muster. It may be a long way to the jail."

Deacon Rose didn't feel up to the trip to the Gould home, but if Kate Gould was to have the truth to pass on to her son, James, when and if he ever came back, the deacon knew he was the one to tell her. Bundled into his great cloak, his head tied up in a wooden shawl, the old man drove as steadily as his ancient mare could manage, too chilled to think much except that he missed Lemuel Haynes. No one, he supposed, realized how he still longed to have the tall, confident, wise young man back in his home. For over twenty-five years he had been able to depend upon Lemuel, who, as an unwanted child of seven, had been indentured to Rose in Connecticut. When Lemuel had worked out his time as Deacon Rose's indentured servant, the deacon had kept him on—a son in the house—had sent him back to Connecticut to study Greek and Latin, believed in his many gifts, encouraged them all.

Lemuel had been so happy when he thought his pupil, young James Gould, would build that bridge. "Few people recognize the boy's real ability," Lemuel had said. "James is so reserved. It troubles me that folks take him for granted. He's a born builder."

Deacon Rose wondered if Kate Gould realized how much Lemuel had meant to her son. The whole town missed the Reverend Lemuel Haynes their minister, but Jacob Rose was sure that Lemuel's leaving for a larger parish had been a real blow to James. Ever since the boy had advanced beyond what Miss Babbit could teach in mathematics, Lemuel had tutored him evenings, but the deacon had observed that their relationship was deeper than teacher and pupil. They had been friends. The old man sighed. Lemuel could help now, but God had called him and he was gone to a church in Torrington, Connecticut.

Driving up the Gould road toward the tall, narrow clapboard house, he couldn't help noticing the sagging doors on the barn and the half-split logs strewn helter-skelter around the wood lot. Kate Gould's youngest boy lacked his brother's get-up-and-go. Poor Mrs. Gould. Her fine eldest son killed at Bennington. Her husband worse off than dead. James, always so reliable, up and gone after that fool, Daniel Shays. But Deacon Rose had come today because he thought so much of James. Because he wanted the boy to know the truth about the bridge he should have built.

He dreaded, as did everyone, having to listen to poor Captain Gould talk of his son William's death as though it had happened yesterday instead of ten years ago. Dreaded the whole visit, but he had it to do.

"Captain Gould is still in his bed, Deacon," Kate Gould said in a faraway, flat voice as she hung up his coat. "He—died this morning right after Horace went to school—the girls to help Mrs. Stiles for the day."

The old man stood looking at her. She was simply returning his look, her back straight as a ramrod, her chin high. He knew she hadn't cried yet.

With the help of his thick cane, Deacon Rose made his way to the settle. "It's been a hard ten years," he said. "It's over now. Captain Gould is fine at last. God will take care of him just fine. You can rest a little."

"You must be cold, Deacon. I'll heat a cup of cider."

More than ever, he wished for Lemuel. The woman needed appropriate words in these moments, a helpful sermon preached at her husband's funeral. One that would give her real comfort.

"I've bathed him," she was saying, as she stirred the cider with a stick of cinnamon. "He's laid out in his uniform. I thought best to do all that before the children got home."

"What about the coffin, my dear? Can your son, Horace—?"

"No, I'll have to pay someone to build that. Horace would try, but bless his heart, he's all thumbs."

"Have you money to pay?"

"I expect so. Enough. If—if James was here. . . ."

"Yes. Yes. James and Lemuel. We need them both."

"At least, Deacon, you know Lemuel Haynes is safe—doing God's will."

He sipped the hot cider. "I expect we can get the minister from the other church."

"I'd rather hear you preach his funeral, Deacon Rose."

"As you wish."

"You'll say something for—me."

"I'll try."

"Will you come see him now? I want him to look nice when the children get home. I'd like you to tell me if I've combed his hair right. It was hard for me to do that somehow."

At the door, ready to leave, Deacon Rose stood holding her work-hardened hands. "God will give you the strength you need now minute by minute, Mrs. Gould. He never gives it a minute before we need it, but always in time."

He had come to tell her about the new vote on the bridge, and he supposed she would want him to in spite of what had happened. "I drove over here to tell you something, Mrs. Gould. Something I wanted you to be able to tell James when he comes home, so he'll know the truth of the way things have turned out with the bridge. James went off—I know he did—after that rapscallion Shays because the folks in Granville refused to pay for that new bridge. Now they've changed their minds. They've voted to build it. The job went to Tom Vernon."

"Because James was away."

"Yes. Won't be half the bridge your son would have built, but tell him when he gets back that if he'd been home the job would have been his."

"Thank you. I'll tell him first thing."

"I keep thinking James wouldn't have gone if Lemuel had been here."

She smiled a little. "I'm not so sure about that. My son has a mind of his own about most things. I doubt anybody could have stopped him. Even Reverend Haynes."

Captain Park Holland knocked before he entered, shook hands with James and Tim, introduced himself, and then sat down before the fire as though he had come for a friendly visit to a sickroom. He was a big man. He spoke like a gentleman, handled himself with ease, but James was guarded and defensive. This man was his enemy.

"Which one of you is James Gould?"

"I am, sir." James looked away from the deepset eyes.

"I fought with your father at Bemis Heights."

"Yes, sir. You wrote to my mother."

"How is Captain Gould? Is he well?"

"You see, sir," Tim answered for James, "Captain Gould's mind was never right since he got home. He never has recognized anybody—even his own family. Just sits there in a chair all day long and—kind of mumbles about the war."

James saw a troubled look cross Holland's strong, bearded face. "I'm deeply sorry to hear that. But perhaps it explains your being here in this trouble. Gould." When neither responded, he went on. "I'm sure you saw me march your comrades off to General Lincoln's headquarters early this morning."

Timothy nodded.

"I knew you were unable to walk, Stiles. My wife said Doc Taylor ordered the hot towels. Gould was left behind to do that."

They murmured their thanks. It would be a risky time for them not to show respect. James had to admit that Holland had been lenient, but it confused him. Almost everything about Holland was confusing. They were prisoners and he was treating them as though they were guests in his house.

"You young men have taken part in a rebellious act of violence against your government," Holland was saying. James felt, more than saw, the power in the steady eyes. Something like the way Lemuel Haynes used to look at him when he had not worked his best. The look itself on the lean dark face was the reprimand, but Lemuel Haynes' reprimands had always been given with the affection and trust of a friend. Park Holland was his enemy. . . .

"General Lincoln was granted authority to pardon as he thinks proper," Holland went on. "I've just come from his headquarters, where I watched the General pardon all but two of your men."

Tim sat up. "He—he let 'em—go?"

James signaled Tim to keep still.

"The men who received this mercy from the General's hands are on the way to their various homes at this moment."

Now James had no doubt. There was something under all this talk. He watched the Captain for a sign that might expose it and hoped that Tim would be quiet.

Holland looked from one to the other. "I doubt that I will ever forget the moment this morning when General Lincoln walked past Shays' men asking what each wanted most. The poor devils gaped at him, then some managed to say that, more than anything, they wanted to go home." He paused. "This is what General Lincoln earnestly wished for them and he told them so—offering sleighs and provisions to all."

"Honest?" Tim's voice cracked.

James stared at the Captain.

"Maybe General Lincoln isn't what some men call a military giant," Holland said, "but he is a handler of men. I've never seen more repentant, more relieved men in my life. Those rebels will never raise their hands a second time against their government."

Park Holland reached into his jacket pocket. "I have here two pardons signed by General Lincoln. It will not even be necessary for you to see him. As soon as you, Stiles, are able to travel, a sleigh and provisions will be made available for the trip back to Granville." He handed one folded document to each of them. "All that will be asked of you is that you act, from this time forward, as though you believe in your country."

It was too easy! James waited.

"Listen to me, both of you." Holland was on his feet now, walking slowly up and down the room. "If you think I don't understand the conflicts taking place inside you, you're mistaken. To you, right now, I represent your government. You are free to go home and begin to help us. Americans are always going to be free to criticize their government. Indeed, we must criticize it, but you're both needed as builders, not destroyers."

Holland could not have chosen a more potent

word. James believed himself to be a builder. Lemuel Haynes had started him believing it by using the word almost every time they talked. "No matter how skillful you are at building something with your hands, James," his minister would say, "it will get you nowhere unless you feel and think like a builder. Builders create bridges and houses and shops and barns for people to *use*. Once a thing is destroyed, it cannot be *used*. There can be no separation of your gift for building with your hands and your need to act like a builder in your relations with other people." James had tried to follow Lemuel Haynes' advice for a while and it seemed workable—even with Horace. Then Haynes had gone away, and James had stopped trying.

"You seem troubled, Gould," Holland said.

"Yes, sir. I am."

"But we are sorry for what we did, James—ain't we?" Timothy's eyes pleaded for agreement.

James walked to the window.

"Don't pay any attention to him, sir," Timothy said earnestly. "You see, he thinks a lot. Why, he was gonna design and build a bridge over the Hubbard River, but there wasn't any money for it because of the rotten courts—I mean because of—well, excuse me, Captain, but what we gotta know is how things'll get any better just because we say we're sorry. I mean, sure, we'll go home and do right, but we'll still be poor. Don't you think it's wrong to throw a man in jail for bein' poor? Don't you think it's wrong for us poor dirt farmers to be taxed the same as those powerful merchants in Boston?"

James looked around at Tim. That was a good question.

"Stiles," Holland began, "and you, too, Gould. No one's denying there is injustice all around us. Shays was right, there. No one condemns the misled followers of Daniel Shays for wanting to set things right. Our country is still new—a new, untried ship. We have no chart of experience to guide us, no map of the past by which to lay our course. We're not yet a decade old. General Lincoln and I—your fathers and brothers—fought beside Captain Shays and many of his older followers in hard battles against a powerful enemy. They are not bad men . . . they are frightened, stubborn men who took the hothead's road. We'd much rather remember their good services to the country than to dwell on what historians may call their disservice. You younger fellows are much like our country. You've grown up with men's burdens on your shoulders and no time to discover wisdom. Your fathers, who could have guided you, have been killed or horribly wounded. We do not discredit you."

James thought, Park Holland talks a lot, but what he's saying makes sense.

"I don't know the solution for our country yet. Perhaps we need a strong central government instead of the loose confederation we now have. I do know violence and rebellion are not the answers. Reason and careful planning by our leaders will one day bring our ship to port, but in the meantime, you young men especially must stay informed. Keep level heads, make up your minds to be builders and hold to your faith in America. America isn't your enemy. The state of Massachusetts isn't your enemy. This new country is your native land. Your responsibility as well as mine."

Park Holland tossed a dry birch log onto the fire. "Well, I congratulate you, Gould, for saving your friend's foot. That called for stamina and devotion. I'm sure you're dead for sleep."

"Did you say my foot will be all right, Captain?" Tim asked.

"Didn't Doc tell you when he was here this morning?"

"No, sir. He just slapped James on the back, made some funny rumbling noises and walked out."

Holland laughed. "Doc Taylor is a little like your friend here, Stiles. He doesn't waste many words, but that pat on the back meant the foot is saved."

The old familiar grin was spreading across Tim's face.

"Of course, you can't travel on that foot for a month or so, but Mrs. Holland is feeling better. You'll both find her an excellent hostess. I leave again tomorrow. We're still hunting for Shays. Rumor has it he may be hiding somewhere around Granville. You can write letters to your mothers. I'll see that they're delivered."

As soon as Tim was well enough, they were free to go home. They would be there for sheep shearing in May. With luck, they could even be home in time to make their maple syrup in April. The Goulds would need to sell both syrup and sugar this year. Nothing had changed for the better, but their pardons were in their hands.

Captain Holland was finishing his lunch alone in the keeping room when James handed him the short letters. They exchanged a few words about the somewhat warmer weather. James wished him a safe journey and said he'd be glad to help Mrs. Holland for board and keep, then turned to leave.

"Just a minute, Gould. I didn't mention this in front of your friend. He's been through enough. But you should know that Doc Taylor says Stiles will be a cripple for the rest of his life. You saved the foot, though. You can be thankful for that."

"Yes, sir."

"One more thing. Tell me a little about that bridge you were going to build."

"There isn't anything to tell, sir. Just no money to build it."

"Is that what you want to do—build?"

"It was."

"Was? Not that much has changed."

"That's the trouble, I guess. Unless something changes, where's the money coming from to build anything?"

"No new houses going up in Granville?"

"Not that I know of."

"Could you build a house, Gould?"

"Yes, sir."

He had not only made the drawings, he had built the addition onto Deacon Rose's house for Lemuel Haynes. "These two new rooms have made the old house look like a mansion," the deacon had said. He could build houses, all right.

"Know anything about surveying?"

"Some," he answered.

"Next to farming and soldiering, that's my work. Ever done any surveying?"

"Yes, sir. A new town road last year."

"The country's pushing out in all directions, son. Surveying is a good way to make a living." Holland stood up. "I'd be honored to lend a hand some day to Captain James Gould's son, if I hear of suitable work for you. I promise to be on the lookout."

James thanked him, hurried from the room—not to Tim but to the parlor where most of Shays' men had slept. Tim would have to get along by himself for a few hours.

He stretched full length on the drafty floor and fell into a deep sleep, a rag rug half covering his shoulders.

Chapter 3

Headed for home in the empty wagon, after delivering six new cedar tubs to Mr. Clow in West Granville, James permitted himself to enjoy the clear October day. The Gould's one horse, Old Pet, knew the road and flicked a friendly ear when James said, "Take your time this trip, Pet." Idly, he counted the straight white birch trunks, relaxed in the warmth of the gold-washed afternoon as the wagon rattled under the arching yellow-leafed branches. Not many birds singing at this time of year, but the blue jays squawked on their way to the ground, then lumbered off with acorns in their beaks.

After only six months back in Granville, he no longer felt a part of the rebellion. "You did wrong, James," Deacon Rose had said after Meeting last Sunday, "but I have to say you fellows stirred things up. There wasn't a man marching with Shays who thought he might be pushing our stubborn leaders into forming a central government. Still, I honestly believe that could happen now. The good Lord knows we need one. Don't see any other way to keep more trouble from breaking out." James smiled to himself. One thing he knew—he no longer felt like a failure. Instead of condemnation when they reached Granville, he and Tim and the others had been treated like heroes. And yet, Granvillians still had those debts and taxes.

He reached into a bag of Greening apples Mr. Clow had given him and selected one. Slightly frosted. Crisp. Just right. He had delivered six well-made tubs. Not a bad joint in the lot. Mr. Clow had placed a lumber order too, and Mrs. Clow wanted him to make her a pine blanket chest. The winter months ahead would be busy. Now that his sisters had gone to Old Fort Schuyler, he missed Mary, but it was a lot quieter without Rachel. Having only Mama and Horace at home made it easier to excuse himself and go up to the attic in the evenings, to work on the lighthouse plans he had recently begun to draw—or just to lie under the bedcovers and think about the future.

He had started to believe in himself and to believe that, as soon as the time seemed right, it would not be selfish for him to leave Granville. His new freedom had begun, he knew, during the weeks spent in the Holland home. Lucy Holland had become his friend; the agonizing months with Shays had begun then to vanish into the spring air. Mrs. Holland had not dwelt on the rebellion. Instead, they had talked about his future.

"You waste so much strength fighting things you can't help," Lucy Holland had said. "Winter comes for the rest of us too, you know. I insist that you stop fighting the cold. Stop fighting the monotony of your life in Granville and spend that energy making plans for what simply has to be a successful life ahead for you! How I wish I could just shake you free of all the tragedy and hardship of your childhood. I can't, but you must. The war is over, and so is the trouble with Shays. Cheer up! I look forward to the day when I can say that I knew the outstanding builder, James Gould, when he was a young man."

In one way being with Mrs. Holland had been much like his hours with Lemuel Haynes. They had read together from the Hollands' library of twenty-four books and James had even felt free to discuss his own dreams. He had told Lucy Holland about his dream of building a lighthouse, and she didn't laugh or appear at all surprised.

Back home, the endless round of work went on the same as before, never finished, seldom rewarding, but even Mama seemed somewhat changed. All the way from Petersham, he had dreaded the first meeting with his mother, but those fears had been a waste of his strength, as Lucy Holland would have said. Mama had stood at her keeping-room door watching him walk up the path and clasping her hands like an excited child. When he had said, "Hello Mama—I'm home," she had buried her face in her hands and wept. "I'm glad you're home, James. So glad. We don't have Papa any more."

The second thing his mother had told him was that Tom Vernon had built the Hubbard bridge. Telling him had seemed difficult for her. Maybe she understood after all. It was hard to believe now that he had ever cared so much about that bridge.

In sight of the Rose house, he could see the old deacon waiting for him out by the main road, a bundle of newspapers under his arm—the latest Boston papers, which still came every month or so from Lemuel Haynes. Back in August, James read that the Federal Convention had finally managed to assemble enough delegates in Philadelphia to start work on a Constitution. Maybe it was finished by now, in spite of the way Rhode Island had acted. In spite of Patrick Henry and Sam Adams and the others who still shouted to keep the states separate and under no obligation to each other. Most of the men with Shays had wanted independent states too, but Lemuel Haynes and Deacon Rose and Lucy Holland were on the side of Washington and Hamilton and Jay and Madison—in favor of a strong central government and equal responsibility among all thirteen states. James knew he hadn't begun to think past the end of his own nose when he marched off with Shays.

The deacon was smiling, his toothless lower jaw wagging up and down. "Sorry I can't invite you in today, son. I've got some letters to write. But we can talk later on. After you've read what's in this batch of papers Lemuel sent us."

James reached down for the bundle. "The way you look, Deacon, it must be good news."

"The best in the world. We got us a Federal Constitution and even better than that, they say General George Washington could be our first president! Now, all we gotta do is get those consarned states to ratify."

As he reached the Stiles property line, there was his friend limping down the path, waving both arms, grinning from ear to ear. Even before James could stop Old Pet, Tim scrambled onto the wagon seat. "I did it—Nancy's gonna marry me! She told me this morning when I took the milk to her house."

Marriage to pretty, hard-working Nancy was right for Tim, James decided as he started again for home. She would make a good wife. They would live out their lives in the Berkshire hill country—Tim farming his rocky soil, hopping crookedly around the dance floor at sugaring-off parties and sheep shearings, managing somehow to keep a roof over the heads of a big family of freckle-faced children.

The marriage would be a relief. He had worried about leaving Tim behind; he had even mentioned it to Lucy Holland and still remembered her disturbing comment: "You tend to be almost too responsible, young man. It's admirable to want to look after your mother, your sisters and brother—even Timothy—but only to the point where you don't hamper yourself. They all need you at your best." She had noticed his puzzled look. "See here, there's a temptation for a sense of responsibility to turn into downright pride. Have you thought of that? Have you thought that maybe you enjoy feeling as though they couldn't get along without you? Maybe your brother wouldn't be so spoiled if you hadn't always acted as though he couldn't manage as well as you. Could it be that you want to be indispensable? More capable than anyone else?"

She didnt know Horace. Oh, she would love him—everybody did, including James—but she didn't know how aggravating Horace could be.

He tried to think of what he could make for Tim and Nancy as a wedding present. Maybe a new settle or a pine chest. Later on, a cradle, if he was still in Granville.

When he thought of leaving, his mind swerved back to Horace. As he had expected, on his return last April, he had found the house, the barn, the harness, the fences—everything around the place—in disrepair. Horace had done only what he had to do. Mainly, what he wanted to do. He had painted Mama's bedroom after Papa died, to cheer her. He had also run up a bill with Peddler Sam for some bright-colored cloth for a new house dress, although she still had to wear her widow's weeds to church. Mama was still praising the crooked frame Horace had put around her old cracked looking glass, but Papa's sawmill had stood silent, the corn wasn't planted, and James had spent every evening for a whole week nailing down loose clapboards.

At the Gould barn, he sat a moment looking disgustedly around at all Horace had left undone today. Bessie and Maude were complaining, their bags heavy with milk. Weeds still flourished in the squash patch, and one glance toward the mill told him that yesterday's lumber had not been stacked.

As he began to unhitch Old Pet, James heard the keeping-room door bang and saw Horace running down the path to the barn, stuffing his mouth with a cookie.

"Guess what, James? Guess what? Wait'll you hear what happened! Aren't you curious?"

"Depends."

"Mama had a letter from Mary, and Rachel got married!"

James whirled to look at him. "You're making that up."

"No, honest. But I'm not supposed to tell you. Mama wants to surprise you at supper."

"Then why did you spill the beans?"

"I couldn't help it! How could I keep a big piece of news like that? You won't act like you know, will you?"

James unfastened the trace from the singletree. "No. I'll act surprised."

"I got a pocketful of cookies—want one? Mama just baked 'em."

"I'm not hungry."

"You think it's good news about Rachel, don't you, James?"

"Sure I do." It was good news. Rachel had talked about nothing but getting married since her eighteenth birthday, and had become harder by the year to live with. He would be glad to have only Mary at home.

"Yeh, we oughta have a good time at supper tonight." Horace followed him into the barn. "Mama's got beef stew and johnnycake besides these cookies. You sure you don't want one?"

"I'm sure."

"But you deserve a cookie after that long drive to old man Clow's place."

"Bessie and Maude deserve to be milked, too." James hung up the harness, bridle on top, and grabbed two leather pails from their pegs by the barn door.

"Aw, gimme those, James. I was just comin' out to milk."

James examined the pails, then handed them to Horace.

"What's the matter? Didn't I get 'em clean again this morning? 'Pon my honor, I thought I washed 'em good. Must have been still sleepy or something. It was kind of dark."

A grin lighted up Horace's well-featured, open face. "You sure have a hard time with me, don't you, James? But you know something? If you'd play some instead of working so hard, I think we'd get along a lot better."

James allowed himself a fleeting smile.

"Don't you like to play ball or pitch horseshoes, James?" Horace persisted. "Is that why you never play with me and the other fellows?"

"Never had time to get good at either. I don't do anything I'm not good at," James answered, taking the pails and heading for the well, Horace trailing along.

"Oh, I know I'm not good at much of anything," Horace said. "But I'm the good-looking Gould, and that should count for something." He laughed.

James scrubbed out the pails and started back to the barn. "Don't you ever think about making a name for yourself, Horace?"

"Me? I've already got a name—Horace Gould."

"That's not very funny."

"Oh, I didn't mean it to be. I just like my name better than yours."

James settled the stool beside Bessie and began to milk.

"Don't you wanta know why I like my name better?"

"All right, why?"

"Because it's a lot more fun to be me than it is to be you."

James squirted him with a stream of milk.

"Aim it at my mouth—I got one cookie left!"

"Do you think you could manage to water Old Pet?" James asked.

"Sure! I was gonna chop wood, but I'll be glad to water Pet instead."

"I thought so."

"Hey, James?"

"Yeh?"

"Didn't old man Clow say something good about your tubs? He's hard to please, but I bet he liked 'em, didn't he?"

"Seemed to."

"How much did you get?"

"Seventy-five cents apiece."

Horace whistled. "We'll be rich in no time at that rate! Hey, James?"

"What?"

"You're not mad at me, are you? I mean, Mama's gonna be so happy about those tubs and Rachel gettin' married and all, we'll have an awful good time at supper tonight if you're not mad at me."

James stood up, laid both hands on Horace's stocky shoulders and looked him straight in the eye. "No, I'm not mad. And I'm not going to get mad at you any more. I'm just going to hope you'll begin to grow up—soon."

"Oh, I expect to—any day now," Horace said seriously.

James mussed his brother's bright, curly hair, smacked him on his bottom, and headed him toward the watering trough.

It had been a good day. He had earned some extra money, the Boston papers were there to read tonight, Rachel was married at last—but best of all, he had discovered that it was possible not to let Horace irritate him. Always before, James had given in to the boy, but nurtured his own anger. I've changed, he thought. Maybe Horace will too.

Mary had been home from New York state almost a week and her mother was still asking questions.

"Is Rachel's husband good to her, Mary?"

"Yes, Mama. He's a good man."

"But it all happened so fast, I declare I don't know how the child had a chance to find out what kind of man he is."

Mary took a deep breath. "Mama, I've told you seventy-eight times if I've told you once, that Mr. Trowbridge is a kind, gentle, loving, patient man. He'd have to be to put up with Rachel. Now don't look that way—you know I love my sister, but John Trowbridge's the one we need to worry about."

"I don't know what's gotten into you since you've been home. You were never snippety about Rachel before."

Mary jumped up, jerking at a tangled skein of yarn. "Maybe it's the way she left this yarn—look at it. Oh, Mama, I don't feel snippety about Rachel. It's just that I've told you all there is to tell. You've got to stop acting as though Rachel's a child—she's far from it. You seemed so happy at first."

"You couldn't possibly know how a mother feels at a time like this, Mary."

"Why don't you ever worry about James or me?"

Without glancing up from her mending, her mother said, "You and James will always be all right."

"How can you be so sure? I mean, James and I have feelings too, you know. Ever since he came home from Petersham, I can see a big difference in him. He's got something on his mind."

"He hasn't said a word to me."

"Has he ever? James and I don't take on about our troubles the way Rachel and Horace do—but we've got feelings too!" She cut off a piece of the tangled yarn and started for the door. "I'm going out to see if James has the yellow dye ready. If he has, my yarn can be dry enough to start your new shawl tomorrow."

"Put something around you. It's cold out."

Standing at the dye vat near the woodshed, James watched his slender, dark-haired sister stride across the back yard, her hands full of tangled yarn.

"Rachel spun this before she left." Mary laughed a little. "Looks just like her, doesn't it? Poor Rachel."

"Poor Rachel?"

"That's what I said." She tossed the yarn into the dye. "Our sister will miss so much and not even know it."

With a long-handled paddle, James punched the yarn down into the dark gold liquid, on which floated chips of willow bark. "You think a lot of Mr. Trowbridge, don't you?"

"Yes, I do. Why?"

"I wasn't thinking about Rachel when I asked. Is everything all right with you, sister?"

"Doesn't the family always expect everything to be 'all right' with us both?"

He watched tears slip down her cheeks.

"Never mind me. I want to know if you're worried about anything, James." She swiped at the tears, making no effort to hide them. "I know you've got something on your mind. I could tell the day you met me at the ferry."

He had planned to tell her that he was leaving some day, but now he couldn't. Not now. "Did—did Rachel just sweet-talk Trowbridge into marrying her?"

"He didn't stand a chance." She laid her hand on his arm. "What will I do when you marry, James?"

"If that's the only thing bothering you, you're lucky."

"Sometimes it's as though you're all I have. Does that sound silly?"

"No." He lifted the yarn and held it steaming in the cold November air. "You'll get married before I do. Girls marry young, and you're a year older than me, don't forget. Is that a bright enough yellow?"

"No, put it back a while. And don't ever say that again because I will never marry anyone." Her deep breath ended on a sob. "Rachel married him last month."

So he had been right.

"James?"

"Yeh?"

"I'll never pry, but there's something on your mind. Just don't forget I'm here—when you need me."

He went on punching the yarn back and forth in the dye.

Two years after he left Petersham, Lucy Holland had sent the book James had coveted—*An Historical Narrative and Topographical Description of Louisiana and West Florida.* He had read it through three times in the past year. Even if the Floridas did belong to Spain—even though it would mean leaving America—his decision was made. At night, he dreamed of building a home of his own near a coastal river, sheltered by tall slash pines, mango trees and live oaks. What if he did have to work through still more northern winters in Boston or Philadelphia or New York? He could wait.

In mid-March winter still clung to the Berkshire country, but on the first day of June 1791, James meant to say good-by to his family. The Gould household would be left well supplied. For a whole year he had carved bowls and made tubs and barrels, extra soap, cheese, candles and dye. He had even bought large pins from Peddler Sam and mounted them in neat wooden handles so his mother would have plenty of candle pickwicks to last until James sent for the family to join him—wherever he decided to settle.

Every night for the past seven months, he had planned what needed to be done, then checked off items on a detailed work list. Now in March, they could set into the maples the spiles which Horace had helped carve on his twentieth birthday. After sugaring time next month, James would never again have to slog through the spring mud, his back aching under the wooden yoke slung with buckets of heavy sap. Soon, he could cross off the sale of their syrup and maple sugar. Then, sheep shearing, plowing, planting—and it would be time to go.

He would sell as much syrup and sugar and wool as they could spare this year to add to what he had already saved from working long hours at the mill, from carving and coopering. From Peddler Sam, Horace had blithely ordered first a new clock for Mama, then a new hat, then a cooking pot, and James had put his foot down. When Peddler Sam came again this spring, no one was to order anything without James' approval. He intended to have enough money saved for two years' taxes and household necessities—and at least seventy-five dollars for his trip.

Sitting on the side of his bed one April night, he found it difficult to concentrate on a new idea which he was sketching for hanging the lamps in his lighthouse. Peddler Sam would be along next month bringing the things James had ordered for the trip to Boston—a new razor, a comb, and the small gentleman's hand lantern he had dreamed of owning. If Mary hadn't guessed that he was leaving, she would surely know when she saw the lantern, too fancy and too small to use around a farm.

He put the lighthouse plans away in his father's old leather portfolio and lay back on his bed. How many nights had he done that? Feeling afraid without William, missing William, wondering through the years why for so long his father could neither get well nor die, puzzling over the mechanical problems of constructing lanterns the wind would not blow out, making fun of himself now and then for being so serious about the lighthouse plans when all he could ever be sure of doing was planting and plowing and milking and chopping wood and running a small sawmill. Worrying, especially this year, because Mary looked so much older, had grown quieter, laughed less, walked often by herself.

He had also been lying on his bed, staring at the

familiar dark knot in the big beam directly overhead, the night he decided to order the little hand lantern from Sam. The first lantern he had ever bought for himself, it came from England, Sam had said; it was made of polished tin, about twelve inches high and tapered at the top, with a design of neatly pierced holes for ventilation and thick beveled English glass on all four sides. Night after night, he had tried to picture the lantern he would carry off into the world some place while he was about the business of making a name for James Gould. "The kind of fine lantern any rich man might carry on a Boston street at night," Sam had declared. It should be a beauty. It was going to cost two dollars.

He would feel strange waking up this summer away from his attic, no longer able to tell the time by the length of the sun streak across the wide board floor. He would have to learn not to worry about Horace and Mama and Mary. Weeks would go by without knowing how they were, but in Boston he would meet new people, see new things. He would be able to finish his lighthouse specifications because there he could inquire about how to figure the cost of hard bricks, how to fasten the lamps to their platform so they wouldn't swing in the wind. He and Lemuel Haynes had studied a picture that Haynes owned of the famous Boston Light. He might even see it.

What if his mother took on and said she wouldn't let him go? He would go anyway. A man twenty-four years old makes his own decisions.

Most of the time, he felt torn between excitement and worry, but the long years of waiting had almost ended. In a little over six weeks, he would begin the walk to the Connecticut River ferry. Even if Horace offered to take him in the wagon, he had made up his mind to leave alone.

He would need the twelve-mile walk to the ferry to shake off the sadness of good-bys—to set his sights on what lay ahead. He would be carrying only one small valise, the lighthouse plans in the big portfolio—and his new tin lantern.

Chapter 4

June-green sumac and elderberry, crowned with wide, flat blooms, stood dense and high on each side of the narrow road. On the air, still moist from the night, were the scents of blossoms and wild animals.

James thought of his mother, standing in her keeping room only an hour ago, waving. "James Gould, if you go, I go too," she had said when he told her he was leaving. "Send for us when you're ready."

At Springfield, the ferry pilot introduced him to elderly Jonathan and Eliza Smith on their way to Marlborough, needing a young driver for their team.

"We've got provisions," Mr. Smith told James. "Provisions and an old wagon and two fair horses. You can ride with us, eat our victuals, if you'll handle the team and keep a fire at night. Mrs. Smith's plumb scared of wolves. We're movin' to live with our son. Lost my farm here in Springfield. High taxes put me under. Too old to start over. Only one word of warning, son—neither one of us talks much. Don't be lookin' for a lot of idle talk, nor money. We ain't got neither to spare."

At Marlborough, James' luck was still running well. Mr. Smith's son engaged him to deliver a fine riding horse to a man in Boston and, as befitted a gentleman with a blooded mount and a shiny tin lantern, he decided to spend his first night out of Marlborough in a tavern, sleeping on a real bed. Who would know the horse didn't belong to him? Why not enjoy the Sudbury Tavern's special treatment for guests riding good horses? Why not experience the luxury of a black boy to tend his horse and the equal luxury of a room shared with only two other travelers?

When he went to bed, wrapped in his travel cloak, the straw mattress felt almost as comforting as his own feather bed. His legs and back ached from the long journey, his hands were skinned and bruised from prying those old wagon wheels out of the mud. But he was on his way at last, alone. Only once, before he fell asleep, did he wonder about Horace and the work at home. Only once did he feel a twinge of guilt over leaving his mother and Mary. He would need a clear head from now on, a mind free, for the first time in his twenty-four years, of responsibility to anyone but himself.

Holding the bridle, he stood beside the restless horse on the Charles River ferry, sniffing the salty air, the pungent mud flats, hearing the city long before the raft reached the Boston side. He was almost there and had to stifle an impulse to whoop for joy as he listened to the din of bells, whistles, shouts, the altogether strange clamor of a thriving city and its people. Twenty thousand, he was sure. Well, there would be twenty thousand and one now, because James Gould was on his way across the Charles River.

The tavern keeper at Sudbury had told him to ride straight out Leverett to Green Lane, then inquire how to find Hanover Street at Brattle Square, where he was to deliver the horse at the Purple Grape Tavern. He intended to ask no one. He would find the Purple Grape himself.

Down what he hoped was Green Lane he cut over to ride beside the huge Mill Pond and then into a busy street he was sure must be Hanover. Who would know, he wondered, if I kept the horse a while longer? What difference would it make if I don't deliver it as soon as I've found the Purple Grape? I want just one glimpse of Boston Harbor. . . .

His conscience silenced, he crossed Brattle Square and rode into King Street, which the Sudbury tavern keeper had said would take him right to Long Wharf.

Down the length of King, he had his first glimpse of the vast, blue-gray water of Boston Harbor. Even the sky was wider than he expected, with no hills to shrink it. Slowly, slowly, he rode out onto the wharf, drinking in the movement and the color, the dream-like sight of what looked to be a hundred ships, their bobbing masts as thick as a forest of hemlocks.

On the wharf, there was even more confusion, more shouting than in the streets. Shops, fish markets, and pubs lined one side of the wharf, and beyond the forest of ships at anchor, his eyes searched what he supposed was the open sea. The Boston Light was somewhere out there, perched on rocky Little Brewster Island. Everything was much bigger and farther away than he had dreamed.

He absorbed the newness for almost an hour, enjoying the fact that no one seemed to notice him. Four or five times he started to leave, each time returning to his vantage point by the dock, reasoning that it was all right for him to be there for a little while, having a good time. He had left no chores undone. He was too far from Granville now to worry about work. "I don't have to hurry," he said aloud. "I've got all the time in the world."

A large schooner was tying up at a slip a few yards away. He rode toward it, drawn by the familiar scent of freshly sawn lumber. Boston must have a dozen or more sawmills. A city this size would need sawyers, coopers, carpenters. It would need builders. . . . His confidence held. The quiet, certain confidence acquired year after year at night in his attic was as much a part of him in the midst of the hubbub of the strange city as the strength in his hands.

Men on foot carrying boxes and bundles, men on horseback and men driving cattle or unloading lumber whistled and sang and shouted all around him. Guiding the horse back up King Street toward the Purple Grape, he caught himself whistling too. Why not?

Chapter 5

He had allotted himself four carefree days in which to roam the brick footways of Boston, spending as little as possible on food, too excited for hunger. At night, hating to part with his hard-earned money for a tavern bed, he rolled himself in his cloak and slept on the Common, which like the rest of the city fell silent by ten o'clock, except for the calls of the watchman. Waking at first light each morning, he began still another day of exploring the shops, buying nothing, comparing his tin lantern with those on sale and finding his better made, more gracefully designed, and, unlike most of the others, equipped to burn either whale oil or candles.

Everywhere he walked, stopping often for a drink at the public pumps, James looked at the new buildings going up, studied their architecture, and spoke with an occasional workman; but so far he had asked no one about a job. Munching buns and apples, he inspected new homes, shops, business houses. There would be work for him, but one more holiday remained, one more day in which to learn the city, to savor every minute alone, accountable to no one for anything.

For a long time he studied Faneuil Hall, rebuilt after the fire of 1761. Inside, before John Trumbull's painting, *The Signing of the Declaration of Independence,* he scrutinized the face of each man in the picture, Thomas Jefferson and George Washington, in particular—men from the South. There was a certain flair about them, a grace and charm somehow denied men who had endured northern winters. He had seen Horace so cold even he couldn't muster any charm; so chilled he would sit in Meeting on Sunday drawing big, gulping breaths to keep from crying. James' determination to move South some day had not lessened in Boston, but Boston was as far as his savings would take him now, and he meant to make the most of it.

Late in the afternoon of his fourth and last holiday, strolling between Old South Church and King's Chapel, he grew hungry for a hot meal. Why not? He had lived mainly on buns and cheese and apples. Whistling, he headed for the Purple Grape. Important men spent time there in the late afternoons, the taverner had told him the day he delivered the horse. He could learn still more about the ways of the city by listening to tavern talk. A stew, with meat and vegetables swimming in gravy, would be just right. When the evening chill settled in a little later on, he might even celebrate with a steaming, frothing flip.

At the tavern door, he looked down at his wrinkled homespun jacket and breeches. What if the gentlemen who frequented the Purple Grape did laugh at him? He had no intention of buying new clothes until he knew exactly what he was going to do. The taverner had seemed obliging enough and had allowed him to leave his valise and portfolio and lantern there each day while he strolled about the city.

He rather liked the taverner, a large man who grinned all the time, his thick arms folded over his barrel chest. He never greeted anyone with "Good morning" or "Good afternoon," James had observed; just began talking as though already in the middle of a conversation.

"Exactly the way I thought it would be," the taverner said, as James walked inside the dark, low-beamed, noisy room. "Yes, sir, I figured you'd be here early today. Figured three days would be enough for you. Come to gather your belongings, eh? Had enough of the big city already."

"No, sir. I like it. I came to eat a meal."

"Been wondering when that would happen, too. You look like you could stand one. Tell you, friend, sit down over there at that corner table with Captain Budge. We're a little crowded today. First mug of beer is my treat, since it's you, son."

His eyes already accustomed to the shadowy tavern,

James glanced down again at his clothes. He had sheared the sheep for wool which his mother had spun and woven into the coarse cloth; he had dug the clay from which the brown dye was made. He was not going to be ashamed. Even though he preferred to eat alone, he would walk right over and sit down with the middleaged, portly gentleman at the corner table. Captain Budge sat beside six emptied tankards and probably wouldn't notice him at all. "May I sit down, sir?"

The florid-faced, neatly bearded man pulled himself to his feet and extended a thick hand at the same moment the taverner set a foaming mug of beer in front of James.

"Sit down, sit down," the Captain chanted. "Sit down, sit down, in your suit of brown. Lift your cup—drink up, drink up!"

A puzzled grin on his face, James straddled the triangular stool, lifted the mug toward his companion, and drank.

The Captain eased himself down unsteadily. "After supper, a flip, a flip. Betwixt the cup and the lip, there will be no slip."

James was grinning broadly now, surprised that he liked this peculiar man on sight; wondering if the Captain always spoke in rhyme.

"My name is Captain James Budge, young man. Sunbury." Twice, the Captain tried to snap his fingers. "There I go, forgetting again! They've changed the name of my town from Sunbury to Bangor. Clean slips my mind. I'm Budge from Bangor." He laughed. "Budge from Bangor. Doesn't rhyme, but has a good sound, don't you agree? Funny thing about that name Bangor." He leaned across the narrow trestle table as though about to impart a secret. "As a selectman, I helped send our most—uh—unusual minister, the Reverend Seth Noble, to the General Court to handle all the fiddle-faddle required to incorporate our town. The Reverend Seth Noble, a poet too, happened to be humming his favorite hymn tune called 'Bangor' when the decision was being made amongst the august gentlemen of the court as to the name of our fair community. You follow me?"

"I think so, sir."

"Well, perhaps composing a bit of verse, or more likely, having sampled too much of the wine from the grape—as is his wont—the Reverend Seth Noble misunderstood the question, thought they asked the name of the tune he was humming, answered 'Bangor,' and Bangor it is and Bangor it shall ever be."

James laughed and took another sip of beer.

"Now that I've introduced myself—who are you? When friends do meet, they fain must greet. But—friend you can't claim, who has no name."

"I'm James Gould, sir. From Granville."

"Ah-ha! And were you among those Shays' rebels, Gould?"

He nodded.

"Shows you have spirit, and no one felt the squeeze following the glorious war with Britain any more than did you western farmers. No one, that is, except us poor souls up in the Penobscot highlands. Why, if a man ate flesh once a week in those days, he feasted." Budge patted his ample middle and winked. "Things have changed now, needless to say, but right after the glorious war, it was nippin' and frizzin'. Some families gave up and moved away. Why, we couldn't even afford oxen to haul logs to my mill. Fishing for profit was at a standstill—no laborers, no salt. Men couldn't leave their farms to trap furs—it was the devil of a time for all of us."

When Budge stopped for another gulp of beer, James asked, "Did you say you owned a sawmill, sir?"

"Indeed I do. Built my first one in Orrington, on the Mantawassuck, opposite the mouth of the Kenduskeag River in 1773, just two years after I sailed into the highlands on a small schooner with my friends the Smart brothers, their sister and her husband, Jacob Dennet, to begin a new life in the beautiful northern wilds. Kenduskeag Plantation, as Bangor was then called, looked the most promising to me, and in a few years I built another mill there. Spring sees the river front crowded with Budge logs now. Budge's Mills—biggest in those parts, if I do say so."

"Is that right?"

"Of course, truth is, nothing's very large up there yet, except our trees. You a farmer?"

"I was. Also ran my father's sawmill."

"Ah-ha! A fellow lumbering man. Taverner! Bring us two more! I can see this lad and I have much to talk about. Ran the mill yourself, eh?"

"Yes, sir. My father was wounded at Bemis Heights and could never work again. He finally died."

"Accept my deepest sympathy. Is your mill large?"

"Oh, no, sir. Very small. We farm too. Depend on the mill for only part of our income."

"What are you doing here in Boston? Who's running the mill?"

"My brother, I hope. I—I'm here to—make a name for myself."

"A man who does not mince his words will never scratch chicken dung with the birds. I like that, Gould. Like my rhyme and like your straightforward answer to my question. Married?"

"No, sir. I can't afford a wife."

"He who waits when Cupid whistles could end up in a bed of thistles. Still, you may be as wise as you are fine-appearing. Yes, fine-appearing." He paused. "If I don't say anything more now for a minute or so, Gould, it's because I'm thinking."

There was so much clatter and laughter in the tavern, he would enjoy himself far more if Captain Budge did think a while. Fingering the thick woolen cloth of his knee breeches, James decided some new clothes might be a good idea after all. Especially since Captain Budge thought him "fine-appearing." Of course, the Captain was in his cups. . . .

"I need to interrupt my thoughts for a moment, Gould, to ask another question. Got a family? Mother? Brothers, sisters?"

"Mother, one brother and one sister at home."

"Sure there's no pretty little lass back in Granville who might draw you home some day?"

"Yes, sir. I'm sure."

"Upon my honor, I think I believe you. A man who lies in his youth, is not a man to trust—forsooth! I do trust you, Gould, and I've a proposition to make. Come to Bangor. We're going to be attracting more people one of these days—primitive and wild yet—but come to Bangor! I guarantee a job in my mills. Can you do engineering maintenance around a big lumber mill?"

"Yes, sir."

"Understand, do you, about the balance of water-wheel shafts and buckets? The temperament of saws?"

James nodded.

"Ever make a timber survey?"

"Yes, sir. I selected all my own timber."

"How old are you—twenty-five?"

"Almost."

"Young, but old for your age, if you follow me. Do you like lumbering more than anything else? Enough to make it your life's work?"

"I could make it my life's work, I guess, but—" He took a deep breath. "I'm a builder."

"Ah-ha! One of these days frame houses instead of log cabins are going to be springing up in Bangor like toadstools." He wagged a big forefinger. "If you're there, established with me in the lumber business, ready to go, you can be a builder! Why, I can hear the word traveling up and down the Kenduskeag and the Penobscot. 'Have you heard?' they'll say, 'have you heard about young Gould, the builder from Bangor?' " The big man smiled. "I like that. James Gould, the builder from Bangor."

"It does sound good, sir."

"The same as done! Come home with me tomorrow. I hold passage on a schooner from Carolina. I'll pay your way. Where's that taverner? Have another beer, sit quietly for a moment, then agree to go."

James stood up. "Thank you, Captain Budge, but I'd better not have any more." His head swam, partly from the strong beer, partly from the proposition he had just received from a man he didn't know and who didn't know him. "I'll walk around a while and think. Will I find you here later? I'm coming back for a meal."

"Most of the night—right at this table, Gould. Later, upstairs, stretched on a Purple Grape Tavern bed. You stopping here?"

"No, sir. I've been saving my funds. The Common."

" 'A penny saved is a penny earned,' as old Ben Franklin said. If I'd made that up, it would have rhymed. No matter. Walk and think to your heart's content. Come back for supper with me here. Share my room tonight—and tomorrow, we head north to Bangor!"

Forcing himself to walk slowly, James circled Brattle Square five times, but he was certain what he was going to do. He wondered what Lemuel Haynes would think of a drinking man like Captain James Budge. His mother, of course, wouldn't trust him at all. "Do you think he'll pay you once you start working for him?" Mary would ask. James liked the warmhearted enthusiasm of the man. It would take time to learn to understand his employer, to know when he was being serious and when he was just making rhymes, but with no more assurance than his own instinct, he trusted Captain Budge from Bangor. Bangor. Still farther north. Even colder winters. Shorter summers. A job in a mill with a man who was drunk when he made the offer. Still he was only walking, stalling, so as not to appear too eager. His decision was made.

Tomorrow, around five o'clock, the Carolina schooner would float out on the tide from Long Wharf into Boston Harbor, and when its sails caught the wind through Nantasket Roads, past Little Brewster Island, James Gould would be aboard . . . looking hard for a glimpse of the Boston Light.

Chapter 6

Bangor, Massachusetts
1 June, 1793

Dear Mama, Mary, and Horace,

Two years ago today, I left Granville. My health is good and I still like my work here with Captain Budge. He is a somewhat eccentric fellow who arrives at decisions on the spur of the moment, but he is generous to a fault. I have received my wages on time and since I last wrote, not only have been given a more responsible place at the mills, but have been paid to build an additional room for myself onto the Budge's log cabin. Both Captain and Mrs. Budge appear pleased with the new room and so am I.

I would judge that in about a year you should prepare to join me. Horace should accept Deacon Rose's offer to buy our house and land. His offer will be fair. Since I am occupied with long hours at the mills these days, kindly request that Deacon Rose advise Lemuel Haynes by letter that I am doing well. I want him to know. I have purchased a large lot overlooking the Penobscot River and hope to have our new home built by next summer. There are 175 people in Bangor now, and with merchant Robert Treat and master shipwright William Boyd at work on their second Bangor-built brig, the signs of growth are all around. We still have no Meeting House and no school building, but Captain Budge, Moderator at our Town Meetings, reports interest in both. Granville will never grow. Bangor will. Captain Budge promises a job at the mills to Horace, and I am certain Mama and Mary will find many friends here. I am writing from my small mill office and must now walk down to the dock in order to send this letter fav^r^ Captain Banks from Castine. Trusting you are well and agreeable to joining me next year.

Y^r^ Obedient son and brother,
James Gould.

Mary folded the letter and tucked it into her reticule, no longer feeling guilty that she always opened and read James' letters first. One reason, she supposed, for staying on to help at the Granville school, was because travelers passing through Granville from Boston always left letters there. For two years, her life had revolved around any scrap of news of her brother; somehow it was important to know—even before her mother and Horace—that James was all right.

Tying on her bonnet, she smiled to herself. If anyone knew how to stay out of trouble, it was James. Another year was a long time to wait, but he still wanted them to come, and that was all that mattered.

"One of these fine days we'll build my wife a new frame house, James," Captain Budge declared. "That's what she nagged me for, you know, when she first learned you're a builder."

James and Budge sat side by side in the cluttered mill office, supposedly going over the June payroll. "I'd certainly like to build your house, Captain, but I expect we'd better finish what we're doing first. The men will be waiting for their pay."

"You handle it. Don't feel like peering at those rows of even figures you line up. Feel like talking." Budge crossed his arms. "Yes, sir, really considered having you start right in and build Mrs. Budge a new frame house when you added that room to our log cabin."

"I doubt I would have had the time then. I had to learn how your lumber business operates."

"Now, why didn't I think of that excuse last night when she was carving me up in little pieces for stalling? All I could think to tell her was the truth about why I'm putting it off—and I didn't dare do that."

"The truth?"

"That it never pays to give a woman too much at once. Especially Mrs. Budge. Of course, there was another practical reason for delay. Until we worked out the means to produce lumber in quantity, we just didn't have material for frame houses. I wonder why I didn't think of *that* last night? Now that we're carrying out your idea of floating those tall pines down to Castine for sale as new schooner masts, I think maybe the time has come to build that house for her. I can afford it—I think I can. We have the lumber. In fact, I'm sure the time has come. Just since we've been talking here, the right time rolled around—sure as a gun's iron. We'll build a two-storied, four-roomed frame house on my hundred acres right away. Mind you, nothing fancy. In a settlement full of log cabins, living in a frame house will delight her enough. When can you start?"

"Any time, but can you promise me a double crew of carpenters and stone masons? I have my own frame house to build within a year."

"I guarantee a double crew of good hard workers."

"Then I'll get right to work putting down a few ideas." James looked at Budge. "I want you to know I'm very grateful for the chance. But what about the payroll?"

Budge waved his hand. "By and by, James. My mind is elsewhere. Now, you have a choice tonight. Either stay in your room and begin to draw plans for the new house, or get all slicked up and accompany Mrs. Budge and me to supper at the home of our Scottish friend, Michael Davidson. You're invited. I understand Davidson's titian-haired sister, Jessie, is due to arrive in Bangor in a few months. You should cultivate his friendship immediately."

James laughed a little and went back to figuring.

"Come, come, which appeals to you most? Drawing plans or spending an evening among convivial people?"

"Drawing plans, Captain."

Budge clapped his hand to his head. "James, I intend to make a fine builder of you, and if Mrs. Budge is right in thinking I drink too much, you may end up running my mills. But alas, I will never see you married at this rate."

"I still can't afford a wife." He pushed the tally sheet toward Budge. "Sign this, please."

"You sign it for me."

"You're the owner."

"All right, all right." The older man scribbled his

name. "I know, you've told me a hundred times you can't afford to marry. You must bring your family to Bangor, build a house, settle them first. Very admirable. Very unromantic. Did you say they'll be here in a year?"

"I figure I can afford to bring them about this time in June next year. Especially now that you want me to build your house."

"Need a loan?"

"I don't like loans."

Budge sighed. "James, you are definitely the salt of the earth. Too bad. You'd enjoy life more if you weren't." He looked out the window in both directions, then whisked a bottle from his desk drawer. "You know I'm uncorking this far too often?" When James didn't answer, the Captain took a drink, wiped his beard on his sleeve, replaced the bottle, "Wouldn't admit it to her, but Mrs. Budge is right. I'm drowning my troubles. The juice from the grape puts the heart in shape." He stood up. "Pay the men, son, and hie yourself to your drawing board if you must. As for me? I go to charm the ladies." He hiccupped. "All except Mrs. Budge, that is."

Alone in his room that evening, James lighted his pipe and began to make a rough sketch of the kind of house he thought Mrs. Budge would want. Poor Captain. Everyone else said "Poor Mrs. Budge." He frowned a little, both at his own still puzzling defense of the Captain and because the roof line he had just drawn didn't balance the wide central chimney. Crumpling the paper, he began again. Why did such a good, generous, lovable man have to drink? In spite of their gossip, the people of Bangor went right on electing Budge a selectman year after year. There was not a man in town more prominent than his employer.

James held the sketch at arm's length. The roof line still did not suit him. A kitchen wing would help, but Budge had said only four rooms. I've got to get it right before I show it to Mrs. Budge. Maybe the best way I can help the Captain is to please her with this new house. I might drink too, if I had to listen to that woman every day. He laughed aloud, rather enjoying the sound of it. Until he had met Captain Budge, there hadn't been much to laugh about. Oh, he remembered good times with Lemuel Haynes, but he had laughed then to please an older man whom he admired. He and the Captain enjoyed jokes on each other—man to man.

He laid down his quill and went to the open window. Enough light remained for him to see three trading schooners at anchor. Schooners in the harbor meant money in James Gould's pocket. Four log cabins had been built for new families since his arrival. Now, he was about to design and build a frame house for one of the town's leading citizens. "My first house," he whispered, "and I'm not scared." He knew his future in Bangor depended upon the success of this house. A risky way to begin, because even those who sympathized with her considered Mrs. Budge sharp-tongued and opinionated. "Impossible to please," the Captain had warned, but James meant to please her, not only for his employer's sake but for his own. With any kind of luck on the Budge house, he mused, and if Bangor continues to grow, in ten years I could save all the money I'll need to go South in style and live well until I can locate in a city where I'll be able to build great houses.

Watching the lavender afterglow deepen to purple, he experienced a rush of gratitude toward Captain Budge. I still have so much to learn, he thought, but he's given me my chance to prove what I've always known—that *I can build a good house.* I can learn here by building. I'll order some books from Boston and spend every spare hour studying classical revival designs—the kind of architecture popular in the town and country homes of wealthy men both North and South. Even if Captain Budge did specify a simple, two-storied, four-roomed dwelling, I can work my own ideas into its construction. And with each new house I build in Bangor, people will be more and more convinced that James Gould is the best.

I aim to build big houses, he thought, and some

day I'll build my lighthouse—just because I know I can. Then, later on, in a pleasant southern city, I'll put up a fine house of my own. He drew a deep breath of cool, pine-scented air. My contribution to this country will be fine buildings. Nothing will stop me because *I know I can.*

Back at his sketch, he smiled to himself. Dreaming would not fix that clumsy roof line on this first small, plain house—his responsibility now—June 20, 1793. He studied the drawing a moment and saw suddenly that the line of the roof was not too steep, as he had thought at first; it was too flat. A few quick changes, and the proportions were right. Tomorrow, if the Budges approved, he would discuss dimensions, figure and order the lumber and field stone, and the building could begin. Captain Budge had promised extra workmen. With any cooperation from the weather and Mrs. Budge, he saw no reason why he couldn't be finished before Christmas.

James earnestly recommended rough-split shingles for siding at least on the north end of the house, explaining to Mrs. Budge that grooved shingles, finished lightly with a drawknife, would shed rain and outlast clapboards.

"I like the design in general, but we will have hand-riven *clapboards* all around the house, Mr. Gould," she answered, giving him no chance to argue.

James suggested no overhang, attempting to convince her that his builder's eye saw overhangs as ill-shapen. "Your house will be the talk of Bangor, ma'am. It should be as pleasing to the eye as possible."

"We will have a *framed overhang,* Mr. Gould, and I insist that you carve the pendules yourself. One thing you must learn, young man, is that *women* know what pleases the eye!"

He had tried and failed to enlist Captain Budge's help in persuading her that the ash pit beneath her oven in the side of the eight-foot chimney would be at ground level—not two feet up from the floor, as she wanted—and definitely not covered with a wooden door to match the paneling on the fireplace wall.

"Mr. Gould, it is *I* who removes ashes to store for the soap which *I* make. If my husband were more help around the house, *perhaps* your idea might be used. Fire hazard or not, *my* oven ash pit will be elevated so that *I* do not break *my* back in order to empty it!"

"Very well, Mrs. Budge, but it must not have a wooden door. It's too dangerous."

"It will *have* a wooden door. Line it with sheet iron, if you like, but outside—wood, to blend with the wall."

"I refuse to pity you, James," Captain Budge said as they worked over the November payroll. "You and I chose the lumber, had our own way with the use of that sturdy queen-post truss supporting the roof, built a stone chimney instead of wood, approved the foundation timbers. Considering that we had Mrs. Budge to contend with, I refuse to pity you—or me. You have borne your burden well—someone should ring a bell!"

James looked up from his figuring, not amused.

"I beg you, James, don't bring your gloom here into our mill sanctuary! You've a long, angular, handsome face. But for the past five months, it's been getting longer than ever—and not handsome. Gloomy!"

James sighed. "I guess I'm—discouraged."

"Discouraged? Why, any man who's managed to come through almost half a year of constant hammering by Mrs. Budge is a man indeed! You've not only built a fine house without neglecting your work at the mill, you've made Mrs. Budge the proudest woman in the state of Massachusetts!"

James stared at him. "Mrs. Budge is—proud?"

"You don't understand my wife. Just wait 'til you hear her extol your virtues before our guests the night of our welcoming party."

"But, except for the framing, the part that doesn't show, she rejected almost every idea I had!"

"You *don't* understand Mrs. Budge," he repeated.

"Of course, neither do I entirely. But you have only one more period requiring patience, lad. Soon after we move into our new abode next month, she will give her party. Then listen to her. You'll see I'm right."

"I dread the party."

"Nonsense. Are you ashamed of your house?"

"No. I—just don't feel it's mine."

"It *is* yours!" He slapped James on the back. "You've built a good house. It'll outlast even Mrs. Budge. Of course, I doubt the carpenters feel too kindly toward you. You worked their fingers to the bone, from dawn to dark, but you made your goal. We're moving in just when you predicted, and my charming tormentor will sing your praises. Remember, son, give in to a woman and you'll—you'll—" He snapped his fingers. "Now, I wonder why I, of all people, can't think of a rhyme for 'woman'?"

"I can see you're pleased with it, Captain. That helps. I suppose I just had the wrong idea of what it would be like to build a house."

He could feel the Captain looking at him. "You can tell me now, lad. It *is* your first complete house, isn't it?"

"Yes, sir."

"So rejoice! You've had your trial by fire and you came out solid gold. Mark my word, from now on, the way is clear—lift up your head and be of good cheer!"

"And would you believe it? Mr. Gould even thought about the beauty and symmetry of the outside of our house, as well as my convenience within. Why, our rived clapboards cover not just the front, they go all around! Tapering in width, because Mr. Gould insisted—all the way to the peak of our gable. That young man is simply marvelous!"

From upstairs in his room in the new house, James could hear Mrs. Budge's penetrating voice praising his work to the early arrivals at the welcoming party. His spirits lifted. It was a well-built house. Captain Budge had convinced him that everyone would think it a palace, since they all still lived in log cabins. Perhaps standing between the Budges as they received their guests in the parlor wouldn't be so bad after all.

He pulled on dark gray pantaloons, fussed with the pink, pleated, slightly large shirt which Captain Budge insisted he borrow for the occasion. His waistcoat buttoned, he slipped into his maroon tail coat and went to the looking glass. A successful-appearing young gentleman looked back at him—lean, hard of jaw, high wide forehead, solemn dark eyes, the proud Gould nose. He stepped closer to comb his almost-shoulder-length hair, tried to flatten the thick brown wave—and decided it looked rather well full. Not a weak face, certainly. Perhaps not handsome, but the face of a man who knew what he wanted and who dared to believe that he was on his way at last.

Between Captain and Mrs. Budge downstairs, he received the compliments of the Jacob Dennets, the Simon Crosbys, the Andrew Websters, the Robert Treats, the Thomas Howards, the Reverend Seth Noble and his new wife. He had worried that he might be tongue-tied before all those prominent people, but they talked so much, he got along quite well and with little more than "Good evening" and "Thank you."

"Right here and now, Gould." Major Robert Treat declared, "I want to engage you to do the same—or better. Will you build a frame house for me? Bigger and better than this one?"

"Why, yes, Major. I'll try."

"No better, Treat," Captain Budge bellowed. "Bigger, perhaps; you've a family, after all—but not better! A house as good, indeed he could—but better? better? Better . . . better . . . what rhymes with better?"

Everyone laughed. They'd never heard the Captain stuck before for a rhyme—and during the merriment two more guests entered the crowded parlor.

James stopped laughing to stare. The gentleman, he knew, was Michael Davidson. The young lady—dressed in bright green, her shining red hair piled under the scoop of her bonnet—looked back at James for an instant, then turned to speak to someone.

"I understand the Budges have the finest, most up-to-date attic smoke room in Bangor, Mr. Gould." He only half heard Major Treat's remark. The girl was walking toward him now on Michael Davidson's arm. Dimly, James realized that Budge had asked a question about how the cornice had been cut, but he was looking at the heart-shaped face, the arrogant nose, the slanting brown eyes set in her proud head like a doe's eyes.

For the year, the hour, the few seconds it took her to reach him, he felt himself loosed and hurtling, falling free—no chance to turn back, to catch himself. He heard his own blood, louder than Mrs. Budge's voice: "Good evening, Mr. Davidson. You know our Mr. Gould, I'm sure . . . so, your lovely sister decided so soon after her arrival to join us after all. How nice to see you, my dear. Welcome to our new home! Miss Jessie Davidson, may I present the architect and builder, Mr James Gould?"

He bowed over the small, gloved hand, received her compliment on the house—spoken with a soft Scottish brogue—excused himself almost at once and hurried out a side door.

He crossed the dark, newly graded back yard, half stumbling, past the woodshed, following the rail fence just completed yesterday, until he reached his makeshift builder's shack.

Palms pressed against the rough sawn wood, he tried to think. No one had taught him how to build a house. He had always known. In a minute or so, away from the noise of the party, he would begin to grasp how to handle this unexplored part of his own nature. If he could be alone for just a little while, he would know what to do with the wildness, the utter recklessness which he already recognized as love. In this too, as with the building of his first house, he would be able to trust the part of himself which had always *known*.

The darkness over the river roared with primal throbs from the throats of a thousand frogs. Far across on the other bank, one frog drummed above the rest . . . or was it the lone, insistent drumming of his own heart?

"Isn't this a peculiar place for the honored guest to be keeping himself—out here with the frogs?"

In the pale light from the star-strewn sky, he could see Jessie Davidson coming toward him, alone.

Chapter 7

For the first time since the night they met, almost six months ago, James was going to be alone with Jessie. He had seen her every day as he worked on the Robert Treat place, but always at the noon meal with her brother present, or on the job when she walked across the meadow—often through snow and spring mud—to inspect and praise his work. Even then, carpenters or stone masons were around so that only his eyes spoke of love as he showed her the shape of the Treat's big fireplace, explained the angle of the stair to the second floor, the sketches he had made for the front door fanlight. He had held her in his arms only once—the night she had followed him to the builder's shack.

They would be alone today in his canoe on the river, and she had suggested it. "You've done nothing but work since we met," she complained. "The Treat house can get along without you at least for one afternoon—I know it can!" His canoe was scrubbed, the paddles oiled. The sky was high, a clear, northern spring sky, the sun warm for May.

It still seemed too good to believe that he was in the finishing stages of his second house, more commodious than the Budges', and with a kitchen wing. If the good weather held, the Treats could be moved in by the time James' family arrived—according to Mary's letter, near the end of June. Jessie had talked him out of his guilt that his own place would not even be started and had seemed to enjoy helping him work out plans for temporary living quarters. Mary wrote of her pleasure that they would all be there for the building of their new home. So it was settled: the Goulds would live temporarily in the Budges' vacant log cabin. Jessie would help him clean and pretty it up in plenty of time. Best of all, Jessie never tired of discussing ideas for the new Gould house. There was little doubt in his mind but that she meant one day to live there as his wife.

He pulled on his new tight knitted pantaloons, hoping Jessie would dress warmly. He would be careful to stay away from the cool shade along the riverbank. He would be careful of Jessie. Always.

Buttoning his shirt, he tried to imagine living with her in their own house on the big lot overlooking the Penobscot, or just walking hand in hand through rooms he had built to please her. His family would live there too, but he would build it to Jessie's liking, and especially their quarters upstairs, where he could lie beside her at night, could possess her in the fury of their love, the peace of their contentment.

For the first few minutes on the river, Jessie talked steadily about all she had heard in praise of both the Budge and the Treat houses. "I'm proud of you," she said simply, tilting her head, a smile in her voice. " 'Guid mornin' to Your Majesty! May Heaven augment your blisses. . . .' Do you know the Scottish bard, Robert Burns, James?"

"No, I'm afraid I don't."

"Then I must read to you sometime. I own a copy of the first volume of his ever published. Those lines I recited just now are from a poem called 'A Dream,' "

"Jessie. . . ."

"Yes?"

"I love you." He watched her smile fade, her eyes grow suddenly wistful. "I love you," he repeated.

Looking out over the river, she murmured, "I know."

"But—you're frowning. Why?"

"Because I'm sure you want to marry me."

"I do, oh, I do. More than anything in the world. I want to marry you and build the Gould house—for us."

She looked at him, her brown eyes honest, seeming neither sad nor happy. Puzzled. "I know you want to do—all that." She touched his hand. "And—there are times I want to marry you."

James laid down the paddle, took her hand in both

of his. "I was afraid to hope. But I have been hoping. I'm not going to stop."

Relieved, he saw her smile return. "Any lass would be fortunate to marry you, James. I wondered if you would ever ask me."

"I'm not—very good with words," he said. "Do you love me, too?"

"Yes, I do love you, I think, in many ways. Perhaps in the ways that matter." Her eyes were serious again. "But do you understand what I mean when I tell you I wish you—laughed more? Were jollier?"

James could feel his face redden.

"Forgive me," she went on. "But, for many of my childhood years, as I remember them—I was weeping. In our old, dark stone house in Dundee, first my mother lay in her coffin, when I was eight. When I was eleven, my father. Then, when I went away to school at thirteen, I cried throughout the long carriage trip home because I knew I would see the new graves of my young sisters whom I adored—twins. My last aunt died just before I left Scotland to come here. I need to laugh, you see? Over and over again I tell myself there will come a time when someone besides my brother, Michael, someone close to me will want to laugh with me." A sudden smile lighted her face and she threw out her arms as though to embrace the whole earth. "I've wanted so long to—play! To be giddy and make jokes and—" She broke off. "Do you understand at all when I say I want to pick flowers, make a garland and throw it around the neck of the man I love?"

Desperately, James tried to manage a smile in return. "But couldn't you teach me to laugh the way you mean? I'd try, Jessie, I'd try!"

They were drifting toward the bank of the river and James quickly guided the canoe back to the sunlight.

"You're keeping me out of the chilly shade, aren't you? You are a very, very dear person. Will your mother like me?"

"She'll like you fine, but—Mama's a lot like me, I'm

afraid. She doesn't joke much either. She's worked so hard all her life."

Jessie smiled. "If I set out to make her like me, she will. Do I sound full of pride?"

He shook his head. "Maybe you can teach Mama to laugh too."

"Is your sister older than you?"

He brightened. "Mary's a year older. My favorite in the whole family."

"And your brother? Is he—like you?"

"Horace? He isn't anything like me. Light, curly hair, stockier—nothing like me."

"He's younger?"

"Four years."

"Is hard work all you think about in the Gould family? Hard work and success?"

He smiled. "Not Horace."

"Sometimes I wonder if I'm still too much a child even to think about becoming a man's wife. Part of me loves you. Part of me wants to be your wife. I'm not sure that's enough."

"For me it is. I'll help you. I'll help you learn to love me the way you've always dreamed about."

"Will you, James? Will you, please—do that?"

He wanted to be alone after he took her home, to relive the golden hour with her, but there was work to be done. The largest lumber shipment Budge's Mills had ever filled must be inspected before the loading could begin tomorrow. Trusting only himself to get the inspection under way, he hurried through the jumble of old chairs and packing boxes in Captain Budge's office, reached his own cubicle and stopped short. A gaunt, bearded skeleton of a man pulled himself slowly to his feet from James' chair.

"I've been waiting for you, Gould," the man said hoarsely, trying to stand erect. "I see you don't recognize me. Wouldn't be surprised to learn I've dropped seventy or eighty pounds of weight since you saw me last at Petersham some six years ago."

"Captain Holland!" The men shook hands. "Please do sit down, sir."

"Thank you. I sail for Boston late this afternoon. Just completed a survey of the great east branch of the Penobscot, from the head of the tide to its source. Set off a tract six miles wide on each side of the river for the use of the Penobscot Indians. The General Court appointed my old friend Jonathan Maynard and me to handle it. Nearly did us both in. Wild country."

Still finding it hard to believe that this wan, shaking man was Park Holland, James asked, "Have you eaten? Do you need a bed? I can drive you to Captain Budge's house in the supply wagon. You're welcome to my room there."

"No, thank you, Gould. I've been well fed. Maynard and I spent the night with the Robert Treats. Looked over his fine new house you're about to finish. You must be proud of it. I was taken aback, I can tell you, when Major Treat told me young James Gould from Granville had designed and built it. My congratulations." He smiled. "I considered offering you a place on my surveying crew. Look at me. You were fortunate I didn't."

"I'm well satisfied in Bangor, Captain Holland."

"Glad to hear it. But I have news which could play a part in your future, should you ever decide to move on. Seems a mite ridiculous in view of your present success. Still, I remember promising you I'd be on the lookout, and Mrs. Holland told me of your interest—at one time anyway—in the southern part of the country."

"Yes. I still hope to go South some day."

"Well, because of the trouble with Algiers, Congress is likely to pass an act to provide naval armament for the United States. Vice President John Adams is strongly in favor. President Washington is said to agree. It will be next year, apparently, before the act is passed, but when it is, the President will have the option to build a fleet of forty-four- and thirty-six-gun frigates. Live oak will be needed in large supply. Such oak, of course, comes from the southern coast. There should be a fine opportunity for a young man with your knowledge of timber to assist in the survey."

James' thoughts were racing. A year before the act might pass. It would be more than a year before a timber surveyor would be appointed. Congress moves slowly. He could see his family settled in Bangor, where Horace would have a good job. He and Jessie could leave for the South together!

"How did you find out about this way up there in the wilds, Captain?"

"I only heard last night when we arrived here. Major Treat learned it through his close friend, the master shipwright, Joshua Humphreys, in Philadelphia. I believe Humphreys has already been engaged by the Government to design the frigates. Robert Treat simply had not thought of you in connection with the survey."

"Did you tell him of my interest in the South, sir?"

"I did not. Never pays to spread news of any kind around a small place like Bangor. Might damage your prospects here."

"Thank you."

"Now, you'll know best, Gould. In no way do I want this to cause dissatisfaction for you. You're respected here. Well liked. I don't think Treat or any other leading citizen would appreciate my telling you. Just keeping an old promise." He stood up. "A young lady in the picture yet?"

"Indeed there is!"

"Good. My best wishes to you both. And my regards to your family when they come. In the near future, I understand."

"The end of next month."

"You must be important to them. It's a long, hard journey." Holland held out his hand. "Well, good-by, young man. You've turned out well. I'll take Mrs. Holland a glowing report."

James watched Park Holland walk haltingly down the path toward the dock.

He was not ready, yet, even to consider the Government survey. That would depend entirely upon

Jessie. There would be time to build the new Gould home, time for Jessie to learn to love him as he loved her. Seeing Holland again had sent his spirits soaring.

Maybe, with Jessie as his wife, he could even learn to laugh easily, to make jokes like Captain Budge or Horace.

Chapter 8

When the spring mud began to dry, the pink lady's-slippers and wake-robins blooming along James' shortcut from the mills to the almost completed Treat house were a welcome sight. He couldn't recall a winter when he had worked so hard. Still, he could cover the mile or so on foot two, often three times a day, yet feel as fresh in the evening as on his first hike to the construction site before sunrise each morning. He owned a good horse, but the walk alone from one job to another had become somehow important. A man in love needed a little time to himself to enjoy the state of his own heart.

He slept well every night and awakened alive and eager before dawn because Jessie would be a part of every day. At midmorning, after several hours of work at his mill office, he would hurry down the woodsy path to the Davidson log cabin across from the Treat house to find her waiting for him, a surprise lunch in the now familiar woven basket. She loved to watch him work, and her interest and praise transformed into acts of magic mundane jobs such as knicking a wooden trunnel for the porch railing, to prevent its working out in the cold, or shiplapping a joint so the dry icy air couldn't pry it apart. Hard work was no longer laborious. He had become a craftsman whose every move was now motivated by love. With no effort whatever, he had molded and fitted into place the intricate joint between the newel post and stair railing—a task he had planned to assign to a more experienced carpenter. Jesse wanted to watch him do it. His stair was perfect.

Instead of walks in the woods and canoe rides, they now spent every spare hour together discussing plans for the Gould house. His mother's room would be on the first floor, convenient for her when she was too old to climb stairs. Rooms for Horace and Mary in one-storied wings on each side, and upstairs, the master chamber for him and Jessie—a large, airy room with a carefully proportioned fireplace, wide enough to balance all the windows she loved.

Now and then, he worried a little that his mother would not care for their new home, that she would think it too large or too pretentious, or would regard the extra wide window sills for Jessie's plants as dust catchers. He was eager to have his family observe his success for themselves, but he would be relieved when they had met Jessie and had begun to realize that he was his own man now—in love, about to be married, his life no longer revolving only about their needs.

Early in June, some three weeks before they were due to arrive, James spread the finished plans for the Gould house on the floor of the Davidson keeping room and studied Jessie's face as she went over every line.

"Oh, good—wide window sills. Don't you think your mother will like them?"

"I doubt she will, but I know you do. The wide sills are for you." He waited a moment, then asked, "Did you hear what I said?"

"Yes."

"Whatever you want, Jessie, I want too. Does that make you happy?"

She looked at him. "Not when it seems to make you so solemn."

"I'm sorry. I didn't mean to scowl, but you know these plans are far more to your liking than—even the Treat house."

"Which could simply mean you're growing more skillful."

"It means I expect you to live in the Gould house as my wife."

She smiled a little. "I don't remember refusing. But, can you be patient until I'm sure I'll be welcomed by your family? Now, don't look hurt, James, but you are a puzzling mixture of humility and bird-dog persistence, you know."

"You don't like that in me?"

She jumped up before he could help her. *"That is not the point.* I'm simply waiting to be certain your mother and sister and brother like me!" After a long pause, "Waiting, too, I suppose, to hear—the bells ring."

"You don't hear any bells when you're with me?"

"Now and then, a soft silvery, contented sound, yes." She took a deep breath, laughed. "I may hear the loud, urgent clang any day, though. James?"

"What?"

"My brother's not here—would you care to kiss me?"

When the schooner from Boston docked on June 10, James could scarcely believe his eyes when he saw his mother, supported by Horace, walk unsteadily down the gangplank. Mary, loaded with bundles, followed close behind. He elbowed his way through the knot of people on the wharf, took his mother's other arm, and then reached around to hug Mary.

"We're early, big brother," Horace announced.

"Oh, James," Mary said breathlessly, "Mama's sick. She's been sick all the way from Boston!"

"Hush, Mary, I'll be fine." Kate Gould held her head higher than usual to prove it, and patted his hand. "I just got seasick, James."

"The trip was so hard on her," Mary whispered.

"Hard on all of us," Horace said. "Bet you never thought I'd get 'em here."

Mary set down her bundles. "Can't we take her some place where she can sit down? Is our rented log cabin ready? James, say something!"

"I haven't had a chance." He laughed nervously. "Guess I'm too surprised to know what to say, except—it's good to see everybody."

"Don't worry about Mama," Horace's voice sounded almost fatherly. "She's mostly just worn to a frazzle. You take the womenfolks wherever it is we're going, James. I'll see to our baggage. You've got a helper now, big brother."

"You didn't answer me," Mary broke in. "Is our house ready, James?"

"No, of course it isn't. We weren't expecting you for three weeks."

"We? Who's we, big brother? You haven't gone and got yourself hitched up to that Scottish lassie you wrote about, have you?"

"No, I haven't. Not yet. But she aimed to help me get the Budges' cabin ready for you." He pointed toward the mill house. "Mama, do you think you can walk to that building down by the end of the wharf? The one with the sign 'Budge's Mills'?"

"I can do whatever you tell me to do, James. We're here because you're here."

"That's a long way," Mary said, peering through the bright sun.

"Yeh, James, a rich man like you must own a buggy!"

For an instant, James fought the old inadequacy, the old helplessness—whatever he did for his family would never be quite enough.

"That big mill where you work?" Horace wanted to know.

"Part of the time. I've got an office there. Mama can rest in my office 'til I get a buggy hitched to take her to the Budges' cabin."

"Whoop-de-da," Horace caroled. "Got his own office! That where I'll work too?"

James nodded, pulling a wide board from a pile of lumber across two kegs. "Sit here, Mama. Mary can stay with you while I run for Captain Budge's buggy."

Horace settled his mother on her makeshift seat and began to fan her with his hat to keep off the herring flies. "Take your time, brother. I'll see to both of 'em."

Halfway across the lumberyard, James saw Jessie driving toward him in the Davidson buggy. He signaled for her to slow the horse, then leaped into the seat beside her. "Jessie, they're here! Almost three weeks early. Mama and Horace and Mary just got off that boat. We've got to get the old Budge cabin fixed up fast." He took her hand. "I'm sorry they came so soon. I'd looked forward to our doing it together. But for some fool reason Horace got an earlier passage, and Mama's all tuckered out. Seasick, I guess. Would you please let me take her to the new Budge house in your buggy? Mary can put her to bed in my room for now."

She smiled reassuringly. "I'll take her myself, James. Introduce me to your family and get back to the mills. I know this is your day to check the Boston orders. I also know Captain Budge is—indisposed. Just leave everything and everyone to me."

"But, Jessie, you can't take care of fixing up the house and Mama too!"

"I can and I shall. I'll take your mother to our house, put her to bed in my room, and start right in settling their cabin. I was cleaning it anyway—just this morning—as a surprise for you. All I lack are some supplies, food, linens on the beds, and a bouquet of flowers! Your brother and sister can help, and when you're through work we'll drive your mother to her temporary home and tuck her into her own bed." She tightened her fingers over his hand. "After all, James, this is the day we've waited for—it just came early. Please don't fret."

"Oh, Jessie—I love you. I love you."

Since the cabin was less than a quarter of a mile from the Budges' new house, James decided to keep his room there until they could all move into their own place together. Mama and Mary would have separate rooms that way, he reasoned, relieved not to have to give up his privacy. He worried a little that in the flurry of settling them and finishing the Treat place, he had not found time to take his family to see his lot overlooking the Penobscot River.

"Don't worry. We've heard all about it," Mary informed him, not long after their arrival, when he stopped by the cabin for his daily visit. "Jessie described the high bluff where our house will stand, the big sweep of the river. She thinks it's beautiful."

His face lighted up. "I know she likes it all right. We picked out the house site together."

"I can't see for the life of me how you found a young lady like Jessie, son," his mother said. "She's got a kind heart. Most pretty girls lack kind hearts."

"She's been waiting to be sure you'd like her, Mama," he said eagerly.

Mary looked at him a moment, then asked, "Why, James?"

He flushed. "She might not marry me if Mama didn't."

"Well, I hope she will," his mother said. "The way she's helped us settle in looks like she's partial to us. Nursed me like I was her own mother when I was so poorly."

"Oh, she does like you, Mama. Mary and Horace too."

His mother began to chuckle. "I tell you, if you could hear the way Jessie and Horace take on together sometimes at the table, you'd think they weren't ten years old apiece!"

"At—the table?"

"Jessie's been giving Horace a ride home in her buggy at noon almost every day," Mary hurried to explain, adding, "He gets a hot meal that way and it saves me packing his lunch."

"Oh," James said lamely. "I—guess I've been missing a lot, haven't I? But I'm all through with the Treat place. They're moving in tomorrow. I can eat here from now on."

There was a short silence, then Mary said, "We're so proud of you, James." Emphasizing each word, she repeated, "So proud of you. Horace tells us you practically run the mills, on top of all your work as a builder."

He was thinking too hard to answer. Jessie had gone to a lot of trouble explaining that she could no longer bring his lunch across the meadow to the Treat house since she was helping Mama and Mary. He was grateful for her help, but he didn't know she had been stopping for Horace every day. He got up abruptly. "I'd better go."

"Not stay for supper with us tonight, son?"

"No, Mama. There's more to do at the office. I'll eat with the Budges later."

Mary stood too. "I'm going with you, James. I want

to see your property. Mama, you don't mind, do you?"

"No, Mary. But don't keep James from his work."

"Why don't you come, Mama?"

"Not this time, son. Jessie said she'd be by again this afternoon to bring me some new plants she's potted for me. Wouldn't look right for us all to be gone. Maybe I can go tomorrow."

"It won't take too long to show me the house site, will it, James?"

"Be glad to, Mary. It's just a ways down on Washington Road."

Mary sat in silence until the mill buggy turned into Washington Road. Finally she laid her hand on his arm and asked, "James, you do know how glad I am to be here with you after all this, don't you?"

Without looking at her, he answered, "Yes, I know."

"I hope you do. And I am so proud of my favorite brother. We all are, but you know Mama and Horace. I can speak for them, though. We're all puffed up over what you've done here."

"I've been lucky this past year, all right."

"Not lucky! You deserve everything you have. Every bit of praise the townsfolk heap on you. Does your life here make you happy? That's what I need to know. You seem so—grown up and strong. But, are you *all right?*"

"Sure. I've learned a lot. I aim to learn a lot more."

I'm not asking the right questions, she thought. At least, I'm not getting the answers I want. Maybe I should hush, just let him talk when he's ready. They rode in silence again for a short distance, then Mary blurted: "James, did Jessie promise to marry you?"

She could see him stiffen. "Why?"

"Oh, nothing. Several of the ladies have called on Mama and me, and they all think it's just a matter of time until you're married. They've seen you together a lot. Jessie's so beautiful, and you're so successful, they've got it all decided. Everybody talks about it."

She took a deep breath. "I just hope you marry her soon if you love her as much as I think you do!"

He turned off the road onto the mowed area behind his acreage and reined in the horse under a maple tree. "I love Jessie with all my heart," he said simply.

Mary ached to put her arms around him. She had seen him change when Mama told him Jessie and Horace laughed and joked together at the table every day. I know it scared him, she thought. I know it did. "James, have you come right out and asked her to marry you?"

"Sure. Lots of times. She doesn't refuse, either."

"Ask her again!"

He had been gazing out over the river. Now he shifted his position so that he looked straight at Mary. "Any reason why you said that?" His voice shook. "I mean, the way she's been going on about how much she likes the site here, you'd think she's already made up her mind to live with us. Jessie would rather walk along that riverbank over there than anything else." His dark eyes bored into hers, his sensitive, lean face suddenly animated. "I know she likes the plans for our house. I designed it just the way she wanted it."

Mary had to look away from him toward the river.

"Why, Jessie's told me a dozen times that she was just waiting to be sure you and Mama liked her."

Only their heads and shoulders appeared in Mary's line of vision, as Horace and Jessie climbed the riverbank. Two heads close together, one a light brown mop of curls and one shining red in the sunlight. She tried not to change her expression as James' earnest voice went on, but when Horace leaned to kiss Jessie, Mary whispered, "Let's go, James!"

"What?"

"I said—let's go, *now*. Just turn the horse and drive off."

She sat motionless beside him, unable to take her eyes from Horace and Jessie, who had climbed to the top of the bank with their arms around each other. They were in full view. Mary made herself look at James. He had seen them. He leaped from the buggy, took a few strides, then stopped, his hands hanging helplessly at his sides, as Horace jerked his arm from Jessie's waist and Jessie covered her face.

For what seemed a lifetime, James stood there, not a hundred feet away. When he started toward them again, Mary jumped from the buggy and ran after him shouting, "James, no! Not now! Wait, please wait!"

She reached him just after his fist smashed against Horace's jaw. Together they watched Jessie fall to her knees beside Horace and begin to cry.

"Come on, James," Mary said. "I'm leaving with you."

"That's all I know to tell you, Mama." Mary's voice was strained, almost cross, as she bustled around the cabin fixing supper. "I don't think Horace will be here this evening to eat with us, and I don't think Jessie will be bringing your plants." She sighed. "It might be a long time before James can face coming again."

"I declare, I don't know what to think." Kate Gould walked aimlessly from one end of the keeping room to the other. "No matter how hard I try, I can't feel bad toward Jessie, though. She's a beautiful, kindhearted girl."

"It isn't Jessie who matters now—it's James! He expected to marry her. James loves her. Can't you understand that?"

Her mother's voice quavered. "I guess I understand. I loved your father. I'm really sorry for James, but he'll marry somebody else by and by. Any girl should be glad to have him."

"Mama, I'd rather bite off my tongue than hurt you, but I don't think you even realize what James is going through tonight! I know Horace is your favorite. I know how much you think of Jessie. But James not only has a heart chock-full of pain, he's going to be humiliated all over this town when folks find out his own brother stole the girl he wanted to marry." She took a step toward her mother. "Mama, please try not to hurt James any more than he's already been hurt."

Kate Gould's tears were flowing now. "Why on earth would I want to hurt my own fine son?"

"You wouldn't. I know you wouldn't. But you have hurt him, all his life, just by taking for granted that he'll be all right, no matter what happens. Me too, Mama. Me too!"

The women fell into each other's arms, weeping.

A soft September rain had begun to fall when James heard unsteady footsteps on the wooden stair—unmistakably those of Captain Budge. He quickly capped his inkwell, hid all evidence of the letters he had been writing, and opened the door to find his employer in his nightcap and shirt, one thick finger to his lips.

"Sh! Let's don't rouse *her,*" Budge whispered.

James motioned him inside and closed the door softly.

"I'll only stay a minute," the Captain sighed, sinking into the one easy chair, "but my old eyes would not shut, in spite of two extra dollops of brandy."

"I couldn't sleep, either," James said.

"James," Budge began, "I don't pity you, but I feel what you're feeling. There's a difference, you know. Feel every heartache, every humiliation, every nerve cracking as you crack your whip over the heads of those poor devils hurrying to finish your mother's house." He sighed again, heavily. "Yes, I had to come up here to your room tonight, to tell you I feel your pain. Feel every pain."

"Thanks. But unless a man went through it, I doubt that he could know."

Budge peered at him. "Good friend James, why do you think I married Mrs. Budge? Why do you think I left my birthplace of Medford at age nineteen and fled to Castine? For my health?"

After a long time, James said, "I'm sorry, Captain. I didn't know."

"Course you didn't know! I've well-nigh forgotten it myself. All, that is, except her dimples and the way my young heart dried and curled up in the face of the ugly humiliation before my home town. The good folk here in Bangor are gossiping about you now, too, as you well know. And I have no sage advice. But they aren't looking down on you. They don't think any less of you than before. You won't believe that, I know, because you think so little of yourself now, but it's true. They aren't poking fun at you, they're simply enjoying themselves. And—*I feel your pain.*" He started to get up, sank back again. "When are you leaving me, James?"

James stared at him in surprise.

"I'm no fool, boy. You wouldn't be rushing that house if you hadn't made up your mind to go. You'll be off to prove yourself in another place. Hope you'll tell me where you're heading, but I'm not asking. Only like to know how much longer I can rest in the knowledge that my good right hand, James Gould, is still here with me."

"The house will be far enough along for me to sail in October."

Budge's heavy shoulders slumped. "One more month of—rest. Well, I'd better go back down and crawl in beside Mrs. Budge." He hoisted himself from the chair. "Good night, son. I hope we both sleep some."

Part Two

Chapter 9

The moon, which had been a thin, sharp sickle in the October sky the night James stood on the deck on the brig *Schuylkill* and watched the Philadelphia waterfront slip away, now hung—a giant round copper—close to the quiet water of the Hampton River on St. Simons Island, Georgia.

Unable to sleep, he had crept out the back door of the newly built tabby cabin which he shared with Captain John Barry at Butler's Hampton plantation on the north end of the Island. The moon was too low yet to give much light, but fearing his lantern would disturb Barry, he picked his way across the clearing where Major Pierce Butler's residence would one day be built, and leaned against a large live oak on the bluff above the water. Sooner or later he would have to let his mind go back—all the way back to an afternoon almost five months ago, when his world had crumbled beside another river far more than a thousand miles away. Miles which stretched along through the Carolinas, Virginia, Maryland, Delaware . . . hundreds of miles of unreal shoreline which tonight had begun to shrink as he tried to sleep in the strange cabin. In the bustle and excitement of Philadelphia, on board the *Schuylkill* during the seven days and nights at sea, he had managed to believe that he was escaping the long months of torment and grief and humiliation. He had clung to this belief by reminding himself that one dream, at least, was coming true. He was sailing south.

All through the hot Bangor summer he had kept to himself, visiting his mother and Mary only when he knew Horace was at the mills. Even during his brief stops with them, Mary had done most of the talking. By day, he had driven himself as mercilessly as he drove the workmen hired to build the Gould house, had hurried from his mill office to the house site, taking the back way through the woods to avoid the prying eyes of people—especially the Bangor women.

"James, won't you please tell me why you're killing yourself to get our house up so fast? You look as though you haven't slept in weeks, and still you won't even sit down when you visit us!" Mary's pleadings had added to his misery, but he told her nothing. His own pain had kept him from reaching toward Mary in hers.

Tonight, the thought of Captain Budge haunted him too. Poor Budge. "I knew you were too good to last, James," the Captain had said, unashamed of his tears when they said good-by. "But, I'll keep your secret. I won't tell a soul you're heading South on that Government survey. You can count on me. Even too much brandy will not pry it from me. I will tell them all, including your family, that you have gone away on business for me. If the good Lord can forgive my drunkenness, He can overlook one small lie to favor a boy who has come to be as dear to me as though he were my own son."

He had built his mother a good house. Not the larger one to please Jessie, but a tight, neat five-roomed cottage. His money had paid for every board and every nail and every pane of glass. He had worked day in and day out from sunup to sundown, and at night he had labored over letters following up on the sparse information Park Holland had given him. Almost five agonizing weeks had passed before an answer came from the first letter addressed to Joshua Humphreys. From Humphreys he had learned that indeed the United States Government was still looking for an experienced timber surveyor to work in south Georgia, and that he should write to John T. Morgan, the Boston master shipwright who would build the frigate *Constitution*. Morgan had offered little hope of assistance, since he was leaving then for St. Simons Island to supervise the first cutting of live oak. Three more nervewracking weeks had passed before the answer to his second letter arrived from Joshua Humphreys urging James to see Captain John Barry in Philadelphia as soon as possible and to give

Budge as reference. No timber had arrived from Georgia, and Barry himself was being sent in October by Secretary of War Knox to discover the trouble and remedy it.

He had been reading Humphreys' letter on his way from the mill to the new house site right after the ship from Philadelphia docked at noon. Deeply in thought, James had been forced to jump out of the way of a buggy rattling down the mill road. In it were Jessie and Horace. The house was not quite finished, but his decision to reach Barry in Philadelphia had been made as he stood mortified and angry in their cloud of dust. "They just didn't know whether or not to wave, James," Mary had tried to comfort him. "After all, you haven't talked to either one of them since—that day."

He didn't need comfort. He needed to get as far away from Bangor as possible. The next day, October 1, telling Mary and his mother that he was going to Philadelphia on business for Captain Budge, he had walked to the Bangor wharf, carrying only his valise, his lighthouse plans in the portfolio and his tin lantern.

Captain John Barry, the naval hero of the Revolution, with whom he had made the voyage South, did not even know Jessie existed. He meant never to speak her name again. Meant never to return to Bangor. In time, he would write to Mary and send his regards to Captain Budge, the only two people in the town whose memory did not fill him with pain and shame—the two people whose devotion he trusted. He was in Georgia only because Barry had known of Captain Budge and was convinced that if Budge had given him so much responsibility in Bangor, James Gould was a knowledgeable timber man.

"God above knows we need you," Barry had said the night James reached Strawberry Hill, the famous man's home, four miles north of Philadelphia. "Don't apologize for knocking at my door, Gould. I'm inclined to think God sent you. I trust His interest in the United States' first navy. And now, especially since we're having such trouble in Georgia securing the needed oak and timber, it wouldn't surprise me at all if the Lord Himself brought you to my door."

Dropping down on a gnarled root of the giant oak beside the Hampton River, James thought about Barry's statement. If God caused Jessie to break his heart, to humiliate him before everyone in Bangor so that he had sought out Captain Barry, then he was through with any thought of God! He recalled his mother's ashen face, her stiff back the day they had learned that William was dead. "If God wills a thing, it's usually hard," she had declared. "But we accept it."

He pressed his head against the bark of the tree. I don't accept it. If God did this to me, I don't accept it—I fight it.

Lemuel Haynes had told him once that grief eats deeper when not shared, but he meant to keep this grief to himself. For him, silence came easy. There would be no more worry about learning how to make conversation, to laugh. She had the world's most entertaining fellow now in Horace.

Across the Hampton River he could see the dark outline of Little St. Simons, a small island wrapped around the north end of the parent Island, separated by the river and a stretch of marsh. The moon had turned white, was higher in the sky, silvering the tall pines and the water with flat, cold light, but the air—unbelievable for October—was still warm. Warm and soft, touching his bare forearms and face.

He should go to bed. Tomorrow would be long and hard. When he and Captain Barry had landed yesterday at Gascoigne Bluff on the southwestern side of the Island, they found John T. Morgan alone at the mill site except for two sick boys, and not a stick of timber cut. Horses and oxen had been aboard the *Schuylkill* too. Thirty sawyers and fifty or sixty axmen were on their way from New London, Connecticut, according to Barry. Until the workmen arrived, no timber could be cut, but James would be occupied learning the Island, studying hundreds of live oaks. He must become as familiar with this strange timber as he had been with northern pine and spruce.

"Can't sleep, either, Gould?" It was Captain Barry.

"I didn't hear you coming, sir."

"Even sound is different down here. Hushed. Dampness in the air, I suppose. The unbroken flatness of the land. Don't think I'd like it for long."

"I would."

Barry stood looking across the river and the marshes toward the low, black, outline of Little St. Simons. "Strange, beautiful sight, I admit, but eerie, somehow. Doesn't it strike you that way, Gould? Those long shadows, all that thick gray moss swinging from the trees like dead men's beards?"

"No, sir. I like it."

Barry eased his muscular body to the ground, clasped his hands around his knees. "I've heard it said that the coast of Georgia strikes men differently from almost any other place on earth. A man either loves this region with the romantic attachment you seem to feel—or he visits and leaves, with no mind to return. What are your plans when we're finished here, Gould?"

"I don't have any. Except I already know I'd like to stay South."

"Rich timber country. No doubt about that. Pine as well as hardwoods. Those frigates will be seaworthy fifty years from now, built of this live oak. Five times the durability of northern white oak, regardless of the pressures on Congress by our New England politicians. I'm a Northerner, but as a frigate captain, I settle for nothing less than Geogia's live oak." John Barry lay down on the warm, leaf-covered ground. "Since your family didn't know you'd be shipping out with me when you left, you'll want to send a letter back. In spite of our problems here, I still hope to have the *Schuylkill* loaded with oak and be on my way to the North again before the month is over. Be glad to see to the delivery of your letter."

"Thank you, sir. If you'll excuse me, I believe I'll get some sleep now."

"Oh, we'll be far more weary tomorrow night. Anyway, this sandy river bank is softer than Major Butler's corn-shuck mattresses. Rest here a while. I feel like talking."

Conversation was the last thing James wanted, but he stretched out near Barry and lay looking up at the blue-black sky, hung with small and large clusters of stars. After all, he wouldn't be in the South except for Barry's confidence in him.

"Your youth and ambition cause me to remember my own beginnings back in County Wexford," Barry was saying. "Your Captain Budge brings to mind the man who gave me command of my first ship when I was twenty-one. A Mr. Edward Denny. The ship we renamed *Barbadoes*. Large, she was, for colonial times. Sixty tons. Tight ship. I won't be any prouder as master of the frigate I'll command one day, simply because the *Barbadoes* was my first. Much the way you felt when Captain Budge gave you the first house to build. Never give up, Gould. The prize at the end of the voyage is worth all the hard work, the uncertainty, the fears."

"I can't believe you were ever afraid, Captain—or uncertain."

Barry laughed. "I'm a man. There's not a man who ever lived without both fear and uncertainty."

"I hate them."

"So do I, but I'm almost fifty. I've learned to expect and accept many things I hate. One doesn't go from cabin boy to ordinary, from ordinary to able seaman, from able seaman to mate and finally to shipmaster without experiencing both fear and uncertainty." Barry raised himself on his elbow. "But we should talk about you, not me. I've already lived through my young years. What is your consuming desire? Your one important dream?"

Would Captain John Barry, so familiar with the sea, think it ridiculous that a young man from the hills of western Massachusetts dreamed of building a lighthouse?

"A tactless question, perhaps?" Barry asked.

"No, sir. I'll tell you. I aim to build fine houses, but more than anything I want to build—a lighthouse."

John Barry sat up. "A lighthouse! Well, now, that's as noble an ambition as a man could have."

Not since he told Lucy Holland of his dream had he spoken of the lighthouse to anyone. Lucy Holland and Lemuel Haynes knew, but he hadn't seen Mrs. Holland in years and was only fourteen when, with Lemuel Haynes, his youthful curiosity and interest in lighthouses had become an obsession.

"Would that more men with your abilities showed interest in learning how to build a practical lighthouse," Barry went on. "Many towers have a kind of lonely beauty, but all do not give dependable light to ships at sea. Tell me, how does it happen that a young man born in the hills holds a dream such as this?"

James was sitting up now, less reluctant to talk. "I don't know, sir, except that a friend of mine in Granville had a picture of the Boston Light. This gentleman was my teacher. We used to sit and look at the picture, and first thing I knew, I wanted to build one."

"Ah, yes, the Boston Light is a good light. Little Brewster Island—perched on the cliff there. Useful. And that's what you must remember, Gould. Lighthouses are not houses, they're lights. Never understood why, in the past, all the way back to antiquity, light towers were generally magnificent structures, pleasurable to the eye by day but often worthless as a snuffed-out candle to a ship working her way through heavy night seas. Tell me, was your friend's picture a likeness of the old Boston Light?"

"No, sir. It was an engraving of the present light. He wrote for a description for me. It's seventy-five-feet-high, octagonal lantern eight feet wide. Conical in shape. The tower tapers from a base diameter of twenty-four feet. Walls seven and a half feet thick."

Barry chuckled. "I would say you have studied the Boston Light, young man."

"I—well, you see, for years I've worked nights on plans for my own lighthouse."

"The one you're going to build some day." Barry's voice held no hint of derision, not even surprise.

"That's right. I've modeled it along the same general dimensions. I hoped for a chance to visit Little Brewster Light. Never did learn how the lanterns were fastened down, but I'll work that out."

"Did you bring your lighthouse plans along?"

"I always take them with me."

"Perhaps I can see them before I sail for the North." Both men stood up. "Hold that dream fast, young man. The world has never had enough lighthouses, so hold it fast. One day the Government will wake up to the fact that if we are to have a navy, if shipping is to prosper, vessels need lights by which to navigate."

The two walked toward their cabin in moonlight as bright now as dawn. At the door, Barry said, "Major Butler will have a splendid plantation here one day. Fortunate for us this cabin, at least, is habitable. Difficult but courageous man, Butler. Like you, he says little. Unlike you, he dreams little, I fear. Thrives on his own often hotheaded opinions, but his hospitality is appreciated. Get some sleep now. Good night, Gould."

"Good night, Captain."

Inside the small room, behind his closed door, he lighted a candle and took out his lighthouse plans.

The memory of Jessie's face, her eyes, her mouth blurred every page. He let the drawings slip to the floor and fell on his bed fully clothed, hoping the thick tabby walls would muffle his sobs.

Chapter 10

James had slept little, but by the time pink streaks began to appear in the sky above the Hampton River, he had shaved and put on a clean shirt, and now he sat waiting for Barry at the foot of the same big oak. A pair of warblers flashed green-yellow, disappeared and darted again around a low-hanging limb of the great tree. Live-oak branches grew wider, hung lower to the ground than any he had ever seen. Thirty feet, he estimated, this branch twisted out and down until the upraised tip was no more than a foot from the earth. The Government's decision to use live oak in the frigates was undoubtedly valid. In the book Lucy Holland had sent, he had read about its toughness, its long life, its resiliency.

Again today, as every day for the past four months, waking up had been a heavy, smothering experience. The first moment of consciousness had widened to admit the now familiar flood of pain: Jessie didn't love him. He would never touch her again, never see her again.

The lighthouse drawings scattered across the floor of the small room reminded him that at least Captain Barry had not laughed; had considered a lighthouse a noble dream.

The drawings were back in his father's portfolio. A new day stretched ahead under the southern autumn sun. A fresh start in a strange place, where no one knew what had happened to him in Bangor.

The *Schuylkill* had docked yesterday on the leeward side of the Island at Gascoigne Bluff, the spot where the British ships had anchored when James Oglethorpe claimed the land for the Crown. The brig had passed near the ruins of Oglethorpe's Fort Frederica on her way south to Gascoigne. James hoped to find time to explore what remained of the ghost town of Frederica—called Old Town by the Negroes at

Hampton Plantation. Some of the houses were still standing, he had noticed as the ship sailed past; a few appeared to be in use. Riding up Frederica Road yesterday with Captain Barry and John T. Morgan, he had seen only three plantation houses, miles apart. From where he sat now, he could see the tall chimneys of the finest new plantation, Cannon's Point, less than half a mile away. Distances were difficult to figure because of the irregular hammocks and bluffs and serpentine salt creeks winding through the marshes and past stretches of the high land, but he judged the Island to be at least ten miles long, perhaps only three to five miles wide. He wondered how many peopple lived here; who owned the land at Gascoigne Bluff where the Government sawmill stood; who owned the land to the south of the Bluff, and tiny Hawkins Island nearby.

Growing impatient both for breakfast and for work, he stood up, stretched, drew deep draughts of the salty-sweet air into his lungs. Examining a clump of hanging gray moss, he found its wiry strands clean, growing in no predictable way but as though by whim. He sauntered to the edge of a small tract of uncleared woods—sweet gums, hickory, a few maples. Later on, there would be some color here among the pines and live oaks and cedars, but there would be no color anywhere to match New England in October. The riot of reds and golds which Jessie loved along their river had already begun when he left.

"Gould!" Captain Barry called. "A servant has brought our breakfast."

"Coming," James replied. He was no longer hungry, but at least the business of the day could begin.

Mary Gould hurried across the lumberyard at Budge's Mills. She had made up her mind to come right out and ask Captain Budge about James. If the news was bad, as she feared from the still-raging gossip, she would need time to decide how to tell Mama.

Mary had visited the mills only once before, but as

she recalled, she could slip in the back way unnoticed. So far, no one had paid her any mind.

She had almost reached the high open double doors at the rear of the mills, when someone shouted: "Mary! Mary—where you heading?"

Horace was the last person she wanted to see. "Oh, hello, brother. I didn't expect you to be out here."

"I didn't exactly expect you, either."

"Uh—is Captain Budge in his office?"

"Now, that's a question nobody can answer without looking. With James gone, I'd say the chances are he's there, trying to figure out how to meet his payroll." Horace frowned. "What on earth are you doing here—dodging in the back way? Did Mama send you to find out about James? When he's coming home?"

"No, she did not, and if you tell her you saw me here, I'll wallop you good!"

"I won't say a word—*if* you'll tell me why you came." He touched her arm, his face suddenly troubled. "Mary, did—Jessie send you? It wasn't Jessie wanting to know about James, was it?"

"I've never heard her mention his name since he left."

He sighed. "I—I just love her so much, I get scared sometimes. I mean, she did almost marry James. If I saw a single sign that she might be sorry she let him go, I don't know what I'd do!"

"Horace, Horace, don't get me upset over you, too. You be happy with Jessie, do you hear me?"

His smile returned. "I am. Once we're married, I'll be fine."

"And that won't be but two weeks."

"You haven't told me why you want to see Budge."

Her eyes filled with tears. "Horace, I have to know if he's coming back. Maybe Captain Budge can tell me."

"I expect he can, if he will, but I bet James swore him to secrecy." Horace pointed toward the back doors. "Go right in there, turn to your right and down the long passageway—and good luck, Mary. I promise not to tell. Honest, I feel bad enough about—about James."

"I swear to you, Miss Gould, that your brother went on business for me to Philadelphia." James Budge fidgeted. She was watching him too closely for comfort. "I asked him to make the trip because—well, a little something is brewing. Uh, by 'a little something' I mean—possible new business. Yes. Possible new business. You see, my dear young lady, a new act has been passed whereby President Washington is free to begin building the first United States Navy. The first United States Navy! Doesn't that sound impressive?"

She nodded. "But what does my brother have to do with it?"

"Your brother? Why, everything. I mean, quite a lot. After all, the frigates will be built of timber, won't they?"

"I suppose so."

"Uh, now, I'm sworn to secrecy—" He lifted his right hand. "No, not by your brother. By—yes, by the United States Government."

"I wouldn't ask you to break your word, Captain Budge, but if my brother is somehow needed in the procuring of the timber, I fail to see why it has to be secret. Is he still in Philadelphia?"

"Haven't heard a word from him, I suppose?"

"Not a word."

"Neither have I, Miss Gould."

"Did he really go for you, sir? Or did he go because he wanted to get away from—Bangor? Please understand I wouldn't be bothering you except that my mother's heart will be broken if—if he isn't coming back. And—so will mine."

"I only know I hated like the very mischief to see him go."

"You didn't answer my question, Captain. Did he really go on business for you?"

He spread his hands helplessly on his desk. "I know nothing more than I've told you, my dear Miss Gould. Where matters of the Federal Government are concerned," he said gravely, "it is not for us to say."

He shuffled some papers on his desk.

"I see," she said.

Budge pulled himself unsteadily to his feet as she

stood. "One thing I know, you never need to worry about your brother, James, getting into any kind of trouble. He's an honorable man."

"I don't worry about that, Captain. I just worry about James himself."

The first two days on St. Simons were spent inspecting the timber on the Gascoigne Bluff tract, land rich in live oak, pine, sweet bay, hickory, red oak, black laurel—and mosquitoes. "No wonder Richard Leake chose to build his plantation home on the mainland in McIntosh County instead of here," John Morgan said, as he rode with James through the tangle of pathless undergrowth. "Not so bad now as it was in late summer, I assure you, Gould. My legs and arms were swollen from bites until mid-September." James hated the pesky mosquitoes and sand gnats, but he was not going to let them spoil his growing love for the Island.

Up before sunrise, eager for a glimpse of the dawn breaking over Little St. Simons Island, he felt his energy return. He was learning how to judge the day with the first sleepy look out the high open window of his room in the tabby cabin at Hampton; gray light at dawn did not necessarily mean a gray day. Some mornings the miasma hung so dense and white above the Hampton River it blotted out Little St. Simons and blurred the sun pushing its way up into a cloudless sky. Often, he carried his coffee and fried meat and cornbread to the riverbank to watch the miasma change from dull gray to gold to pale green as the day came on. A day that would not chill his bones, that would not chafe and split his fingers as he worked. The mosquitoes and deer flies and sand gnats were everywhere, but at least he could slap at them; could set a wad of rags smoldering on the ground outside his bedroom window at night to discourage them. During the day, the smoke from his pipe helped as he walked from live oak to live oak, estimating the lengths each would yield.

The timber cut from Richard Leake's land at Gascoigne Bluff would not be difficult to load aboard the *Schuylkill* for shipment North when Captain Barry was ready to go, but far more timber was needed than this one tract could supply. The oxen and horses they had brought from the North would be none too many. Oak logs, too heavy to float down the rivers and salt creeks to the Gascoigne landing, would have to be dragged from other parts of the Island. One frigate alone required 27,540 cubic feet of live oak, cut to size and conformed to the molds. Much of each great tree would be unusable. He secretly enjoyed the prospect of being forced eventually to survey other sections of St. Simons.

Riding back to their lodgings at Hampton on the evening of their third day on the Island, Captain Barry slowed his mount to an easy trot and began to talk.

"The problems here are worse than I anticipated, Gould."

"I know, sir. We've got to clear a road, for one thing."

"And that means renting slaves from these plantation owners."

James was aware that the Southern economy revolved around slavery. The Hampton Negroes had washed his clothes, cleaned his cabin, served his meals, yet until now no one had used the word "slave." He said nothing except, "When do you think we can expect the workmen from New London?"

"Who knows? Two days, a week. Every ship doesn't find the smooth sailing we encountered. We need slaves first, though, to open up that road. I might as well admit my shock that almost nothing has been done. I don't blame Morgan. The Collector of Customs at Savannah—Habersham, I believe he is—has sent neither men nor provisions nor tools. Not even utensils for cutting the molds."

"Does Habersham hold the timber contract with Leake, Captain?"

"Yes, and I can't figure a reason for his laxity. There must be a serious misunderstanding. Habersham is well recommended. Of course, Christopher Hillary, the Brunswick Collector, has been helpless too."

"Are we free to cut timber anywhere else on the Island but Leake's land?"

"This I must also find out. I believe the Government has empowered Habersham to make further contracts if needed. Where we cut should be your decision, Gould. I've kept my mouth shut. Hesitated to embarrass Morgan, but now that I've seen the lay of the land, I feel convinced he is not to blame. I intend to ask some direct questions first thing in the morning."

James had little time to enjoy the sunrise the next day. Before first light, they were saddled up and ready to ride south again down Frederica Road.

The sun was still burning off the miasma over the river as they reached the makeshift mill at Gascoigne. Except for the tethered horses and oxen and master shipwright Morgan pacing up and down, there was no activity at all.

"Not a very thriving shipyard, Morgan," Barry called, as they hitched their horses.

"Hard to look busy when you're alone." Morgan shrugged. "But my two boys seem stronger today. They can at least help with the road clearing—if we can manage to rent some slaves. We've got to have a road."

"I'm sure we'll get cooperation from some of these plantations. Right now, if you don't mind, Morgan, I need some answers. Only you can give them."

"At this point, I wonder if there are any, Captain Barry."

"Tell us exactly the terms made with the owner of this land."

"Habersham merely told me that I might cut what timber I wanted off Leake's land, on terms as good as he could get anywhere else in the state."

James and Barry exchanged glances.

"That doesn't mean much," James said.

"Do you have anything in writing, Morgan?"

"No, sir. It's so vague, how could it be written down?"

Barry was pacing now, scratching at the sand gnats in his hair. "That's no contract at all." He strode to his horse, took ink, quill, and paper from the saddlebags, sat down on a barrel pulled up beside a sawbuck, and began to write. James watered the horses, listening as he worked to Morgan's nervous assurances while Barry went on writing. A cutter had been promised from Savannah with at least some tools and stores and perhaps fifteen men. Morgan repeated what they already knew, that a sloop was coming from New London with the expert sawyers, carpenters, and axmen. Nothing more.

Barry finished, folded the paper, tucked it in his jacket pocket. "I'll see Mr. Habersham as soon as I can leave for Savannah, but meantime, he'll have an idea of my disgust. We can send this letter back with the promised cutter—that is, if she comes. Now, Morgan, what plantations are down here on the south end of the Island where we might rent some slaves?"

"Only one of any size. Owned by James Spalding. Not in residence at present. On his way to the legislature in Augusta. I feel his overseer will rent slaves, though. He knows of Spalding's interest in our project."

"Gould, you and Morgan will ride to the Spalding place to inquire?"

"Yes, sir."

"After Spalding, where?"

Morgan thought a minute. "Well, some small landowners scattered about, most with only a handful of slaves. I'd say we stand a chance at Major Wright's place, Orange Grove, on Dunbar Creek. Might get a few from Harrington Hall, where the Demeres live, farther north. Major Pierce Butler's overseer will rent a dozen or more, I'm certain. And without a doubt, the Scotsman, John Couper, at Cannon's Point, will do what he can to help."

"All right," Barry said, rubbing his hands together. "We'll decide where that road should go, eat an early lunch, gentlemen, and you can be on your way."

"Look, Captain," James called from the edge of the

bluff. "That must be the Savannah cutter rounding the bend!"

They waved toward the ship, and Captain Barry shouted: "Hurray! We're about to begin at last, gentlemen! Get those Negroes and let's go."

That night, weary from miles on horseback, James excused himself early and by eight o'clock lay on his bed listening to a steady rain peppering the tin roof of the tabby cabin. Major Butler seldom visited this place; had not even started the big house. The atmosphere here was almost that of a military post. The Hampton Negroes were not permitted to visit other Negroes, even across Little Jones Creek at Couper's place.

Today James had been exposed for the first time to owner-managed plantation life when he visited Cannon's Point. Couper's holdings were larger than any he had seen, except Hampton. A hundred or more Negroes milled about the fairly neat, white-washed quarters, swarmed across the vast cottonfields, or tended the botanical garden, where their owner experimented with rare trees and plants never before grown on St. Simons Island. Cannon's Point was more prosperous than the others, and busier. John Couper's people operated his cotton gin, his carpentry and blacksmith shops, and cared for his stock and a large stable of fine horses as well as his fields.

James had his first glimpse of the Scotsman when he and Morgan rode down the lane of oaks toward the big house. He had liked Couper on sight—well over six feet, wearing a white shirt with long, flowing sleeves, his clean-shaven face alight with anticipation as he waited for them to ride up. James had let Morgan do most of the talking, but had felt almost at once that he could converse with John Couper as he had with Lemuel Haynes. Like Haynes, Couper talked a lot, but he also listened. The slight Scottish burr had at first reminded him painfully of Jessie, but before long, John Couper had his full attention.

Staring up at the whitewashed low ceiling of his cabin room, James let his thoughts wander. The owner of Cannon's Point was plainly a happy man. In the middle thirties, he supposed, but the thatch of dark red hair, the expressive, straight brows gave his ruddy face a look of both youth and wisdom. Never boasting of his extensive holdings, the man possessed a contagious kind of joy that James envied. John Couper seemed to have nothing to prove to anyone and could laugh as easily at himself as at a good story.

The house at Cannon's Point had caught James' eye as he and Morgan walked with their host up the sun-spattered lane. It was spacious, square, three-storied. The ground floor, an English basement, was, like his cabin, made of the mixture of shell, lime and sand called *tabby*. The upper floors were of clapboard, painted white with green shutters. Across the second story ran a wide piazza reached by a gracious flight of steps. Glancing upward to the third story, he saw that fan louvers had been built into the handsomely proportioned dormer windows, with arched transoms which opened for ventilation. That intrigued him. He had seen only the central hall downstairs, and the parlor; had glimpsed the book-lined library across the hall and assumed that a dining room and very likely a bedchamber made up the first floor. Perhaps one day Mr. Couper would let him examine the construction and the plan of the entire house.

"I mean Cannon's Point to be the most welcoming home I can manage," the Scotsman had declared as James and Morgan sat their horses, ready to leave. "I'll not only loan you fifteen or twenty of my people; I extend a warm invitation to you both to come again soon—and often. You must meet my wife and infant son."

"I doubt if I get back," Morgan had said as he left James at Hampton Point. "You must go again, though, Gould. Your stay will be indefinite on this isolated Island. After all, my work is in Boston, building the *Constitution* from the timbers you find. I salute you, young man, for the courage to tackle such a lonely piece of work. I hope you'll see John Couper often. He's a tonic for anyone—especially a young single fellow so far from home."

I wonder if Couper liked me, James thought, or if he's just pleased to have guests, no matter who. I'm a good listener, though, and he's a good talker. I might have something to offer in the way of friendship. Turning on his side, he looked out the small open window. The rain had stopped.

I'd like to know what part of Scotland John Couper came from, he thought, feeling drowsy. I hope not Dundee.

Chapter 11

In addition to surveying the Leake tracts on St. Simons and Hawkins Island, James had supervised the building of the road over which the oak logs would be dragged to the mill site at Gascoigne. The forty-four Negroes from Cannon's Point, Hampton, Orange Grove, and the Spalding place worked well; they seemed more interested than he had expected and went at the back-breaking labor of removing tough palmetto roots as though it were a game, vying with each other in hacking out the biggest ones in the shortest time. He saw no signs that any one of the forty-four thought of running away. Crude huts had been erected for the blacks at Gascoigne. Escape would have been easy but capture inevitable, he supposed, on an island five by twelve miles.

Since James preferred to listen rather than talk, he found the garrulous Negroes good company, especially Couper's people, who laughed more, sang more, and appeared pleased, even excited when James explained that they were all helping to build the first United States Navy. Each day he was able to understand more of their Geechee dialect. He enjoyed their jokes and tall tales and superstitions and felt honored that they shared them so freely with a strange white man.

The new road was finished just in time. On October 22, earlier than anyone dared hope, the sloop from New London docked at Gascoigne Bluff, and the axmen, sawyers, and carpenters received a rousing welcome, not only from James, Morgan, and Barry but from the Negroes too.

Toward the middle of November, when the tupelos and sweet gums had reached the peak of their color, when every marsh margin tossed great white clouds of blooming sea myrtle, the *Schuylkill* was loaded at last, with newly cut and molded timbers. Captain Barry and John Morgan shook the hand of each workman before sailing for Savannah, where Barry hoped to set the contract trouble straight with Habersham and obtain a guarantee that the promised ships and supplies would be forthcoming.

"We've done well so far here, Gould," Barry said as he shook James' hand. "So well, our main problem may soon be the matter of prying enough ships from Habersham to carry your timber north."

"I'm sure you'll manage, Captain," James said. "And I hope you know I'm grateful to you for taking me aboard as you did."

"I doubt I've ever done a smarter thing," Barry smiled. "You've planned well in keeping your surveys ahead of the sawyers. You're in charge. Neither Morgan nor I will return. We won't need the borrowed slaves now that the road is finished. Can you escort them back to their owners?"

"Yes, sir. I was wondering if you think I should build myself a lean-to down here at the mill? After all, Major Butler is your friend, not mine."

"Nonsense. Unless you dislike the ride down each day, enjoy the privacy of our tabby cabin. I doubt if these palmetto roofs on the huts here keep out much rain. I'll let Major Butler know you're staying on."

James stood on the wharf and watched the *Schuylkill* weigh anchor and move slowly out on the tide, as the square canvas filled with wind. He would miss Barry and Morgan, but with the sailing of the *Schuylkill,* James Gould was in charge. He had been on St. Simons Island only one month; still, except for the Negroes, who were leaving too, no one at the site knew the Island as well. The foreman of the work crew down from New London would have to handle any friction among his men. James' work was his own. As the surveyor, he was responsible only for giving the foreman instructions. It would be up to the foreman to see that the instructions were carried out.

As the *Schuylkill* rounded the bend in the Frederica River, a great shout went up from the cheering men. The first load of timber was on its way at last.

James returned the slaves, one group at a time, thanked each and felt a lump in his throat when Couper's fine-looking Johnson made a simple speech of gratitude to James for having been a good master.

On his way from Cannon's Point to where Couper Road forked into the Hampton lane, he thought about Lemuel Haynes, the only Negro he had ever known well. It chilled him to think that Johnson, with his quick, facile mind, his straightforward manner, might have become a great clergyman like Lemuel Haynes, had Johnson not been born a slave.

Captain John Barry was back in Philadelphia watching over the construction of his frigate, but within two weeks on St. Simons Island, James could see fresh results of the Captain's final session with Habersham in Savannah. The contracts now included all parts of the Island where suitable timber could be found, and according to his latest letter from Habersham, there seemed hope as well that sufficient ships would eventually arrive to take the timber north to Boston for the *Constitution,* to Philadelphia for the *United States,* to Norfolk for the *Constellation.*

James had not only surveyed and made his selections over the entire Leake holdings, he had covered the old Spalding woods and part of Orange Grove, and was spending the first week in December surveying Cannon's Point, in pleasant company with John Couper. The main object of his search now was a live oak from which the huge stern post of the *Constitution* could be hewn. The tree must stand twenty to twenty-five feet in its unbroken trunk, must be four to five feet in girth, and must be flawless.

"Live oaks are deceivers," Couper declared. "I'd have thought we'd have found it six times over!"

"We have found it, Mr. Couper," James said, as they rode together down the Cannon's Point lane late on a brisk winter afternoon. "The Island's only sound oak tall enough and not branched too low. Right there, in the center of your fine garden."

John Couper slowed his horse to a walk, glanced at James, then looked long at the almost perfect tree, its thick symmetrical trunk offering wide leafy branches to the sunset, every strand of lightly swaying moss tinged with gold light. If ever a tree belonged in a particular place, James thought, this one belonged there.

When at last Couper spoke, his voice was hushed, sorrowful. "My beloved, eh? Always called that tree 'Beloved.' I situated my house as much for the tree as for the river."

"I was sure of that, sir."

"Hoped to be buried 'neath it some day. Pictured my children and their children playing under its big protective arms." His strong face softened into a smile. "Childish of *me,* I know. Oh, I couldn't withhold the tree, Gould. Not from the nation I've come to love. Don't worry. It's just that you took me by surprise. When I agreed to give timber, I thought of my woods."

"So did I, but we've scoured those woods. Plenty of good usable trees there. I marked some fine hull pieces today." James touched the rough bark of the great tree, looked up into the gnarled, fern-covered limbs. "This one contains the stern post. I'm—sorry."

Couper shook his head. "My wife, Miss Rebecca, is only nineteen. Still a child in many ways. 'Twill be hard for her to give it up."

"I certainly understand, but do you suppose we could cut it tomorrow? I've promised the stern post in the next Boston shipment."

John Couper was silent for several moments. Then he said, "Aye. Why delay? I'll tell Mrs. Couper and all my people tonight. The people will be heartbroken too, but we'll be waiting—all of us, for you and your sawyers and axmen tomorrow morning."

"You'll be remembered for this," James said gravely.

"Ridiculous! The Coupers will be the ones to remember this day in the month of Christmas, seventeen ninety-four, Gould. Not every man is called upon to supply the stern post for so great a ship as the *Constitution.*" He was smiling again. "Now the first shock is over, I'm quite exalted. I'll ponder some tonight about how we'll mark the stump for posterity."

He saluted James. "See you in the morning, Gould. I'm really not a sentimental Scot anyway. I'm an American. We won't weep—we'll celebrate!"

The early morning threat of rain had passed. Tumbling gray clouds were lifting above the ocean by the time James rode into Cannon's Point with his sawyers and axmen.

"Even the Almighty seems willing for His masterpiece to come down," John Couper tried to joke. "I prayed for rain . . . and my dear wife, although she wept at first, appears to be sufficiently pleased that her renegade Scot loves America enough to sacrifice our tree. She too, is determined upon a mood of reasonable celebration. May even bring our infant son to observe the historic event."

While the axmen sat in a group, honing their broadaxes, expertly stroking the blades with whetstones, James began to figure the fall of the great tree. Where possible, he meant to protect Couper's plantings.

"We'll limb the entire south side, sir, and let her fall free toward your lane away from the house. I'll be glad to have my men move those citrus trees and your banana plants."

As James spoke, a long line of Negroes—men, women, and children—began to file silently into the garden from the direction of the quarters. They stood, off to one side, the men with their hats in their hands, as though waiting for a burial. Not one spoke.

Couper looked toward his people, then back at the tree. "Limb her?" He shook his head. "That's considerate of you, Gould, to want to save my citrus grove, but the tender trees will undoubtedly freeze next month anyway, without the old tree to shelter them. Don't limb her. Leave her whole to the end." He walked to the trunk of the oak, laid his hand on it for a moment, then stepped back. "Let the saws rip—any time—Mr. Gould!"

His arms folded, John Couper watched the first pair of sawyers work in rhythm with their heavy crosscut saw until the blade began to run heavy, when he moved closer to observe how they freed the blade by tapping a persimmon wedge into the cut.

When the cut showed three-fourths through the giant trunk, Couper called, "Could you stop them a moment, Gould?"

"Why, yes. Time to change sawyers anyway. Is anything wrong?"

"No. It's just that death is never easy, and before I send for Mrs. Couper I'd like to walk out my lane and see old Beloved standing, once more."

"Take all the time you need. I hate to see her fall, too."

Gould is a puzzle, Couper thought, as he strode to the far side of the garden toward the lane. He's all business, yet somehow understands my feelings at this moment. Hope he'll decide sometime to talk to me freely. Very knowledgeable about timber, but he seems too gentlemanly for such a life as lumbering.

The Scotsman stood still, fixing in his memory forever the vision of the mounds of leaves against the sky, the limbs reaching all the way to the corner of his house—dark, dark green against the white of the clapboards and the clouds.

He raised his hand to the tree in farewell and walked quickly to call his wife.

A fresh team of sawyers assigned for the final rip, James stationed himself to one side alone, looking from the men to the Coupers as the rhythmic, final thrusts began. Rebecca Couper, holding her baby, leaned on her husband's arm, her eyes wide with horror and anticipation.

High in the tree, James caught the brown and white flash of a hawk's wings as the bird hovered, landed on its familiar hunting perch, turned its ferocious head this way and that, then swooped to the river's edge and disappeared.

The sawyers' "Halt!" rang out. The saw stopped. James caught his breath; the two men ran for safety. Only an inch or so remained uncut; still the tree did not fall, did not even quiver. A cardinal flew onto a branch and began its ticking sound as though to count off the remaining seconds. Cautiously, moving up to inspect the cut, James saw the line of Negroes, some with their hands clasped in prayer; the Coupers clinging to each other as motionless as the oak.

On a signal from James, a sawyer eased toward the tree, timber chisel and sledge in hand: one, two, three heavy blows of the hammer, and at his partner's warning shout, he ran again to safety as the great oak shuddered, began to lean toward the lane, and with a thunderous splitting away of her life seemed almost to sing as she crashed to the ground.

Throughout the afternoon the sawyers and axmen worked at limbing the tree, James inspecting each limb as it fell. Live-oak knees were excellent for ship's joints, and Mr. Couper's tree proved more valuable than most. The Scot followed James from branch to branch.

"She's going to be as useful as she was bonnie, eh, Gould?"

"Right, sir. The trunk was so tall, I don't think you'll find too much damage to your citrus trees, either. Her wide limbs propped her up. Can't tell 'til the branches are cleared away, but I'm hopeful for most of your small trees."

"Ah, don't worry about that. Tell me, what happens next?"

"Well, once she's trimmed down to her trunk, the men will knock in their dogs and chain her to that team of oxen you've loaned us. Then we start the slow drag to the mill. Down there, they'll saw her to size, trim her with adzes to the molds—they're already made—and she'll be ready for her voyage North. The whole process should take two, maybe three days."

"I'd like to watch," Couper said. "May I?"

"Glad to have you."

"Good. I wouldn't rest if I failed to see Beloved all the way into her berth in the ship's hold."

After dinner, James sat with John Couper on the river piazza, out of sight of the hole against the night sky where the tree had stood. A pine knot burning in its flat iron holder gave just enough light for them to see each other as they talked.

"I suppose you and your timbermen think me a sentimental fool," Couper said, "but I must confess I'm experiencing a kind of grief tonight—as though a member of the family had died."

"I understand how you must feel." James sipped Couper's mellow Madeira. "I'd much rather build than destroy."

"Admirable. Of course my tree has just changed occupations in a way. In a sense the tree had assumed an active role in the history of the greatest nation on earth. Gould, I've just decided how I'll mark the poor stump! My blacksmith, Cuffy, will weld an iron band, and in it we'll inscribe: *U.S. Frigate Constitution, Seventeen Ninety-four*. Do you like that idea?"

"Oh, yes Fine. I guess I also like it that your oak will form the sternpost for the frigate that's being built in Massachusetts. I was born in the western hill country."

"I welcome that link with your life too. Tell me, have you always wanted to have a hand in building ships, Gould?"

"No."

"Just happen to be chosen for this timber survey in Georgia, eh?"

"You might say."

"Were you working in Boston?"

"No. Bangor, to the north."

"I don't know why I haven't suggested this before, but what's to prevent your moving over here? With us you'd be as near—or should I say as far—from the south end of the Island as at Hampton. Mrs. Couper and I would be delighted to have you share our home for as long as you're on St. Simons." John Couper leaned toward him. "You must be lonely over there. I believe that might be the best idea I've had in weeks!"

"I have to admit I can't think of anything I'd like better."

"Splendid! Your belongings can come from Hampton tomorrow. I'll send a boat." James thanked him, settled back in his chair. His host reached for the decanter, poured a glass for each of them, and raised his own. "To the beginning of a long and genuine friendship, James Gould!"

"Thank you. I wish I had the words to tell you how glad I am you'd want me."

"You could be here at least a year, you know," Couper said, propping his feet on the piazza railing, "The longer the better, for us. We like people. Our first few months in this house, a young couple came for their honeymoon and stayed through the birth of their second child!"

"I hope I don't impose that long. But in his latest letter, Mr. Morgan wrote that he's bought the entire Richard Leake tract down at Gascoigne. The Government doesn't want to take a chance on running out of oak. I'll have to do another survey. Leake would allow just so much to be cut as long as he owned it."

"Undoubtedly Morgan will hold the land only until the timber demand ends. Why don't you buy it then?"

"Me, sir? I don't have that much money."

Couper laughed. "My cotton crop permitting, I could lend it to you next year. The land will be cleared, ready to plant."

"But—I'm not a planter, Mr. Couper."

"If you were born in western Massachusetts, you must have farmed. I can teach you the science of planting cotton. Fascinating way to live. You can't tell from one year to the next whether you'll be the richest man ever or the poorest mouse in the church! I've been both. Find it invigorating. Adventuresome uncertainty."

"I don't like uncertainty."

"All of life is uncertain, my boy, but I don't intend to waste a moment of it on worry. When we ride up Frederica Road after my tree is safely aboard, I'll show you another piece of fine land you could buy right now."

James grinned. "I don't think I'd like the life."

"But I can see that you truly, deeply enjoy what I have here at Cannon's Point. You're not a—vagabond.

More the country squire. You should own your own land, your own servants, rear your children with their roots down in a place to which they can turn for all their days."

James was silent a long time. "I admit I've never been in a house that makes me feel as I feel here. I—don't want to move from pillar to post, but—"

"But what?"

"I—doubt I could handle a plantation."

"Give me one good reason."

"I couldn't be a slave owner."

"Ah! So that's it."

"Excuse me, sir, but—how do you manage? Do you have any discomfort about owning Cuffy and Johnson and Sans Foix and the others?"

In the dim, yellow glow of the flickering pine knot, James saw him look away, out over the river. "Aye, I do mind owning other human beings. Still, the coast of Georgia is where I make my home. I earn my livelihood by planting cotton—the kind of longstaple cotton which grows best in coastal Georgia. I couldn't do it without my people. My people couldn't live without my protection. I would be bankrupt without them and they without me."

Couper fell silent. James waited.

"True, I don't pay wages. I tell myself I pay them in clothing, food, shelter, and medicine. Perhaps the day will come when somehow our government will find a way for planters to survive and slaves to go free. I hope so. The system is evil, and it's what we have." He sighed. "I confess to you that after some years of owning slaves, it doesn't bother me as it once did. Perhaps I've grown calloused. Perhaps also, I've grown fond of my people and would worry about them if I turned them loose. Does that sound—like a weak-kneed rationalization, Gould? How does it strike your Yankee ears?"

"As honest."

"Thank you. We mortals are created so as to dream dreams. My dream has always been to be a planter. To watch a sprout grow from a tiny seed is life itself for me. I don't believe that I could enter your business.

Trees must be cut if man progresses, but confound it, I don't want to see things die. I want to see them *grow.*"

"I know what you mean."

"Do you?"

"Yes, I feel the same way about building."

James knew the alert eyes were studying him.

"So that's it," the Scot said at last. "You don't want to be a planter because you hope to be a builder, eh?"

"I am a builder already. I supervised a lumber operation in Bangor, but I also designed and built houses."

"Then this timber survey is, as I suspected, a sideline?"

"I wanted to come South. It was a way to get here."

"But we're an agrarian society down here. What do you hope to build?"

"Excuse me, sir, but someone had to design and build this house."

Couper chuckled. "True, though plantations are few and far between."

"I know I'll have to settle eventually in Savannah or Charleston or New Orleans. I'm only trying to pile up some security over the next few years. My one big dream is some day to build—a lighthouse."

Chapter 12

By midafternoon of the third day after the felling of the big tree, James and Couper were cantering north over the narrow shell road that bisected St. Simons. Couper rode ahead, reliving, James was certain, the high excitement of having seen his tree worked to its mold and swung onto the anchored brig.

James was enjoying the gallop on Major, the fine black horse which Couper insisted was his for as long as he lived on St. Simons Only one difficult task lay ahead for tonight. He must delay no longer in writing to Mary and his mother. After dinner, he would excuse himself, go to his new room and get the troublesome task behind him.

Up ahead, Couper was slowing his horse, signaling for James to stop. They were in sight of Orange Grove, the Wright place, and Couper was scrutinizing the woods to the east.

"Here we are, Gould," Couper told him. "Right about here—don't have the exact area in mind—but for more than a thousand acres north and south, before you stretches one of the most fertile, best-drained pieces of real estate on the coast of Georgia! Runs, I believe, all the way to the Black Banks River and across the marshes to join little Long Island over by the ocean. I own that. Wish I owned this too. Someone is going to do well here on the old Sinclair-Graham tract one day. And due to its unusual history, I don't doubt but that it can be bought at a reasonable price right now."

James winced. Why was his host determined to make a planter of him? He had told Couper that he was a builder, had even spoken at length of his cherished dream.

"The north end of this tract may have belonged to Archibald Sinclair, the tithingman at Frederica. No one seems to know for certain, but adjoining what we call Sinclair, or St. Clair, is a property once owned by another Scotsman named John Graham," Couper went on, "back before our Revolution. Owned at least five hundred acres here, along with a thousand down around the St. Marys River, plus various other large and small holdings scattered over the colony of Georgia. Some say twenty-six thousand acres in all. Well, John Graham was just beginning to develop his Mulberry Grove Plantation near Savannah, when he had to flee to East Florida because, you see, the poor benighted fellow remained loyal to the Crown of England. Had no better sense. So, after the Revolution, this land, along with his other vast possessions, was confiscated by the new state of Georgia, and the only thing the Crown did to ease Graham's distress was to bestow upon him an altogether empty title, Lieutenant Governor of the Province—or some such—a title which I've heard brought not a shilling of pay." Couper chuckled. "I'm a dog to laugh, but the man did make a poor choice. With a chance to become an American citizen, to choose the Crown—I can't find much pity for him. And, d'you know, they not only confiscated his plantation and home at Mulberry Grove; along with all else, they took the poor fellow's tomb in the Savannah cemetery too? Nathanael Greene got both the Savannah plantation and the burying place! Does the tale strike you as funny? Or would all that bad luck for remaining loyal to the Crown strike only a convinced patriot like me as humorous?"

"I can see the humor in it," James said.

"A fine piece of land, this. Graham bought well, in spite of his bad taste in loyalties. The Sinclair tract is high and rich, also. Good piece of land Morgan is buying at Gascoigne, for that matter. Hawkins Island included. Hawkins is extremely fertile. Once leased by the Trustees of the Georgia Colony to a Dr. Hawkins and his spirited wife, who came with Ogelthorpe. The Hawkinses built a house there. I'd like to own that too."

'Why don't you buy it when Morgan sells? Along the Sinclair-Graham tract?"

per laughed. "To tell the truth, I'm overbought

now. Of course, 'tis only money, but I try to curb myself—not much—just enough to see Cannon's Point the way I dream it. Intend to write my partner, James Hamilton, about the Gascoigne land, though. He'd like that river flowing past." Couper looked at James a long time, a smile on his sensitive face. "I know I'm only burdening you with my desire to have you own some Island land, Gould. There's a saying that once a man gets a bit of St. Simons sand in his shoes, he finds a way to stay. I hope it's more than a saying where you're concerned. I want you for a neighbor. Want my old boyhood friend, Hamilton, here as well, but"—he threw back his head and laughed—"I don't do so well influencing Hamilton. Unlike me, he's a *stubborn* Scot, y' know."

"I'm not easily influenced either, Mr. Couper. But I am honored you want me."

"You're not influenced and I'm not finished with trying." He turned his horse. "Now let's race to the forks in the road. Suddenly I can't wait to see what Sans Foix has prepared for our dinner. I think I'll get Johnson to play his bagpipes tonight. Started him on the chanter myself. By now, he's more skillful than I ever was. Wait, hold your horse a minute, Gould. I've just had an idea. My wife needs some new pieces of furniture; two of my people possess real skill but need tutoring. Will you work for me at least another year after you finish with the survey?"

James was silent a moment. "I don't know what to say. You're—too generous with me. Could we just see what happens next year?"

Couper laughed. "You are a hard one to pin down, lad. Perhaps you can teach me a bit of that Yankee caution, but beware—I don't give up easily."

At the small writing desk in his room at Cannon's Point following the evening's festivities, James tried to concentrate on the letter to his family. He sharpened a quill, wrote: "St. Simons Island, Georgia. 19 December, 1794. My dear Mother and Sister. . . ." He laid down the quill. Bangor seemed far away, another life to which he felt bound only by his love and duty to

Mary and their mother. The memory of Jessie. . . .

Johnson, in the garden at sunset, an old tam-o'-shanter on his head, had stirred the memory tonight with the wild screaming skirl of Scottish reels and marches. The primitive rhythm still sounded in James' mind. His letter was harder to write because of those pipes. Only the thought of Mary's anxiety, his mother's worry, forced him to try:

> When you receive this letter more than two months will have passed since my departure. I signed on with Captain John Barry of Philadelphia, to do a timber survey in Georgia where live oak is being cut for the building of the first United States frigates. I am well and find St. Simons Island the most beautiful place I have ever seen. Undoubtedly you are enduring winter, while we ride about without jackets.

He walked to the open window. A soft wind breathed through the long needles of the pines, touched his face. He could still hear the pipes sounding over the ancient marshes and tidal rivers. The scent of evergreen was much the same here as along the Penobscot. Had Jessie married Horace yet?

Back at the desk, he scribbled rapidly:

> I may be here another year or more. My living accommodations are the best, in the home of Mr. John Couper of Cannon's Point, a gracious, kind Scotsman some eight years my senior.

Scotsman. He buried his head in his arms. I can't even write to my mother and sister, but she crowds in!

He had told Couper nothing, meant never to tell him. He dipped the quill again.

> Mary, Captain Budge is holding two months' wages which belong to me. You are to collect them when the need arises. Before that amount is gone, I will send more. I am being paid well. Your letters will reach me fav^{r} Captain Budge by way of Boston. We are shipping timber almost every week to the North. Give my warm regards to Captain Budge.
>
> Your Aff^{te} son and brother,
>
> James Gould.

At least his conscience was eased.

He undressed and slid his weary body between fresh linens on the comfortable bed, determined to dwell on the present. Couper had not laughed at his dream of building a lighthouse. Had listened courteously, but had gone right on extolling the beauties and joys and rewards of life as a St. Simons Island planter. Let him extol, James thought, as sleep came. Couper is a good man, seems to like me for myself. I feel welcome, but I intend to do my own thinking. Stay only as long as it seems right. . . .

Chapter 13

Jessie was lifting loaves of bread from the oven at the side of their fireplace when Mary hurried in from her mother's room, closed the door and leaned against it.

"Mary, what is it?"

"I don't know whether it's Mama's body or her mind. If there isn't a letter from James when the boat docks from Boston, I think she might collapse. He's been so good about writing twice a month for the two years he's been gone—I guess she's spoiled. But her headache's worse."

Jessie set the tray of bread on the table and walked to the window, her back to Mary. "James is her favorite now, isn't he?"

Mary sighed. "I think she's stopped having a favorite. The sun still rises and sets in Horace, but James is gone. He's been gone so long, Mama's sure she'll never live to see him again. Talks all the time now about how valuable James was to us."

"You speak as though he's dead."

"He is, in a way, to Mama. Two years this month since he went away, Jessie. I don't think he's coming home again, either. I still miss him as much as the day he left."

When Jessie turned to face her, Mary saw tears in the slanting brown eyes.

"It's my fault. I broke James' heart by loving Horace. I try, Mary, but I can never make it up either to you or to Mother Gould. I don't know how to try harder."

"Jessie, none of this is your fault. You couldn't make yourself love James. You're a good wife to Horace. You've been just right with me and with Mama. I'm sick inside that you still feel guilty, but I'm going to stop trying to talk you out of it."

"Don't stop, please! I need help!"

Mary put her arms around her sister-in-law. "None of us can change what's happened. Other people have had to overcome broken hearts. James isn't the first. I know my brothers—both of them. If one had to be jilted, I'm glad now it was James. He'll learn how to handle his broken heart better than Horace would."

Jessie stepped back to look at her. "Horace is—tender. He must be loved." Jessie's voice softened. "He is loved. Oh, he is loved."

"Well," Mary said, "I think I'll heat some milk. Mama likes fresh-baked bread and hot milk better than anything else. Maybe she'll eat." At the fireplace, she poured milk from a crock into a small kettle and stirred. Without turning around, she said, "I suppose I manage not to worry too much about James because, from experience, I know it's possible to learn to live again."

"Are you happy, Mary?"

She thought a while. "No. I'm content. But in a way, James is better off than me. A man can find a new life for himself. That's what I pray for him, that he will unlock his heart enough to find someone else to love him. I think my brother, James, needs to be loved every bit as much as Horace. More, maybe."

Mary emptied the hot milk into a bowl over the bread Jessie had crumbled. "Mind to take this to Mama? I'm going down to the dock. Nothing would help as much as a letter from James."

As she hurried along the wharf, the whole town of Bangor seemed determined to detain her with small talk, but the long-awaited letter from James was in her hand and Mary managed, at last, to reach the wooded area south of their house. As usual, she had to read first what he had written. If, as with his other letters, he had said almost nothing personal, she would need time to think up words to read aloud to her mother—between his sparsely written lines.

Her hands trembled as she broke the seal:

Cannon's Point Plantation
St. Simons Island, Georgia
4 October, 1796

Dear Mama and Mary,

I know more than six weeks have passed without a letter from me, but unexpectedly I have had extra work to do. As I wrote, my Government survey was not completed until early summer of this year, when Mr. Morgan sold his land at Gascoigne Bluff to Mr. Couper's business partner, James Hamilton. It fell my lot to make another survey, partially in the pay of Hamilton and partially in the pay of Morgan, as to the timber left standing on the tract, including small Hawkins Island. This is now finished and I am, as I have been almost from the first, still living in comfortable quarters in the excellent house of my friend, John Couper. The Coupers treat me warmly, as a member of the family, and I have had the privilege of watching their only child, James Hamilton Couper, begin to grow into a little man of more than two and a half years. He was an infant when I came.

Mary closed her eyes and breathed a prayer of thanks. He was telling them more about himself.

St. Simons Island holds little for me from now on except my friendship with the Coupers and the indescribable beauty of the place. (I am surely at home here.) Of course, I will have to find work of a more permanent nature soon, but I am in no hurry except that, once my usefulness to Mr. Couper has ended, I cannot accept his hospitality. Since finishing the surveys, I have been designing and building furniture, while tutoring two of his Negroes who seem skillful and quick. The Negroes, Johnson, who plays bagpipes, and Margin (so named because he was born one day as his black mother picked greens along the marsh margin) are both capable workmen and will surely be able to proceed without me by early next year. Mr. Couper wants me to stay on indefinitely, but of course, I refuse. I may go to Savannah to hunt work as a builder.

There was a little more. He hoped Mama was feeling better, that Mary had been well, but her heart caught on the sentence about hunting work in Savannah. James was not coming back. She had posted a letter to him last week telling of Mama's worsening condition. That might influence him, she thought. I'd never try to persuade him for my sake. Horace and Jessie have made me feel welcome. But Mama needs James. Mama needs him in order to get well.

Before she reached their fence, Mary could see Horace sitting by himself on the front steps, his head in his hands.

She unlatched the gate and hurried up the path. When Horace raised his head, he was crying.

"Mama's dead. Mama–died–just now. Jessie's bathing her."

Margin, his round alert brown face shining with sweat, rested his oars a moment and asked: "Be you goin' back up Norf, Mausa Gould? Soon as me an' Johnny gits good 'nough at de cab'nit work?"

Four Couper Negroes were rowing James to Frederica for supplies. The mood of all five occupants of the plantation boat was leisurely. The tide was right; the boat moved evenly through the clear, quiet water of the Hampton River.

"I honestly don't know what I'm going to do, Margin," James said, his eyes following a towering white cloud. "Got to get back to work at something. I'll stay 'til we finish that table for Miss Rebecca's Christmas present. I don't suppose I'll go before the first of the New Year. But I can't get along without working."

"You ain' done nuffin but work, Mausa Gould, eber since you come to lib wif us at Cannon Point. You be de hardest-workin' white man Margin eber seed. Why don' he stay wif us?" Margin directed his question at the other oarsmen, who grinned and nodded.

"I'm pleasured, Margin, that you'd all like to have me stay."

"Oh, all de niggahs, dey like you fine, suh. Me and Johnson, we sho' gonna miss you. Mausa Couper, he like you too. He do take on to hab you stay."

"Your master is a remarkable man."

"You spoke de truf, suh."

James thought for a while. "Margin, where I come from, at the North, there are almost no–slaves. Do you ever despise Mr. Couper because he owns you?"

James honestly could not decide what Margin's sudden frown meant. "Perhaps I had no business asking a question like that," he said.

"Oh, you kin axe me, Mausa Gould. Margin jis' wanna git yo' meanin' straight."

"You're a slave, just by the accident of having been born black in the section of a country where slavery is legal. Doesn't that ever make you angry? Doesn't it make you hate somebody?"

Margin shook his head. "Gittin' hate in yo' heart ain' gonna change de color ob yo' skin. Bein' black fo' a white man lak Mausa Couper's better'n bein black fo' anybody else."

Margin resumed rowing, as another oarsman rested. For a long time, no one spoke. After a while, the black men began to sing—the improvised rowing song which told other Islanders, long before they saw the boat, that Couper's oarsmen were coming. The song was about their Mistress, Rebecca Couper:

Red bird fly—eye—eye
Thru de sky—eye—eye
Ain' no purtier, ain' no fairer
Den Miss Becky, den Miss Becky.

Blue bird sing—ing—ing
On de wing—ing—ing
Ain't no song, ain' no song
Lak Miss Becky—lak Miss Becky.

James knew the oarsmen well—Margin, Eddie, Tom, and Peter. These men lived at Cannon's Point as comfortably as many whites in Granville, or in Bangor. Lived better than some, because there was no such thing as hunger along the Georgia coast. The ocean was their inexhaustible pantry, and John Couper fed, clothed, housed them well and allowed ample time for their own gardening. The cabins in the quarters at Cannon's Point were kept in repair, whitewashed, floored with wood—most with an area called a hall, two sleeping rooms and a loft for the children. Every man had honest work to do, an allotted task each day according to his ability and strength. Yet it troubled James to see intelligent, capable men like Cuffy and Margin and Johnson totally dependent, even upon a kind man such as Couper. Though Margin's answer had helped some, it was not enough. Still, it was the only answer a black man dared have, James supposed, and live with himself.

Nearing the bend above the town of Frederica, the oarsmen—now in a primitive, nasal tone, were chanting:

Good-by, Brother—
  Hmmh
I'm goin' to leave you—
  Hmmh
For you cain' go wif me—
  Aye, Lord,
Time is drawin' nigh.

A sad song seemed the same as a gay one to these men, and James wondered if that could be their secret. Whatever they felt, they framed it in song—black sorrow, clear joy.

At the Frederica wharf, James watched the muscular brown bodies tie up, then unload the boat, still singing. Perhaps the wise course was the one John Couper had chosen: stop trying to understand. Don't think about what it really means to own a man. Don't try to think what it means to be owned.

On the return trip, James sat in silence, staring straight ahead—seeing none of the copper or gold or pale green of the late autumn sunset tinting the deathly quiet water, as the oarsmen hurried their strokes to reach Cannon's Point dock before the tide ebbed too low for landing.

He had read Mary's letter only once. It said only one thing of importance. Mama is dead.

Slowly, the realization crept over him that right now, at least for the remainder of the trip up the Frederica to the Hampton River, he *needed these slaves.* White men would have asked questions. The four slaves were simply taking him home, knowing instinctively not to sing, their oars stroking the water almost soundlessly, their strong hearts open to whatever misery twisted his soul.

Chapter 14

Through the short winter days and into the lenghening days of spring, James worked from morning to night making needed repairs at Cannon's Point—improvements in the large, many-ovened kitchen. He had built new, carefully designed banisters on each side of the wide front steps—a design which he felt better suited the architecture of the big house. Two months had been spent surveying the Couper woods, both at Cannon's Point and at Couper's holdings on the South End of St. Simons. He had directed the Negroes in the proper thinning of the thick stands of pine and oak and hickory as the giant woodpiles were replenished to supply the kitchen, the fireplaces in the main house and those in the cabins at the quarters.

He had intended to be gone from the Island early in 1797, but beyond having reached the South, he had not moved any nearer his dream of making a name for himself. It was the end of February, and he was still living with the Coupers. He could afford to buy at least a small part of the Sinclair-Graham tract, could start with a few Negroes, and would himself be an extra hand because hard work had been his life. The monies from the Government survey lay untouched in a Savannah bank. He had been able to send regular drafts to Mary out of the extra he had earned from Couper and Morgan and Hamilton. Where his security was concerned, he was free to choose his next step. Could go to Savannah or Charleston and build houses. With his mother gone, there was no reason ever to return North. Mary could join him some day. Why, he wondered, with the way clear, did he hesitate to take the next step?

As usual, when troubled, he retreated into himself; evaded conversation with John Couper; spent hours alone crabbing in the Hampton River, plowing barefoot through the sticky black mud at low tide to fill baskets with oysters, frequently roasting them for himself over a small fire built out of sight of the big house. He would miss the smell of the marshes, the laughter and barking dog and crying babies and the ring of Cuffy's hammer in the blacksmith shop. These were not the sounds that stretched a man's nerves; they were safe sounds, enclosing him in the sequestered life of his friend's plantation.

Another man from Massachusetts named John Adams had just been elected President of the United States. Adams from Braintree, a farmer, too, not a national wartime hero, like George Washington. Adams was not the kind of man people idolized. James had seen him once on a Boston street. He still recalled the effect on him. Merely glimpsing the rotund, unprepossessing gentleman had somehow reassured James that he, too, could reach his own goal. By only one vote, to be sure, but a Massachusetts farmer now held the highest office in the land.

Poling John Couper in a small bateau across the quiet waters of little Jones Creek between Cannon's Point and Hampton on a sunlit afternoon toward the end of the first week in March, James told his friend that he was leaving. "I've stayed too long as it is, John. I mean to ask Major Butler at dinner tonight if he knows of an opportunity in Charleston."

"Is that why you agreed so promptly to go with me to old Butler's dinner party?"

"I suppose it is. You know by now I'm not much for parties. I—don't know how to thank you for all you've done for me. I stayed so long—because Cannon's Point is the way I always thought home should be."

"Give yourself more time to recover from your mother's death, James. When a man's mother dies, he needs more than ever to feel at home somewhere. I know. No lad ever wanted to escape the shackles of family more than I at sixteen. But when the letter reached me here that my mother had died in Lochwinnoch, the first thing I wanted to do was run back to Scotland. I didn't run. Neither will you, but what you do next may be the turning point in your whole life. Let this be your home a bit longer."

James tied the bateau at the Hampton dock, and the two friends strolled past the big oak under which James had sat his first night on St. Simons Island, and across the wide, fenced front yard of the new Hampton Big House. James dreaded the evening. Major Pierce Butler was John Couper's opposite, he had heard. Stiff, dogmatic, overly strict with his people, but an important man in government and in Charleston. To stay near John Couper would mean strength and comfort, but the time had come for him to begin again to depend only upon himself. In all the world now, he had no one but Mary, and with Mama gone, even Mary seemed a part of another life.

The newly built plantation house at Hampton Point lacked the charm and elegance of the Couper home. James had watched it go up—solidly built, staunch, unyielding like its owner, who lived most of the year away from his plantation. For dinner, two soups—clam broth and chicken mulligatawny—were served first; then fish, shrimp pies, crab in shell, a lamb and a beef roast with vegetables. After a simple dessert of tartlets of orange marmalade—the oranges from Couper's trees—dried fruit and nuts, the great punch bowl was carried in filled with a heady mixture of rum, brandy, sugar, and lemon juice. Major Butler handed around heavy goblets to John Couper, to James—and to the third guest, whom James had watched all through the meal. A middle-aged, flamboyantly talkative gentleman known as Don Juan McQueen, Commander of the St. Johns and St. Marys Rivers in Spanish East Florida.

In spite of his natural mistrust of a man who talked as much as McQueen, James felt uneasily drawn to him and listened to every word he had to say about East Florida, his adopted land.

"Perhaps I should explain to our young friend, Gould," John Couper said, "that Mr. John McQueen—"

"Don Juan McQueen, if you don't object, Mr. Couper," McQueen interrupted courteously. "In all ways I have become His Majesty's subject, Don Juán McQueen."

Couper smiled, bowed. "I beg your pardon, Don Juan McQueen. You see, sir, it was my pleasure to have met you while you were still an American named John McQueen."

"I fully understand and accept your apology, sir."

James found himself enjoying this man, who seemed unaware that his conversion not only to the Catholic faith but to the Spanish Monarchy was somehow comical. Couper obviously was highly amused by McQueen. Tolerant, almost affectionate smiles flickered, even over Pierce Butler's stern face.

"As I was saying," Couper went on, "perhaps our friend Gould should understand that we are honored by the privilege of your company, McQueen, since you rarely visit Georgia these days."

Don Juan McQueen shifted his chair so that he could stretch his scarlet-clad legs and unfasten a gold-washed button or two in the jacket of his lace-trimmed uniform. "The honor of this visit is mine," he declared. "But tell me, Mr. Gould—are you not from my old land at the North of these United States?"

"Yes, sir. Massachusetts."

McQueen drained his glass, set it firmly on the table. "Transplanted humanity! More's the pity, I say, that man finds it so impossible to put down his roots that his progeny might grow up and flower in a place called—home. Still, when a man—uh—is transplanted as I have been privileged to be, to the land of flowers and sunlight, he can only give thanks." He raised his refilled goblet. "To His Royal Majesty, Don Carlos, by the grace of God, King of Castile, of Leon, of Aragon, of the Two Sicilies, of Jerusalem, of Majorca, of Seville, etcetera, etcetera—as well as of my adopted, beloved land, East Florida!"

The others raised their glasses with him, even Butler unable to stifle a chuckle.

"As I was saying," McQueen plunged on, "when a man has the good fortune to have been set down in a land so fair as the land of my Spanish adoption, then some of the heartbreak of leaving wife and home and beloved children is lessened. Especially, my enjoyable friends, when there is no such thing as a tax! The compensations far outweigh the tragedy of displacement—even for a loving father such as I, who longs by some laudable means to collect enough to pay his debts before he goes to his long home."

James was beginning to piece together the parts of Don Juan McQueen's story. Obviously, he had been forced to flee to East Florida because he could not pay his Georgia real estate taxes. Entertaining, graceful, even with a certain appealing innocence, Don Juan McQueen could not be termed a stable citizen, and yet James could not dislike him.

"Where, may I inquire," Butler asked, "did you come upon that rather—unique uniform, McQueen?"

McQueen straightened his shoulders, quickly rebuttoned his jacket, so as to give them the full effect. "Designed it myself the minute I learned that His Majesty was about to bestow upon me the lofty title of Commander of the St. Johns and St. Marys Rivers!"

Butler, warmed by his punch, seemed to be relishing the exhange. "What do you command? What does it mean to be the commander of a river?"

"Why, sir, it means that I command the banks! And along the banks of both the St. Johns and the St. Marys lie veritable gold mines if one is alert."

"In captured runaway slaves?"

"And in timber, Major Butler! Your new President, Mr. John Adams, will do well not to listen to his biggety young Vice President, Mr. Thomas Jefferson, in alienating Spain. Adams must see only to vastly improved relations!"

Pierce Butler snorted. "John Adams, indeed! It's more than my stomach can endure to realize that pompous, puckery, Yankee son of a harness maker is actually our President."

James knew Couper was watching him, but he kept silent. What difference did it make if Butler despised John Adams? Butler and every other American would find out that the affairs of the country during the next four years would be handled with sanity and wisdom. He disliked his host more than ever, but he would not stoop to argument. Adams needed no defense.

"That domineering little Federalist will send the country to hell, you mark my word!"

Couper said, "Ah, Butler, don't decide, just because Adams gaveled you to silence in the Senate the day you tried to dissolve the Union in a speech in defense of us cotton farmers, that he'll wreck the ship of state!"

Butler's face was red with anger. "I'm your host and your longtime friend, Jock Couper, but I cannot hold my tongue when that man's name is lauded. Not only has Georgia lost all hope of Federal payment for her escaped slaves because of the stiff-necked Yankee Puritan, he's a boor besides! He so insulted me that day—when he was merely Washington's Vice President—I had no choice but to challenge him to a duel."

James could see that Couper was enjoying himself. "Did you now? And did Adams accept?"

"Accept? Of course, he did not. He's a coward as well as a monarchist. Ignored me entirely!"

After an awkward silence, Don Juan McQueen began again. "Gentlemen, it seems to me that our conversation should move to loftier themes. I extend to each of you a warm, enthusiastic invitation to visit me in St. Augustine. I am a poor man, though contented, but I confess I yearn for such company as yours. I can promise a table almost as laden as our host's and fruit more succulent than you have dreamed of eating." He turned abruptly to James. "You, in particular, young man, should visit me. Spanish East Florida needs you. You need Spanish East Florida!"

"Why, sir?"

"Why? For one thing, there is a shortage of accomplished, well-recommended beaux in Florida. For another, with your qualifications as a timberman—" He broke off, jumped to his feet. "Why have I been so remiss? I hereby offer you the golden chance to take up life in Spanish East Florida at once—in the paradise of the Spanish East—the St. Marys River!"

"I thought you lived on the St. Johns," Butler said drily.

"I do. But it just so happens—how it slipped my mind, I cannot say—that I know of a lease to be had at Mills Ferry some thirty miles up the St. Marys, Gould. A sawmill in reasonable repair stands on the banks of a flowing millstream—called, I believe, Cabbage Creek—there are at least seven millhands waiting for operation to be resumed. How long these restless crackers will wait, I cannot say. But the land is owned by old Mrs. Drayson, who resides still in her tall frame house by the mill. Her son, who operated the mill, was—uh—killed in a fight with slave traders. The elderly lady is, of course, dependent now on these millhands for everything. Good workers, but a degraded lot at best."

"How large is the tract?" Couper asked. "Who owns the lease?"

"Ah, we have reached the interesting part of the story." McQueen sat down again. "Nine hundred acres of magnificent oak and pine—giant tree standing beside giant tree, waiting to fill the pockets of some experienced young man like you, Gould. Why, the trees are of such incredible size that one could make a fortune in squared timber alone!"

"Who owns the lease?" Couper persisted.

"Why, Don Juan McQueen owns it."

"I thought so," Butler said.

"I declare to you, gentlemen, in all the land ventures in which I have succeeded—and lost—none has been so rich in future possibilities. If some courageous, qualified gentleman fails to see the future in this operation, alas, it too will be lost."

"Lost?" James asked the question this time.

"Well, lost to me, of course. On my way to visit my dear wife and children in Savannah last month, I obtained it from the griefstricken Mrs. Drayson. I can see her now, watching me as my skiff left her dock—waving from her window—praying for my return or the arrival of someone like you, Gould. She is at the mercy of those loutish millhands—and the Creeks."

"I expect one needs to be on the lookout for Indians in that Godforsaken spot," Butler said.

"Ah, that is one service I can provide. The Florida Indians are hostile to Georgians because you are not Spanish sympathizers. I have—shall we say—contact with them. I could almost guarantee you would not be bothered, Gould, taking the lease from me."

Couper laughed. "An 'almost guarantee'? I doubt even you can control those Creeks. McQueen. They hate Georgians now as much as they revered Oglethorpe and his Colonials."

James asked, "Do you know the land where the lease is located, Mr. Couper?"

"Why, yes, but don't tell me you're interested in taking a gamble on this wilderness frontier?"

"I am. That is, if you'll be present when the deal is discussed. May I impose once more?"

Couper clapped his hand to his forehead. "Of course, of course. But for a quiet, retiring young man like yourself, you do jump to decisions."

"I'm interested. I know timber and mills."

McQueen was on his feet again, his hand extended. "Accept my heartfelt congratulations, young man! You'll never be sorry a day of your life—and since seventeen ninety, now that my esteemed friend Governor Quesada is there, it is no longer necessary to renounce your Protestant faith or your American citizenship. I highly recommend doing both, but neither is required."

"I know that," James said.

"Well, then, I leave tomorrow when the tide suits." McQueen turned to Couper. "May we close the deal at your place, Jock?"

"Gould and I will be waiting for you first thing in the morning, but I warn you, you old robber, I know this lad. He'll not be easily fooled."

Some two hours later, after the short trip back across Jones Creek, James and Couper walked slowly up the path from Cannon's Point landing, James' tin lantern lighting their way. In the bateau, neither had spoken of the St. Marys lease.

"McQueen's an eccentric, my friend," Couper said at last, as they entered the garden. "But he does know good timberland. With me present, I don't think he'll try to put his price out of your reach. 'Tis a dangerous wilderness on the Spanish side of the St. Marys, but a good opportunity. I wouldn't try to persuade you to turn it down. I know the way you think now, James. You've got it in your mind to make enough money in your own timber operation so you won't have to take just what comes—as a builder."

Would he ever feel as comfortable with anyone again as with Jock Couper? Life on the St. Marys River among a gang of cracker millhands, risking Indian attacks, border fights with slave smugglers, would not fulfill his dream, but it seemed the next step. He could invest his earnings, work hard and in a few years be his own man.

"If you consider his offer good, I'm going."

They stood at the bottom of the wide front steps, the lantern throwing long, splintered shafts of light through its beveled glass panels, picking out green palmetto and yucca spikes, a bright patch of coral azalea freshly in bloom.

"Our prayers will follow you," Couper said. "Now, I know its late, but what I have to say, I don't want to hold 'til tomorrow."

They sat down on the steps.

"I'll hate leaving, Jock."

"I know." Couper's voice grew serious. "I have discovered a few things about you since you've been with us. You're proud to the point of being stubborn. Determined to make your own way as far as possible. To be your own man. I admire this, but it can also handicap you when you're about to leave to work in a foreign country—a violent, often criminal wilderness where everyone will be a stranger. I don't want you to go without learning a wee bit more about how to receive from those who want to help you."

"I've done nothing but receive from you and Mrs. Couper."

"Hold that lantern higher so I can see your face. Are you scowling? Good, you're smiling. Do that more often, James. You've a disarming smile. The more so, I suppose, because you use it so seldom. In a roundabout, awkward way I'm leading up to something. I've decided to give Margin to you. He has no family. The fellow's grown attached to you. I've had the papers drawn up ever since I first began to suspect you'd be leaving us. We can go to my desk and settle it tonight."

James said nothing for a moment. "You mean you'd *give* Margin to me—to own?"

"That's exactly what I mean. Will you make me happy by accepting?"

"No, John. I couldn't."

"There you go being obstinate again. Rebecca has her heart set on it too. When she finds out you're about to leave for the wilds of the St. Marys, she'll want more than ever to know Margin's with you. I beg you not to disappoint us, my friend."

"I wish I knew a kinder way to say this, but I—cannot own a slave."

After a long time, Couper asked quietly, "You *will* not, or you *can*not?"

"I cannot. In spite of my wish to please you, I cannot accept."

"But, do you mean to go off—all alone?"

"I've always gone that way."

"I see. Very well, the subject's closed." Couper stood up.

In a moment, James asked, "Do you understand at all why I can't take Margin?"

They climbed the steps. Couper held open the door. "I not only understand; I think I envy you. Let's go to the cupboard now and discover what Sans Foix left out for us to nibble before we retire. Hungry?"

"Not very."

"Then we'll find a drop of claret to whet your appetite. I do own Sans Foix, and there's no merit whatever in letting his culinary efforts go to waste. He's already informed me that for your farewell dinner—a pleasure we will now all have to forego—he had planned to create his famous secret roast turkey." Couper removed the crystal stopper from the decanter as he talked; filled two small glasses. "Do you know that Sans Foix bones a turkey, then reassembles it—working, if need be, under a clean linen cloth lest even the kitchen help discover his secret—so that when he's finished, the bird looks once more whole?"

James lifted his glass. "To your health and happiness, Jock. I will never forget you."

Couper raised his own glass. "Success to you, my friend, success. I won't say farewell tonight, tomorrow morning—ever, James Gould. I mean only to wave you off with McQueen, then wait for the day we can welcome you back to Cannon's Point."

Chapter 15

A flurry of rain squalls began to slow their progress southward as the McQueen longboat entered the Cumberland River, and it was late morning of the second day when the weary oarsmen landed James and Don Juan McQueen at the wharf in St. Marys.

The hurried farewells at Cannon's Point, the exhausting trip, the surprisingly busy St. Marys waterfront, and the eccentric Don Juan McQueen, who scanned the crowds furtively while giving James advice, made for a sense of nightmare, half frightening, half ridiculous.

"My stay here will be limited," McQueen said, smoothing the limp lace of his uniform. "I am not exactly welcome in Georgia, you know. The town of St. Marys is still in Georgia. I will not breathe freely until I'm safely across the river in my beloved Spanish East Florida, but I must see to your welfare. My Christian conscience will not permit me to do otherwise."

"You may trust McQueen," Couper had said, when he approved the cost of the lease. "I don't think the man is dishonest. He's a lovable, not very wise opportunist, but he does know timberland—as I've said. I give you my blessings, James. Think of McQueen as a gentleman whose intentions are good, who carries off his enforced exile with style and dignity. Before you reach St. Marys, you'll come to like him, perhaps even to trust him."

Couper was right. James did feel foolish trailing around St. Marys with the Commander in his gaudy uniform, but he trusted the connections McQueen made for him—Randolph McGillis, the Camden County Sheriff, Collector of the Port of St. Marys, and James Seagrove, who according to McQueen was "Camden County's most prominent citizen," Creek Agent and member of the legislature. In less than two hours, McGillis had found James a good secondhand cypress canoe and had directed him to trustworthy merchants for flour, coffee, sugar, blankets, shot, and powder; and through Seagrove, a strong-bodied Creek named Comochichi had signed on with James, not only to make the more-than-thirty-mile trip up the St. Marys River to Mills Ferry, but to live and work at the new place in whatever capacity James needed him.

McQueen delayed his own depature until James and Comochichi had loaded their canoe, and he was still standing on the St. Marys dock waving his gold-braided hat in farewell as they rounded the first bend in the St. Marys, the crookedest river in the world, according to McQueen, "with water so clean it could be carried halfway across the globe before it spoiled."

With an earlier start, the distance could have been covered in a day, but still some fifteen miles from Mills Ferry, they were forced by darkness to camp for the night.

Rolled in a thick blanket on a pallet of pine branches woven by Comochichi, James lay looking up into the now cloudless sky and knew he would not sleep. He had slept on the ground night after night on hunting trips with William, with Shays' men, and along the Penobscot on timber surveys for Captain Budge, but in spite of the warmth of the blanket and the fire by which Comochichi still sat, the dampness of the semitropic spring night chilled his bones. Even the stars seemed frighteningly close. He shivered; anxious, apprehensive. It was only, he told himself, that he had grown soft from more than two years in the comfortable house at Cannon's Point; was suffering from the sudden uprooting, the quick jump into a dangerous, uncertain new venture. On the word of a quixotic exile who dramatized everything, he had invested most of his savings, his very life in what could turn into a rousing success or a crushing failure. The uncertainty alone could account for his fear, and yet, hadn't he leaped as suddenly into the proposition made in a Boston tavern by tipsy Captain

Budge? Why had he felt no fear on the schooner to Bangor?

He sat up and saw the Indian glance toward him without moving his half-shaved head. "Don't you sleep, Comochichi?"

"When Comochichi sure, he sleep."

"Sure we won't be attacked by the cats?" James meant to joke.

The Indian nodded, his face solemn. "Wildcat or Creek."

James scrambled stiffly to his feet and sat down by the fire across from Comochichi, where he could study the smooth brown stoical face. "Are we in danger from your people here?"

"Spanish Indian always dangerous."

"You mean the Creeks who are on the Spanish side —against Georgians."

The Indian nodded.

"These Spanish-loving Creeks live near here?"

"Live where stealing good."

"How do they feel about you?"

Comochichi shrugged.

"How will they feel about me coming to run a sawmill on the Spanish side of the river?"

"Hm."

The Indian reached for a handful of oak branches, tossed them onto the fire. In the flare of bright orange light, James looked at the blunt-featured face, the small black eyes, at nostrils sensitive as those of a deer. "How is it you came with me, Comochichi? Weren't you better off in St. Marys, since you're not friendly with the Spanish?"

"Comochichi like wilderness. No people."

"You dislike—all people? Or just white people?"

"Herds—any kind."

"I see. So do I."

For the first time, they exhanged direct looks.

"You sleep," the Indian said. "Still long trip."

James stood up, stretched, peered into the shadowy forest crowding the hammock land where they camped. I don't think I fear Comochichi, he thought. He's the Indian I've hired. I have to trust him. If he decides to kill me in the night, there isn't one thing I can do about it anyway.

He lay down, dread closer around him than his blanket. After a while, Comochichi slept. James did not.

"Mr. McQueen said we'd have no trouble recognizing the place by the old lady's tall, narrow house. Said we'd see the chimney as soon as we round the bend at the mouth of Cabbage Creek. Right after we see her house, we spot the mill on the creek bank."

The Indian paddled in silence for a mile or so, then James asked: "If you and others of your tribe don't favor the Spanish, what do you think of Georgians?"

Comochichi shrugged.

"Nothing, eh?"

The Indian shrugged again.

"While I stayed on St. Simons Island, I read of the Englishman, Oglethorpe, who settled the Colony of Georgia for the Crown. He seemed to be one white man who got along with Indians."

"White man change since then."

"Don Juan McQueen feels sure we won't have any trouble."

Comochichi swerved suddenly—an enormous alligator missed his mark, slid under the canoe—and before James could restack scattered supplies, both men saw the black smoke rising from what had been the old lady's house. They rounded the bend at the mouth of Cabbage Creek and, across the clearing beyond the still-burning ruins, saw the Indians streak away into the forest. As soon as the last horse and rider vanished, the air was split by a prolonged, wild whoop.

Mrs. Drayson's body lay in the smoking rubble which had been her parlor, a heavy iron candelabra still clutched in her hand, her scalp gone, the room littered with broken, charred furniture.

By evening, the millhands and their sallow-faced wives and children had straggled back from forest hiding places to their shacks. After a brief visit to each cabin—where he was received with neither hostility nor welcome—James helped Comochichi bury the old lady and once more settled for the night on the ground, beside another campfire.

"Millhands stay—work for you?" the Indian asked.

"They say so, *if* I protect them from another Creek attack." He sighed. "Who can do that?"

"Send letter. Don Juan McQueen."

James sat up. "That's right! A letter to McQueen can't do any harm. If I can tell the millhands I know him, have written for help—"

The Indian nodded.

"Comochichi, will you take a letter back to St. Marys tomorrow?"

"You not afraid stay?"

James laughed a little. "Frankly, I am. But until I can get more familiar with this territory, I think I'd be just as afraid with you here. I'll write the letter first thing in the morning. How soon can you be back again?"

"Morning of third day—if no trouble."

"What kind of trouble do you mean?"

The Indian shrugged. "Alligators."

James grinned. "Get some sleep. That's a long trip with no one to spell you. No need to watch our fire. The smoke from the old lady's house will keep the cats away. Goodnight."

"Good night—friend."

Chapter 16

"Hit don' do no good fer you to come bellyachin' 'bout that danged Injun to us, Gould. You jist up an' showed us how green y'are 'bout these parts by lettin' 'im take yer onliest canoe by hisself all the way to St. Marys. Been gone two weeks! He ain't comin' back."

James glanced at Sam Webber, then looked away down the empty river as Webber walked off. He especially distrusted Webber, an expert axman, and Leaven Kyser, who handled the mill.

Feeling the need to learn more about the people on whom he would have to depend, he determined to try, at least, to talk to Ebba, Leaven Kyser's wife. He found Ebba at the well and began to question her.

"I ain't rightly his wife, but clost enough," Ebba drawled. "Ain't no better millhand in these parts than Leaven. Yo're plumb fortunate he's still here. But whut I wanta know is—do you mean to stay on here at Mills Ferry?"

"Of course I do," he answered, studying Ebba's watery blue eyes for some sign of intelligence he might trust. "Why do you ask?"

"Effen yo're aimin' to stay an' make money lak the ol' lady's son did oncet, then I don't aim to leave Leaven. Him bein' the bestchu got an' all, he makes good when the mill's workin' full time."

"I see."

"I wonder d'you see? Us womenfolks's gotta look arter ourselves. Me an' t'others, we stays or we shifts to another man. Oh, I kin stummick Leaven, bad teeth an' all, long as he's makin' good. One man smells purty much the same as t'other, anyhow."

"I plan to stay, all right, and your husband is a good millhand. No reason why he won't stay too. Mrs. Kyser?"

"Whatchu want?"

"How long have you and Leaven been here?"

"Purt' near three year. We come over from Georgie. He stole us some cattle an' a horse, then we heerd 'bout this mill. Effen yo're awantin' to know has them Injuns kilt here afore, the answer's no. Leaven, he thinks they done it to skeer you off."

"But I didn't decide to take the lease until a few days before I got here. How did they know I was coming?"

She spat a long arc of snuff juice and laughed. "Them Injuns knows things afore they happen! They're conjures—ever last one of 'em. Out-an'-out devil's conjures. Got full sway, the devil has. Ain't nary a church anywheres, so ol' Satan, he's got full sway with everbody." She took a step toward him. "Mister, effen yo're awonderin' 'bout the rest of us white folks here, I kin give you a piece of wisdom."

"I'd be grateful."

"Except fer a smart woman like me, that knows how to take keer of herself, you stay away—keep yer distance from the womenfolks. Now, you don't need to spurn me. Ebba, she knows what to do. Leaven Kyser's a dumb ox. But watch yer sparkin' with me so's to keep the other womenfolks from talkin' amongst theirselves. You do that an' you'll git along jist fine. All our men kin work good. Course, you cain't trust 'em no further'n you kin throw a ox, but lessen you rile 'em by botherin' their womenfolks, you'll do all right. All except me, Ebba. I kin look arter myself."

James felt his stomach turn. The woman stood batting her pale eyes at him, twisting back and forth on one horny bare foot.

"Don't worry about that, Mrs. Kyser," he said stiffly and turned to walk away.

"Aw, now, hold on. I didn't aim to rile you by whut I said. Butchu don't need to worry 'bout no trouble with Ebba. She knows her way through these woods. Jist any time, when yo're off surveyin' an' huntin' new timber, Ebba, she kin findju. Jist count on me. Letcher heart down, purty man, an' don' pay no mind to them other wenches."

"I order you never to follow me into the woods, is that clear?"

Ebba stepped back, her loose mouth hanging open in surprise. Then she grinned. "Well, didju hear that—he *orders* me! He *orders* me!" She was rocking back and forth on her heels. "You know what I'll do? I'll jist bide my time. A fine-lookin' young feller like you'll git woman-hungry 'fore long in this wilderness—so hungry fer a woman, he cain't sleep nights. I ain't rushin' you none. Jist lettin' you know gentle like that Ebba kin take keer of Leaven—when yo're ready."

From that day, he stopped attempting any kind of conversation belong instructions to the men, as they began to repair the mill wheel, make new water buckets, reinforce the dock. He saw to it that he was never alone, even with the millhands' stringy-haired little girls, and permitted no one to come inside the temporary lean-to he had built for himself and Comochichi, still hoping the Indian would be back.

Within a month he had built a new skiff, and the first square pine timber had been spiked and chained together into a raft, ready to be poled around the sharp bends in the snakelike river to St. Marys for shipment to England. The supply of sound timber seemed inexhaustible, and as yet he had surveyed only a small portion of the tract. Economically, he had made a wise move, but he trusted no one. Comochichi, the one person on whom he had relied, had not only stolen his boat and deserted him after one night at the mill; there was a strong chance that the Indian had signaled his tribesmen that the new mill operator from Georgia had arrived.

Near the end of the third week in April, as he worked on the foundation of a cabin for himself, James spotted a canoe with a lone man aboard, poling, not paddling, around the bend in the river. He reached for his gun, ran across the clearing and onto the dock. Comochichi was tying the canoe to a piling.

For a moment, James could only stare at the Indian, who now stood facing him. He laid down his gun and walked toward Comochichi.

"Where have you been?"

"With squaw."

"I didn't know you had a squaw!"

"Comochichi near death." He pointed to an ugly, fresh scar on the front of his left thigh. "Rattlesnake bite. Squaw save life."

"Did you get to St. Marys to post the letter to McQueen before the snake bit you?"

The Indian nodded. "Rattler strike night I start back."

James sank down on a piling, weak with relief. "I don't know what to say, except that I've never been so glad to see anyone. I was sure you had betrayed me, stolen my canoe. I didn't know what else to think."

"Only sickness keep Comochichi away." He pointed to himself, then to James. "We friends."

"I believe that now. I won't doubt it again. I promise."

"Good. White millhands no friends."

"You're right about that, but they do work. See what we've done while you were gone?"

Comochichi looked at the reinforced mill house, the new buckets on the big wheel, the heavier dam to store up the flat tidal waters, the foundation of James' new cabin, the raft of squared timber chained by the dock. "You do good. We do better—together."

"I hope so. Maybe the old Commander of the St. Johns and the St. Marys can persuade the Creeks to leave us alone. After all, I paid him well for this lease. He'll share in the profits."

"No way know about Creeks."

Three years after James had finished his own log cabin, Comochichi still insisted that he preferred to sleep at the edge of the clearing. He took shelter only when it rained, in the woodshed attached to James' house. James had learned not to question when his friend stated a preference. Perhaps he did rest better on his bed of woven pine branches, but he could also stay on guard if he slept outside.

Not once again had James heard the Indian mention the squaw who had cared for him. Comochichi had thrown in his lot with the Gould Mill, with the owner. What he did with his wages, James had no notion.

James' mill was prospering. Even the white crackers seemed satisfied, and in three years there had been no news of an attack anywhere between his place and the town of St. Marys. Don Juan McQueen's mysterious contact with the Creeks seemed effective.

Checking through his meticulously kept account ledger at the end of the year 1800, James was gratified with the steady increase in his own income. McQueen had prospered through his efforts, too, and each time James went to St. Marys to ship more lumber—squared timber mostly, bound for England—warm, verbose letters of praise awaited him from the ailing but still ebullient Commander. "How I long to be able to bless you in person," McQueen wrote again and again, "and to realize at last the privilege of extending to you the delights and civilities of St. Augustine. Do honor me with a visit, my friend Gould, and perhaps face to face I can convey my gratitude to you for the superb work you have done on the St. Marys River tract. Beyond my wildest expectations!"

Although he replied regularly, enclosing detailed reports on the enterprise at Mills Ferry and commiserating with McQueen because of his "troublesome gout," visiting the volatile McQueen did not interest James. But he did look forward to the autumn of 1801, because by then, the additional men he had hired would be able to operate the mill in his absence, and in October, always his favorite month on St. Simons, he planned to spend a week at Cannon's Point, on his way to Savannah to sign what could turn out to be a substantial new lumber contract.

A letter from Habersham in Savannah, dated October 2, 1801, lifted James' spirits still more. The lumber order, which would take three years to fill, could easily net him enough to sell the Mills Ferry lease, move back to civilization, and begin, at last, to build houses and other things.

Comochichi accompanied him as far as St. Marys,

and in October 18, James booked passage on a small cotton packet with a scheduled stop at St. Simons Island.

The week at Cannon's Point went fast, but it was long enough for James to realize how lonely he had been. He and Couper brought each other up to date on all their business transactions and spent hours reading and discussing the news in the Savannah papers—a luxury James had sorely missed. He informed Couper that the Habersham deal could make him a well-to-do man; Couper told him laughingly, that the Sinclair-Graham tract was still for sale. There seemed little left unsaid, but as they sat once more in the book-lined library on their last evening together, a sadness hung between them.

"I don't know when I've enjoyed a visit more, James," Couper said, his voice unusually solemn.

"Even knowing how you exaggerate, I'm gratified, Jock. A man hears so few civil remarks down there in the wilderness. Wasn't at all sure I'd still remember how to converse or to conduct myself in a gentleman's home. Hope I haven't disgraced you."

"You couldn't disgrace me, James, no matter what you did or said. But I do worry about you . . . no romantic attachments?"

James laughed. "I don't see a decent woman at St. Marys more than four or five time's a year."

"Not good. Still you couldn't ask a lady to live in that wilderness." Couper shook his head. "No ladies, no civil society. Do you even know your nearest neighbors?"

"I've met them. We accommodate each other when possible with mail, supplies from St. Marys. When they go, they're nice enough to come out of their way to my place just to collect any letters I might need to post."

"Who are they? What manner of folk?"

"British family named Howsam. He inherited a grant of eight hundred acres some ten miles down the river from my place. Somehow the land is still in their family from the British occupation of the Floridas."

"Odd. I thought the Spanish had chased every Britisher out."

"I keep thinking they'll lose their grant any day, but they feel secure. Man and his wife about your age, I'd say, with two sons and an infant daughter. Own something like thirty or forty slaves. He's an indigo planter. Doing well. They seem to like it."

"Do you—like it, James? Or do you just endure?"

"It's my home for now."

"Do you know that your sister and brother in Bangor are well?"

"My sister writes regularly. I hope to have her join me later on in Savannah or Charleston. My wilderness doesn't appeal to her. I'll never go back to Bangor."

"Still no slaves, eh?"

"Still no slaves."

"To your wilderness, James! May money grow on every tree. I don't know how you tolerate it, but if it suits you—I toast it!" He set down his glass. "Don't wait so long to come again, friend—and God's blessing on your trip to Savannah."

Chapter 17

Christmas back at Mills Ferry was no lonelier for James than any other day. Except during the two years spent with the Coupers, he had never celebrated the holiday, and both he and the millhands were eager to work on the new lumber order from Habersham in Savannah. The reputation of Gould lumber had spread all the way to Charleston, according to Habersham, and contracts for the second, still larger portion of the order would have to be signed there in March of the coming year. Success had given James added zest for work. Not a man at his mill worked longer hours than he, but by February of 1802, he found himself counting the days until he could leave for Charleston, a colorful, bustling city he had never visited.

Just after daybreak, on a chilly morning toward the end of February, he was startled by harsh, terrified screams from the shack where Ebba and Leaven lived down by the mill creek. On impulse, he ran into the yard. As suddenly as they began, the screams stopped. Hurrying back inside, James realized that he should not have permitted himself to be seen. The crackers hated interference in their private affairs. If he spoke of anything beyond the business at hand, their faces went blank—a warning to keep his distance. Leaven Kyser beat Ebba when he pleased, but there was a difference in her screams today. Her husky voice seemed to be crying for help, not just shrieking in fury or sheer animal pain.

He cooked his breakfast, worked on the account books for an hour, then went outside to mix soot in a bucket of water to the right inky blackness. This was the day set aside to line the trees his sawyers were bringing down on the north end of his tract—fine, straight slash pines, each of which should square at no less than twelve to fourteen inches. The sale of this shipment would buy his new steam sawmill. For three years, he had wanted to be rid of the tedious band saws, laboring up and down, inching their way by water power dependent on the tides; doing their job, but far too slowly.

The trees he planned to line today should top out at from forty to sixty feet. From a ball of strong cord, he measured a length sufficient to line the big beauties, cut the string with his pocket knife, and immersed it in the sooty water. Carrying the bucket in one hand, his gun in the other, he headed for the mill.

Leaven was there, securing the iron dogs on an oak log, ready to begin his day's work. James nodded; the man returned the nod, his big-nosed, scruffy face expressionless. Sam Webber kept his back turned as James passed the log pile beside the timber bridge. Five other hands were on their way to the mill, where they would keep Leaven supplied with fresh timber to cut. He could hear his sawyers and axmen already at work half a mile to the north. Everything seemed in order as he entered the woods by the worn, pinestraw path behind the mill.

As usual, when he could be alone in the Florida wilderness, even on a crisp winter morning such as this, the lush, soft green calmed him and gave him a sense of repose and confidence. He didn't own this rich, productive land outright, but he could work it, live on it, enjoy its practical value as well as its beauty for as long as he chose to stay. The distant, familiar sounds of saw and ax heightened the silence along the empty path. Only the sun entered with him, barely warm, penetrating down into the dense shade in long shafts of pale light, pointing up a red-brown pine cone picked clean of its seeds by peckerwoods and jays, turning a tassel of gray moss almost white, illuminating the aging palmetto fronds until they looked spring green.

For the time being, he was contented here, in spite of his deep dislike of the crackers, as they so proudly called themselves. The week spent among the warm-hearted, responsive Negroes at Cannon's Point had made the whites who worked for him seem more contemptible. He tried to pity them, but with little success.

A shingle of pine bark the size of a man's hand hit him on the head, and he looked up to see if he could spot the Lord-God bird which had sent it sailing down. There it was, a huge, black-backed, red-crested pileated woodpecker—the Negroes' Lord-God bird, chipping off pine bark as expertly as an adzman. He smiled, not only because the woodpecker always struck him as funny, but because it inevitably brought pleasant memories of Cuffy and Margin and John Couper's other people. Slaves, bound by law to their master, but in their bondage moving about far more freely, less violently, with less resentment at life than the white crackers who worked for wages. Would Cuffy and Margin and Rhina and Sans Foix and Johnson and the other Couper slaves change if they had a choice? He didn't know.

Midway to the north tract, he heard a rustle, repeated, like footsteps carefully placed, stealthy. Indians patrolled his woods at will, keeping watch, Comochichi said, or hunting. These steps were too heavy for an Indian. He walked on a short way, then stopped. There was only the sighing of the pines in the breeze off the river, the rapid scratch of a squirrel, the Lord-God bird still axing away.

Then he saw Ebba behind him on the path, her unborn eighth child filling the square, stolid body so full she looked about to choke. Her face was blotched and puffy, and he could smell her ten feet away. For over four years, she had obeyed his order never to follow him. Because of this he had almost forgotten his loathing; because of Leaven's cruelty, he had begun to feel near compassion for her.

Now he wanted to shout as to a stray dog: "Get out of here!" But he had learned, when possible, to let them speak first. He set down the bucket, leaned his gun against a tree, and waited. Ebba seemed to be waiting too, glancing furtively around her. At last, she raised her hand in an awkward greeting and began to walk toward him, heavily, breathing so hard and with such labor, James wondered if her time would come right there in the woods alone with him. He broke his rule of silence: "Ebba, what are you doing here?"

"I need holp, Mr. Gould. Honest, I wouldn't acome effen I didn't needju to holp me!"

James frowned. "What kind of help do you need?"

"I jist gotta know somebody cares somepin' 'bout what happens to me—to me an' my baby that's acomin'. Holp me, Mr. Gould!" She was coming closer, closer, her arms raised in the air as though surrendering. "Holp me! Holp me!"

From the thicket to his right, James heard a metallic click, then a blast, and before his eyes, Ebba's face blue up in pink and white and red fragments. He flattened himself on the ground as the faceless woman toppled, a dead weight across his legs.

In a matter of seconds, Leaven, his blunderbuss still smoking, stood astride the path where James lay.

"Ain't no use'n lookin' like a snake bitchu, Gould. I tol' 'er I'd kill 'er effen she throwed herself atchu one more time. I tol' 'er, she done it, an' I kilt 'er." A grin spread slowly across Leaven's face. "Ain' no law on the St. Marys—whatchu gonna do 'bout it?"

James freed his legs from Ebba's body and stood up. "I'm going to fire you as of right now. I want you off the place by dark. I don't care where you go—just get out!"

Leaven's mouth contorted with laughter. "Now, ain't that smart? Here you countin' on makin' all that money on them big timbers, an' effen Leaven don't run that saw, who will?" He nudged James in the stomach with the blunderbuss. "You know I'm the onliest one, Gould. You can't fire me. Effen you do, who's to stop me akillin' you t'night in yer bed? We uns knows yore Injuns' done gone to St. Marys."

James could handle the mill himself. His father's primitive saws had been far more difficult to control. But Leaven was right. Spanish East Florida *was* lawless. Even when he got back, Comochichi couldn't guard him day and night. Threatening to operate the saw himself would settle nothing. He decided to try a different tack. "I've got a question for you," he said; his voice hard. "Who will look after your children, now that you've murdered their mother?"

"I'll git me anothern. We got some young uns runnin' roun' here, dontchu fergit. Don't ack like you ain't took no note a them high-titted young wenches. How come you don't gitchu one too?"

His fist cracked against Leaven's ribs, and before the sawyer could get to his feet, James picked up his bucket and gun and strode off toward the north tract. If he did not call Leaven Kyser's bluff now, he never would. He walked fifty yards, a hundred—not hurrying, walking steadily, without looking back.

At the edge of the clearing where the sawyers and axmen were resting under a live oak, he stopped, listened, and decided Leaven had not followed.

"Good morning," he said briskly, as he joined the men. Only one or two returned his greeting.

A young lumberjack named Hop and his brother, Jake, scrambled to their feet as James began to pull the length of saturated cord from the sooty liquid. The trees to be lined lay about on the ground, already topped to their best lengths and bark-stripped. James handed Hop one end of the black dripping cord and pointed to the tree he wanted lined first. The brothers, one at each end, began to tighten the cord along the tree's length, pulling as hard as they dared without breaking it. James, at the center of the trunk, twanged the taut cord. A perfectly straight line lay on the timber. They repeated the process on all four sides. One piece of timber was marked off square. The adzmen could go to work.

Before moving to the next bark-stripped pine, James said, "You men heard a shot a while ago, I suppose."

They only looked at him.

"I know you heard it. Leaven Kyser just killed his wife."

Still no one spoke.

"I told him to get out by tonight," he went on. "Until I can teach one of you or find someone else to operate the big saw, I'm taking over his work."

Without another word, James turned, retraced his

steps along the pine-straw path. Nearing the thicket from which Leaven had fired, he considered taking the long road home. I dare not act afraid, he told himself. I'd better go back the way I came.

He kept on walking. Ebba's body was still sprawled across the path, but Leaven was nowhere to be seen.

From his window at sundown, James watched the eldest Kyser girl head for his cabin, her yellow hair blowing about her peaked face.

When she knocked on the door, he said, "Good evening, Mattie. What can I do for you?"

"You kin bury Ma."

"You mean your father hasn't done it yet?"

"Please, Mr. Gould, kin I come inside?"

Mattie must be thirteen. He decided against it. "I'll come outside with you," he said, closing the door behind him.

"But if Pa sees me on yore porch, he'll skin me." The soiled, childish face twisted. "It be bad 'nough havin' Ma dead. Somebody oughta put 'er in the ground. I—I gotta be Ma—to the kids—but honest, I don't know how—to bury a person."

"Listen, Mattie. Go home now. I promise, first thing tomorrow, I'll see to it."

"I'm obliged to ya, but I don't know kin I sleep tonight with Ma alayin' out there—the dew afallin' on her—cold—all by herself."

James watched the girl walk away, her body bent as though she dragged the whole of her grief behind her, the whole of the new responsibility which had just fallen on her scrawny shoulders.

He built up his fire and sat down. It was not his place to bury Ebba. With luck Comochichi would be back from St. Marys this evening, but if he and the Indian buried her, the other whites could think of a dozen evil reasons. A storm of anger rose in him. Anger toward Leaven Kyser—more brute than man. Yet there came at last a sickening pity for all his white millhands and their families. He thought of Mattie—a child—but she had shown some sense of human kindness, some willingness to look after the family. Most of the men worked responsibly. Perhaps what he was trying to admit was that in Mattie, he had seen a capacity for a kind of devotion. The child's face haunted him—her thin voice whining, "I don't know kin I sleep with Ma alayin' out there—the dew afallin' on her. . . ."

Ebba's face haunted him too. Her pleading look just before her head blew up into those fragments of bone and muscle. . . . What had Ebba been trying to ask him? What kind of help did she need? This time, she was not trying to give him her body, in spite of what his sawyer thought. Did Ebba want him to promise to help her children in case Leaven did kill her?

The only way he could help Ebba now was to keep her husband on at the mill.

James, handling the big saw, had not closed down until almost sunset. He had worked among the men all day. No one but Mattie had even mentioned Ebba's death.

He had promised the girl for first thing in the morning, but unless he told someone in the settlement what he intended to do, he wouldn't dare lift a spadeful of dirt. The right man to tell was Leaven Kyser.

His heavy jacket buttoned around his throat, James set out by the light of his tin lantern across the clearing along the millstream, where the people lived in a cluster of rickety shacks. At the Kysers' door, he knocked firmly and waited. A small boy called, "That you, Ma?" Someone else whimpered. Then, except for Sam Webber's dog barking down the lane, there was silence until Leaven flung open the door.

"Evening, Leaven," James said.

"Whatchu want, Gould?"

"Two things. May I come in?"

"Don't see no reason."

"All right. We can talk here. The first thing I want to talk about is Ebba's body out there on the path. Would you like for Comochichi and me to bury her in the morning?"

"Yer Injun ain'tchere."

"He will be tonight or early tomorrow. I want you to answer my question. Would you like for us to bury your wife?"

Leaven let go a snort or a dry sob—James honestly couldn't tell what the sound was. "Effen you want to. Somebody better."

"No one has died since I've been here, except the old lady—dead when I came. I said some kind of prayer over her grave. What do you want for Ebba?"

"She warn't religious."

"Would you like your neighbors to bury her instead of me?"

Leaven shrugged.

"Well, if you don't care, will you tell the others I'm going to do it for you, tomorrow?"

"Don't see why you cain't tell 'em yourself."

"All right, I will. The second thing I want to say—" He stopped. Leaven's face was as inscrutable as ever, but in the lantern light, James could see tears rolling down the weathered cheeks, as the man stood there both cocky and remorseful, his long arms hanging at his sides. "The other matter has to do with you and me. I still feel the same about you as I did when I knocked you down this morning. But—you may have your old job back."

A smirk twisted Leaven's face. "Heh! One afternoon of shovin' them heavy levers an' guidin' them iron-dogged logs through them saws's too much fer a feller like you, huh? I knowed it would be! I'se just abidin' my time, Gould."

James clenched his fist. "I don't expect you to believe this, but you've got your job back because—God pity them—your seven children have to eat!"

There was a brief silence; then Leaven began to laugh. "An' on top a that, effen you'se to go all the way to Savanny, Georgie, you'd not find as good a head sawyer as Leaven Kyser, huh?"

The convulsive laugh went on so long, James walked off the porch. At the foot of Leaven's path, he called back, "Report to work at the usual time tomorrow."

"Don'tchu worry none 'bout that Gould. I'se aimin' to be thur alla time!"

At dawn, as soon as Comochichi got back, before they unloaded the skiff, they buried Ebba's body in the woods under a big hickory, near the path where she fell. When Comochichi had packed down the last shoveful of black woods loam, James asked God to watch over Ebba's children.

On their way back, about halfway between the grave and the clearing, Mattie met them, a bunch of sugar-berried cedar in her arms.

The child passed them on the path without slowing down, but James heard her murmur: "I'm much obliged to ya, Mr. Gould."

Chapter 18

Charleston, South Carolina
4 March, 1802

My Dear Sister, Mary,

I had every intention of writing from St. Marys so that my letter could travel North by the same boat which brought me here to Charleston two days ago. But every waking moment in St. Marys was devoted to work and the gathering of supplies which Comochichi took back to Mills Ferry. There was also great activity at St. Marys due to the near completion of a magnificent ship, the *General Oglethorpe,* commissioned to be built there by the son-in-law of Don Juan McQueen, a Mr. Robert Mackay. Mr. Mackay's enthusiasm over his newly launched schooner aroused my own long-buried ambitions for new adventure, although I cannot say that life on the St. Marys River is ordinary. It is far from ordinary, but certainly a lady would wish to avoid it. Be sure my dream of becoming a builder in a more civilized place is still intact, and I pray the day of our reunion will not be too many years hence.

I am in Charleston for the signing of further lumber contracts and expect to be almost opulent soon. If a statement such as that from your otherwise restrained brother causes you amazement, I am not surprised. As I write this, my first leisurely composed letter in many months, I confess that I often dumfound myself. The contradictions within me are not always understandable, even to me. For all of my nearly thirty-five years I have exercised rational restraint and caution while at the same time leaping from one situation to another on the spur of the moment. I confound myself by staying in Spanish East Florida, however prosperous my enterprise, when I really long to build fine houses. I hold to my dream and yet refuse to embrace it. Both Savannah and Charleston offer opportunities for building. Instead, I contract for bigger lumber shipments and escape back to the wilderness once the ink is dried on the agreements. I do not like to burden you, but there is no one with whom I can talk.

My dear sister, I now approach the most startling part of this letter, which I request you keep to yourself. I aim to marry a young lady whom I have not even seen. I heard of her only yesterday from a crusty old sailor, met by chance on the Cooper River dock, here in Charleston, as I waited for the broker's office to open. The sailor was shucking oysters and since I was lonely, we fell to discussing severe storms. He described a crossing from Nassau, New Providence, some four years ago, when the ship encountered a tropical storm of such violence that even the crew lost hope. Among the passengers was a pretty girl aged fourteen years, traveling alone, so courageous and spirited the old sailor still vows she saved the ship and all aboard. I became so absorbed in his praise of her, I shocked myself by saying, without a moment's hesitation, "If I can manage to meet that young lady, I am going to marry her." The mariner laughed uproariously, but gave me his blessing and informed me that she is now employed as a tutor for guests in the home of an acquaintance of mine, Major Pierce Butler, the same who owns the plantation adjoining John Couper's on St. Simons Island as well as a residence in Charleston.

I have left my card at the Butler house and now wait like a nervous schoolboy for some word from Major Butler. If Butler is in Charleston, he will surely, out of courtesy to a friend of John Couper, invite me to call. The rest will be in the hands of Providence and your brother's good fortune or lack of it. If she will have me, will I take her back to the wilderness? I do not know. It is an agonizing question already, since I will need at least three years' time to fulfill the timber contract which I will sign here. Still, I am overcome with loneliness and have at last faced my need for companionship. I advise you not to try to make sense out of what must seem merely another impulsive act on my part.

Your usual money and a little extra, accompanies this lengthy letter, with my love and devotion and esteem.

Yr Bro. James Gould.

Send your next letter to St. Marys as always. I shall claim it eventually, but I do not expect to leave Charleston until I have met her, however long that may be.

Since the new timber contract was not to be signed until the next day, James posted Mary's letter and wondered what to do with his time. Charleston had fascinated him on sight. Following the initial timber negotiations, he had walked its narrow, sun-drenched streets, studying the architecture of the better houses. Built mainly of wood, they were large and airy; two- and often three-storied, with piazzas running the length of both upper stories. Sensible architecture, he thought, in a climate where every breeze counted. Most were built gable end to the street, a style peculiar to Charleston, so far as he knew. He liked the ornate, wrought iron gates set in brick walls, opening from the streets into private, walled gardens.

He had not by any means seen all of Charleston yesterday, but, afraid to stay away from his room too long, he headed back after only an hour, hoping for some word from Major Pierce Butler.

Striding around the corner from Broad Street to Meeting, he loosened his short brown jacket, annoyed with himself because he still had not learned that after a rain even early March days can turn warm in the South. Dress clothes irked him after the years at Mills Ferry, where he worked in shirt sleeves or in no shirt at all. Major Butler would not come in person, he felt sure, and wondered why he had bothered to dress so carefully in the new gray waistcoat and woolen jacket.

Forgetting for the moment that a proper gentleman does not leap puddles on a city street, he hurdled a wide pool of muddy water, felt better for it, and repeated the performance almost in front of his lodgings. This time both feet landed in the far edge of the puddle, thoroughly splashing his dark pantaloons. He would surely have to sponge them before his appointment tomorrow. He hurried through the iron gate into the garden of his rooming house, muttering some ungentlemanly words, and did not notice the young lady at the door until he had to excuse himself for almost knocking her down.

"It's quite all right, sir," she smiled. "I suppose a

horse galloped past just when you reached a mudhole."

Later, he tried to remember exactly what she wore—blue, he thought, a high-waisted blue dress, the color of her eyes. On her head, a straw bonnet . . . chestnut curls falling over her forehead. Her nose was perfect, but not haughty—not like Jessie's. He did not think of beauty. He thought of how natural she was.

"If you let your trousers dry first, I don't think you'll have much trouble removing those spatters." Her laughter was as gay as a reel, her speech cultivated British, suiting her well. "I got splashed by a dray last week," she went on. "Don't worry. The mud comes right off when it's dry."

"You're very reassuring."

"Are you calling at this house, too, sir?"

"No, ma'am. I have lodgings here."

"Then perhaps you can help me." She took a folded note from her tapestry reticule. "I've brought a message for a Mr.—" Suddenly, she laughed. "Wouldn't it be jolly if my message turned out to be for you? By any chance, *are* you Mr. James Gould?"

He stared at her blankly.

"Are you?"

James nodded.

"An acquaintance of Major Pierce Butler?"

"Yes, ma'am."

"Then I've performed my mission. You see, I work at the Butler house. I offered to bring Major Butler's message and his regrets on my way home. He left Charleston this morning on a business trip." She held out the note.

James stuffed it, unread, into his jacket pocket. "I hope you'll excuse me, ma'am—"

"For what, Mr. Gould?"

"For staring at you this way. In fact, I'd be honored—more than honored, if you would allow me to explain it. I promise to tell you the whole story. May I, Miss—?"

She curtsied. "Harris. My name is Jane Harris. I don't think I need to apologize for not telling you, need I? As merely the bearer of a message, I thought—well, to tell you the truth, I didn't think at all!"

"Would you mind if I wrote you a short note—requesting the pleasure of your company? Soon? I'm only in town for a few days."

"Since you're a friend of Major Butler, a gentleman he would have invited to dinner had he been able, I'm sure my father would not object."

James bowed. "Thank you. Oh, thank you ever so much."

"You're quite welcome. I've enjoyed our—curious encounter."

Her nose crinkled, he noticed, when she smiled. "It's far more important than you know, Miss Harris—this meeting of ours."

"You will certainly have to tell me what you mean by that! Good-by, Mr. Gould."

"Good-by." As she turned to leave the garden, James called, "Where may I deliver my note?"

"I live on Elliott Street, the third house from the corner."

The day his contract was signed, James found her reply to his note under the front door of his lodgings. He had driven a hard bargain during the closing of the timber negotiations; had come off better than he dared hope. Now taking the stairs two at a time, he burst into his room, tossed his copy of the contract on the bed and stood holding the small sealed letter, almost afraid to open it. Uncertainly, he broke the seal with the initials J.H. and began to read.

> Miss Jane Harris wishes to inform you that her father, John Hartley Harris, agrees to your visit on 8 March at 4 o'clock, teatime. We are a noisy but happy family of five children, in addition to a loving mother and father. We all unite in hoping you find us acceptable company.
>
> Jane Harris.

Wishing he had not chosen to wear his expensive new riding jacket, James climbed the worn wooden steps of the old frame house on Elliott Street promptly at four o'clock, still finding it hard to believe that she had arranged the meeting for the very next day. He knocked.

Almost at once, the latch clicked, the door burst open, and a lad of nine or ten shouted cheerily: "Good afternoon, sir. As you'll see, we've been waiting for your knock. Mums has even made both tea cakes and scones."

"Well, don't you think you'd better invite our guest inside before you list the menu, Charles?" A gentle, scholarly-looking man of fifty stood behind the boy, his hand extended.

"How do you do, sir? I'm James Gould."

"And I'm John Harris. This is my son, Charles. Come in, come in."

Inside the large shabby entrance hall, a plump, smiling lady came toward him. "Welcome to our home, Mr. Gould. I'm Mary Harris, Jane's mother. We're delighted to have you call."

A baby began to cry at the rear of the house, and Mrs. Harris excused herself.

"That's our baby crying," Charles explained.

"He knows that, dummy," another somewhat older boy chimed in from the other side of the parlor, where he had just spread a linen cloth on the low tea table. "I'm John Mackay Harris, sir," the young man said, his straightforward naturalness reminding James somehow of Jane. "We all know you didn't come just to see us, but every suitor my sister has is forced to pass family inspection."

James' heart constricted. The excitement of seeing her again had so overwhelmed him, he hadn't once thought about other suitors.

Mr. Harris pointed to their best chair. "Won't you sit down, Mr. Gould?"

"Thank you."

"Are you a Republican?" John Mackay asked with enthusiasm.

James grinned. "I'm afraid I can't answer that without some thought."

Mr. Harris asked, "Do you believe it quite polite to inquire about a man's politics first off, John Mackay?"

"Oh, it's no secret about him, Father," the boy answered. "He wears his hair short—in a crop—brown, the way God made it. No powder on it. Fairly obvious, I'd say. Most young gentlemen like Mr. Gould are Republicans. Jeffersonians. Not often Federalists. That's for staid old men."

"Actually, I've been out of touch with American politics. I live in Spanish East Florida. I'd be laughed off my land if I wore long powdered hair."

Both boys whistled in admiration, then Charles asked, "In the wilds of Spanish East Florida? Or in St. Augustine?"

"In the wilds, I'm afraid. I'm in the lumber business."

John Mackay whistled again. "You must be rich!"

"Comfortable," James said, looking toward the stairway.

A grin broke over Charles' face. "Do you think my sister's going to come down those stairs any minute? She won't. Isn't home from work yet. Sometimes Janie has to stay with the children she tutors until their mother arrives—whether she wants to or not. We never know, do we, Father?"

"We know this time. I see her running up our front walk." John Harris hurried to open the door.

James jumped to his feet, watched her embrace her father, kiss each brother, then walk straight to him.

"Can you forgive me, Mr. Gould? To be late for your first call is rude, I know, but I decided not to get flustered." She smiled. "It's nice to see you—here in the Harris castle."

"I doubt that any of you knows how glad I am to be here," James said, bowing over her hand.

"Oh, I think we know, all right," Charles drawled.

Jane removed her bonnet, tossed it on a table. "You'll just have to learn about my brothers, both of them, Mr. Gould. They say exactly what they happen to be thinking at the moment. Our parents encourage that in us—within the bounds of courtesy."

"We've got another brother, too," Charles offered. "Well, I suppose you could call him that. He's still rather a baby. Four years old. Stephen, in case you're interested."

"Oh, yes, I am interested."

"Well, I'll run to the kitchen," Jane said. "Mums will need help. Excuse me, gentlemen?"

"We're not a very sedate family," Mr. Harris chuckled.

James sat on the edge of his chair, not ill at ease, but wishing that he could share his feelings fully with this kind, intelligent man. Wishing he could tell John Hartley Harris that he already loved his daughter, that he thought a warm, congenial home life must be the most important gift a father could bestow. Instead, he said, "Your family is fortunate, sir. Fortunate to be together—happily."

"We agree. I have considered moving to Savannah, some time in the future. My nephew is Mayor. Keeps insisting we come. Says schoolmasters earn better fees there."

"Mayor Charles Harris is your nephew?"

"I'm his namesake," Charles piped. "Cousin Charles used to live here with us until he became both famous and wealthy by marrying Cousin Kitty McIntosh," the younger son elaborated.

"Oh, it didn't spoil Cousin Charles. He's as jolly as ever," John Mackay declared. "Besides, he didn't get to be Mayor just by marrying a McIntosh."

"Well," Charles said, "it helped."

The men talked until Jane and her mother came bearing tea and hot scones and cakes. From then to the end of the visit, James remembered little that was said, except that, as he left, the girl he loved asked him to come again.

"By all means do," her father said. "I'm afraid we've done all the talking today. When do you leave Charleston, Mr. Gould?"

"I—I'm not certain, sir; I still have business," James lied, looking at Jane, who was looking straight back at him.

"If it's convenient, I'd be delighted to have you walk me home from Major Butler's tomorrow, Mr. Gould. Four o'clock?"

Chapter 19

He hadn't walked her home the next day; they had run—through a sudden torrent of rain—all the way from Major Butler's house to the Harrises'. There had been little chance for conversation, only small talk and laughter, as they splashed, soaking wet, through the puddles, James' arm around her waist. Once they had reached her home, of course, there was the family.

Alone by the small window in his room that night, rain still falling, he at first felt disappointed, then decided that perhaps the unexpected rain had helped. Miss Janie had made a game of their puddle-dodging, and he had known a kind of exuberance so new to him, of such sheer delight, that he felt he couldn't wait for tomorrow, when he would see her again. At the Harris home, the family had joined in the fun—the boys spreading James's soggy cloak to dry by the fire, Mr. Harris insisting that he borrow a shabby, once-elegant jacket for the trip back to his lodgings.

He went to his clothes press to examine the old tweed coat more closely. British made, lined with heavy, though frayed, silk. Made in London years ago, he was certain. The Harrises had made him talk some about himself, but they had spoken freely of their own beginnings in London. An army officer, gentle John Hartley Harris had been retired early due to ill health and had apparently never been able to do more than feed and clothe his family on his earnings as a schoolmaster. "Our hopes for the future are in our sons," he had said, making no exaggerated apologies for his own failures.

Miss Janie was like her father; she embroidered nothing. Life together seemed enough for the Harrises without their attempting to appear better off than they were. He had met both young Stephen and baby Caroline. Only the Harrises' first-born, Elizabeth, was missing; she had married well-to-do Captain Samuel Bunch in London several years ago and gone with him, after he left the Army, to Nassau, where, James gathered, the Captain had met reverses.

Of the two older boys, James felt Charles would be the more successful, although at nine, it was hard to tell. John Mackay, twelve, was by far the handsomer of the two; heavy black curly hair, ruddy cheeks, dark eyes that seemed somehow, in spite of the difference in color, to be like Janie's eyes—always holding a shining secret, not yet divulged. Charles was a towhead, restless, wiry, with a mind that snapped up new ideas faster than a warbler snaps gnats. The mother, patient, easy of manner, had, he felt certain, held the family together in all the practical ways. Her obvious devotion to her husband impressed James deeply. He could not imagine that they had ever quarreled.

He had never felt as comfortable in any family circle. Not even at Cannon's Point. The difference was Janie. This was her family, and they had accepted him so swiftly, so naturally, that he felt somehow as though he already belonged. He wanted Janie with all his being, and he wanted her family too.

The next day, when he called again, the talk was of the eldest sister, Elizabeth Bunch.

"Wait until you meet Elizabeth, Mr. Gould," Janie said. "Won't he love Elizabeth, Mums? She's the steady, dependable one—rather like you, Mums, really."

"Elizabeth has had ample opportunity to prove her steadiness," Mary Harris said. "Her life has not been easy."

"My sister's husband, Captain Bunch, got wiped out by red spiders," Charles announced. "He was about to be even more wealthy, then suddenly they were poor—"

"Crop failure can happen to anyone," the boy's father interrupted.

"We hope Elizabeth and Samuel will be coming to this country to live," Mary Harris went on. "I believe Captain Bunch will choose Savannah rather than

Charleston, but at least they will be close by. The Captain bought a cotton plantation in Nassau with his inheritance, but he lost everything." The concern in her voice was unmistakable.

"They're moving to Savannah because he's decided to become a cotton factor," John Mackay said.

"That's a lucrative business and getting better," James said. "Now that the gin's been put in use. I don't see how the Captain could fail."

"Oh, my sister's husband is awfully good at failing," Charles remarked.

"That's enough, dear," Mary Harris said. "Don't let my son give the wrong impression, Mr. Gould. Samuel Bunch is a lovable, good young man."

"And very handsome." Janie served him another tea cake. "When Samuel Bunch walks into a room—even where he's not known at all—everyone turns to look at him."

"He struts."

"No, he doesn't strut, Charles! He merely has a military bearing. I'm devoted to Samuel. I lived with them for a year, Mr. Gould, on their beautiful plantation, and even away from Mums and Father, I was happy. Samuel and I played all sorts of games together." Jane was giving James her full attention. "They were like second parents to me—even though they're only a few years older than I. I really can't wait for them to come to America!"

James looked at her for a moment. "You're fortunate, Miss Janie, to have even one set of parents."

Her eyes grew tender. "That was thoughtless of me. I'm really so sorry you lost both your father and mother. Please help yourself to mine!"

"Thank you. I'd like that."

For a moment, no one said anything. Charles broke the silence. "It won't surprise me one bit if you two get married. I certainly never heard Janie offer Mums and Father to anyone before!"

"Charles!" Mrs. Harris' voice was stern.

"Shame on you!" Janie's voice was not stern.

"Why should I be ashamed? Isn't he courting you?"

"Yes silly, of course he is," John Mackay said loftily,

"but we're all supposed to act as though we don't know it."

James had overstayed his planned time in Charleston by a full week before he mustered enough courage to invite Janie for a drive in a rented gig.

"I wondered if you'd ever ask me," she said, as they rode along the Battery.

She sat beside him looking straight ahead; her nose in profile was exquisite. "I'm not very good at this sort of thing, Miss Harris. I've lived in the wilderness too long, I guess."

"What sort of thing, Mr. Gould?"

"Putting into words what I—I really feel."

"Are you going to keep your promise made that first day we met?"

"Did I make a promise?" The words were no sooner out than he remembered. He had begged to be able to tell her the whole story of how it was he knew he wanted to marry her even before he had learned her name. "Yes. I'll keep my promise."

He reined in the horse, pulled the gig to one side of the shell road, and began uncertainly to tell of meeting the old sailor. As he talked, she turned toward him, listening intently, and by the time the story was finished, he was looking at her. "I know it must sound awfully strange to you, but I swear it wasn't only because I'd been so lonely. I love you. I want to marry you."

She sat perched on the edge of the seat, almost motionless for so long that he was frightened. The clear complexion was paler than ever. Her lips parted, as though to speak, but no words came. If only he knew what she was thinking. "Have I—upset you, Miss Janie?"

She nodded, biting her lower lip. Nodded again. "Yes—you have, Mr. Gould." Her voice was barely audible. "What if I had looked like—a witch—ugly, hideous? With crossed eyes and protruding teeth?"

"He told me you were lovely—even at fourteen."

"But, *how* did you know you would love me?"

"I can't answer that. All I know is—if you won't marry me, I'll never marry anyone."

She leaned back. "Of course, I don't believe that for a single minute, but you're going too fast. I need time to recover from the—insult."

"Insult?"

"*I* think it's an insult. You see, a woman, especially if she's vain like me, wants to feel the man she loves desires her because she's beautiful—now—not because she showed some kind of courage or spirit at the age of fourteen!"

"Miss Jane, did you say 'the man she loves'?"

"Yes. I love you. I've loved you from the afternoon I met you with mud on your trousers."

He had not allowed himself to dream that anyone so beautiful as Jane Harris could love him at first sight. He had deliberately pushed aside his recurring questions about taking her to live in the midst of the violence and lawlessness of the Spanish border. He intended to move to Savannah or Charleston one day—but Janie loved him *now*.

He reached for her hand. "Miss Janie, I—I don't understand about any of it, except that I love you more every time I see you—and if you'll marry me, I promise I'll sublease my timberland down there and move anywhere you want to live. I'll gladly give it all up."

"You'll do no such thing! I heard you tell my father you would have to cut and ship lumber for three years in order to fulfill the contract you've just signed. I'll go there with you."

His fingers tightened over hers. "I can find other work. I'm really a builder, anyway."

She sat up straight again. "James, I'm not a forward young woman. I'm just—me. I know you haven't talked with my father yet, but the truth is—I want to marry you now and go home with you to the St. Marys River. Or anywhere."

Chapter 20

John and Mary Harris had helped him convince Janie that they should wait at least a year to be married. "He loves you too much to permit you to live in such danger," her father had said. "Give the man a chance to change the circumstances of his life, my dear. He'll know when the time is right."

Back in his cabin at Mills Ferry, James could still see her eyes blaze, could see her standing alone and helpless in the Harris parlor demanding: "Why is it that *no one* understands that I love him enough to want to share his life—no matter where he is?"

She had wept like a heartbroken child when he held and kissed her for the last time before boarding the schooner. Once on the boat, out of her sight, he had wept too.

His men worked well in the woods and at the mill as the weeks dragged into autumn. Gould timber went regularly by way of St. Marys to Charleston. Even Leaven Kyser and Sam Webber seemed satisfied with their increases in pay for the longer hours required to meet the demands of the new contract.

Christmas came and went, unnoticed in the settlement by everyone except Mattie Kyser, who baked James a cake. Janie and her family sent a box filled with Christmas delicacies—sugar cookies, seafoam candy, plum pudding, Janie's letters were both a comfort and a torment.

> Mr. Broadfoot did well with your Christmas buying for us, beloved. Of course you spent far too much money, but the boys adore their new guns and greatcoats and Mums and Father were deeply touched that you had made such a careful list of gifts all the way from Caroline's doll to the much-needed suit and dress for my parents. My heart never aches more for you than when I look at my own face in the exquisite silver

looking glass you sent me. Am I really as beautiful as you deserve? I've always thought myself pretty enough for any man, but now that I belong to Mr. James Gould, I fret. I count the days unil you come for me. Every empty day between now and March is down on a list which I mark off—one slow day at a time—and shout "Hurry! Hurry!" I can tell you are working too hard. Stop it. You need not try to fulfill that contract ahead of time, sir, because I promised to wait for one year only. When you come again, I am returning with you to the St. Marys River as your wife.

There was no way to shorten the time. The Charleston firm through which the British purchases were made expected the lumber in spaced lots and would pay him accordingly, over a period of three years. He looked around the one large room of his cabin—well constructed, tight against storms, clean because he took care of it himself—but too crowded for a man and wife to live in any kind of comfort. Of course, he could add rooms, and would build her a beautiful house on the bluff away from the settlement squalor as soon as the fall shipment was ready. "She'll live in this cabin with me until I can do better," he assured himself. "I'll despise myself every day until Janie has a decent house, but I can't wait beyond this year, either."

He had written to her regularly, carefully evading any mention of the fact that they would have to live in his cabin, perhaps for a year or more. As the weeks wore on, he began to face the unfairness of his letters. If he could not wait to marry her, and if he would be too occupied with his work to begin their new house, she deserved to know. His letter, dated January 15, 1803, was no longer evasive.

I cannot tell you how I will loathe your having to live in this cabin, but your determination to come back with me in March forces me to tell you that this is where we will live until I can find time to build our new home. I will add two rooms to the cabin before I leave Mills Ferry for Charleston. I will buy anything you want in the way of furnishings, linens, silver, etcetera, up there. I will do all in my power to make you happy, and I will love you and cherish you. But once you are here, I will not draw an easy breath while I am away from you during the day. You will not be safe, my dearest. It has been quiet so far, but there is danger of Creek attack. There is always danger from the low class of men who work for me. How I can let you come into this wilderness, I do not know. How I can live longer away from you, I know less.

The letter could not be posted for a week. There would be ample time to read and reread it, to test his feelings again each day. Once it was mailed the die would be cast.

Whistling as he cooked breakfast a few days later, James glanced out his cabin window to see Mattie Kyser climbing the steps to his front porch. Still wary, he stepped outside.

"Morning, Mattie."

"Morning, Mr. Gould. I was hopin' kin I talk a minute?"

"Why, yes, if you make it quick. Haven't had breakfast yet and I'm due at the south tract right now."

"I seen a–dress–the purtiest dress–all flowered and ruffled–in a old book that said I could send off for yard goods to Charleston. I was wonderin' kin I clean your winders er wash yer clothes er scrub yer cabin floor? It's the onliest boughten material I ever seen–much less *had*!" She twisted her fingers, her eyes pleading with him. "Please, Mr. Gould! Please let me work a dollar's worth! I ain't never had no boughten goods in my whole life!"

He had never permitted any of the millfolk inside his cabin.

"I'll come arter you go an' be gone afore you git home, I promise!"

The girl knew his predicament. She had shown her gratitude to him in as many small ways as she could manage. "All right, Mattie. If we work it that way.

Go home 'til you see me ride out. You'll find a bucket and a broom in back. I'll leave your money on the kitchen table."

Thunder had rolled all afternoon, as James and Comochichi surveyed the newly opened south tract, riding two horses James had bought last month from a half-breed Indian Negro. The two had worked swiftly, hoping before the storm came to mark enough trees to keep the sawyers busy tomorrow.

As they galloped back toward the settlement, low slate-gray clouds pushed across the sky. The tops of the trees flailed each other in the driving wind, dead branches splintering around them; the horses shying.

"If this keeps up, you can't go to St. Marys tomorrow," James shouted. "Too bad. I wanted you to post an important letter."

At the barn, they hurriedly removed the saddles, watered the horses and headed for the cabin, rain coming down in torrents. Their heads lowered as they ran, neither man noticed until they reached the porch that the cabin door was standing wide open. Inside, the chairs were overturned, papers from James' makeshift desk were strewn about the room, and the linens were half torn from the bed. Jagged pieces of broken glass from a window littered the floor, and in a corner stood Mattie's scrub pail and broom.

James lighted his lantern, and without a word the two men began to search the cabin. Nothing had been stolen. Even Mattie's dollar lay crumpled on the floor by the table where he had left it. "He wasn't a thief," James said.

Comochichi pointed to a trail of blood which led from the table leg across the room to the rear door.

Mattie lay on her back at the foot of the steps, her blood-soaked dress almost covering her face, her thin legs spread-eagled in the muddy water, flowing now in rivulets from under the house.

"We'll have to carry her to Leaven's place," James said. "He'll never believe our story, but we can't take her back inside my cabin."

James watched as Comochichi cleaned the blood from Mattie's head and body and applied cooked-herb poultices to her wounds.

"She needs sleep and food, Leaven," James said. "Will you see that she gets both tonight?"

Leaven Kyser looked up from his coffee. "Mat's the cook. Reckon she left somepin' in the pot." Then he glared at James, his eyes slits. "You gonna tell me who done it, Gould?"

"Mattie's the only one who knows that."

"I aim to kill the skunk that raped my girl."

"If you find him, I wouldn't blame you," James said. "Most likely, he's half way to the Okefenokee swamp by now."

Together, Comochichi and James cleaned the cabin, heated a kettle of white beans and onions, tried to eat their supper.

"Was she able to talk at all, Comochichi?"

"Enough."

James set down his tin plate of food almost untouched. "You know who did it?"

"Half-nigger Indian."

"The fellow who sold us our horses."

Comochichi nodded.

James began to pace the room. "I was sending a letter with you to St. Marys tomorrow. Planned to get married in March. Had decided to bring my wife back here to live."

Sitting on the floor, his legs crossed under him, Comochichi watched as James paced back and forth, striking one palm over and over with the fist of his other hand.

"Planned to bring a lovely, refined young lady back to this hell of blood and mud and rattlesnakes and—murderers." He jerked the letter from his pocket, tore it into shreds and threw it in the fireplace. "I'll break her heart if I refuse, but I—can't let her come."

"You think no tonight," Comochichi said, watching the scraps of paper curl and turn black. "Tomorrow, rain stop. Sun come out."

James stood for a long time, his back to the fire.

"Comochichi? How do you live so contentedly away from your squaw?"

The Indian shrugged.

"Do you love her?"

Comochichi thought a while. "Love her when with her."

James sighed. "I see. No, I don't see! I can't live without Miss Janie and I can't let her live here. What does a man do under these circumstances? What does a man do?"

Comochichi got up, stretched his long arms over his head, yawned. "A man sleeps night away first."

Sometime after midnight, when the rain had stopped, James got out of bed, dressed hurriedly, and pulled on his heavy jacket against the fog he knew would be rising from the river, reaching its penetrating fingers all the way into the woods. He lighted his lantern and went outside to walk; to walk and think until he reached a decision. Not tomorrow when the sun came up again—tonight, while the ground was slick with mud, the trees still dripping; while the ghostly miasma hung over the evil wilderness where he had chosen to live his life—while the floor of his cabin was still stained with Mattie's blood.

He walked deeper and deeper into the woods, along the logging trail, until the flame in his tin lantern began to flicker. He had forgotten to put an extra candle in his pocket. Deciding to risk a shortcut back to his clearing before the light went out, he started to run, as though driven. Suddenly, for a reason he did not try to understand, he had to reach the warmth and the light of his cabin before his lantern went out. He was in sight of the clearing when a palmetto root caught his foot and threw him to the ground. How long he lay there until he could bear the pain of standing he didn't know. He smelled the smoke before he remembered dropping the lantern. Behind him, a thin, bright worm of flame wriggled across a scattering of pine straw. He hobbled to the spreading flames and stamped them out, tears flowing from the pain.

Weeping, finding relief in it, he crawled about on the forest floor, feeling in the dark among the vines and palmetto roots until he found his lantern still hot, its candle gone.

Toward the middle of the night, hunched near his fireplace, he knew the decision had been made for him. A man was not meant to be alone when pain struck. When pain struck his body or his mind or his heart, God meant a man to have a woman to comfort him. Across almost seventeen years, the strong, gentle words of Lemuel Haynes still reached him. *Take yourself a wife one day, James, and cherish her. She will be God's gift to you because He will know your needs. You're a strong young man, but a strong man's needs run deep.*

He sat holding a mullen poultice on his swollen foot until almost dawn. The injured ankle would have to heal quickly. In March, in a little over six weeks, he had an urgent appointment in Charleston.

And somehow, between now and then, two more rooms must be added to the cabin.

Part Three

Chapter 21

Janie broke off her thread, smoothed the wrinkles from the new flowered sofa cover and stood back to admire her handiwork. The sofa had been James' bed when he lived alone in the cabin. Now, freshly covered to match her new curtains, and stacked with plump pillows from Mattie Kyser's geese, it was the comfortable place where they sat together for tea each afternoon.

Hurrying about the three-roomed cabin "fixing," as James called it, for their evening together, she wondered what made this house seem better, more livable than most small houses. Most large houses, for that matter. James had explained all the possibilities of danger; yet in their cabin she felt safe, shut away from the hostility which he said hung in the very air outside.

She placed a kettle of fresh water on the fireplace crane for brewing her strong oolong tea. "Oh, Elizabeth," she said aloud, and her thoughts raced. How I wish your restless Samuel had some of my James' strength of character! How I long for a sign that your Captain has begun to stop dreaming of great fortune—has begun to see himself as he really is—a warmhearted, well-meaning man who could find his happiness right under his handsome nose, if he'd only look.

Elizabeth and Samuel Bunch had arrived in Savannah from New Providence just in time to make the trip by boat to Charleston for Janie's wedding, but Samuel, as cocky and disarming as ever, full of gaiety and laughter, had almost spoiled the day for Elizabeth. As guests arrived at the Harris home, Elizabeth overheard her husband boast that he had sold thirty-five of the Negroes brought with them all the way from New Providence.

"It cost a lot of money, Janie, to transport our people from Nassau," Elizabeth had explained in tears. "They would all have been happier if he had sold them there where they had always lived, where they had friends and relatives. Nothing would do Samuel but that we must bring them to America with us. Two days in Savannah and he was determined to open his factor's office on Commerce Row without enough capital. Our poor people brought a good price, eleven thousand dollars, but not enough. Now they're miserable and afraid in a new country—and so am I."

The strained, courageous smile on Elizabeth's face as the bride and groom had waved good-by to the family on the Savannah dock still haunted Janie. James agreed with Elizabeth that Samuel Bunch's new cotton brokerage would be underfinanced, and to Janie, her new husband's keen judgment in business affairs was sure to be right.

She slid fresh-baked scones from the tiny oven, covered them with a napkin, and went to the kitchen window to watch for him. Any minute, he would come striding out of the woods to take her in his arms, to sit beside her on their sofa. He had complained a little about teatime at first. Arranging his work to arrive at four o'clock had not been simple, but he seemed to like the idea now. Besides, she meant to protect him. He had worked too hard all his life.

Who else in all the world, she smiled to herself, can have tea between kisses with Mr. James Gould, propped close to him on such a magnificent stack of down pillows? "Only me, only me," she sang, as she ran to their one looking glass by the door, smoothed her blue striped skirt, tucked a stray curl under her house cap, and bit her lips and pinched her cheeks to heighten their color.

He'd stop first, of course, at the well, where he kept a basin and soap to wash. Maybe he knew and maybe not, but every day she hid behind the kitchen curtains and watched as he stripped off his work shirt, exposing his broad strong back.

She examined their tea tray again, set with the elegantly shaped cups selected in Charleston, with James beside her, just before the wedding. "Lowestoft china for a cabin at Mills Ferry, Janie?" Why not? No matter that he worked so hard, she had married a gentleman and meant never to let him live without beauty around him. Never.

Her grandmother's gold watch on its baroque brooch read ten past four. It was time to run to their bedroom for the next part of the daily ritual—his freshly laundered shirt, unbuttoned, ready to slip into.

Back at the kitchen window, she saw him already in the yard, splashing soapsuds at the washstand by the well. I think I love him more than when he left this morning, she thought.

Between the first and second cups of tea, he kissed each finger, her wrists, her arms as far as he could push up the sleeves of her white shirtwaist.

"I wish we had been the first man and woman on earth, don't you, James?"

He laughed. "You mean Adam and Eve in their garden? Maybe we are. Why, Janie, you're crying!"

"You'll just have to learn that I cry sometimes when I'm happy. I'm surprised you haven't discovered that. We've been together for over four weeks."

James released her long enough for her to prepare his second cup of tea—just right, the way he liked it, one lump of sugar, not a drop too much hot milk. Plenty of butter on his scones.

"Every day of my life, if I live to be a hundred and ten, I will wonder how I ever managed without you, Janie."

"Please do live to be a hundred and ten," she said, her face solemn as she sat down beside him. "I'll be a wrinkled old woman when you're a hundred and ten, but I'll still want you close to me. Do you hate the thought of death?"

"Yes. More than ever now."

"Are you afraid of it?"

"No. I just hate it."

"I've never been afraid of it," she said, "but I am now, because it would mean I'd have to be away from you."

He said thoughtfully, "Before you came, I was like

a—a frosted persimmon. Too shriveled up to have any room, even for much fear." He set both their cups on the table, grasped her hands. "Janie, I don't think I should take a chance on staying in this place any longer than the time I need to honor the agreement with Broadfoot. I'm not accepting any more lumber orders."

"But I like it here, James! I like being shut away—with only you in my life. What about the new house we've been planning?"

"I've never told you, but the first day Comochichi and I set foot on this place, the old lady's house was still burning. We saw the Indians ride off."

She turned away slightly.

"I never mean to do anything but obey you," she began slowly, "but if you leave this successful enterprise you've worked so hard to build just because you're afraid an Indian will scalp me before tea some afternoon, I will feel dreadful."

"Janie, that could happen!"

"I'm not going to let myself be afraid. When I hear a strange noise outside—here alone—I just remember that some fear is part of our life. James, I was more afraid in Charleston without you than I am now."

"Another thing, you'd better stop visiting at the settlement."

"Why? We're having sewing classes!"

"I don't worry about the women and children."

"But the men make such a good living working for you, they wouldn't dare molest me."

He stretched his lean length on the sofa and eased his head into her lap. "I wish I believed that."

For several minutes, she massaged his forehead, her fingers tracing the dark lines of his eyebrows, smoothing away his frown. "No more frightening talk, James," she said at last. "I don't want to leave Florida as long as you're doing so well. We can visit my family often. I'm really not very afraid"—she kissed his nose—"and anyway, I want to watch you draw this evening. Please make some more sketches of our new house out on the bluff! Your supper's ready. I can serve it to you right here—while you draw."

His eyes were closed, but in spite of himself, he was beginning to smile.

"What are you grinning about, James Gould?"

He sat up, hugged her. "The way you handle me."

"But I'm not handling," she said seriously. "I want to watch you build a house—all the way from those impressive sketches and funny marks and measurements to the setting in place of our front doorknob! Even if you decide to move away from here some day, I will have had the pure joy of watching my husband build something."

He sighed. "We can't leave for well over two years, anyway. If a new house is what you want, I'll build it, as soon as I can."

"We have lots of time for everything we ever want to do, dear James."

"I don't feel as young as you. Do you realize you were just learning to walk when I went off to fight with Shays' rebels?"

"And I don't want to hear any more talk about that dreadful time in the freezing cold with Daniel Shays, either! I want to watch you draw our house."

"All right," he laughed. "Run get my portfolio."

In a minute she was back with the bulging leather folder, a sly smile on her face.

"Do you know that, more than almost anything, I've wanted to open this sometime when you were out working and look at everything in it?"

He chuckled. "Why?"

"Because you've always taken it wherever you've traveled. I'm jealous. This portfolio knows more about you than I know."

"Why haven't you peeped, then?"

"It's your private property."

He took his father's old portfolio but, instead of opening it, sat looking at her, marveling still at her naturalness. At his ease with her. Who would believe laughter had become a part of him? Now and then, he had to stop and listen to be sure it was he, James Gould, able to laugh so easily, share himself so freely. He pulled her down beside him, spread the portfolio open on their knees. "I have no secrets from you," he said. "I'll never need to have any."

"Draw what our house will look like from—let me see—from the back!"

"You mean a rear elevation?"

"Is that what it's called?"

Rummaging through the folder for fresh paper, his hand fell on the yellowing batch of lighthouse sketches, the sheaf of specifications. He took them out, flipped through them.

"What are all those important-looking papers?"

He drew a deep breath. "I'll sketch for you all evening if you want me to, but here's something it's a wonder I didn't show you long ago. These papers are not worth anything now at all, but I guess they were the most important thing in my life until I found you."

"If you want to tell me about them, I want to know."

"A dream. That's all they mean. A dream I've had since I was a boy. I've nothing to show for it except this set of plans—for the one thing I've ever really wanted to build."

"What? What is it?"

She was looking at him with such concern, he said, "You wouldn't laugh at all about a boyhood dream, would you? I mean that I've kept these—carried them with me all these years."

"James, I could no more laugh at a dream of yours than I could bear to die and leave you."

Through supper and until the cabin filled with darkness, he talked to Janie about his lighthouse. Even before she lighted the candles, after he could no longer see her face, he could feel her concentration, her sharing of each detail. From the first time Lemuel Haynes had shown him the engraving of the Boston Light to the strange kind of consolation he had received through all the hard places in his life, just from knowing that his drawings were there in the old portfolio and that the day might still come when James Gould would actually build a lighthouse.

When he finished, he put some wood on the fire, sat down beside her, and waited. Not anxiously. She had lived every moment with him. He had intended to add, "Of course, it was only a silly boy's dream. Little by little I've let it go. Far more important matters to attend now." But he merely waited.

Finally, she stood before him, silhouetted against the orange and blue flames. "You'll build that lighthouse, James Gould. I'm sure. As sure as that we love each other. Some day, somewhere, you and I will stand together—*looking* at your lighthouse."

"Thanks for hearing me out," he said after a while. "But don't talk nonsense."

"Nonsense? That's your *dream!*"

"I'll leave the dreaming to you now."

"I want you to dream."

"Not any more—not that way. Dreams are for filling the empty places in a man's life. Substitutes for what he knows he can never have. I don't need that old dream now. I'm in the lumber business." His voice was sharper than he intended. "Let's not mention the lighthouse again—and how do you expect me to draw elevations without a quill and ink?"

Chapter 22

The new steam mill, one of the first in the South, was installed and ready for use by the end of their first year together, and James turned down an additional lumber order from St. Marys so that the more versatile saws could be put to use cutting sills, joists, rafters and flooring for their home. He had selected a site on the highest point of his land—a twenty-foot bluff overlooking the St. Marys River, some two miles from the mill settlement. Janie's days would be quiet there, away from the quarreling children and barking dogs, away from the constant whine of the saws, the hiss and chug of the new steam mill.

He would build a sturdy, two-storied, braced frame house of clapboards, with a single central chimney, since they needed fire for warmth only three or four months out of the year. Janie's kitchen, off their small dining room on the first floor, would have cross ventilation, and water piped from the artesian well. He designed a smaller fireplace in the parlor side of the chimney for them to enjoy on chilly evenings. Their master chamber, on the second floor, shared the chimney. In the attic above, he would smoke meats and fish.

The basic plan had been made for months, but even after the bricks which came by raft from St. Marys had been laid, ready to receive the heavy foundation sills, he was still amusing Janie at night by drawing elevations of the interior. One night he would draw the fireplace wall in their parlor, paneled in oak; another night, the row of three wide windows through which light and air from the river would enter their bedroom. She had seen a window-sill sundial once as a child in London, and James promised she would have one on her wide kitchen sill—with Roman numerals from I to VI and from VII to XII spaced along it—so that, on sunny days, at least, she could play at being primitive and plan her work according to the shadow moving across the sill.

By the middle of August, the frame braces and studs had been tenoned and pegged into place. Janie, too, could envision their house now. It looked so much larger than she had dared imagine—larger and taller the day the roof beams were set.

"Oh, James, I can see our garden too! I do thank you for designing the house with a walled garden, even here in our wilderness. Gardens should always have walls. We played in a lovely, overgrown, walled garden, Elizabeth and I, in London."

Janie knew his first reason for such a wall was for her safety. He hadn't said so, but he had shown her the iron sliding bar forged at the St. Marys blacksmith shop where the rosehead nails, flooring brads, and scuppers had been made. She understood that the heavy black latch would be on the inside of the wooden garden gate. A man would have to scale a seven-foot brick wall if he meant to harm her.

"Do you think your family will like our new place?"

"Oh, Mums will be tearful with joy over it! She'll adore the English garden, and I can see her settled on the upstairs piazza like a queen surveying her realm. Father will be so proud"—a note of sadness crept into her voice—"and Elizabeth will be glad for me. Unselfish Elizabeth. James, how can a man love a woman as deeply as Samuel loves her and go right on causing so much sorrow?"

"Captain Bunch is probably far more frightened under all that boasting than your sister, Janie."

"Samuel frightened?"

"No man has to swagger and put on such airs unless he lacks confidence in himself down underneath. Has he had more bad luck?"

"Of course he has, and this seems to me the saddest of all. For both of them. Would you like me to read part of the letter Comochichi brought today?"

"If you like."

She took the letter from her apron pocket. "I

wasn't going to tell you, James. I'm embarrassed about my poor family's misfortunes—I won't read it all—oh, yes, here's the sad, sad part. 'I know, Janie, I should not burden you with our troubles, but these days in particular, I am never without pain and pity for Samuel. All the money from the sale of the Negroes is gone, and on Tuesday, the second of August, his favorite possessions and some of mine were sold at public outcry at the Court House by virtue of an attachment.' "

"His cotton brokerage failed, then?"

"Utterly! That's later on in the letter, but what breaks my heart, dear James, is right here—listen: 'Sold were his cherished Arabian Horseman's sword, his double-barreled gun, his prized pearl-handled dueling pistols and all of my silver. I confess I wept, since the silver was Samuel's first proud gift to me. I suppose I should give thanks that for some strange reason none of this seems to depress Samuel. Already he is about the business of borrowing money to buy a hotel!' James, did you hear that? His debtors are coming right into Elizabeth's house to take her silver and Samuel's trying to get himself embroiled again!"

"I heard. He tried to interest me in that hotel when you and I were married. First time I met the man."

"Oh, how dreadful! I'm so ashamed for him, for my family."

"No need to be. I think I have the Captain sized up."

She folded the letter. "I love you, James Gould. And I thank God *you're* my husband. You, not anyone else."

"You think you might keep me, do you?"

For answer, she held his hand in both of hers possessively.

At the open cabin door, they watched the copper moon rise to the top of the pines, and when it reached the tallest tree, James said, "I want to go to bed, Janie."

"Are you so tired, my beloved?"

"No. I need to be close to you."

They were in the new house by Christmas, 1804. Most of the furniture ordered through James' London agent was in place, every piece gleaming because Janie polished it two or three times a day. The heavy mahogany bedstead, his special gift to her, smelled so of lemon oil, he made her promise not to polish it again for at least a week.

"It won't be easy," she pouted. "I'm here all alone so much of the time with nothing to do."

"You lie very prettily, Janie. No woman without help has time on her hands."

"Hush. Do you suppose anyone else on the St. Marys River has six Queen Anne chairs around a dining table as graceful as ours?"

"Yes. The Howsams' furniture is just as finely made; but I want to discuss hiring some help for you."

"James, you're all the help I need. Gracious, you can make candles and soap, and with Comochichi running in and out through the day, I do very well. Do you know the piece of furniture I like best of all? Our pine hutch you made. I like it better than all the furniture you bought for me!"

He chuckled. "That's ridiculous, Janie."

For Christmas he gave her silver, complete with satinwood knife boxes decorated with delicate mounts and inlays. "If you love this old man enough to live in this desolate place," he said as they sat together before a roaring fire, "the least I can do is see that you're surrounded with beauty."

"You're not old and I'm no happier than I was in our cabin except that I love you more."

"My old teacher, Lemuel Haynes, once told me it was fine to own beautiful possessions, just so long as they didn't own me. Said God created all beauty. I aim to see you always have it, Janie."

"Is it true or are you teasing me, when you vow your family didn't celebrate Christmas?"

"It's true."

"But what did you do when Christmas came—just nothing?"

"One year, to please my British father, Mama let my brother William and me drag in a Yule log."

"Does it still make you sad to think of William?"

"I wish we'd been able to know each other as men."

"Didn't your mother believe that Christ the Saviour was born at Christmas?"

"She believed it, but her God was very different from Papa's God, I guess. Mama's God didn't believe in celebrating anything."

"Do you mind not having a church here?"

" I guess I hadn't thought much about it."

"I do sometimes. But this is holy too—this night right here in our isolated castle. James?"

"Hm?"

"Do you think we might visit my family any time soon? Now that they're moving to Savannah, the distance isn't as far as Charleston."

"Not very soon, I'm afraid. I can take you to St. Marys and see you safely on a Savannah schooner, if you want to go without me."

"I don't!"

"I've spent so much time working on our house, it could be almost a year before I can leave again. When they're settled, they can come here. Are you unhappy that I can't go for a real visit now?"

"Yes. But if you think for a minute that I intend to go without you, you're wrong. I love you more than I love my family."

"The last thing I ever want to do is disappoint you."

"I know, and I'm a spoiled child, but in just a very little while, I'll be all over it—probably about ten minutes from now. When I am all over it, we can celebrate Christmas properly with carols on my new pianoforte."

He gave her a long, grateful kiss.

"I think I'm over my disappointment already," she breathed. "But when you know whether it will be a year or less than a year, will you tell me? I love to count off days. Now, I'm going to play 'God Rest Ye Merry Gentlemen'— and you're going to sing!"

Openly disobeying James, who had ordered her never to leave their walled garden without him, Janie unlatched the gate and slipped out into the bright, sunlit May afternoon. She had finished her ironing, had dressed their bed in clean linens, had made his favorite cookies; her bread was baked for the week. What harm could possibly come to her if she tucked a small bundle of sugar cookies in her apron pocket and set off, a little way down the pine-straw path to meet him? I may just teach him a small lesson, she told herself. If we're to live here, something must rid James of his fears for me. She sang as she walked—a made-up ditty:

> Why wait longer
> Than a maid has to wait
> To see the man she loves?

A squirrel leaped from a branch and startled her. She laughed, slowed her pace a little so as not to venture too far from the clearing behind her. James might disapprove a bit less if she hadn't come so far to meet him. She delighted in the tiny, ticking sounds of the woods . . . the vast, empty silence. No other sound but the distant wail of the mill saws and a brown thrasher scratching in the undergrowth.

Moving softly so as not to miss James' step on the path, she marveled at the loud noises her own feet made, snapping last year's dead twigs, splintering a dry, silvered cone as her slippers scrunched in the straw itself.

I will surely hear him a long way off in those work boots he wears. *Clomp, clomp, clomp.* She stamped one foot hard after another, like James. Then stopped, whirled to stare into the thicket beside the path. Something was crashing through the winter-dried weeds, cracking branches—coming nearer. James? No . . . not boots on the path. From the woods! A man's boots, pounding, heavier than James' wiry stride. He's trying to frighten me, she decided, and began again to tramp as heavily as she could, to stamp the ground, to chant in a low, meant-to-be-giant voice:

"Who goes there through the woods this day? Who—goes—there—through the woods—this day?"

The footsteps stopped.

Janie stopped too, then shouted in the bass-giant voice: "I know you're there, King James! I can wait if you can wait. I—can wait. . . ." Her voice trailed off.

There was no answer. Terror gripped her, held her rooted to the path. She whispered, "James?" Screamed, "James!"

Somewhere in the tangle of scrub oaks beside the path she smelled the strong, sweaty stench of a man; forced her body to turn and begin the staggering, nightmare flight toward home. The heavy boots were following close. One slipper came off, and stobs and pine cones tore at her bare foot as she tried to run faster, screaming for James until there was only enough breath left for running.

In sight of her house, she heard a shot. Something fell heavily, and James voice shouted: "In the house, Jane! Get to the house!"

Inside the garden, she leaned against the brick wall, shaking uncontrollably as James slid the iron bar securing the gate.

"Did you—kill him, James? Did you—kill that man?"

"No." He grabbed her shoulders. "Janie, why did you do it? Why?"

"Scold—me later," she sobbed. "Shouldn't you—see—about him?"

"Comochichi's there. It's only a leg wound. Don't change the subject. What in the name of God made you do a thing like that?"

"I—I just meant—to—surprise you."

He lifted her in his arms, pushed open the door and carried her upstairs.

"Don't put me on the good bedspread, James!"

She wiggled free, turned back the thick woven counterpane, tumbled onto the bed and fainted.

He was stretched beside her when she opened her eyes. She looked at him for a brief moment, then buried her face in his shoulder.

"What am I going to do with you?" He had never spoken harshly to her before. "Whatever possessed you to leave the garden? I've told you a thousand times to stay out of those woods!" The ordeal had been enough for her—why couldn't he comfort her?

"Who was it?"

"Sam Webber. I should have killed him. I wish I had!"

"James!" She sat up on the side of the bed.

"I will kill the next man who even looks like he aims to lay a finger on you!"

She swiped at her eyes with a corner of the sheet, stood up, taller than he had ever seen her, and looked straight at him.

"That is enough of such talk, James Gould. I've done a desperately foolish thing and I'm sorry. But you're talking like a madman and I want you to say you're sorry. Not to me, to God. It may take a while for you to believe this, but your wife—your spoiled little-girl wife—has just grown up."

He could only stare at her.

"I will not cause you more worry by ever going out alone again," she went on. "Neither will I plague you to take me to visit my family. Not ever again. I know your heart. You will take me when you can, and that's when we will go. From now on, you will come home from work each day only when it's right and convenient for you to come. Not earlier, just to please a pampered little girl playing house. And I'll be here, inside the locked gate. I've stopped being a child. From now on, I'm a woman. Will you take back what you said about killing Sam Webber?"

He nodded, too startled, too in awe of her to answer.

"I forced you to say such an evil thing, James. Forgive me, please. I mean never to take advantage of you again."

"Yes! Yes, I'm sorry. I—I guess I was just wild at the thought of—what he might have done to you."

Janie had managed to do what no one else had ever been able to. She had taught him how to play, laugh, share his heart without fear of betrayal, of being hurt. "But don't change," he whispered. "I want you always to be—my girl."

She laid her hand on his cheek. "Poor James. Are you afraid we won't laugh together any more because I've grown up? The best laughter I've ever heard came from behind the door in my parents' bedroom. I honestly thought I knew *when* to play games. We know now I didn't, but there's no reason to worry. Nothing bad has happened to me, and nothing will. You'll see."

He went to the window. "It's harder here for you," he said after a while. "I'm with people all day, even if they are brutes, most of them. You need some human society. Friends. We could visit the Howsams Sunday, would you like that?"

"Not as much as being alone with you on the one day you can stay at home."

"I wish I could bring myself to buy a good black woman for you!"

He felt her hands on his shoulders, turning him firmly around to face her. "You do not believe in owning slaves," she said, "and I will not be the cause of your acting against your own principles."

"How do you feel about it?"

"I suppose I haven't thought about it, as you have. Samuel had people, of course, in Nassau. Elizabeth still has four. I imagine Mother and Father would own one or two servants if they weren't too poor. I used to watch the dreadful business at the slave market in Charleston until I'd have to run away and cry, but often I prayed that I would some day be able to buy them all."

"To free them?"

Janie had changed. The realization was breaking over him. They were discussing a serious subject together—a subject other than their own happiness, their own love, the wonder of their life together. They were not making love or playing games. Janie was not hopping from one topic to another. They were talking to each other.

"Did I want to free them?" She repeated his question thoughtfully. "I don't know. I was too young, I suppose, to want to do more than protect them from what I saw at the slave market. What would they do with freedom? What has a white cracker like Sam Webber done with his?"

Before his eyes, she was becoming more than his adored wife, even more than the desired object of his love. Janie was becoming his friend.

Chapter 23

There was a hint of autumn in the duller green of the sweet gums, the tinge of yellow that tipped the leaves of the wild grapevines, as James stood watching Comochichi round the bend in the river and swing the small, loaded supply skiff alongside the dock. He could not imagine life on the St. Marys without Comochichi. The Indian had been as dependable as the sun, protective of Janie, of James himself. Comochichi's hawkweed poultices had probably saved Sam Webber's life when gangrene had spread in the gunshot wound. Webber had been back at work for over two months, his leg as good as ever.

James called a greeting and caught the mooring rope which the Indian tossed.

"Good journey."

"I know you had fine weather. At least, we didn't have a drop of rain here."

After he secured the skiff, James began to help unload boxes of staples, gunpowder, nails, a supply of writing and drawing paper, some new sewing materials for Janie.

The men worked a few minutes in silence; then Comochichi said, "Good trip, good weather—bad news. Creeks burn house at Roses Bluff. Comochichi see smoke today from river."

Still holding a heavy keg of nails, James whistled softly. "That's just about three miles from the town of St. Marys! Little over twenty-five miles from here. Are they coming this way?"

Comochichi shrugged. "May go off for black-drink ceremony. May come this way next year—next week. May not come."

James set the keg on the dock. "Any mail?"

Along with the sheaf of invoices for the supplies, Comochichi handed James a letter from Savannah for Janie, stood watching while James flipped absently through the invoices.

"I'll study these later," he said. "My mind is on one thing—getting Mrs. Gould away from here. We've done well this summer. Our fall shipment's headed for London by now. I'm taking her to Savannah. If I go too, maybe she won't suspect the real reason for leaving. We'll stay at least a month, until the present danger is past."

"Comochichi no be able to save new house if Creeks come."

James sighed. "I know that. Just try to warn the people—and save yourself."

On his way to the house, James decided not to tell Janie until after she had read her letter. He decided also that they would travel the thirty miles to St. Marys by land in the mill wagon. That way, she wouldn't see the burned plantation house at Roses Bluff.

Janie chattered above the humming of the teakettle—something about needing two more flower boxes, then excitedly broke the brown blob of sealing wax on the letter from her mother, unfolded it and began to read aloud:

Savannah, Georgia
16 September, 1805

Our dear Jane and James,

We are well settled in our new house and although I use the word *new* with caution, it is as comfortable, at least, as the Charleston place. Our cousin, Mayor Charles Harris, has been generous to a fault. He has not only moved us here, supplied our every need, but made your father happy by procuring for him a position as School Master, and has arranged for him to serve as a member pro tem of the Board of Health. This latter entails some indelicate chores, since he and the other Board Members must pass through the city inspecting yards, enclosures and *privies*. Not elevating, but important to the welfare of the citizens.

Janie stopped reading. "Poor Father. Still, I'm sure being a member of the Board of Health is very important, don't you think so?"

He nodded vigorously. "Anything to help keep down fever." She seemed satisfied, he thought, and tried to settle back for the remainder of the letter.

> I dare not count the months since we have seen you. We never want to burden you with pleas for a visit, but are certain you both know our hearts long to be with you. Elizabeth and Samuel are well and Elizabeth speaks often of how she admires and respects you, James. Dear Samuel has managed so far to pay the rent on their drafty house by manufacturing candles, but I dare say they will have to move into ours one day. We are all in good health and John Mackay, who has just had his fifteenth birthday, talks of nothing these days but his wish to join you in Florida and learn the lumber business.

"Oh, James, was it an imposition for Mums to mention that so casually at the end of her letter? I never want my family to take advantage of your generosity."

"John Mackay, eh? No imposition at all. Sounds interesting." He touched her hand. "We can talk about it with the boy face to face. I've changed my plans. You and I are leaving the end of next week for Savannah."

On September 25, the schooner *Electiva* docked at Savannah. Standing beside Janie, James helped her scan the wharf for a glimpse of the family. There had been time to get a letter to them by Howsam. The Harrises would all be there to meet the boat.

"They're here! We just haven't found them yet," Janie cried. "Mums, Charles, John Mackay, little Caroline—can you believe she's past four now? And Stephen. Oh, James, Stephen's seven years old!"

Her happy voice went on as they waited impatiently for the docking to be completed, but there was no sign of the waving, welcoming Harrises in the handful of people on the wharf.

"I don't understand. Father would know when our boat arrives. Where are they, James?"

He put his arm about her reassuringly. "Hold your

horses, young lady. We're just missing them in the crowd, I guess."

"No! There aren't that many people. Something has happened, or they would all be here."

After what seemed an eternity, the gangplank was finally swung into place. Holding her close to his side as they hurried onto the wharf, James could feel her tremble.

Then there was Charles, standing alone, taller, his straw-colored hair plastered to his head, his drawn, thin face a mask of suffering.

"Charles!" Janie almost screamed his name.

The boy moved woodenly toward them, allowing himself to be knocked about among the shoving people.

James released her arm and watched her run to her brother.

"Hello, Janie. Hello, Mr. Gould," the lad said, his voice hoarse, his eyes red-rimmed. "It's John Mackay. He died yesterday of bilious fever. We had to bury him the same day. Papa said it's the law."

Janie understood, seemed almost grateful, James thought, when he arranged to stay away from the Harris home on business for hours at a time. "I remember when we found out William had been killed, we just wanted to be by ourselves a while," he had told her on the second morning as he dressed to leave the Harris house on the South Common.

His Savannah business had been quickly finished the first day. An investment in a local hotel, made for him by his broker, had doubled in value. He sold his interest for cash, but the satisfaction was dimmed by Janie's grief. The final papers on the almost completed three-year lumber contract were in Charleston, but he dared not leave her. I'll have them sent here, he decided, as he walked slowly down Drayton Street toward the Bay, his thoughts tumbling with anxiety over Janie, over what might already have happened to their home in Florida, to his mill, to all his holdings there.

Within sight of the river and the towering masts of

ships at anchor, he paused to look across the Strand at Factor's Walk. Cotton production was eight times what it had been before the widespread use of Eli Whitney's gin. More than fifty million pounds were being produced in the Southern states, and one of the centers of activity was Factor's Walk on Commerce Row, along Savannah's waterfront.

If Samuel Bunch had been wise enough to increase his capital just a little before opening his own brokerage office, the poor man would still be in business. James had talked for a long time last night with Elizabeth. What a pity her husband lacked her calm, practical mind. A fine woman, deserving of a far better life than her quixotic Captain would ever manage to give her.

"I didn't marry him, Mr. Gould, so that I could amass possessions," she had said. "I married Samuel because I loved him. I still do. He's one of the most warmhearted men on earth. Of course, if he could be satisfied with less, we'd have more."

Hard to believe a man could fail in Savannah as a cotton factor these days, James thought, ambling west along the Bay. John Couper had written that he had taken full advantage of the gin and was prospering, along with his factor. "Almost keeping up with my spending. You won't approve, I suppose, James, but I now own over two hundred people, and Cannon's Point thrives in every way."

James hoped he and Janie might stop on their way home for a visit with John Couper. The lumber expert, Reuben King, could come down from Darien for a talk. Income from the Gould Mills depended in part upon the lumber measurements King made. It would be helpful to talk face to face. Besides, John Couper had not met Janie. His hopes for me may rise a little, James smiled to himself, once he sees the wife I've found. After St. Simons, they could continue south with a stop at Dungeness on Cumberland Island. Was he putting off the return to Mills Ferry? He would have to take one day at a time. As yet, there was no way to know he still had a home in East Florida.

His hands thrust in his jacket pockets, he stood looking across at Commerce Row, reading the signs that hung above the thriving establishments: Habersham; Lively and Buffton; Mein and Mackay. He wondered how many of those tow bags of cotton stacked on the wharf had been picked from the Cannon's Point fields. He missed John Couper. I'm successful beyond my own hopes, he thought, but Janie and I both need friends. There are some excellent town houses here. Perhaps I should consider buying one now. Rentals would return my purchase money. Then, later, if Janie wants to settle in Savannah, we'd own a comfortable place until I could build one to her liking.

On the south side of the Bay, near the corner of Whitaker, a crowd had gathered. Some sort of sale was in progress. He crossed the street to investigate.

Had he noticed the crudely lettered sign, he would have turned back:

AUCTION OF VALUABLE SLAVES

In Charleston, he had, when possible, avoided the slave market behind the Exchange, his stomach turning at the sight of human beings forced to stand inspection like cattle. Today, he found himself watching when a stocky mulatto, as light-skinned as Lemuel Haynes, stepped onto the rickety, foot-high platform.

The auctioneer, a modestly dressed, graying man with a pock-marked face, went about his business in a matter-of-fact way, gesturing from time to time toward the young man on the block.

"Gentlemen, I have the pleasure to offer a most unusual mulatto named Frank, aged about thirty-two. Has been in this country seven years, is an excellent coachman and hostler, understands perfectly well the management of horses and is, in every respect, a first-rate character, except that he will occasionally drink. Though, I hasten to assure you, he is not an habitual drunkard." He stroked the Negro's heavily muscled bicep with the back of his hand. "Now, ain't that the truth, Frank?"

James saw the mulatto lower his head.

"Well, I see the cat's got Frank's tongue today," the auctioneer went on affably, "but now—what am I bid? For this splendid specimen, do I hear twelve hundred dollars?"

Bidding began at six hundred, the auctioneer droned on, and James moved to the edge of the crowd, where he could see the other slaves lined up. A child no more than five clung to its mother's tattered skirt; a young man in his twenties; a grizzled old Negro with deep white scars across his bare shoulders. Last in the straggly line, a little apart from the others, stood a tall young woman, her long, faded pink dress spotless and mended, her head proudly erect, her deepset eyes looking deliberately off over the small crowd of bidders and onlookers. James thought he had never seen a more noble-appearing woman, black or white. He stepped closer to wait through the sale of the others, for her summons to the block.

"All right, Larney"

The woman moved with dignity, stepped up onto the box and stood looking toward the river. She was near Mary's age, James supposed, undoubtedly a house servant, capable, well trained, but he seemed to see more, and his head began to throb with hatred for the auctioneer. This slave was no longer black. *She was Mary* standing there, alone, unprotected—for sale.

"Yes, indeedy, my friends," the auctioneer was saying, "we have saved the best to the last. Larney will not be sold for pennies! She is here for sale only because her mistress died in Richmond a month ago and her master, old and infirm, went to live with his son. Larney, thirty-odd, born in Virginia, of fine sturdy stock, washes, irons, cleans, cooks—her rice pilaf would make your mouth water even before you taste! The perfect house servant, worth her weight in gold!" To prove his next point, the man casually ripped the neck of her dress to expose one brown shoulder and a breast. "Perhaps best of all, Larney is a proven, first-rate brood matron—look at that!"

James had pushed his way to the front of the group of men nearest the trading block, unable to leave until he learned the woman's fate.

"Ah, I see one interested gentleman," the auctioneer said, pointing at James. "Your interest only indicates your discrimination, sir. As further proof of Larney's worth as a breeder—note the width of the pelvis." He slapped her buttocks sharply. "No problem at all for Larney to increase your investment manyfold with little black pickaninnies. She's borne three fine sons already. All three brought a good price last year back in Virginia."

The woman had closed her eyes, but held her shoulders erect, her head high.

"See what I mean about her quality? Look at those wide, powerful shoulders. That chin in the air. You can't make Larney cringe and beg like other black wenches."

A sweating man with powdered hair shouted: "Nine hundred dollars!"

"For this excellent property? For this superb piece of black flesh? An insult! Let me hear a sensible bid, gentlemen!"

"Nine hundred and fifty," the man shrilled.

"Nonsense."

"Turn her around, so's I can get a better look. Maybe I'll raise it!"

The auctioneer turned the woman all the way around, touching her breasts with his gavel, her buttocks, noting again "the ample pelvis."

"One thousand dollars!"

James saw her open her eyes to look straight at the red-faced man who seemed about to buy her. She swayed slighty, shuffled one bare foot, then closed her eyes again and waited.

"One thousand and fifty dollars." The bidder's voice shook with annoyance. "No one in his right mind will go higher than that!"

"Eleven hundred!" James called out. She opened

her eyes again. "Eleven hundred dollars," he repeated, to help her locate him in the crowd.

"Eleven hundred and fifty, by damn!"

"Twelve hundred dollars," James shouted. He heard the gavel bang three times against the platform where Larney stood, as the auctioneer began his detached explanation: "One half cash and the other half in notes at six months, drawn and endorsed to the satisfaction of the vendor, with special mortgages on the slave until final payment. Sold to the gentleman in the gray cape for twelve hundred dollars!"

James' profit from the hotel investment was in his pocket. "I'll pay cash," he said and began to count out the money. His head ached. He was still angry, but one relieving thought crossed his mind: Mary and Janie will be glad I saved her.

A minute ago, she *was* Mary, her eyes Mary's eyes: searching, wise, lonely, but somehow offering to help. Now Mary had turned into a strange brown woman named Larney.

A slave named Larney, who belonged to James Gould.

He paid for her, signed the necessary papers with as few words as possible, turned toward the woman, then whirled and sent the huckster sprawling to the ground. A few men guffawed. "You've got your twelve hundred dollars," James said, glaring down at the auctioneer, "and you've also got a tangible idea of what I think of a man who earns his living as you earn yours!"

Larney, who had not moved, stared at him.

For a moment, James wondered what to do. It was against Georgia law to free her. She was his legal property. His responsibility. People bought and sold Negroes every day. No one in all Savannah would think anything unusual had happened, he told himself.

His first impulse was to help her down from the block, but he realized what people would think, nodded instead and motioned for her to follow.

As he walked rapidly up Bull Street toward the Harris house, Larney a respectful distance behind, only one thing came clear: no matter how well he meant to treat this woman, he had sinned against the one person he had ever wanted to be like—Lemuel Haynes, son of a Scottish indentured servant and a black slave.

Chapter 24

Mills Ferry
St. Marys River
East Florida
21 April, 1806

Our dearest Mary Gould,

I am writing this letter because James asked me to see that your money reaches you near its regular arrival date. He has been away in Darien, Georgia, on business for ten days. It is convenient for him to make his trips now since we have our fine Larney. I don't believe that James has told you, but I am certain he would not have permitted me to return to Mills Ferry from Savannah last year if he had not bought Larney. He finally admitted to me that we went to Savannah because he feared an Indian attack. There has been none, however, and already, in half a year's time, we have come to depend on Larney for almost everything. She seems content, her only worry being that as yet, there is no baby in our household.

James is as attached to Larney as I am, but he still suffers over being a slave owner. More so than ever now—and I think he prefers me to tell you—because he owns fifteen others besides Larney. Four months ago, on impulse, as with Larney, he bought the fifteen men. My feeling is that he has not been able to bring himself to inform you, and so I will try to relate the story as it happened. He was surveying a new timber tract some distance from the mills and ready to ride home one evening when he heard from across the river sudden rough shouting, moans and sharp cries. When James rode to the riverbank to investigate, he saw on the other side a small band of Negroes being brutally forced to swim the river under the curses and whips of white and Indian slave smugglers. James, unable to tolerate the cruelty, shouted across that he would buy them all, then rode home for a boat to transport them downstream to makeshift quarters near the settlement.

Now, we have a large vegetable garden and James has leased additional acreage to be cleared for planting indigo. Once the white millhands learned that the Negroes would not be working the timber with them, they appeared satisfied. In spite of the heavy guilt which I know James carries, the new venture seems to absorb him, even to the erection of quarters for the field hands and the construction of his indigo vats.

Still, he needs help from you somehow, Mary. I do not mind if you tell him of this letter. I keep nothing from him, but because of his Massachusetts upbringing and a Negro minister who befriended him in his boyhood, James cannot accept what he has done. I'm sure you know that no one has influenced James as the Reverend Lemuel Haynes did, and I feel James considers himself as having betrayed their friendship, even after all these years. Please, Mary, do try to assure him that his purchase of all these people is not dishonorable. He saved them from terrible fates. I fear I do not worry about principle as James does. I am content knowing that at least our sixteen people are well treated, but then I do not reason as deeply about such matters.

Even though this letter is already long, I must tell you again that your bother has made my life all joy. He was so kind and sensitive and generous with my family during our bereavement, and he thinks of the small things that make me feel important to him—such as stopping for an extra day in St. Marys last year after a month in Savannah, to indulge a whim I had of having a silhouette made by the traveling artists, Raphaelle Peale and his brother, Rembrandt. Our only anxiety—constant to us all here—is the danger of Indian attack. We have escaped thus far, and I try to keep my fears from James. After a while one does learn to live with danger. He has ordered rare and beautiful plants, shrubs and roses for me, by way of the ships which transport his lumber abroad, and most of the year our walled garden is a picture. We feel now, since all seems quiet, that we will stay indefinitely and pray always for a visit from you. Please remember me to Mr. Horace and Miss Jessie.

Yr Affectionate Sister-in-law,
Jane Harris Gould.

The first indigo crop was profitable. When Comochichi brought the mail from St. Marys in September, James was not only surprised by the size of the payment received from his new venture, there came in the same post a request from a London firm for a lumber shipment larger than any previous single order. The quality of Gould timber was now known abroad as well as along the eastern coast.

Shuffling through the bundle of letters and invoices, James strolled toward the house, feeling gratified, savoring his success. Don Juan McQueen had so far been able to keep them free from Indian attack. Janie seemed content, now that Larney was with her. He knew he could build houses in Savannah and Charleston, but he was almost forty. The practical side of his nature told him to leave well enough alone. No sensible man pulled up stakes with not one, but two successful operations going smoothly.

In the mail was a letter for Janie from her mother, one for him from Mary, and a rare treat—word from John Couper. Janie and Larney would still be sewing; wouldn't worry about him if he slipped away into the woods beyond the clearing to read the letters from Mary and Couper by himself.

Not far from the path, he sat down on a fallen hickory and opened Mary's letter first.

Bangor, Massachusetts
30 August, 1860

My dearest James,

This is a personal letter to you, although since Janie's letter, written during your absence last spring, apprised me of your troubled conscience, you must feel free to share this with her. Last Sunday, the Reverend Lemuel Haynes filled the pulpit in our church. He is famous in New England now, and is considered, as you know, one of the most prominent divines. Still, after Meeting, he gave me all the time I needed to try to explain how troubled you are at being a slave owner. As I talked, he smiled and seemed to understand even before I finished. "Tell James that I do not condemn him for what he has done," he said. "This is simply the price a man of conscience must pay for living in a part of the world where slavery is still legal. There is no simple solution. I will pray that James can grasp this. In some of life's dilemmas, one cannot draw a sharp line between good and evil. The issues are too complex, too related to circumstances over which we, as individuals, have little influence. My old friend James may have no choice but to learn to live in this blurred time in history, when men of principle are forced to make the best of bad situations."

As nearly as I can remember his words, I have written them down for you to read and reread, James. When we parted, the Reverend Haynes repeated that he still has the highest regard for you and sends his promise to continue to pray for you. He told me that he has not failed to pray for you every day of the past twenty years. He even remembered how long it had been since he last saw you.

I will write a joint letter to you both soon.

Yr Loving Sister,
Mary Gould.

James read the letter twice and for the first time since Sunday Meeting in Lemuel Haynes' church back in Granville, knelt by the fallen tree and tried to make peace with Lemuel Haynes' God—and with himself.

He stayed alone in the woods as long as he dared without causing Janie anxiety, then started toward the house. Well into the clearing, he remembered the letter from John Couper, ripped it open, scanned the brief, deftly penned lines, crumpled the page and stuffed it in his pocket. Couper had sold to the United States Government, for one dollar, four acres of his land at the South End of St. Simons Island for the erection of a lighthouse. The Government was now advertising for a builder.

Walking faster, James experienced no conflict—only a wrenching grief. No responsible man his age would even consider giving up a lucrative lumber business for the few thousand dollars he might be paid to build one lighthouse. Janie must never know that he had been given the chance. John Couper's letter would go directly into the fire. For over twenty years, the lighthouse dream had been his. The grief would be his alone.

In their parlor, he tossed the crumpled note into the fire and as cheerily as possible called, "There's a letter from your mother, Janie!"

Word from Savannah always made her so happy, he would only have to listen, nod now and then and try to smile.

"Don't come in here, James," she called back from the sewing room at the rear of the house. "Wait right there—for a surprise!"

At the window, he looked out onto the glassy water, reflecting even the thinnest clouds stretched across the sunset, pale blue and rose and gold. A lighthouse on St. Simons Island. A lighthouse on St. Simons Island. If the chance had come from a thousand miles away, he could have borne it better.

From the doorway, Janie was impatiently clearing her throat for his attention. When he turned around, she stood like a princess, smiling, holding out the ankle-length flowing skirt of a new gown she and Larney had just finished—shell-pink mull, intricately trimmed with yards and yards of white lace and insertion.

"Well, now," he managed to say, "I've never seen anyone so beautiful."

"You're supposed to be looking at the dress, not at me, James! Aren't Larney's tucks perfect?" She dropped the skirt. "What's wrong?"

He had never lied to her: "I—I got some important mail today. I was just thinking. . . ."

"Well, don't think now. Larney's bringing our tea, with her biscuits and gallberry honey. Sit down and get comfortable."

"Did you hear me say there's a letter from your mother?"

"Of course I heard. We're going to read it together just as soon as I take care of my husband, so hush."

She filled his pipe, held a lighted spile. He puffed, wishing this time that she would forget her little ritual of massaging his tired feet, sliding them into his house slippers.

"I do declare, Mr. James Gould, you seem more interested in that letter from Mums than I." She stood looking down at him, her hands on her hips. "Would you like a small glass of wine before tea? You seem awfully tired."

"No, thanks. Just tea."

Janie sat across from him, opened the letter and began to read. " 'Nine September, eighten six. My dearest Janie. . . .'"

James saw her lips tighten, the color drain from her face. "Janie! What is it?"

"It's—my father," she said in an anguished whisper. "Father died the seventh of this month."

In the doorway, Larney stood holding the tray with the tea service.

"Oh, Larney, I'm glad you're here," James said.

"Larney?" Jane whispered.

"Yes, Miss Janie, Larney's here."

"My—father—died."

Larney set the tray on the table and went to stand beside her. "Ah heerd, honey. Ah heerd."

"Mums says—she—will—be afraid—of September—from now on. John Mackay died in September too."

"Dis be a bad ol' month fo' feber."

James watched the two women in silence. His wife had stopped talking to him. She looked at no one, but she was talking to Larney. Then she was in the tall woman's arms, weeping like a stricken child; Larney weeping too, smoothing Janie's hair with her wide brown hand.

As he slipped from the room, he heard Larney say, "Death be a part ob life, chile. Now dat you gonna hab a baby, you kin see dat to be true. Death jus' be a part ob life."

James stopped outside the door. She had told Larney first!

"Do Mausa James know yet, Angel Miss? Do dat good man know he gonna be a papa?"

"I was planning to tell him tonight. But he won't mind that you knew first. He understands the way we are, Larney. You see? He's left the room. He knew I needed you before I knew it."

"You want me to git 'im now?"

"Not yet. I need to splash my face with rose water. I must look a sight."

"You don' hab to do nuffin' yet, chile. Jus' git all de cryin' past—right here on Larney's shoulder."

James knew Larney was embracing Janie; he could hear the black woman's comforting sounds, soft unintelligible croonings. Then he heard Janie say:

"Tell me about your—father, Larney."

"Don' 'member much 'bout 'im, honey. 'Ceptin' dat he were big an' black an' laugh a lot."

"Did—did he die when you were young?"

"Maybe Papa daid by now. He'd be sixty-odd." Her voice filled with pride. "Ah allus heerd Papa he bring Mausa a big price!"

"I see. Your mother?"

"Look, chile, why don' Larney go git Mausa Gould right now?"

"No. I have to know—about you, too. You know all about me."

James hurried upstairs, feeling guilty for his long eavesdropping, admitting that he didn't want to know more of Larney's tragic life. Until Larney called him, he would wait, would let himself think of nothing beyond the fact that he was going to become the father of a child, at last.

On the evening of April 3, 1807, when Larney came wearily down the stairs carrying his black-haired, squalling son, James' first question as he rushed to her, was, "Will Miss Janie be all right? Will she live?"

"In de night, ah warn't sho'."

"You're sure now?"

She nodded. "You kin go on up, Mausa James. Angel Miss all bathed an' waitin'."

Then he looked at his son and, without a word, began a systematic examination of the still squalling infant: a careful check of every inch of the tiny, warm body—the feet, finding them straight; both arms, finding them strong. Gesturing to Larney to hold the baby higher, he inspected the spinal column, the sturdy shoulders. Last, he placed both hands around the velvety head—and nodded, approving the shape.

Abruptly, the baby stopped crying, seemed to look defiantly at James.

"See? He don' want *nobody* pokin' 'roun on 'im!" Larney hugged the infant to her. "It be *his* bi'ness how dem li'l arms an' legs be made. All his parts b'long to him!"

"I just had to be sure he was all right."

"Inspectin' 'im lak he be a new pile a lumber," she grumbled. "Now, Mausa James, you git on up dem steps an' leave us be."

"Can't he sleep a while upstairs with his mother? You must be dead for rest, Larney."

"Git! Angel Miss up dere all by hersef!"

Her dark-ringed blue eyes were open wide, her arms reaching for him. On his knees beside the bed, all he could say was, "Janie, Janie, you're all right. Larney pulled you through. I didn't lose you."

Her voice was weak, but with enough of the familiar cheer to lift his heart. "I've simply had a baby, James, that's all. Tell me how you like our son, James Gould Third."

"Is—is his name James?"

"I'll consult you on the name of our next child, but not this one. He could have no other name but yours."

"There won't be any next."

She tried to laugh. "There will be a next and a next and a next. So, don't scold. Just kiss me and get some rest. You look miserable!"

Chapter 25

On a bright Sunday morning late in April, James and Janie sat on the upstairs piazza, the baby's cradle between them. James rocked it gently with one foot. A breeze off the river stirred a thick rope of wistaria—grown in only three years to the second story—fanning one heavy lavender clump slowly back and forth. Each time the blossom swung near, Janie tried vainly to touch it.

James watched a while, then teased, "I'll pick it for you if you want it that much."

"That would spoil my game."

He stretched his legs, let the cradle come to a standstill. "I thought the Howsams' visit yesterday a very convivial one, didn't you, Janie?"

"Mrs. Howsam certainly approved of Larney's torte! I like our neighbors. Isn't their little girl pretty?"

He nodded. "The younger boy seems unusually bright. Robert, is it?"

"Yes, Robert. Fifteen. Thomas intends to plant indigo with his father, but Mrs. Howsam told me Robert wants to become a doctor."

"Heaven knows we need one. What might have happened to you without Larney when the baby came, I don't dare think. I was sure I'd have time to get Dr. Hunter from St. Marys, but—"

"Jimmy and I fooled you, and don't start blaming yourself again because I didn't count the day correctly! Jimmy's here." She brushed a fly from the baby's forehead. "I'll be stronger soon, and best of all, we're together in all this peace and beauty. Except for my heartache over Mums without Father, I'm happy. Did you hear me, James? I'm contented here."

He smiled at her. For a long time, neither spoke. Their shared sorrow over John Hartley Harris' death, the joy in the birth of their son had somehow lessened his pain over the St. Simons light. But the cutting disappointment was still there, surfacing especially in moments of silence as he rode to and from his work through the woods, and at night before he fell asleep. It was there now. Couper's second letter, received a few weeks before the baby was born, had helped a little. "A man from Connecticut seems likely to build the light, if his sureties are in order. But you James Gould, would have built a better one." I'm an ungrateful wretch, James scolded himself, to go on grieving over the collapse of a farm boy's dream. I have more to be thankful for than any man I know. This year, at least, I'm in far better condition financially than John Couper. Lumber is safer than cotton. The weather can only delay a lumber shipment, never destroy it. Couper, along with every other St. Simons planter, had suffered from a hurricane this year. James was sure Couper's loss would be enormous.

His letter from Mary, after her talk with Lemuel Haynes, had greatly eased his conscience. He would try to follow his old teacher's advice. The time he had spent alone by the fallen tree the day Mary's letter arrived had helped. He had enjoyed working with his people more since then. He had lost at least some of his guilt and had begun to face the situation with a clearer mind. He could do no more about abolishing slavery than he could change the animal existence of his white millhands. Better to concentrate on what he could handle. He had got up from his knees still despising his own helplessness, but fighting it less. Time, he supposed, and the changing pattern of the days—death, birth, success, more and more work—would eventually ease the conflict. Larney seemed happy; the fifteen men down at the quarters showed no sign of wanting to escape. He was pleased with the spring indigo planting. When the first good blue began to show as the men stirred the fermented contents in the new vats, John, the most intelligent of the lot, had beamed as though full credit belonged to him. John was so capable, he could run an indigo plantation himself.

James looked at Janie, who had dozed off. He felt

drowsy too. Today was good. Comochichi had heard no rumors of attack; seen no warning signals for months. Old Don Juan McQueen apparently still wielded enough influence over the Spanish Indians to keep them east of Mills Ferry. But James was well aware that the newly passed law prohibiting the importation of slaves into the United States could bring increased violence. Slave smuggling among the Indians would undoubtedly be rampant. The Florida Creeks broke the white man's laws as freely as the white man had cheated them.

"James, something has just come to me!"

"I thought you were asleep."

"I dozed a minute. Have you noticed John and Larney lately?"

He sat up. "What do you mean?"

"I think they've become quite attached to each other."

James slid back down in his chair, laughing. "Janie, your imagination is never idle. Even when you doze."

"I am not imagining. I'm observing. And wouldn't it be lovely if John and Larney got married?"

"Why, yes, I suppose so, but—how would they do it? I mean, do you know how Negroes marry? Or if they really do?"

"Certainly, I know. Larney told me. They gather their friends around them, hold hands, sing and jump over a broom."

"Is that right!"

"Marriage has to do with whether you love each other anyway. Larney explained—God understands that jumping over a broom is simply an African custom. Negroes' marriages are made in heaven, the same as ours."

"I suppose that's right," he said, only half listening. He had caught a glimpse of a man in the thicket at the river, dodging nearer and nearer the house. Without arousing Janie's suspicion by getting up, he watched until the figure appeared again near the barn.

"James," she went on, "I think we should encourage a marriage—right away. I feel it in my bones that Larney really loves John!"

Janie began to change the baby, and James got up—as calmly as he could—and sauntered to the porch railing. If the man were headed for the house, he would have to cross the clearing by the barn; would come in full view. In a moment, at the edge of the thicket, the myrtle bushes parted, framing the face of an Indian streaked with blue and yellow paint.

James stood motionless. If the Indian vanished, it probably meant that he was a scout and they were in for trouble. If he only intended to steal and run, why did he wear paint? How did he manage to get so close to the house without Comochichi knowing?

"What's wrong, James? What are you staring at?"

"Nothing," he lied. "I was—just looking around."

As James spoke, the Indian darted out of the thicket, took the clearing in long strides. Familiar strides. And the set of the wide, lean shoulders was familiar. Comochichi!

When James called to him, the Indian's finger flew to his mouth—a warning to be silent.

"James, what is it?" She was beside him now. "What's wrong?"

Without answering, he ran down the outside stair to the yard and into the clump of oleanders at the end of the house where the Indian waited.

"Comochichi—what on earth's gotten into you?"

"Creeks on trail," his friend gasped. "Drinking black drink *now* between here and Howsam place. Danger. Get wife, baby and Negroes in boats fast. Leave! *Leave now.*"

"Leave? Today?"

"Before two hour."

"But why are you hiding like this? Why the paint? I almost didn't recognize you."

"Creeks always send scouts ahead. Comochichi hide behind war paint like scout. No talk. Comochichi go. Not see you again. Great Spirit watch over you." The Indian vanished into the woods behind the house.

The day James feared most had come.

Two hours. Two hours to pack what they could and run for their lives. The new plantation bell! Ring it first. Take that chance. No other way to get the people assembled without wasting precious time. They couldn't gather even the bare essentials and pack the two large boats without making some noise, anyway.

He raced to the back of the house and began jerking the bell rope.

Janie, her face white and drawn, resisted, then obeyed when James ordered her to sit with the baby inside the house until time to leave.

"Larney can pack what we'll need—at least, all there's room to take. And please, don't make it harder by begging for any of your treasures."

He held her a moment, led her to the chair beside Jimmy's cradle, feeling her fear, her physical weakness, as she clung to him.

"Could I take just one cup and saucer?"

"No, Janie. Nothing but essentials. Nothing. I've given Larney her instructions. My God, what if we didn't have her? What if we didn't have John and the other men?"

"Where will we go, James?"

"St. Marys first, if we can make it. We'll talk later. Just wait right here. Don't leave this room—and try not to be afraid."

In less than two hours, the boats were loaded: three smoked hams, a side of bacon, rice, sweet potatoes, flour, and a trunk containing James' lighthouse portfolio and other papers—into which Larney also somehow packed one cup and saucer among a change of clothes for Janie and the baby, blankets for them all, and her master's old tin lantern, too small for use on the trip.

The oarsmen were in their places when James led Janie across the walled garden, through the gate and down the path to the dock. Seven blacks with John at the tiller would man the supply boat; there were seven, with James steering, in the boat where Larney and the family would sit. Carrying the baby, his face shielded from the sun, Larney climbed in first. James helped Janie to the seat in the stern beside her, then took John aside.

"You're in charge of the lead boat, John."

"Dat be good, Mausa Gould. Best me an' de niggahs be first. But ah don't lak you standin' at de tiller in dat rear boat. You gonna be a plain target be dey Injuns watchin' us."

"We're all targets. I'll feel better with us steering. Remember, watch the currents a mile or two downstream. Stay to the middle of the river and keep the men rowing smoothly. Not too fast, they'll wear out. They're all trained oarsmen now, thank God, but we've a long way to go in loaded boats."

"Trus' me, Mausa Gould."

James looked at the square, brown, earnest face. "I do trust you. Hope we can trust the others to keep rowing, no matter what we hear or see along the banks. We dare not stop for at least ten miles or so, until we hit the straight stretch where there's only marsh. Up to that point, the Creeks can watch us from the thickets along either bank. Don't forget, no slacking off until we've reached Howsam's place."

"Ah'll 'member, suh."

"Chances are, they're somewhere between here and the Englishman's. We'll all make good targets, so keep the men rowing and watch me for signals."

James took his place at the heavy tiller in the family boat, repeated his instructions to his men, gave a sign to John. The two big boats slipped into the river's channel and gathered speed through the dark waters.

One mile, two miles . . . three. The sun glare was so bright it was blinding, heightening his fear. Even standing up, facing forward, he could not tell whether Creeks lurked in the dark tangle of the river's banks. His oarsmen pulled evenly, fairly sure of a clear channel over this stretch. So far, no one had spoken. Even the baby was quiet. James, glancing down now and then at Janie, tried to concentrate only on the tricky currents, on John's boat ahead, on the strenuous effort of his own arms and shoulders as he gripped the tiller, forcing the big rudder to keep the loaded boat rounding the bends safely in the twisting river. His oarsmen were supplying good power . . . the heavy pull . . . the short pause . . . the heavy pull . . . the short pause . . . the heavy pull. Their boats moving swiftly now past the dense stands of hickory, magnolia, bay and palms. Was Janie strong enough to handle such fear? Was she aware that at any moment one or all of them could be toppled into the water by a rain of poisoned arrows? He felt far away from her, helpless to do anything but force his arms and shoulders and back to pull and push the all-important tiller—his hands already tender and burning against the wooden bar.

Three more miles and they would be in sight of the Howsam's landing and the straighter stretch in the serpentine river, where a mile or so of marsh—an unlikely hiding place—spread on either side. Two cypress swamps lay ahead to be passed first, then they would see the enormous live oak which sheltered the Howsam's dock. If they could reach that dock alive, there was hope of making it to the Georgia town of St. Marys.

He looked down at Janie. She leaned white but wide-eyed against Larney's shoulder; he saw her glance at the baby in Larney's lap. The black woman nodded up at him reassuringly. His responsibility was terrifying, his work laborious, but he was better off than Larney or Janie, who could only sit there, enduring the gnats and the hideous heat. And the fear.

His skin prickled when the baby began to cry. Even Larney's comforting whispers sounded as loud as gunshots in the silence which had held them all. His own voice seemed a shout when he said, "It's all right, Larney. Let him cry if he wants to." What difference would the cry of a baby make if the Creeks were there, stealing through the dense vegetation, watching the boats, deciding whether to kill him and Janie and the baby and capture the Negroes or to move silently beside them until exhaustion forced them to stop? If hostile Indians were around, as Comochichi believed, their scouts had been watching from the moment the boats left the Gould dock.

"We'll be in sight of the Howsam oak in a few minutes, Janie," he said. Speaking aloud lessened some of his panic. Senseless not to have done it before.

The baby grew quiet again as James and John called short, terse directions to the men, for they were in a section of the river made hazardous by fallen trees and alligators. In a few minutes, over the rhythmic rumble of the oars in the oarlocks, he could hear Janie and Larney whispering. Abruptly, Janie turned to look up at him.

"James! We smell smoke!"

He had already caught the acrid stench. He saw thick, wavering black columns over Howsam's bluff. Around one more bend in the river, they would be able to see the house.

"Put your backs into it," he shouted and the oarsmen quickened their strokes. In sight of the big oak, James glimpsed plumes of flame from the kitchen at the rear—and the one remaining wall of his neighbor's home collapsed as they watched. He saw John slowing his men, waiting for a signal to tell him whether to hurry past or run the risk of stopping to offer help.

"We must stop, James. The Howsams would help us!" Janie's voice was suddenly full of courage.

She had decided for him. He signaled, and both boats moved toward the dock.

Climbing cautiously up the steep path, just ahead of John, James found the body of a boy first, a mulatto child sprawled on his back at the top of the bluff, his scalp half cut away, his skinny chest gashed by a tomahawk.

The two men stared down at the wide-open eyes. "Maybe they only killed this boy," James whispered. "If the others are alive, we've got to help them."

Inside the picket fence of the Howsams' front yard, James called: "Mr. Howsam?"

"Ain' no use," John whispered. "Nothin' livin' 'roun' here but dem birds up dere."

James looked up. Five wide-winged turkey buzzards circled, swooping and sailing, using the wind currents to move them out and down toward the smoldering ruins of the English family's home and a feast of human flesh.

"We've got to make sure," he said.

Picking their way through the hot rubble, among smoking trees and shrubs and weeds, they found the Howsams: the little girl face down at the foot of the veranda steps; the mother on her way to the child—murdered by an arrow; Mr. Howsam and his two sons sprawled near the burning barn, tomahawked, their scalpless skulls still glistening.

"It—couldn't have happened more than an hour ago," James whispered.

"Ah kin git de men. We kin dig de grabes fast, Mausa Gould."

"I wish we dared. We can't take the time."

Headed once more for the safety of St. Marys town, James laid to the tiller for a few minutes, then leaned over the side of the boat and vomited.

Janie tried to get to him but fell back in her seat as the boat veered sharply to starboard.

"Effen you kin hol' de baby, Mausa Gould," Larney called, "Tapo kin steer. Ah kin pull his oars."

James regained control of himself, righted the boat. "Stay where you are, Larney."

"Oh, James," Janie cried. "James, please don't be ill!"

"I swear I'm all right. I'll be fine."

The nausea left him dizzy. His head throbbed, but he would keep steering.

"How much farther, James?"

"A little under twenty miles. But if the Creeks have moved in the direction of our place, they'll likely go on to the Okefenokee when they've finished there. I think we can all rest easier now. With luck, we'll make it to St. Marys by daylight."

When John steered the lead boat into the first available docking space early the next morning, there was already activity at the town's wharf.

"Look, James," Janie said, pointing to the sky. Fair-weather clouds piled in the east caught the sun's first color—clouds shading up, up into a high dome, soft blue, blue, dark blue where touches of the night still lingered. "Look at the dawn. It's—for us."

He maneuvered their boat to the dock beside John's, sank to his knees and took Janie in his arms. "We made it down the river, Janie. We're going to be safe now."

Janie seemed strangely heavy, a leaden weight. She had fainted.

Chapter 26

Sitting alone by the waterfront in the fog-blurred light of the second morning at St. Marys, James tried to decide what to do next.

He and his family, with Larney, were staying in the home of James Seagrove, the Creek Agent. Because the memory of the Howsam massacre still tormented him, he had slept little, had eaten almost nothing. He was numb with fatigue and worry, yet he felt compelled to make a few plans.

The Seagroves' house was small. He would have to decide first where they could go until Janie regained her strength. They would be welcome, he knew, at Dungeness on Cumberland Island, only five and a half miles by water from St. Marys. And thirty miles north of Cumberland, the John Coupers would welcome them on St. Simons for as long as they needed to stay.

Savannah was his ultimate destination. From now on, Janie was going to have the chance to live in a civilized society near her family. Questions jabbed at his weary mind. Why had he stayed so long at Mills Ferry? He got slowly to his feet and began to walk. What good now were the fine profits he had made from the lumber shipments? His home and new steam mill undoubtedly lay in ruins. More than five thousand dollars in logs, ready to be rafted, jammed the river below his dock. The timber still standing was worth nothing to him now without his millhands, who had surely fled the Creeks too. True, he had some twenty thousand dollars in a Savannah bank and the lumber stacked at Darien, but his nearly twelve years of hard work had been wiped out.

He owned no land. Nothing of any value but his Negroes . . . *his* Negroes.

He laughed drily, picked up a dead branch, snapped it into small pieces, and threw them at the ground.

Past the cluster of waterfront buildings, he reached the fields south of town. The thick fog rolled off the water and churned around him, sucked this way and that by a changing wind from the Sound. Dirty weather for ships at sea. The thought intruded: dirty weather at sea. The kind of weather a seaman needs a light to sail by. A lighthouse.

He wanted to stop on St. Simons, wanted Janie to meet his friends there. But Couper would surely insist that they ride down to see the progress being made by the man from Connecticut who, by this time, would be building the new light. "People will be talking of nothing else on both St. Simons and Cumberland," he said aloud. "I'll see if I can take my family and all my people straight to Savannah by schooner."

At the Seagroves', after breakfast, he felt up to a serious talk with Janie, and took a fresh pot of coffee to the spare room where she still rested in bed, the baby beside her.

"Where's Larney?" he asked, seeing the neatly folded blankets, Larney's pallet on the floor by their fireplace.

"She's washing our clothes. Have you decided where we're going, James?"

"First, tell me how you feel—the whole truth."

"Ever so much better! I'm not pretending. I slept nine hours last night."

He took a deep breath. "You'll need every hour of rest you can get here. I tried early this morning, but I can't book passage for all of us. The Seagroves say we're welcome to stay a few more days, but there are nineteen of us, with the baby. I'll put you and Jimmy and Larney on a Savannah boat as soon as you're able. Captain Bunch and Charles can meet you."

"Come here, dear James. Sit down beside me on the bed." She took his hand, looked straight into his eyes. "I hope I won't sound like a foolish child, but after—what happened, I cannot bear the thought of being away from you. I think I feel as well as I'll feel for days to come. Well enough to make the trip in our own boats, just the way we left Mills Ferry."

"Janie, it's almost ninety miles!"

"I know. But we'll be together. Any time you're ready, we can start."

"Will Jimmy be all right?"

"Yes. Larney will see to that." She blinked back tears. "Oh, my dearest, I couldn't go to Savannah without you. Not Savannah, or any other place."

Three days later, when the two plantation boats had been loaded with supplies and their few belongings, James called John and the other Negroes to one side of the St. Marys wharf.

The men, still wearing the clothing in which they left Mills Ferry, had been sleeping in the loft of the Seagroves stables. Two had caught colds, but as James studied each face in the little circle gathered around him, he felt pride in his people. Felt the need of sharing his plans with them. They had served him so faithfully, he could not bring himself merely to order them to take their places in the boats once more.

"I'm on my way in a few minutes, to Mr. Seagrove's house to fetch Larney and Mrs. Gould and my son," he began. "You have all been more than helpful. We could not have escaped the Indian attack without each one of you. My funds are low until I can get to my Savannah bank, but I have bought new clothing for all of you as a small token of my gratitude. You will find the shirts and trousers in that large box on the dock beside John's boat."

James thought they seemed pleased.

"I have tried to book passage for all of us on a schooner, but we are too many. Mrs. Gould feels she will regain her strength more rapidly at her mother's home in Savannah. Savannah is a long way. I regret having to give you an order like this, but I am giving it to myself too. I'll be steering along with John again, of course. Mr. Seagrove has promised to send a scout to Mills Ferry and report to me in Savannah as soon as possible, but I won't be surprised to learn that I have lost everything. I did not own the land we worked. I only leased it. We will probably remain in Savannah and if so, I promise on my word of honor, that if it becomes necessary to—to sell some of you, it will be only to an owner who I know will be a good and fair master, as I try to be. Between here and there, even after we arrive, you will have ample opportunity to escape. I pray you mean me well. You will be kept informed of all my plans, whatever develops." As he turned to go, he added, "I suggest you bathe yourselves as best you can in the river before donning those new clothes. I'll be back in an hour or so with Mrs. Gould and we'll head for Savannah."

Chapter 27

Still unable to sleep, James rose before dawn the morning after they reached Savannah, scribbled a note to Janie, slipped down the stair of the Harris home and out into the murky half light of what would surely be a rainy April day. Good weather had held just long enough for the two loaded boats to cover the ninety miles in only three days. He would never forget either the silent exhaustion of the Negroes, matching his own, or the helpless look on Janie's face when she fell at last into her mother's arms. Larney, weary too, had managed to get the baby to sleep soon after they arrived, in spite of his painfully sun-blistered little face.

James' own face felt raw and drawn, too burned to shave. Even after a night's rest, his spirits were as low as the leaden Savannah sky. He was so spent, he found walking an effort. Unable to thrust his bruised, swollen hands into the pockets of the dark green riding jacket borrowed from Samuel Bunch, he felt awkward, almost feeble, as he turned toward the Bay. He had waked often in the night with the nightmare picture of their house in flames, Janie's china cracking in the heat, the curved staircase on which he had worked so hard breaking loose from the second-story joists to crumble into a charred heap in the hall below. As a businessman, he should have worried about his mill—the toolsheds stacked with broadaxes and adzes and crosscut saws—but his nightmares were of their house, their furniture, Janie's silver and glassware, the baby's cradle he had fashioned with skill and pride. And what had happened to Comochichi if the Creeks, who considered him a traitor, had captured him?

Of course, there was a slim chance that, drunk on their heady black drink, the Indians had lost interest, drifted south into the Florida wilderness or returned —passing Mills Ferry—to the Okefenokee swamp to hunt and fish a while. If the place still stood, and if they had escaped, there was no telling how long Leaven Kyser and the others would stay around, waiting for work to resume. He meant never to go back, but did he dare hope to salvage something by attempting to sell the lease to another mill operator? The almost new house and steam mill should increase the value of the holdings, if anyone could be persuaded to move there.

As soon as his bank opened at seven-thirty, he would stop by to discuss the prospects of building contracts in Savannah, inquire about good town houses on the market. He had no intention of imposing on Mother Harris any longer than necessary. Shelter would have to be found for the fifteen Negroes, too. Samuel Bunch had sold all his slaves but four in order to finance himself as a cotton factor. James did not blame Bunch for this, foolish as it turned out to be, but he could not think of his own people as mere property. He would find a way to look after them until he knew his own next step. The men had his promise not to sell them at auction.

He had reached the Exchange Coffee House on the Bay with half an hour to wait for the bank to open. Across the Strand on Commerce Row, a sign hung by one chain: Samuel Bunch, Factor. The windows of the small office were barred over. Janie's brother-in-law troubled him, mainly, he supposed, because he liked the man, even enjoyed him, although James felt he could see through Samuel as through a pane of glass. He had never known a more charming, courteous fellow, perpetually enthusiastic, well-intentioned, but James had been sure, since their first conversation some four years ago in Charleston, that the red spider was not the only reason the Bunch plantation in Nassau failed. Samuel Bunch, he was certain, had never bothered to learn any business from the ground up.

The Captain had a notion of himself as a prosperous, promising man of property, but in spite of having been born to money, that was as far as it went. It was an out-and-out imposition for him to have moved himself and his wife into Mother Harris' house.

True, there was plenty of room, but James guessed the Bunches contributed little to the living expenses, although Samuel was still making candles. Their four Negroes had to be fed and housed too. Samuel Bunch had told James that he got along on four or five hours' sleep a night, was up and out "making contacts" early each day. Too bad, James thought, the man can't find a solid outlet for all that restlessness.

A cup of hot, strong coffee would help pass the time until the bank opened, he decided, and entered the Exchange Coffee House. He had just poured cream into his coffee when the front door swung open and in strode Samuel Bunch, doffing his stylish buff hat in greeting to the proprietor and the waiter. His affable manner and striking appearance caused everyone in the room to turn and look. The last thing James craved this morning was conversation with his brother-in-law. He kept his head down while the Captain strolled to the hatrack, stopped before a looking glass to adjust his cravat, started toward a table across the room and turned back abruptly.

"Well, upon my word, if it isn't my brother-in-law, James Gould! I didn't see you! How will I ever get ahead in life with these nearsighted eyes of mine? Good morning! Good morning!"

The men shook hands, and since there was nothing else to do, James motioned toward the other chair at his table.

"I was absolutely certain," Bunch went on, "that I had left the Harris home long before anyone else was stirring. You *are* a man after my own heart, James. Never let a blade of grass grow under your feet, eh? Two servings of biscuits and sausage and two cups of coffee, please," he called to the waiter, unfolding his napkin.

He rushed over James the way Horace used to do when he was about to ask a favor. James stood up. "Nothing for me, Captain. I have business first thing at the bank."

"But the bank doesn't open until eight o'clock. Once opened at seven-thirty, I understand. Eight o'clock now. Why stand at the door across the street and wait when we could be enjoying breakfast together? I insist, James. I really do."

James sat down, unable to avoid noticing the frayed cuffs of Samuel's cutaway. "Won't be very good company today, Captain."

"Indeed, I'm surprised to see you up and around after your horrible ordeal. Did I extend proper sympathy and concern when you and your little family arrived last night? I hope so. Elizabeth and I both long for words to let you and Janie know how deeply sorry we are."

"You're very kind, all of you."

"Still, you did escape with your lives, and we can be grateful to Providence for that."

"I hope Janie and the baby will be all right. I could never tell you what they went through."

The Captain leaned across the narrow table, his nearsighted blue eyes filled with sincere concern. "Tell me, did you lose everything for which you'd worked so long on the St. Marys?"

"I won't know that for at least a week or more."

"Hard to imagine those docile Indians shuffling along the streets of Savannah—murdering in cold blood, burning down a man's house."

"Not for me, it isn't."

"Of course."

The waiter brought their breakfast and Samuel popped half a biscuit into his mouth. "Try some of this honey, James. Delicious." He buttered another biscuit, poured honey over it, ate it in two forkfuls, then a cake of sausage in two more bites. "Ah! That's better. Don't know when I've been so hungry. Eat very little, really. Delicate digestion."

James stifled a smile, remembering that his brother-in-law had consumed a thick slice of ham and two bowls of hominy, "keeping them company with a late snack," when they arrived last night.

"Strange and wonderful coincidence, our meeting here like this at, of all places, the Exchange Coffee House," the Captain declared, buttering another biscuit.

"I expect a lot of folks meet here."

"Ah, but you don't understand, brother," Samuel said, leaning across the table again in a most confidential manner. "You see, I plan to lease the franchise for the Exchange Coffee House any day now. Have several interested backers. Merely a matter of choosing the gentleman with whom I'd enjoy working."

James glanced up from his plate. Just last night, this persuasive man had tried to borrow five hundred dollars in order to go into the business of making soap. If the man didn't have five hundred dollars to start a small soap and candle factory at the rear of the Harris house, how could he lease the Exchange Coffee House franchise? James doubted the existence of even one interested backer.

"You see," Samuel went on, "Savannah is growing by leaps and bounds. The Exchange is central to the progress of the city. Everyone of any importance in the business life of the area stops here for refreshment sooner or later. Look at it!" He swept his hand around the large, drab room. "Needs paint, new furnishings. This could be the most fortunate day of your life, sir, instead of one of the most unfortunate. After all, how much better to keep a thriving enterprise like the Coffee House in the family."

James doubted that anyone had ever resisted the Captain's infectious smile. "You mean you'd turn down all those other interested backers so that I could finance you—in both the Coffee House and a soap factory?"

The broad, even features seemed to crumple. Every muscle in the powerful body sagged. He sat looking at James, all artifice gone, his young, ruddy face suddenly lined, tired. "You make me feel—like quitting," he said quietly.

James thought a moment. "I didn't mean to do that."

"I know you didn't. Do you mind that I trust you, James?"

James was at the barn door again back in Granville with Horace, examining the dried milk left in the leather buckets, showing them to his brother, watching the smile fade, hearing Horace say: "What's the matter, James, didn't I get 'em clean? I thought I washed 'em good. Must have been sleepy or something. It was kind of dark." For an instant he despised both Horace and Samuel Bunch.

"James? Do you mind that I trust you?"

"You don't know me well enough to trust me or mistrust me, Captain."

He didn't want another Horace in his life. He had always given in to his brother, and this man was an important member of Janie's family.

"I don't enjoy being a failure, you know," the Captain said, pushing biscuit crumbs idly around his plate with his fork, after the last drop of honey. "I'm ashamed of it. The red spider cleaned every plantation in Nassau that year, but the other planters recouped. I had overextended my credit. I quit while I still had a plausible excuse."

"Does Miss Elizabeth know this?"

"I imagine she does. But I can't talk to her as I'm talking to you. I go on acting at home as though success is just around the corner." He pushed back his plate, a boyish hope on his face. "And you know, I feel sure it is! I *feel* prosperous, James. I believe in my future. I believe in the candle factory, the soap factory, the Exchange Coffee House. I'm sure I won't go on—just missing. This is a thriving city! There has to be a means for me to come by some of the money in circulation in Savannah. Don't you agree?"

"I agree there's no more promising city right now. I wish you well. You're part of Janie's family. About the only family I have." James looked at his watch. "Time for me to get across the street to the bank. I'd like to pay for our breakfast, if you'll allow me."

The Captain, his poise fully regained, was smiling again. "Not at all. I urged you to stay. And, according to my watch, your banker won't be in his office quite yet. I've got it straight that you are not going to—go into business with me. I won't mention it again, I promise. But please stay a bit longer. It's nippy outside still." He reached into an inside pocket. "Here's the newspaper. Even if you just sit and read over one more cup of coffee, I'll be gratified."

James smiled a little, took the newspaper. "I warn you when I read the paper, I don't talk."

"I'm quite agreeable," Samuel said, ordered more coffee and fell silent as James opened the *Columbian Museum and Savannah Advertiser*. The room was filling with people and noise; the clatter of china and silver disturbed him. He liked reading a newspaper when he could concentrate. Looking at page 1, his mind was still on the possibility that Samuel was merely trying another tack on him. Another means of extracting a loan—feigned honesty, almost innocence. He discarded the suspicion. Samuel Bunch had simply not grown up yet. James had gathered from Mary's letters that Horace had at last settled down; maybe Samuel would too, although he must be in his early thirties.

For several minutes, over the Coffee House hubbub, there was only the scrape of Samuel's spoon against the thick cup as he stirred his coffee rhythmically, on and on. James scanned an article predicting that the new law banning importation of slaves into the United States would increase the smuggling of Negroes across the Florida-Georgia line. He knew that already. On page 2, he experienced his usual revulsion at the printed Notices of Slave Auctions, started to turn the page, and jerked the paper open again to the Notices, unable to believe what he saw:

HERE PUBLISHED BY ORDER OF HONORABLE ALBERT GALLATIN, AUDITOR OF THE UNITED STATES TREASURY, A PROPOSAL FOR THE BUILDING OF A LIGHTHOUSE ON ST. SIMONS ISLAND, GEORGIA. A BUILDER IS SOUGHT BY MEANS OF THIS NOTICE, WITH SURETIES, EXPERIENCE AND SKILLS SUFFICIENT FOR THE ERECTION OF A LIGHTHOUSE ACCORDING TO THE HERE PUBLISHED PROPOSAL:

James' eyes raced down the page:

THE LIGHTHOUSE IS TO BE OF HARD BRICK, THE FORM OCTAGON; THE FOUNDATION OF

STONE TO BE SUNK EIGHT FEET BELOW THE BOTTOM OF THE WATER TABLE. . . . THE LIGHTHOUSE TO HAVE 6 WINDOWS, EACH TO HAVE 12 PANES OF 8 BY 10 INCH GLASS IN STRONG FRAMES AND A SUBSTANTIAL PANEL DOOR WITH IRON HINGES, LOCK AND LATCH COMPLETE. . . . ON TOP OF THE BRICK WORK ARE TO BE A SUFFICIENT NUMBER OF IRON SLEEPERS BEDDED THEREIN AND SLOPING FROM THE CENTER WHICH ARE TO BE COVERED FIRST WITH SHEET IRON . . . WITH COPPER OVER THE IRON, THE WHOLE TO BE RIVETED TOGETHER SO THAT THE FLOOR OF THE LANTERN THUS PREPARED SHALL BE PERFECTLY TIGHT AND STRONG, THE TRAP DOOR TO BE COVERED WITH SHEET COPPER. . . .

His heart pounded as he hurried through the remainder of the Government specifications in fine print. Months had gone by since he had looked at his own plans, but they were startlingly similar—even to the octagonal shape!

The Notice was signed by a Mr. Joseph Turner, Collector of the Ports of Brunswick and Frederica, St. Simons Island.

Holding the newspaper up to conceal his face, he tried to compose himself, but all he could think about was that apparently, after many months, no one—including the man from Connecticut John Couper had mentioned—had yet been found qualified to build the St. Simons light!

He jumped to his feet. "Excuse me, Captain. May I keep this paper?"

"Certainly. But what's happened? You look as though you've seen a ghost!"

James grabbed his hat from the rack. "In a way, I have. Perhaps I can explain later—when I see you next. Right now, I must get to the bank, then try to book passage on the first boat to St. Simons Island."

Chapter 28

Past the Tybee shoals and safely over the bar, the schooner was forced to drop anchor when the wind died altogether. Barely seven miles from the city, at the mouth of the Savannah River, they had to sit aground all night. With a long glass borrowed from the Captain, James studied the old Tybee light, which had once used candles. Before dark, he made rough sketches and checked the fixed beam of the lantern off and on throughout the night. The light appeared to him inadequate. His own plans called for a revolving lantern, showing red, white and blue. The Notice in the *Savannah Advertiser* had stated that "Separate Proposals would also be received for building the lighthouse agreeable to the above plans." He clung to that. At least he could submit some of his own ideas. Most lights were merely oil lamps, crudely constructed. James believed that parabolic reflectors with a glazed lantern, operated by a system of weights similar to the works of a clock, would greatly improve the usefulness of most American lights. Perhaps now, he might have the chance to test his theory.

While the schooner waited for daylight and a rising wind, he lay in his berth in the dark, trying to recall details of his sketches and specifications. They had been put away so long, the pages were yellow. There had not been time even to take them out of his father's old portfolio before he set sail for St. Simons. At the bank, he had merely checked his money on deposit and informed his banker that Mr. Seagrove from St. Marys would be reporting on the condition of his Mills Ferry holdings. He had not even inquired about Savannah houses for sale. *If* he received the contract to build the St. Simons light, he would want to be its keeper for a few years anyway, provided Janie was willing. Janie. They had been able to spend only an hour together before he sailed. Just long enough to tell her about the Notice, to make certain that she wanted him to bid on the lighthouse.

After breakfast, watching the reddening sunrise from the ship's deck, he took her note once more from his pocket:

> Beloved James, builder of the St. Simons Light!
>
> I am with you every mile of your voyage, every minute on your beautiful St. Simons Island. Even though I have never seen it, I will love your Island because you love it. I am yours, and "whither thou goest, I will go." With joy, with joy. Our son and I will be waiting to welcome you upon your return and to salute you for being the one man in the whole world destined to build the St. Simons Light!
>
> Your Devoted Janie.

The schooner was moving again. He tucked Janie's note away, his heart swelling with joy—and apprehension. He had never built a lighthouse. The Notice specified a man with experience. The search for a suitable builder had gone on for more than two years. The Government standards must be high.

Janie might be certain. He was only hopeful.

Following a stop at Gascoigne Bluff, late in the afternoon, they moved up the river toward the Frederica dock. Rounding the bend just south of Old Town, he could see the ruins of Oglethorpe's fort. Sections of the tabby walls still stood among the rubble of the colonist's English-style town houses which once lined Frederica's wide main street. Before the gangplank was let down, he noticed a new store had been built and two or three cheaply constructed frame houses. He was heading for George Abbott's store. Young Abbott would let him borrow a horse for the ride to Cannon's Point.

On the narrow wharf, he saw that one of the new buildings was an office, bearing a sign which read: JOSEPH TURNER, COLLECTOR OF THE PORTS OF BRUNSWICK AND FREDERICA—the gentleman whom he would have to convince that James Gould could build the St. Simons light.

At dinner with the Coupers, James had mentioned merely that he and his wife and infant son were spending some time with Janie's family in Savannah. The Couper family had increased. James Hamilton was now thirteen; there were Ann, nine, another son, John, seven, and the elder John's orphaned nieces, Ann Mary and Jane Elizabeth Johnston. Conversation around the table was lively because the Coupers believed children should be included. Enjoyable as it was, James was impatient to be alone with his friend.

When at last he had paid his respects to his hostess and the cook, he followed Couper to the library. They sat down before the small fireplace and filled their pipes.

"It's been a long, long time, James."

"Too long, Jock."

"We've had a bit of excitement to spice our lives since you were here," Couper said. "The Honorable Aaron Burr was a guest at Major Butler's plantation. As he explained, he wished to withdraw from public view following his trouble with Alexander Hamilton."

"What did you think of him?"

"I took no sides in his difficulties, merely found him good company, a man of impeccable taste—especially in his estimate of my wine cellar. Aside from Burr's sojourn, there was the added interruption of a vicious hurricane. As you can see, we survived both."

"I heard about the storm. Were your losses great?"

"Just over one hundred thousand dollars. I'm a poor man, at the moment, but never mind." Couper drew on his pipe. "Now that we've pretended this is merely a friendly visit," he said, "I think it's time we got down to facts. You've aged, James. There's something weighing on your mind. We've all the time in the world. Start at the beginning."

"My wife and child are in Savannah because we were forced to make our escape from Mills Ferry—hostile Indians. Murdered our neighbors ten miles to the east. My man John and I found their bodies."

He would have to go back further than that. Couper

did not know that James, too, was a slave owner now. He went all the way back to the day he purchased Larney and talked steadily for an hour or more, encouraged to speak freely by his friend's genuine concern. "Except for several thousand dollars in a Savannah bank and some lumber stacked at Darien with Reuben King, the St. Marys venture is ended. I'm starting over."

"James, to say I'm deeply sorry wouldn't tell even a wee bit of my sadness for you. I suppose there's no way to recover anything from McQueen on the lease?"

"My banker is looking into it for me. I doubt it."

Couper brightened suddenly, jumped to his feet. "The lighthouse! We don't have a builder yet, my friend. You can build your lighthouse on the land I deeded to the Government—right here where you've always wanted to be!"

James took the news clipping from his jacket pocket. "That's why I'm here, Jock. I figured, since I found this Notice only yesterday, that maybe I do stand a chance."

John Couper rushed to his wine cabinet, poured two glasses of his oldest port. "To my beloved friend, James Gould, builder of the St. Simons light—builder of a lifetime dream!"

James set down his glass untouched. Not even a toast from the heart of his most trusted friend could close the wide chasm which had stood for so many years between a boy's dream and a man's despair of ever making that dream come true.

"You do still hold your dream, James?"

He nodded, unable to find the words that would let Couper know how important the dream had again become—and how afraid he was to permit himself real hope. "Yes, more than ever, I want to try it, Jock," he said.

"Then I don't know why you look so worried! First thing tomorrow morning, we'll go to Joseph Turner's office at Old Town. I know him well, if any man does. It's good you came to me before seeing Turner, though. He's not an easy one to deal with. For instance, he will never let you know it, but finding a builder for that lighthouse will relieve him tremendously. Do you realize we've advertised north and south for a man with the sureties and skills and dependability to build that light? Turner and Gallatin of the Treasury Department in Washington have written letters back and forth until I'm certain when either man sees the other's script on a letter, he wants to run and hide."

"What's been the main obstacle? Why has it been so difficult to find a builder?"

"One or two have had proper recommendations, but no experience."

"I've never built a lighthouse."

"How many men have? There just aren't very many lighthouses in the United States. The Connecticut builder I wrote to you about seemed to qualify in every way. We thought we had found our man, but he lacked sureties to guarantee emergency funds should the need arise during the erection of the tower." Couper sat down, a small frown creasing his forehead. "In view of your recent catastrophe, James, are you able to qualify financially? Could you support emergency materials or workmen's wages should a delay arise in Washington where payment is concerned? Under normal conditions, I would gladly supply funds, but Cannon's Point runs on credit from my factor 'til its next crop of cotton."

"As I said, I have ample funds in my Savannah bank. And fifteen or twenty thousand feet of lumber stored at Darien."

"Well, then, I see no reason why the contract is not yours. You have the skills, the building experience, the common sense."

"Do you really believe that, Jock?"

"Aye!"

James unfolded the clipping again. "Right here in this Notice is a proposal for a lighthouse so similar to my own, my wife swears it's a good omen. I think it will break her heart if I don't get the contract. She has no doubts, either."

"And you are a born doubting Thomas, or you'd be as believing as Miss Janie. It's your stubborn Puritan set of mind." Couper chuckled. "You've always expected the worst. Listen to me, James. For nigh three years, ever since I deeded that four-acre tract to the Government, I've known you were the man qualified to build the lighthouse. I'm elated. Something had to get you out of that Florida wilderness and back into civilized society. I should have guessed wild Indians would have to accomplish it."

"I wasted a lot of time," James said. "Risked the lives of my wife and my son by being so pigheaded about leaving."

"Why were you pigheaded? You don't love money that much."

"No. But for the first time, I was successful. Saw no end to the prospects. Wanted enough in reserve to build Miss Janie a fine house in Savannah."

"I see. Well, I understand that, but tonight is all that matters. How do you feel tonight about your chances with the lighthouse? Confident?"

James turned his glass thoughtfully. "Not very."

"Why not?"

"Jock, I've always thought work could gain a man anything he wanted. I've worked hard over the past decade! I didn't just supervise at Mills Ferry. I worked, right along with my men."

Couper was silent a moment. "I suppose you consider yourself a failure."

James nodded.

"Well, you're not! And the most important thing I can do to help you get that lighthouse contract is to convince you that you must not, under any condition, walk into Turner's office tomorrow acting uncertain. Joseph Turner is a good Collector, conscientious to a fault, but he's a tedious little man. Meticulous, feisty. Doesn't talk much. That's one of his traits I find so irritating when we hold meetings of our new vestry. We plan to build a church as soon as the Island planters regain some of their losses. Hamilton, Dr. Grant, Demere, Major Page—the others among us speak up, let our opinions be known. Joseph Turner sits in silence until we're all finished, then—more often not—disagrees. Hand him your credentials and he'll study them for half an hour without uttering one word, leaving you to wonder. *Don't give him the chance to scent your pessimism."*

"Is the final decision up to Turner?"

"In effect, yes. Of course, Congress will have to pass on his recommendation. Appropriate the funds. How long will it take you to estimate your bid?"

"Except for checking the cost of local labor—stone masons, in particular—it's all ready. I worked it out on the ship coming down."

"Good. We can check wages tomorrow at Old Town before we see Turner. George Abbott's our man. No one as versed on the local economy as a storekeeper, you know. I don't believe all this depends on luck, James. The facts are on your side. So's the Almighty."

"I wish I could believe He is."

"Didn't He give you the capacity to hold that dream all these years?"

"I suppose so."

"You're worn to a frazzle. I only want you to tell me one thing and then we'll retire. Are you convinced in your own mind that you're the man to build the light?"

"Yes, Jock. I'm convinced."

Uncomfortable on the straight-backed bench in Joseph Turner's office, James sat erect, balancing the worn portfolio across his knees. John Couper stood, his back to the tiny, cluttered room, looking out across the wide expanse of river and marshes, while Turner flipped page after page, comparing James' plans with those specified by the Department of the Treasury. Couper had been right. No one had spoken a word for well over half an hour.

"Would you mind sitting down, Couper? Makes me nervous knowing you're on your feet all this time." Slight, balding Joseph Turner spoke without raising his eyes from the papers.

Couper turned, grinning. "Didn't know I was old enough yet to cause you so much concern. I'll glady oblige."

"Your handwriting's hard to read in places, Gould," Turner said.

"Sorry, sir. I wrote those specifications a good many years ago."

James unbuckled the portfolio, then buckled it, sat tapping the end of the leather strap against the case. I should not have apologized, he thought, remembering Couper's instructions to appear confident.

For the first time since James had spread his plans and specifications before him, Turner peered up over his gold spectacles. "Reckon you could leave that case shut or open, Gould?"

"Now, see here, Turner. You've found your man and you know it," Couper said amiably. "I can guarantee the best lighthouse anywhere along the coast, if James Gould builds it. I've known him well for more than a decade. His sureties are in order, his experience beyond any we've considered, I proudly stake my own reputation on his personal integrity."

Joseph Turner glanced over his spectacles again. "I'm accountable to the United States Government, sir. Which gives me the right and the duty to scrutinize every word of this man's proposal."

Couper nodded politely. "You've the right. We'll wait."

"Good."

Almost an hour later, James watched Turner roll up the Government proposal, tie it carefully with a string; then, without comment, begin to stack the frayed pages of James' sketches and specifications.

Finally, James said, "Mr. Turner, I'd like to offer one or two suggestions for changes I think will save the Government some money. According to my understanding of your published Notice, this is in order."

"It is."

"Their proposal calls for hard brick. I recommend cutting the tabby from the ruins right here at Old Town for use in the tower's foundation, except for the brick paving. Further, I recommend that tabby be used entirely in the construction of the tower. We can make it from the plentiful supply of oyster shells and sand here on the Island. Importing hard brick will be costly."

Turner removed his spectacles, folded them, tucked them into his pocket. "Tabby, eh?"

"By Jove," Couper slapped his knee. "An excellent idea!"

The Collector looked at Couper. "You think so, huh?"

"Indeed I do."

"Well, you're using your head, Mr. Couper. So do I."

"I would also request that funds be appropriated first for the building of the keeper's house," James went on. "Materials for that will be available in Georgia. Those orders can be placed now, but it will take time for delivery from the North of the necessary sheet iron, copper and other supplies needed for the lighthouse itself. I feel certain I'll apply for the position as keeper, at least for a time, until I can be sure the light is functioning properly. I'll need quarters for my family during the building of the light tower, so I'd like to put up the keeper's house first."

"How big is your family?"

"I have a wife and infant son."

"Who'd you marry?"

Unable to see what bearing this had, James flushed, then answered, "Jane Harris. Her people live in Savannah."

"Harris, eh? Any relation to Mayor Charles Harris?"

"*Former* Mayor Charles Harris is my wife's cousin. He's Alderman now."

"He'll run again this fall, though, mark my word. Get elected too." Turner's eyes were almost twinkling with sudden interest. "Your wife's cousin, eh? Course, Harris came into his money and prestige by marrying General Lachlan McIntosh's daughter, but from all I hear, Charles Harris knows how to handle both himself and his fortune."

James' annoyance made it difficult to sound pleasant. "My sureties do not depend in any way upon Alderman Harris. I've noted the name of my banker on my proposal, attached a copy of my contract with the United States Government when I headed the timber survey on St. Simons during the building of the frigates. You also have at hand an appraisal by Mr. Reuben King at Darien, specifying the amount of my lumber stored there. Locally, Mr. Couper will supply recommendation."

"Just the same, the name of Harris won't do you any harm." The Collector stood abruptly. "Good day, gentlemen. I'll write the Honorable Mr. Gallatin and submit your bid and proposal, Gould. Thirteen thousand, seven hundred and seventy-five dollars is a lot of money."

"It's my final and best figure."

"I gathered that. In addition to funds for a keeper's house."

"Correct. To be built first—by me."

Turner shook hands. "Come back on the fifth of June. Right here. Same time of day. In view of the three wrecks on our outer bar in the past two years, the Government should reply immediately. One way or another. President Jefferson is said to be strong for lighthouses all up and down the coast. Mr. Gallatin will be as relieved as I will be, if you're the man."

Chapter 29

On his first day back in Savannah, James bundled Janie into a rented carriage and took her to be examined by a physician.

"I could have told you, I'm perfectly all right, dear James," she said, as they drove from the doctor's office toward the Bay. "I'm sorry you had to find out I fainted the day I looked up from my book, to see that harmless old Indian standing outside Mums' parlor window. I'm really ashamed of myself."

"If that's all the harm our St. Marys ordeal caused, you've no need to be ashamed. Sure you feel well enough to wait for me while I visit the bank?"

"I'm fine. Really. It's you I worry about. Even with all the excitement over the lighthouse, I know you won't rest until you hear from Mr. Seagrove." Her eyes saddened. "I'm anxious, too. But, if everything we owned was burned, I still have you."

"Yes," he said. "You still have me."

He stopped the carriage in front of his bank. "We're never going back, even if our house is there. In that case, I promise to send for every cup and saucer and every stick of your furniture."

As he hitched the horses at the rack, she leaned out of the carriage. "If our belongings haven't been destroyed, why not just have them sent to St. Simons Island? I know that's where we're going to live."

"Janie, Janie, don't get your hopes too high. I don't want to see you disappointed."

Half an hour later, she watched him push open the wide front door of the bank. In his arms, he held a heavy wooden box. His expression frightened her. His mouth was drawn into the thin line which meant he was suffering, holding back his feelings.

Slowly, wearily, he carried the crate down the steps and across the sandy sidewalk, then stopped beside the carriage, and looked helplessly up at her.

"James! What do you have? It must be very heavy."

"All that's left of everything we owned. Your silver."

After a moment, she said, "Is there any word of Comochichi?"

"No."

He set the box on the ground and pried open the lid. On top lay her beautiful satinwood knife boxes, blistered, their delicate mounts and inlays blackened; the silver she glimpsed was warped and twisted.

Tears were rolling down Janie's cheeks, but in a moment, she smiled at him and said as buoyantly as she could manage, "It's all right, James. We've just made a splendid trade—for your lighthouse! With my poor silver thrown in as good measure."

Janie insisted upon going to St. Simons with him for the meeting on June 5. At Cannon's Point, in conspiracy with John Couper, she set about persuading James that she should accompany him to Frederica.

"I quite agree with you, Miss Janie," Couper declared at breakfast. "This is the time for a man and his wife to be together. You're outvoted, James, two to one."

"Three to one. I agree, too," Rebecca Couper said.

"Mr. Gould has always chosen to be by himself when he's anxious," Janie explained, "but I see no reason why I shouldn't be there today." She turned to James. "After all, my dear, we'll need to celebrate—all the way home from Frederica in Mr. Couper's boat."

He smiled nervously. "My mother always taught me not to count my chickens before they hatched. Of course, you may go, Janie. If you won't mind a long wait."

Promptly at nine o'clock, James knocked at the door of Turner's Old Town office and was told to enter. He shook hands with the Collector and took his place on the same straight bench.

"If you're ready, Gould, I'll simply read two letters

received—one yesterday and one the day before—from the Honorable Albert Gallatin at the Capitol in Washington."

There was no tiny clue from Turner. James could only shift positions and allow the Collector to proceed at his own maddening pace. First, Turner checked the dates on each letter. Next, he took his gold spectacles from a desk drawer, blew on each lens, polished them painstakingly.

At last, he cleared his throat and began to read:

Treasury Department
25 May, 1807

Sir,

An adequate appropriation having been made during the latest session of Congress for building the Lighthouse at St. Simons, you are now authorized to contract with Mr. Gould in conformity with the proposal you had published, but adding and including the alterations and substitutions of tabby mentioned by him. As he requires a considerable advance, you will be pleased to attend particularly to the sufficiency of his sureties. A remittance payable in Savannah will be made as soon as you shall have informed me that you have completed the contract. The President approves the proposals; but it will be necessary that you should transmit to me the contract itself, in order that it may receive his formal ratification.

I have the honor to be, Sincerely,
Albert Gallatin
Auditor
United States Treasury Dept.

Tears filled James' eyes, and he was thankful that Turner smoothed out the second letter without glancing up.

Treasury Department
26 May, 1807

Sir,

I informed you by the last mail that you were authorized to contract with Mr. Gould for building the Lighthouse at St. Simons. I now enclose the description and approval of a dwelling house for the Keeper, after the design of the Keeper's house at Franklin Island, Massachusetts, in order that it be attached to the Proposals.

I have the honor to be, Sincerely,
Albert Gallatin
Auditor
United States Treasury Dept.

Without a word, Turner reached for the contract, already drawn, and handed it to James. "Mr. Gould, you are now in business with the Government."

For over an hour, the two men discussed sources of supply for materials, local labor, altering a point here and there in the contract. The meeting went like clockwork until James looked at the description of the one-storied keeper's cottage, with kitchen.

"Something the matter, Mr. Gould?"

"Is there room for negotiation on these plans for the dwelling?"

"None. This is what Congress decided. The same as the keeper will live in at Franklin Island, Massachusetts. Seems adequate for the purpose."

James' mind raced to Janie, waiting outside across the green under a big live oak. How could he ask Janie to live in the heat of St. Simons in a skimpy cottage such as the letter described? Good to keep a family snug in Massachusetts, but after what he'd forced her to endure, how could he bring himself to set her down on the hot, treeless beach in such a house? He did not have to build the St. Simons light. He had not spent all these weeks waiting for word from the Treasury Department because he was penniless. James Gould's future did not depend upon signing his name to the agreement on Turner's desk.

"What we need is a builder, Gould," Turner was saying. "Course, we'll need a keeper too, by and by, but it could take three or more years to erect this light. Surely for this length of time the cottage will be good enough for your family to inhabit. What matters is that ships are wrecking on our bar."

James looked at Turner a long time, then said, "You're right. The light is what matters." Slowly, deliberately, he signed his name. "I'll order materials for the dwelling when I take my wife back to Savannah next week." Without another word, the men shook hands. James scooped his old lighthouse plans into the portfolio, hurried from the Collector's office out into the sunlight and ran toward the big oak where Janie was waiting.

From across the green, he saw her leap to her feet and begin to applaud.

When he had almost reached the tree, she clasped her hands and said in a solemn voice: "Build a light, James Gould! Build a light—your light—the finest in the world."

He had meant to take her in his arms, no matter how many people watched from the Old Town wharf. Instead, he could only look at her as she was looking at him, solemnly, in awe of the moment which had come at last.

Part Four

Chapter 30

Not once since he left Bangor had James been homesick for a Massachusetts winter, but neither did he like the long, damp nights of early 1808 on St. Simons Island. Alone in the shack he had put up for himself at the South End building site, he could only read and reread old Savannah papers, write to Janie, fuss with minor changes in his lighthouse plans, fidget, and wait for sleep and the chance to get up and go to work again. The bright, brisk days seemed to mock him; stimulated him to activity, then chopped off activity with sudden, fiery sunsets and the quick-falling dark.

There had been no word from his banker in Savannah concerning the possibility of returning the St. Marys lease to Don Juan McQueen. McQueen had no funds anyway, he was certain, and when he received the ratified contract from the United States Government on January 9, in his own mind he wrote off the years at Mills Ferry. He was going to build his lighthouse, but he chafed at what, to him, was the ignominious beginning—the erection of the ill-conceived little four-roomed keeper's cottage. With the help of six men the house was half finished when he left for Savannah to spend Christmas with his family. Heavy rains had held up the work so that only now, in February, had he been able to dismiss the carpenters.

Not that the house was ready for Janie. The rooms were cramped; even the porch too scanty for three Goulds to enjoy; the steps too steep. He had built it, as agreed, according to the Government specifications, but he was determined to finish the interior himself. He might not be quite so mortified to bring Janie inside their new home for the first time if he at least, at his own expense, put in some good woodwork, including a mantel for the bronze French clock he had given her for Christmas, and built a proper safe for the kitchen.

There were a few more lonely weeks to endure without her, but he supposed absorption in his work would make the waiting bearable. He drove himself more than ever, consoled in his weariness as he used to be when he finished Horace's chores, certain that only he, James Gould, could do them right. He was responsible to the United States Government, as he had been to his mother. No one else could be as trusted to handle the work.

"When y'er ready to build that lighthouse tower, Mr. Gould," one of the carpenters had said the day James dismissed him, "jist don't holler fer me. I reckon I know a little something about buildin' too."

He hadn't meant to offend his workmen. He experienced for the first time in years the feeling that he was misunderstood, and the almost forgotten aloneness caused him to withdraw more and more into himself. He lapsed into old habits of not responding, of sitting in preoccupied silence, even on visits to Cannon's Point.

"Your trouble," Couper said, during a late-February visit, "is that you've grown accustomed to sharing yourself. You've learned how with Miss Janie. Now that she's not here, you're back in your shell. Miss Janie's well, isn't she? And the baby?"

James tapped the dead ashes from his pipe onto the hearth. "They're both fine. I'm thankful to say."

"Are you truly thankful, James? What kind of letters do you write her?"

"Not very cheerful, I'm afraid."

"Of course, knowing she's missed pleases a lady, but I believe I'd try to show my gratitude by lifting her spirits a wee bit. God has treated you kindly."

"Jock, I despise the shack I've been forced to build for her!"

Couper gestured with his large freckled hand. "Mark my word, you'll not be living in that house for long. A man with your abilities will *not* remain the keeper of a light. Keepers are courageous, devoted men, but building the light is your dream. Not climbing steps to polish reflectors and trim wicks. Why, a lighthouse keeper seldom gets an unbroken night's sleep. Once the light is built and operating, you'll move on."

"Where?"

"Up the Island—to the Sinclair-Graham tract, of course. It's still for sale. We need you in our community. Need you on the vestry of our little church. With the decision about to be made to build a chapel at last, the advice of a man of your experience would be invaluable. Naturally, you'd have to become a communicant. Dreams and success and loving families are essential to a man, James, but so is some touch with the Almighty."

"Jock, no one could operate a plantation the size of the Sinclair or Graham tracts with thirteen Negroes in the field, and I'm not ready to buy any more."

"Thirteen? I thought you owned fifteen people."

"Two of the younger men ran away while I was in Savannah at Christmas."

"I saw you at the signing of the final contract in January. You didn't tell me."

"It's not a subject I discuss easily—with you or anyone else."

"You advertised, didn't you? Offered a reward for their return?"

"No. They'd all been working in Samuel Bunch's new soap and candle factory at the rear of the Harris home. It helped him out." James did not add that he too had "helped him out"—with the five hundred dollars Samuel had originally mentioned. "But when I told them I'd be bringing them here to plant some cotton on the land I'm renting from you adjoining the lighthouse property, two of the younger ones ran away."

"You should have made them more secure, James. You lost almost two thousand dollars' worth of property when they left."

"Locked them in, you mean? Where? The poor devils had been sleeping in a neighbor's stable until I put up a little outbuilding while I was there. Those boys wouldn't have escaped if I hadn't mentioned planting cotton."

"When do you plan to bring the others down?"

"When my family comes in a month or so. For one thing, they're my oarsmen. I'll need my boats here."

"Well, at least you'll have a chance on that small tract at the South End to discover how you like planting cotton." While Couper refilled his pipe, neither spoke. "I'll make a wager, James, that within a year after you build your lighthouse, provided the cotton market stays steady, you'll purchase the Sinclair-Graham property—at least part of it."

James got up to stand with his back to the fire. "If I used my good judgment, I'd buy a house in Savannah right now, rent it for income until I finish the light, move there and make a predictable livelihood building dwellings. I'm almost forty-one, Jock."

"Do you want to live in Savannah?"

He was silent a long time. "No. That's the trouble. I'm at home here. Don't ask me why. The Island weather isn't that different from Mills Ferry or Savannah—except—"

"Except?"

"It suits me. I like knowing it's an island."

Couper rested his head in the hollow of the high-backed leather chair. "How well I understand what you mean. I was nigh to being ill the first time I had to leave St. Simons back in seventeen ninety-two. Mind you, I'd only been here for a few days, too. I didn't buy this place only because it was a good investment. I bought Cannon's Point because I had to buy it. In those few days, the Island had become my home." He sat up. "James, I'll let you have enough Negroes to work the Sinclair-Graham tract until you make it pay. I want you for my neighbor."

"I believe you'd do that." James grinned. "Sorry, Jock, but you'll have to let me move at my own pace. Right now, for me, after Janie and the boy get here, there's nothing but the lighthouse. I know my schedule can be slowed by bad weather and late shipments, but I've got it all planned out, step by step. Once the cotton's planted, we can begin to dig the lighthouse foundation. With any luck in the weather, that old tabby can be cut and dragged to the site for laying the bedrock in May. It will be June at least before the stone can be quarried to my measurements and shipped from the North. I figure the supporting twelve-by-twelve timbers can be in place and the brick flooring laid by the first of August. With the foundation prepared, the shell and lime ready, if the sheet iron and copper have arrived when promised, it'll be time to start the tower itself."

Couper was smiling broadly. "Aye, James, I can see by the way your face lights up that you must be left free to think now only of your light. You drop ten years just telling of it."

"I don't plan right now, beyond the tower."

"But remember yourself as you were a minute ago, James, talking more than you have for weeks. Few men are given the chance to see a dream come true. Don't crab at being alone now, and don't let me or anyone else stay you from your work."

"I don't intend anyone will."

Couper sank back in his chair. "Aye, why should you think beyond the day when that indestructible tower goes up to defy the gales? I worry about you when I needn't. 'Twon't hurt you, James, to be to yourself a wee bit longer. You dreamed your tower alone through the years, and"—he chuckled—"I do declare, I sometimes think you almost enjoy being lonely as a lighthouse!"

Chapter 31

After hard August rains, Frederica Road was deeply rutted over the seven-mile stretch from Old Town to the lighthouse property on the South End. Oxcarts and heavy wagons loaded with timber and chunks of tabby had plowed up the narrow road. James would see to its repair, but there was little use to set his Negroes shoveling sand and shell back into the holes until the last load had been delivered to the building site.

The big wagon, borrowed from Couper and drawn by a team of dappled grays James now owned, lurched and swayed, axles grinding, high sides and weather-warped bedboards creaking as James drove the team himself with an important load of squared timber beams salvaged from the old Frederica barracks. On top of the weathered beams, he had placed a thick section of partition from the colonists' storehouse and at least a half load of English-made brick from the rubble of the magazine's walls. He could rework the partition into a strong trap door to serve as the entrance to the lighthouse lantern room. The well-made bricks could be cleaned to lay as walkways from the Gould cottage to the light, and later on, when there was time, to border the flower garden he meant to plant for Janie.

Although forced by the tricky roadbed to keep a tight rein on the horses, his thoughts roamed back over the five months they had lived in the new house perched on the sandy mound a few yards from the wide gray beach. The stolid little building had been to him what the Negroes called a "sore-eye" until Janie came—Janie, exclaiming at all he had done to transform the ordinary one-storied dwelling. "It's a tiny castle, to be sure," she said, "but wherever you live with me, I live in a castle!"

Jolting along, he smiled, remembering how she had looked—as proud as any queen in her soft yellow muslin. With Larney's help, she had further transformed the small, square rooms with bright new pillow covers and curtains, and in no time, flowers bloomed in wooden boxes built to her order. "It's rather like living in a doll house. I'm enjoying myself," she assured him each time he grumbled at bumping into a chair or a table in the crowded rooms. "I've always loved the sea. Now, I live beside it. Best of all, you're building your lighthouse—and having you work so near home is heaven. Please be happy here. I am."

He did not doubt that Janie was drawn to the ocean. Especially on the days when she insisted that they sit on their high, narrow front porch in spite of a wind so strong it rocked her chair. He enjoyed it too, during the rare hours when the wind laid. He found himself eager to see each morning's sunrise—saffron, if fog rolled above the waters of the Sound; on a clear day coral, sometimes flame. The sea breeze had certainly been welcome this summer, keeping him and his workmen free for long spells from sand gnats and the heat.

Once the tower was under way and the road repaired, he meant to buy a carriage and drive Janie around, partly to visit their neighbors, but also to give here a chance to see the rest of the Island—the leeward marshes, the bluffs to the north. Peculiar, he guessed, for a man who'd spent his life longing to build a lighthouse, to be drawn to the woods and the rich high land away from the sea.

He was passing Orange Grove, the home of the newly married Abbotts, George and Mary. He must take Janie to visit them. Just today George Abbott had invited him to bring his wife to service at Christ Church, held for the time being in a small tabby building at Frederica. Abbott was now on the new vestry with John Couper, Major Page, James Hamilton, Dr. Grant, Alexander Wylly, Raymond Demere and Joseph Turner. Janie would like going to church again; he would enjoy going with her, eager for all the Islanders to meet his beautiful wife.

"They certainly need a church building," he said aloud, a habit he had formed during the months alone. "I doubt the beams in that old tabby structure are safe." If Janie wanted to join the church, it was all right with him. Couper had said the vestry was planning to call a rector soon. A man by the name of Best. He was glad the Island's one parish was Episcopalian. Janie had been reared in the Church of England. To him, one church was the same as another. It was enough to be riding down Frederica Road again, to be able to look into the dense green tangles of grape and smilax and honeysuckle crowding the roadsides, to gaze up into the streamers of airy moss dressing the trees.

He had passed the Abbotts' cotton fields; now on either side stretched the Sinclair-Graham tract, the undergrowth so thick, the trees so tall that only occasional shafts of sunlight penetrated, to fall in straight white bars across the shadowed lane. Because the acreage had gone to woods, this section of Frederica Road had always been his favorite. He did think it a shame, though, that no one made use of the Sinclair-Graham high land. The combined tracts, if he remembered correctly, extended west almost to Dunbar Creek, east to the marshes and south beyond the winding Black Banks River. It was bounded still farther south by Kelvin Grove, the plantation of a man named Thomas Cater who had died, he believed, just after the timber survey for the frigates. Major William Page, now owner of the Spalding place, had not only become guardian for Cater's son, Ben, but was overseeing the Kelvin Grove plantation until the boy reached his majority. The Negroes in the Cater fields waved as he passed. Page needed a good black driver there and had offered twice to buy John. Well, John was not for sale. James had no idea what he would do with his people when the lighthouse was finished—there were too many to farm the small acreage rented from John Couper—but for once in his life, he was going to try living just for today.

A buck deer darted from a strip of woods, came to a sudden stop, flicked its tail, and vanished back into the underbrush.

By January he had received no word concerning the sheet iron, brick and stone—more than four months overdue. He decided to use the English-made bricks from Frederica to build the arched vault, twenty by twelve feet, for oil storage. The lighthouse foundation, eight feet below the water table, had long ago been dug; its thick walls formed by slabs of tabby. But there would not be enough usable old brick to pave the surface of the foundation so that its slope would shed water, and it was late February before the weather let up enough for plastering the oil vault inside. Janie sympathized with him daily over the delays, and he redeemed the time by making needed pieces of furniture for her—another pine hutch, exactly like the one at Mills Ferry, a new oval table and a set of chairs, a blanket chest, another cradle for their second child, due sometime in October.

A bill of lading reached him for the copper and sheet iron in August, another for the long-awaited brick and cut stone in the middle of September. The months of waiting seemed endless. But he had improved his plans still more, their house was shipshape, and the garden was planted.

On the morning of September 27, 1809, he noted in his builder's log that the brick floor had been laid over the newly arrived stone. He was now ready, at long last, to begin the tower itself.

The stone masons from Darien were not due until the first of next week, and after bringing his journal up to date, he permitted himself the pleasure of strolling down the garden path toward the new foundation some fifty yards from the house. About halfway, he stopped to indulge himself in what had become a steadying habit during the long months of waiting: to look toward the square, sturdy foundation and see in his mind's eye, standing between him and the water, his finished tower.

He was still there, braced against a strong wind and holding onto his battered old hat, when young Lewis Jones rode up beside him.

"Afternoon, Mr. Gould. I brought your mail down from Frederica."

"Much obliged, son."

The boy stared at the lighthouse foundation, the brick floor laid as smooth as a table top. "How thick are the walls of that foundation?"

"Five feet, Lewis. Five feet thick, twenty-five feet square."

The boy whistled. "That's thick! Won't no hurricane blow this lighthouse down. Are ya ready to build the tower now, Mr. Gould?"

"Just as soon as the stone masons get here next week, she'll start to go up."

"My brother, Joseph, saw the Tybee Light once when he went to Savannah, but I never saw a lighthouse. What will she look like? How tall will she be?"

"Seventy-five feet over-all—not counting the lantern—shaped like a tapering octagon."

"A tapering—what?"

"Octagon." James laughed. The Jones boy was about the age James had been when he first began to dream of his lighthouse. "An octagon is anything with eight equal sides. From the surface of that foundation there to the top of the tower, the tabby walls will be graduated, tapered—all done in twelve-and-a-half-foot sections—six sections in all. The first section will taper in thickness from four and a half feet at the bottom to three and three-quarters at the top; the next will go up from three and three-quarters to two feet, three inches, and so on all the way to the top of the tower, where the wall will be only one foot, eight inches."

James demonstrated with his hands as the imaginary tower went up and up, and when he finished, the boy was staring at least two hundred feet over their heads, seeing, James was certain, what would have been the world's tallest light tower. "Come back any time, Lewis. I'll be glad to explain things to you as we go along."

Young Jones looked at him awestruck. "You must

be the smartest man in the whole state of Georgia, Mr Gould!"

James grinned. "I hope I'm smart enough. Lighthouses are built to save men's lives, you know. I am obliged for the mail, son."

"I'll likely bring it often from now on. So's I can watch some. Oh, I nearly forgot. Mama made me promise to ask when Mrs. Gould's baby's due. I guess everybody's waitin' to know about the new baby. I expect because you're so famous around here, bein' a lighthouse builder."

"Tell your mother the baby's due sometime next week. Probably about the time the tower starts up. Mrs. Gould is just fine."

Lewis whistled again. "Sure will be a lot goin' on around here. Well, good-day, Mr. Gould."

Young Jones rode off and James hurried home, his spirits soaring like the boy's imagined lighthouse. Janie was sewing on the baby's layette in their tiny parlor when he handed her a letter from an old friend in Charleston and a copy of the *Savannah Advertiser.*

He bent to kiss her. "Still feel all right, Janie?"

"Chipper as a robin. I'm an experienced mother now, don't forget. Who brought our mail?"

"Lewis Jones rode down with it. Seems to be pretty excited about getting a lighthouse on the Island."

Janie opened the newspaper, her face wistful. "I'm glad our baby won't be born in September. Next week will be October."

He patted her head. "I know September scares you. It's almost over this year, though, and everyone's all right."

"Could we sit on the porch together a few minutes, James, while I look at the newspaper and read my letter? It's from a lady who used to be Major Butler's housekeeper. One of the first people I told when I fell in love with you."

He chuckled. "That wind's so strong, I may have to anchor your rocker."

His arm around her, they walked out onto the porch. Janie sat in the one comfortable chair. James settled himself, as usual, on the top step. He noticed that she picked up the *Advertiser* first, leaving the letter. "You'll have a time turning pages out here in this gale," he told her.

She stuck her tongue out at him without looking up from the page, then he saw her eyes widen, her features contort with shock.

"James," she gasped. "James!"

He jumped up, seized the paper—opened, as he should have suspected, to the Obituary Notices. Janie walked to the top step, leaned heavily against the post. A gust of wind blew her ruffled house cap across the porch. James caught and held it while he searched the page she had been reading:

> Departed this life, yesterday morning, in the 18th year of his life, Mr. Charles Harris. His native modesty so prepossessing a quality in one so young, his promising talents, strict integrity and virtues of an exalted kind, commanded the affection and love of those who knew him sufficiently to appreciate his worth and merit; and though he left this transitory world in a well founded hope of future happiness, his death must be lamented as the loss of one who bid fair, in a more advanced period of his life, to be a worthy and useful member of society.

James looked up in time to see her sway, then plunge off the narrow porch and lie like a broken doll on the ground.

"Larney," he cried. "Larney, help me!"

Shouting for John as he began to saddle one of the dappled grays, James' hands shook uncontrollably.

"Miss Janie fell off the porch! Ride to Oatlands for Dr. Grant as fast as you can."

John finished saddling the skittery horse, swung onto its back. "De doctor he come back to S'n Simons early?"

"I don't know! He wrote he'd be here next week—but you've got to get him. Now!"

Back in their bedroom, James found Larney bending over Janie, who lay, still dressed, on the bed where he had left her, the black woman trying to bring her to with cold cloths on her head and neck, alternately fanning and slapping Janie's bloodless face.

Larney glanced at him. "You got to feed yo'sef, Mausa James, but eat! Dey's stew in de pot, co'n pone in de cupboard."

"Is she—going to die?"

"We ain' neber lie to each other," she said, still working over Janie. "Larney can't tell you nuffin' 'cept she gonna do all she can to—to—" Her voice broke.

"John's riding to Oatlands, but Dr. Grant may not be back from his mainland place yet. Can't—can't you tell me—*something?*"

"No more'n dat de good Lord know Angel Miss fainted an' fell down dem steps." She straightened up. "De same Lord, He know—de baby done fell wif 'er. Now, git out, Mausa James, an' lemme work."

He turned to go.

"Ah wish ah could hep you too. My hands, dey's full."

For two hours he walked the beach. Back and forth from the house to the water's edge, each time able to walk out a few more inches as the tide receded, exposing the wet, firm sand, lavender from the setting sun and pocked with bubbling holes where clams and crabs worked out of sight. Pipers scampered in even rows, parted, regrouped, parted again. Gossipy, strutting oyster catchers went about their evening business, as though Janie were not suspended between life and death.

In Savannah, a doctor could have been with her in less than an hour—would be with her now, helping her. He trusted Larney to do all she knew, but Janie had fallen down four steep steps—the hated steps off the hated narrow porch.

Even if, by some chance, Dr. Grant had returned from his mainland plantation early, another hour would be required for the ride down from Oatlands. He thought of the rutted shell road. The afterglow was fading. A horse could stumble in the dark on a road like that, and Dr. Grant was not young.

Twice he went to the parlor, where Jimmy slept, tucked in the coverlet, then back outside, afraid even to look at Janie. Each time, he had heard only Larney's footsteps in their bedroom.

Pacing the beach again in the lingering afterglow, he passed and repassed the lighthouse foundation almost without seeing it, thankful only that the stone masons were not due until early next week. By that time, he would know whether Janie would live or die. If she left him, thoughts of following her rushed through his mind. Larney could take two-year-old Jimmy to Bangor to grow up, or to Elizabeth in Savannah.

John had been gone four hours. Did that mean Dr. Grant was still on the mainland? If so, why wasn't John back? Why didn't Larney tell him something? What was she doing in there?

On impulse, he hurried inside and straight to the bedroom. His ear pressed to the closed door, he could hear Janie sobbing convulsively. *What was Larney doing?* Was their child born—dead?

"Larney! Larney, in the name of God, can't you tell me something?"

Her answer came sharply, full of stress. "Go 'way, Mausa Gould! Please go 'way!"

The fear in Larney's voice.... He reeled away from the door; then, all control gone, heard—as if from a long way off—his own voice pleading: "Tell me something! Tell me *something!*"

When Jimmy began to cry, James picked him up, forgetting the boy's blanket, and ran from the house, down the garden path along the brick wall to the lighthouse foundation. He sat on it, peeled off his warm jacket and wrapped it around his son, cradling him in his arms, and began to rock back and forth.

The light was gone from the sky except for a faint red streak above the line of dark water over the Sound. The tide was at its lowest ebb. There was no wind. Only a gentle, ghostly breeze moving the limp fingers of the sea oats on the dune below him, rustling the lone cabbage palm he had planted near the lighthouse.

The child had gone back to sleep.

Only five or ten minutes had gone by when James heard a horse trot up the shell lane. Not two horses. One. Jimmy began to whimper when James jumped to his feet. The horse halted and he could hear John calling him. Left alone, the boy cried furiously as the two men met on the path. "Didn't you find a doctor?"

"Doc Grant, he ain' back yit," John gasped.

"Then where've you been?"

"Ol' Prince be wore out. Ah ride plumb to Cannon's Point. Mausa Couper, he say 'nother doctor be visitin' at de village. Ah ride dere. De lady she say he done gone to a party at Fredericka. Ah ride to Fredericka, but ah couldn't gallop ol' Prince no more."

"And—the doctor wasn't there, either."

"He be dere all right, but he be bad drunk."

Without another word, James walked wearily back toward the lighthouse foundation and picked up his son.

"Ah be de sorriest man," John said helplessly, following a few steps behind. "What kin ah do, Mausa Gould? What kin ah do to hep?"

James handed the boy to John. "You can take him to the house and feed him. He's frightened. Maybe something more to eat will quiet him."

"Miss Janie?"

"Larney won't tell me. If you can get her to tell you, I'll be glad to hear. If she won't tell you either, don't bother to find me."

Not until he heard the soft, slurring sound of the water did he realize he had waited six hours. The tide was coming back in.

Six hours between tides. There had, at least, been no bad news for more than six hours. He got stiffly to his feet and plodded toward the cottage.

Before he reached the garden path, he could see John lighting candles in the parlor. In a moment the little house, dark all night except for the dull yellow glow from the bedroom window, gradually filled with light. He was climbing the steps when Larney opened the front door, came slowly on to the porch, her shoulders hunched with exhaustion, her voice hoarse, but like Larney.

"You kin res' yo' heart now, Mausa James. Dey's bof gonna be all right. Angel Miss, she got a bad ankle from dat fall—but she also got a lil' girl. Ain' no lady lak Angel Miss." Larney tried a chuckle. "Ah b'lieves de angels be partial to her."

He could say nothing except "Thank you. *Thank you.*"

"Git on in dere, now. Dey's two ladies awaitin' to see you. But don' stay long."

He knelt by the bed, kissed the limp, white hands. "Janie," he whispered. "Janie, Janie, you—didn't die. I've still got you."

"Poor James." Her voice was so weak, he bent closer to hear. "Instead—of—one, you have—two of us now. Mary—and me."

"Don't try to talk." He touched the baby's head. Brown hair, like his. "Just nod yes or no, but did you call her Mary?"

She nodded.

"Even if you didn't consult me, that's good. I'm glad to name her for your mother."

"For—your sister," she whispered. "If—if ever anything—happens to me—you'll have another—Mary—to look after you."

Keeping the coverlet carefully in place, he slipped his hand under the tiny head and lifted his daughter into his arms. A warm, new assurance flowed over him. This little girl was going to be his very own, in some secret, holy way. "Hello, Mary," he whispered. "I'm your papa."

Chapter 32

St. Simons Island
22 July, 1810

My dearest Elizabeth,

I am sitting in my rocker on our front porch (the porch James somehow still blames for my fall last year). He pampers me by joining me here often, in spite of his dislike of the wind, while I am bewitched by the constant changes it brings to the sea and the sky. Little Mary, now almost ten months, sleeps in the cradle beside me. Larney and Jimmy (who, as you know, had his third birthday in April) are off gathering the last of the late blackberries. I fear Larney handles Jimmy far better than either of his parents. He is a handsome child, tempestuous, with dancing black eyes and a will of his own. He has grown so much and seems utterly at home with every gull, willet and piper. Baby Mary is her father's pride and joy. From the moment James saw her, he was hopelessly smitten.

The tower is beginning to be recognizable as a lighthouse, although my main concern these days is that James will exhaust himself before its completion. I fear my dear husband has not learned the first thing about patience with the slower, more deliberate pace of the workmen here. He seems reconciled to owning Negroes, but aside from his deep love of the Island and his fondness for the weather and Larney's cooking (especially her red-eye gravy and biscuits), James has in no way become a leisurely Southerner. I have witnessed his first real fits of ill temper because his lighthouse carpenters and stone masons simply do not work fast or carefully enough to suit him. The tower is behind schedule, but after all, the near hurricane, just when the scaffolding had been erected around its third section, caused weeks of added slavish labor. So severe was the wind that in spite of all they did to secure it, I looked out our window and saw wide boards, ropes, capstans—even wheelbarrows—sailing through the air like leaves. The tower itself was not damaged, and only one man was injured when he grew frightened and jumped from the scaffolding, severely twisting his leg. That is all behind us, however, and of late, at least, I have spent fewer evenings calming James.

Each time we see Samuel's little Notices in the Savannah papers advertising Bunch soap and candles for sale, I can feel James' anxiety and concern for all of you. With no reason whatever, he also seems to fret about me. I had a narrow escape from the fall, but with no ill effects, and I am blissfully contented in this modest cottage by the sea. James has been officially appointed keeper of the light by President Madison, at a salary of $400 per year. The Appointment came 4 May and he was, in spite of the small pay, plainly proud to be trusted with the keeping of his beloved lighthouse. He appears also proud of the tower, so far, but what he insists is my discontent, I feel is somehow his own. I simply try to make him laugh and attempt to understand what it is he really wants to do with his life once the lighthouse is completed and he has been its keeper long enough to be satisfied that the lantern and all else is in order.

We attend Christ Church Frederica every Sunday the weather permits. The vestry, reorganized the year we left Florida, 1807, seems to be in a dreadful quandary by now. With high hopes, the gentlemen laid their plans for a new church, retained a builder, a Mr. Burroughs, bought lumber (ten thousand feet from James, most of what he had left at Darien), retained a rector, the Rev. Dr. William Best, decided to abandon the old tabby building at Frederica and begin to hold service temporarily in the Becks' home. Now, due to the inability of the vestry to come to the same conclusions at the same time, and also due to the uncertain state of the nation, the lumber lies rotting in the churchyard and I understand from Mrs. Abbott that the poor rector's salary is far behind. They have moved from the Beck house, and this Sunday we will worship in the home of a Mr. Mazo!

I don't understand about the uncertain condition of the country due to some trouble with Britain, but because of it the vestry decided, after a stormy session, to let the rector leave and postpone building the much needed church. I find myself praying that by the time the vestry is once more able to think about the new church, James will be interested too. I wonder if he wouldn't be less restless if he learned something of the secret of trusting God now and then, instead of James Gould. You can read my meaning as I write this, I know, dear Elizabeth. James could not be more loving, or more considerate, or more dependable, if he went to church every day of the week! I simply feel he would be more peaceful, and I long for that.

Before I end my already lengthy letter, I must tell you that our beloved Larney and John finally "jumped over the broom," and James is now building a new cabin for them to share.

I still cannot believe Charles is gone. I send my deepest love to Mums, Caroline, Stephen and Samuel.

Tell them all that James has completed "twelve and a half feet Number 3." I try to make jokes about the now famous twelve-and-a-half-foot sections of the tower. There remain only two more such segments, and my husband will have, after a dream of over twenty years, built his lighthouse.

Your Affectionate sister,
Jane Gould.

In gratitude for their encouragement and faith during the long months in which one heavy tabby block after another had been poured to its mold as the lighthouse tower inched its way off the drawing board into reality, Janie felt they should celebrate with a barbecue for all their St. Simons neighbors. "I know it's a difficult decision for you, James," she said carefully. "I'm sure you would prefer to celebrate quietly—with no one from outside, but I wonder which would be better."

He had grunted in answer. Janie didn't worry about such responses these days, aware, as she had been all this past summer, of his growing dread that somewhere he might have miscalculated. Night after night, she had listened, as he went over each detail in the installation of the delicate mechanism which would control the heavy iron lantern and its full set of lamps suspended by chains. She knew the procedure by heart and understood his concern that when at last the lantern was hung, the testing time at hand, the contraption might not raise and lower smoothly. He had also gone over and over the measurements and operation of the large weathervane which had to be set so as to control the venting of the lamp smoke in such a way that the smoke would always be to leeward. Evening after evening, she had climbed the spiraling lighthouse stair with him as he inspected and reinspected the day's work—the eight corner stanchions of the lantern, each built down into the wall to a depth of ten feet, the fit of the copper sheeting which covered the five-foot arched dome of the tower. Of course he was apprehensive. The Islanders had kept a steady surveillance of his work from the beginning. His future acceptance among them depended entirely, he felt, upon his success as the builder of the St. Simons light. More than that, Janie well knew, James' own acceptance of himself depended upon it.

Larney was her stay. Janie wondered daily at the black woman's understanding of her master. Of Janie herself.

"You stop fidgetin', honey," Larney said one morning as they cut out a new dress for Mary. "Me an' you, we knows how to handle dat good man. He be scairt dat light won' light, dat's all. When you reckon he be ready to try it fo' de fus' time?"

Janie sighed. "I hope by November. Six weeks from now. Everything moves so slowly in Washington, I suppose President Madison won't really commission the light until next year, but Mr. Gould is already the keeper. He'll light it the minute he can."

"November be a fine month. Nice cool, sunny afternoons. My John say he kin cook de bes' pig. Ah knows ah kin stir up de bes' sauce—thick an' hot. Why don' we jist go on an gib Mausa Gould a celebration oursef? You an' John an' me. John, he kin ride 'roun to invite folks to come. Dat way po' Mausa James, he don' hab to decide hissef 'bout habin' a celebration."

"But what if something goes wrong that night when he lights the lamps with all the people watching? What if they don't work right?"

"Dat been ticklin' mah brain too, but what wrong wif us habin' our own testin' ob de lamps—jist you an' Mausa James an' the chillurn an' John an' me—de night befo'? Ain' nobody on Sn' Simons kin see de lights 'cep' where we is down here on de water by oursef."

Janie laughed. "Larney, when will I ever learn to ask you first, before I worry? That's exactly what we'll do."

John Couper's blacksmith, Cuffy, had wrought the heavy iron lantern to James' specifications—eight feet in diameter and ten feet high—at the Cannon's Point forge. The day it was brought down Frederica Road to the lighthouse in an oxcart, both James and Couper rode along beside it.

"I'll send Sandy and Old Dick to help your men hoist her up to the lantern house, James," Couper said, as the two friends stood surveying the tower, its fresh coat of whitewash gleaming in bright autumn sunlight. "Both of those Negroes have an innate 'hoistin' sense.' That's what they call it, and I've never seen men more skilled with a block and tackle."

"I'd be much obliged, Jock. At this point, so near the end, I need all the 'hoistin' sense' and skill I can get."

"Miss Janie tells me she's planning a barbecue in your honor. I like the idea! Can you give me a date yet?"

James frowned. "I wish she wouldn't, but nothing else will do her. I expect sometime around the middle of November should see me as ready as I'll ever be."

Couper looked at his friend a long time. "If that isn't like you, James. You've carried a dream most of your life—now you're about to see it fulfilled—and you want to hide your light under a bushel. What troubles you?"

"That it might not be perfect."

"Nonsense. It will give light, won't it?"

"As much as any other. More than most. *If* my reflectors are set right."

"The tower will withstand the fiercest gales, the worst battering the elements can give, won't it?"

"I trust so."

"Look at it, man. Isn't it a beautiful sight—a work of art?"

"To me, it is."

"Then enjoy it! There stands the solid, sturdily constructed proof that James Gould cannot, will not settle for less than his best. That's all any mere mortal can manage." The two men walked toward the cottage for tea. "I need your advice about something, James. I've a surprise in store for Miss Janie. I asked the date of the barbecue celebration because I plan to book passage down from Savannah for Miss Janie's mother and her sister and brother-in-law in time for the festivities. Should I tell her now? Or keep it a surprise?"

"I think she'd enjoy having it to look forward to, but Jock, you're too generous. How's a man ever to match your big heart?"

Couper laughed. "By being himself—if his name's James Gould."

Just before dark on the mild, overcast evening of November 14, John finished digging a wide pit two feet deep and covered it with the iron grate he had welded for roasting the freshly butchered pigs. He had already started his big fire, with green oak and hickory, and the flames gave a good bright light for the digging of a small connecting trench through which he would push live coals into the pit itself. John had not had a chance to show the Goulds his skill at roasting pig and he hummed as he worked, stepping back to look now and then, making certain his trench sloped just right. He was permitting no one but Larney to help him. Bozey could sit up with him through the night to keep the fire burning, keep the fresh coals coming down the trench, and to baste the pigs—cut in four sections each—with a mixture of lemon juice, vinegar, water, salt, and secret dried herbs gathered in the woods a week ago. But for this all-important step of preparing the pit, the coals, and later for the "lifting on of the pigs," John wanted Larney. She would bring him luck.

The big crimson sun was sliding down behind a

low bank of clouds when he saw her coming down the garden path from the Gould cottage, lugging a heavy kettle of her special sauce, which had simmered over the kitchen fire for two days. He dropped his shovel and ran to help.

"Git yo' hands off mah sauce, John! You aimin' to spile mah cookin'? Ah ain' seen Bozey nor nobody hepin' John wif dat fire! It be bad luck to let anybody touch mah sauce but Larney."

He hurried along beside her to a separate small fire he had started under an iron crane already set in the ground for her kettle. "Ah loves ya' so much, Larney, I plumb fergits my common sense. Ah wasn' thinkin' 'bout de sauce. Jis' you."

She hung the kettle on the crane, turned to give him a big smile, hit him playfully on his shoulder, and said, "Hush. Hush, an' listen to Larney. Dis night be de mos' impo'tant night in Mausa James' whole life. *Dis night,* when he test his lamps befo' his homefolks, an' *dis pig* fo' when all de folks comes to de gatherin' tomorrow. So, you do right!"

"Ah allus do right fo' Mausa Gould," John fussed, heaving more green oak on his fire. "When dem sixty-some folks gonna git here tomorrow?"

"Miss Janie, she say dey begin to 'rive 'long 'bout noon, she specks. Time dey git dere own work outa de way, git dere chillurn loaded in de wagons an' carriages. Some ob 'em got a piece to come. How long you roast yo' pigs, John?"

Something in the way she asked that made him feel good, as though Larney really respected his skill. "Twelb, thirteen hours anyway. Dem folks aimin' to stay here wif us tomorrow 'til after dark?"

"Co'se dey is! How dey gonna see de christenin' ob de new lighthouse effen it ain' dark?"

"Dat po' man done worry hissef 'bout dat light, Larney. You sure be smart to git 'im to try it out fus' on us tonight."

Larney nodded, stirring her sauce. "Ah declare, Miss Janie, she gonna be glad when he git dat behin' 'im. Dat po' li'l thing done worry herself pert' near sick wif dat good man awalkin' up an' down, nervouser an' nervouser."

"She better be glad she got a man lak Mausa Gould," John declared.

"Angel Miss, she ain't complainin'. She jist gonna fidget long as Mausa James fidget. What you speck?"

John leaned on his long poker to look at her. "Ah tells ya what I speck. Ah speck dem two white folks be pert' near as fixed up together as we be, Larney."

"To be niggahs, we'se de mos' blessed critters on God's earth."

He slipped his arm around her waist. "Ah's glad ah's a niggah, Larney. Ah couldn't sleep 'longside you at night effen ah wasn't no niggah."

She snapped his arm away. "Standin' here wif yo' arm 'roun mah middle! Ah gotta git back to de house to fix supper fo' Mausa James. Maybe you better come on wif me, John. We kin eat in de mausa's kitchen tonight. An' you better eat fas'. He gonna wanta be out dere to test dat light jist as soon as de sky git dark."

John threw on a few pieces of hickory and followed her to the house.

"Ah done tol' Miss Janie you'd carry de boy out to de lighthouse when de time come after supper," she said over her shoulder. "Too much rubble layin' on de groun' yit fo' Jimmy to stumble 'roun in de dark by hissef. Ah's gonna tote de baby, so's *dey* kin march toward de light—arm in arm. Miss Janie an' me, we's got it all plan out."

At exactly seven o'clock, the little procession, led by James and Janie, moved slowly down the porch steps, along the garden path and out across the brick walk toward the tower.

In one hand, James carried his old tin lantern; he held Janie's hand firmly in the other. Behind them, side by side, came Larney and John with the children. Even Jimmy, absorbed in the mysterious doings of this night, fascinated by John's fires burning on the beach, was quiet. Nearing the spot James had selected for them to watch from, Jimmy wanted to know what smelled so good. When Larney explained that her sauce was cooking for a big party tomorrow, he seemed satisfied, asked no more questions until, about fifty feet from the tower, his father kissed his mother and disappeared inside.

"Where's Papa going?"

Larney said, "Sh. Dis be de biggest night in yo' papa's life, Jimmy. Sh."

"But where's Papa going, Mama?"

Larney looked at her mistress, standing a little apart, her hands clasped anxiously. "You bes' tell 'im, Miss Janie."

"Of course." She hurried to where John stood holding her son, took the child's hand. "This *is* the biggest night of Papa's life, dear. This is the night, the very, very special night when Papa is going to light the lamps in his lighthouse for the first time. You'll see, Jimmy, if you keep watching, way up at the top of the tower—that's where Papa will be working on the lamps and that's where the light will come on."

Jimmy leaned his head back so far he almost tumbled out of John's arms. "Not yit, Jimmy," John chuckled. "Yo' papa ain' had time to climb clear to de top yit. Effen yo' keeps yo' head back lak dat 'til he git all de way up dere an' light de lamps, yo' neck gonna' git cricked."

"John's right," Janie laughed. "But let Mama tell you what to expect. First, when Papa's done all the things he has to do, you'll see one, then two, then lots of lamps light up. Then, if—*when* the mechanism Papa built begins to work, you'll see the lantern start round and round, very slowly, and through the colored glass Papa put in—glass that came all the way across our ocean from France—you'll see first red, then white, then blue lights! All turning round and round."

"An' effen you was de cap'n ob a big ol' ship way out on de water," Larney said softly, "you'd see yo' papa's light and know zactly where you was at."

"Red, white and blue is America—Papa told me!"

"*You* gonna' be smart lak yo' papa," John said.

"But we gotta start lookin' now—way up dere at de top, Jimmy."

"Sh, John," Larney whispered.

"Sh!" Jimmy said. "Sh! Sh! Sh!"

Watching the tower, they waited, shivering in the chill wet fog which had begun only minutes ago to roll in from the sea.

"Dat some fog comin' in," John said under his breath.

"If only he'd light the lamps while we can still see them clearly," Janie said.

"We see all right," Larney assured her. "Ah specks dey kin see eben better 'cross de water."

"I'm just nervous, Larney. Is Mary still asleep?"

"Soun' asleep. Lak a little warm possum."

"Sh!" Jimmy ordered, hanging his head backwards again over John's shoulder. "Now? *Now,* Mama?"

From the lantern house, one lamp flared.

"Mama! Mama! Now!"

Janie caught her breath. "Yes! Yes, Jimmy—look!"

Two, then three, then four, five lamps glowed, so brilliant and clear, their light seemed to blot out the tower.

"Papa's light! Lemme down, John. I wanna get down! Papa's light! Papa's light!"

The boy wriggled from John's arms and stood clapping his hands as the full set of lamps burned in the dark sky and then—and then—began to turn slowly, showing, just as they were supposed to show, the red, then white, then blue, penetrating the fog.

"You've done it, James," Janie breathed. "My dearest, you've built your lighthouse!"

When it seemed almost time for him to come running down the spiral stair, Larney took John and the children back to the cottage, leaving her to wait for him alone.

Chapter 33

By the next morning, James was looking forward to the arrival of his neighbors. *The light worked.* He could enjoy himself at the task Janie had set for him of finding suitable boards, left over from the building, to use for long tables. Jimmy ran along beside him, dragging useless scraps of lumber.

Best of all, Janie had been so happy she had wept when, about ten o'clock, her mother and Elizabeth and Samuel climbed out of the Couper carriage.

The Coupers had followed in a second carriage, and by early afternoon, in wagons and buggies, by boat and on horseback, the Islanders arrived in a mood of high excitement and anticipation, eager to help celebrate the first public lighting of the lamps.

Strolling from table to table, James did not lose sight of Janie's pleasure at having her mother and Elizabeth there to assist her in her duties as hostess. Out of the corner of his eye, as he greeted his guests, he noticed, too, how proud Larney and John seemed to be, heaping plate after plate with hot barbecued pork, Brunswick stew and biscuits. The children ran on the beach, gathering olive backs and conchs and sand dollars—a special treat for those whose homes stood inland on wooded areas of the Island, or beside the tidal creeks and rivers.

Even Joseph Turner dropped a little of his official manner.

"You've done a commendable piece of work, Gould," Turner said, as he and James descended the tower after Turner's private inspection. "I'll write to Washington tomorrow. That is, *if* it works when you light it tonight. President Madison won't commission the light, you know, without my full statement as to its efficiency."

As the afternoon wore on, Couper, Demere and

Abbott each told James that Joseph Turner had only praise for the new light.

"Truthfully," John Couper laughed, "one would think the Collector of the Ports of Brunswick and Frederica had built it himself!"

When the sun, a fiery orange, started to sink over the Sound, the grownups visited, sitting about on quilts spread on the beach; the children built silvery-gray sand castles, and the Negroes entertained with ring plays, shanties and work songs, Couper's Johnson leading them with his "violane" until Couper signaled for the singing to stop. Johnson laid down his fiddle, set his old tam-o'-shanter on his head and picked up his bagpipes.

"Haven't we had enough entertainment, Jock?" James asked. "By the time I climb the tower, the sky will be nearly dark. I want to get on with it."

In answer, Couper leaped onto one of the empty tables.

"Friends and neighbors," he began, "the moment for which Mr. James Gould has worked, the moment for which we have all waited, is almost upon us. The Almighty has seen fit to begin to lower the light in the sky, and our beloved and respected friend and neighbor will climb to the top of his magnificent tower and officially light the full set of lamps in the lantern of the St. Simons Lighthouse!" Couper permitted a moment's applause, then held up his hand. "I have planned what I hope is an appropriate accompaniment. My Johnson, known to you all, has, at my request, brought his pipes and even now stands ready, on a signal from me, to herald this glorious occasion—as James Gould, the builder of the light, proceeds to the tower."

The last thing James wanted was all this fanfare. The lighthouse itself would be its own announcement. He had intended simply to slip up the stair and light the lamps, but when he glanced toward the grinning Johnson, then at John Couper, he saluted.

A murmur of anticipation rose from the crowd. John Couper gave his signal, and after one sustained blast from the drone under Johnson's arm, the air was split by the ancient skirl of the bagpipes, as James, carrying his tin lantern, walked toward the lighthouse, pushed open its heavy door, and began the climb.

From the top of the tower, in the glow of the beach fire, he could see Couper urging Johnson to keep playing. With fire from his lantern, he lit first one lamp and then another.

When the full set of lamps flared and the big lantern began to revolve, the pipes were drowned by cheers and applause.

The next afternoon, James and Elizabeth Bunch sat before the cottage fire.

"You must be most gratified, James. I wish I could tell you how happy I am to see one man's dream fulfilled."

Captain Bunch had driven Janie and her mother up the Island to call on the Abbots at Orange Grove. James was glad of this time alone with Elizabeth, who was looking at him now with a slightly puzzled expression.

"You must excuse me if I appear awkward with your long silences," she said pleasantly. "You see, with Samuel, I mostly listen."

"I expect he's easier than I am in a lot of ways."

"Whatever Samuel is, he's my very life."

"Elizabeth, what can I do to help? I know you miss your father."

He read the whole story in her eyes as she sat, struggling with herself, he felt, turning over in her mind the wisdom of confiding in him. "You have already helped—perhaps more than you should," she said. "Your kindness leaves me almost speechless. I don't know what anyone can do now, or ought to do." She nervously adjusted a comb in her hair, then held her hands motionless in her lap.

"I doubt we'll be alone like this for much longer," James said. "Whatever you need to tell me will remain between us."

"Samuel's so in debt he can't even take a chance on

the dislike of a tallow salesman, and so pays far more than he should for the materials he uses in his soap and candles," she blurted out. "Oh, James, I shouldn't say any more. I won't, except that my real pain is for Samuel himself. I'd give anything—anything to see just one of his dreams succeed."

"Is there a chance he might make good in his new sideline—selling real estate?"

"Oh, there's always a chance. He does seem about to close the deal on the property on Skidaway Island, adjoining the Lillibridge estate, but—"

"But what, Elizabeth?"

She looked at him helplessly, then said, "I don't know. I honestly don't know. Perhaps you might convince him to pay that commission to Mums. We're so far behind in helping with the rent." She sat up straight. "No. Don't waste your time. Samuel has already earmarked it, I'm sure, for still another venture."

James went to the window. "Come here, please, Elizabeth . . . You see those breakers out there on the bar?"

"Yes."

"What I'm going to say may seem to have nothing to do with your troubles, but to me it has. Some time ago I ordered much needed buoys to mark the channel. The buoys finally came. Well constructed. Bells have a clear, carrying sound. But the buoys are still lying on the beach behind the lighthouse because whoever saw to the shipping in Philadelphia neglected to include anchors and chains. My buoys are useless without them."

She sighed. "Samuel needs an anchor and chain. But what, James?"

"Maybe just a hand up by an older man who cares about him."

"You?"

They went back to sit by the fire.

"Is Janie really happy here? Wouldn't she like it better in Savannah?" he asked.

"With all my heart, I wish I could tell you that I believe my sister *would* be happier in Savannah. Selfishly, I wish that. But, James, I don't believe it. I've never seen her so contented—so delighted with life."

"Well, I'm considering buying a Savannah house, just the same."

"As an investment?"

He nodded. "And to move you and the Captain and Caroline and Stephen and your mother into it, rent free, for the time being anyway. Just might give Samuel the anchor he needs. Of course, I'd expect him to be responsible for keeping it up. Could help give him confidence, looking after a good house. I'd also know that if Janie ever wanted to move back to Savannah, we'd have a place to go."

She was silent for a long time. "James Gould, you may well be the most kindhearted man I've ever known."

"Nonsense. The house would be an investment."

"Not a very good one if you put your wife's poor relatives in it!"

"But, Elizabeth, I think Janie worries about all of you more than she tells me."

"So, that's it. You love her that much."

"Yes, ma'am. For half my life, the idea that I might some day build a lighthouse was more important than anything else. I did it. Janie's all that matters now."

"Do you feel a bit let down now that the lighthouse is built?"

"No, I'm just beginning to enjoy it." He took a deep breath. "That is, if I can get any cooperation on its upkeep. Those buoys over there in the sand could be rusted out before the Treasury Department answers my letter *or* moves against the Philadelphia firm for neglecting to send the sinkers and chains for them."

"I can tell that's worrying you."

"Some. Not as much as Janie living in a house like this! My pride, I guess."

"Well, your kind of pride's a good thing so long as it doesn't make a man ungrateful for what he has."

"So, that's what you think I am—ungrateful." His tone was suddenly defensive.

"I didn't say that, James. You're such a good man,

so generous and thoughtful, it distresses me that you're not content."

His irritation showed, he knew, and he could sense her carefulness. "John Couper the same as called me an ingrate, too."

"Why?"

"Oh, I suppose I was complaining about the keeper's cottage." He got up. "Elizabeth, my brother Horace, who never had an ambition in his life, lives in a better house than this. I know. I built it myself."

She didn't move. The room was oddly quiet, too warm. "You've given my sister security, as well as love," she said at last. "Janie and I have never been accustomed to large, lavishly furnished houses. She's contented here. I beg you, please be grateful, James. Please be contented for Janie's sake. For your own." She paused. "As for doing any more for Samuel, talking to you has helped me to see clearly, dear James, that you mustn't permit Samuel to become dependent upon you in any way other than as a friend. When—*if* he succeeds, it must be due to his own efforts. You're ten years his senior, established. He could begin to put you in the place of the father who always pampered him. This would only harm Samuel and become a burden to you in the long run. I'm very grateful, but I believe you'll agree with me when you think about it."

Chapter 34

Not only had the anchors and chains not arrived; neither had the necessary funds to hire men to sink them. All winter he was occupied with apparently futile letters to Washington, his regular keeper's reports and the daily tending of the light; and with the care of his rented cotton fields and a big garden added through the spring and summer of 1811, he let the purchase of a house in Savannah slide. The St. Simons Light was formally commissioned by President Madison late that summer, but its operation and maintenance grew more burdensome. The Government was obviously too occupied by the trouble with Britain to give thought to the requests of a lighthouse keeper on an island off the coast of Georgia.

Without the buoys on the dangerous outer bar, James felt the beam from his light needed even closer attention. He tended the lamps religiously. Not once, he was certain, except in fog so thick no light could penetrate, had ships at sea found the South End of St. Simons dark. His weariness increased. He had never been able to sleep in the daytime, and for more than a year had not slept through a single night. Often as many as three times a night he checked the lamps, replenished their oil, cleaned reflectors, trimmed wicks. He was growing irritable, he knew, with some of his people, impatient with himself when he overslept. He missed the leisurely evenings with John Couper, spent what little time he could with his children—ate—tended his light.

The lantern atop the white, octagonal tower had become a new kind of symbol: his care of it a measure, somehow, of himself. He would be remembered by the descendants of the Islanders as the builder of the St. Simons Light. A lighthouse, as Captain Barry had said so long ago, was only as good as its beam.

His frequent trips to the tower each night disturbed Janie, he knew, but she only made a game of warming his feet, of welcoming him each time he crawled back into the comfort of her arms. Either Abraham or Bozey could spell him a few nights a week. Both had offered, but the light was his responsibility.

When he had finished his ten o'clock round on the night of November 18, Janie was embroidering in the living room, as though it weren't already past her bedtime.

"I've heated some milk, dear James," she said when he bent to kiss her. "I thought it might help you sleep."

Sipping from his favorite thick ironstone cup, he picked up the most recent edition of the *Savannah Advertiser*. "Anything of interest in the paper, Janie?"

"I haven't looked. Why don't you read to me? That always makes us both drowsy."

He studied her tired face. "We won't live this way forever. I promise. When those buoys are finally sunk, and as soon as I'm sure about the reflectors in all kinds of weather, I'll begin to let Abraham and Bozey help me. Without at least one buoy out there, the light is twice as important."

"Have I complained, James?"

He opened the newspaper. "No. Not my girl."

For a few minutes, they sat in silence, as he looked over the front page. "England is really causing trouble for our ships these days," he commented. "Boarding American trading vessels on the high seas, capturing our sailors at gun point. Pressing them into British duty."

"Will that lead to anything serious?"

"Suppose it could. Some of our leaders in Washington want to go to war with them right now."

"What a dreadful thought!"

He folded the paper back to another item of interest locally—the published Presentments of the Glynn County Grand Jury. John Couper had been foreman of this session.

He began to read the first Presentment aloud; stopped short, gripping the paper.

"What is it, James? What is it?"

He read it to himself, all the way through, hurled the *Advertiser* across the room, grabbed his old jacket, lit his lantern, and rushed from the house.

Breathless, he hoisted himself through the trap door, into the lantern room, and stood staring out into the arrested beam of his light—reaching only a few feet now into a mass of fog billowing like a giant thunderhead.

An hour ago, the beam had been clear. An hour ago, there had been no fog. Of course, the light would "not be visible a short distance from the land" on a night like this! The words of the Grand Jury Presentment blazed in his mind:

> It has been proven to us that the St. Simons Light is not visible a short distance from the land and that the buoys (particularly one brought from Philadelphia, at the expense of 500 dollars) are allowed to lie and rust on the beach, which neglect must certainly endanger the lives of seamen bound on this coast and led to expect a Light and Buoys off the South End of St. Simons. . . .

James Gould publicly accused of neglecting the light! He struck an iron stanchion with his open hand. There wasn't a lighthouse on the coast of the United States as carefully built as this. Not once, since the first time the full set of lamps had flared against the black sky, had the light been permitted to go out, even to dim.

He peered into the fog, whipping about, ghostly and sinister, on the wind which had pushed it in so fast. What made the gentlemen of the jury think he could sink buoys without chains and anchors? What made them think any man could keep a light bright enough to penetrate the gray, eerie blanket out there tonight?

Why hadn't the members of the Grand Jury questioned *him?*

He would have had no objection to their inquiry—the people had a right to know all the facts—but to humiliate him, to make a fool of him by printing such accusations without a hearing! That was unendurable.

He sat down on the cold iron platform of his lantern, and buried his face in his hands.

How long he sat there before footsteps roused him, he didn't know. He looked down through the open trap door and saw Janie climbing the last turn in the steep spiral. Numbed by his rage, he made no move to give her a hand as she hoisted herself up into the lantern room.

"I read the Presentment, James. I came to be with you."

"You shouldn't have. It's cold up here. Bad wind on the way."

"Do you want to ride to Mr. Couper's tonight? Bozey and I can tend the light."

"Not tonight or ever."

"He's your friend. I know he'll have some explanation."

"Mr. Couper is my friend—Judas!"

Her arms went around his waist. "No! He believes in you. More than any other person on this Island, he's been your friend."

James stood, his arms at his sides. "John Couper was the foreman of the Glynn County Grand Jury. His name heads the list of signers. I don't intend to go crawling to him. I'm not guilty of neglect and I don't mean to give Couper or anyone else the pleasure of—of—"

"Of what?"

He pulled away. "I don't know! *I don't know.* Can't you see I need to be by myself?"

When she started down through the trap door, he grabbed her arm. "Just—just for right now, Janie. I'll be coming to bed—later on."

"All right. Give yourself time to think it through. There has to be an explanation. I know you're hurt—your pride's hurt."

"What's wrong with pride?" he shouted. "What's *wrong* with a man having pride?"

She looked up from the shadow of the stair, her face white. "Nothing's wrong with pride—or with suffering—so long as it doesn't cause you to shut out the people who love you most."

He listened as her footsteps faded down the wooden stair, watched her lantern move unevenly through the darkness below, the wind whipping her long cape. She stumbled. He should be helping her, but he could only crumple once more on to the lantern platform.

The wind had begun to slam tons of water against the lighthouse bulkhead. At least the fog was blowing off. If the gentlemen of the jury were on a ship out there now, they could see his light!

In the gusts knifing around the windows, the lamps flickered. From habit, he jumped up to add oil, to trim and relight one lamp at a time, his fingers stiff with cold.

Blowing now at gale velocity, the wind screamed past the lantern house, dimming the roar of the waves, buffeting the tower until he could feel it shake beneath him as he stood by his lamps, his whole being suddenly threatened. Not by the gale, by what seemed to be voices on the wind. Insistent, unwelcome voices, invading his sanctuary—the tower he had built from nothing but a dream in an icy Massachusetts attic. The attic where a skinny boy had lain alone at night, listening to another wind, to the sharp crack of nails popping out of winter-shrunken wood. There were sharp cracks now because of the wind that rocked his lighthouse. The carefully mortised joints in the tower frame creaking and groaning, in what seemed to be the same wind that howled around the corner of the Granville attic . . . bearing the voice of his demented father, and Mary calling: "James, where are you?"

He clamped both hands over his ears, but William laughed, his mother scolded, and Janie whispered, "I've come to be with you." . . . His own voice shouted her away. He shut his eyes, stopped his ears more tightly, but Lucy Holland chided: "Could it be you only want to think you're more important than your brother? A strong sense of responsibility often turns to sheer pride!"

"Your pride's hurt, James." That was Janie.

Pride has shut you away from your family for all these years, the wind itself accused. Shut you away from your friends in Bangor. From friendship with your own brother. You've built your lighthouse, the symbol of your own indestructibility, but one false accusation and you go to pieces—still afraid people will think less of you.

Well, I won't think less of myself . . . something in him answered. Without pride in myself, I'm lost! I don't know where to turn. . . .

"Where to turn is a question which haunts every man at least once in his lifetime, James. But wherever you turn, God will be there. Even if you turn away from Him, God will be there, looking for you, waiting for you."

The memory of Lemuel Haynes' words only angered him. He stood up. "Why should I heed a black man? I own them! I *know* where to turn! I can go to Janie. I can always turn to Janie!"

Hurtling down the narrow stair, he felt the tower sway, and stopped to reassure himself that the slight motion was only enough for safety in the wind—exactly as he had planned it.

His lighthouse would stand.

At the bottom of the stair, he threw his weight against the door, forced it open in the wind and ran to the cottage calling, "Janie! Janie! Janie!"

Chapter 35

Bundled into a crimson riding coat and warm knee breeches, a thick muffler around his throat against the chill of the early morning, John Couper galloped down his lane and headed for Frederica Road.

That a visit to James Gould could fill him with dread seemed impossible, and yet the published Presentment was in his pocket. Signing it had been the hardest thing he had ever been forced to do. Voted down by the members of the Grand Jury in spite of his insistence that there was some explanation for the alleged negligence, he had added his name, too. Now, certain that by this time James had seen the *Savannah Advertiser,* there was no choice but to try to make his position clear. Not once in the years of their friendship had he seen a single sign of irresponsibility in James Gould. No, the man expected too much of himself, seemed almost driven to see to it that whatever he undertook would be at least a shade better than anyone else could have managed. Couper recalled the big oak, now the sternpost in the U.S. Frigate *Constitution.* Knowing how I loved it, that my entire garden had been planned around it, most men would have settled for a lesser tree. Not James Gould.

Time after time, Couper had ridden down this road in order to experience the sheer exhilaration of watching his friend at work on the lighthouse, aggravating the area's most skillful craftsmen by his insistence upon excellence, even in the portions of the tower which no one would ever see. "I have to know," James had said, "when *I* look at it, that every joint is perfect, every nail driven true. For my own satisfaction."

Couper recalled, too, the months James had spent at Cannon's Point teaching the Negroes how to make fine furniture. Being Gould, he had gone beyond duty: Johnson and Margin and every black man with whom he had worked still kept the tools honed and oiled, hung just so, always available, never lost or forgotten in a clump of weeds. Perfection in everything he did was this man's way of setting himself apart. There had to be an explanation for the rusting buoys.

In sight of the lighthouse, he braced himself and slowed his horse to a trot.

"I haven't seen my husband at all today," Janie said, when Couper knocked at the door. "He slipped out before I was awake."

"I'm sure you know I've come about the Presentment, Miss Janie. I must talk to him. Do you think he's at the lighthouse?"

She bit her lips, nodded.

"Then I'll go right up." When tears began to flow down her cheeks, he patted her shoulder. "I'll try to help."

John Couper pushed open the trap door and pulled himself up into the lantern room. He could see James on the gallery outside, scraping salt spray from the windows. It was apparent he had not heard Couper's footsteps, and for a moment he looked startled, then angry.

"I'm here to talk," Couper called. "Will you come inside?"

Slowly, methodically, James dried the freshly washed pane, wiped off the flat blade with which he scraped salt, then climbed in. His eyes were suspicious, his mouth as tight as the window he banged behind him.

"I supposed you'd be too proud to come to me, James. I've come to you."

Couper's hand was ignored. He thrust it into his pocket and brought out the creased page from the Savannah newspaper. "You've every right to your anger," he said carefully. "But no right to refuse to talk it over."

"If I'd been ready to talk, I'd have ridden up."

"I didn't vote against you. Didn't feel the Grand

Jury made a thorough investigation. Simply sent someone here to be sure the buoys were still lying on the beach. I know you too well to believe you've willfully or carelessly neglected the public welfare. Why didn't you tell me about the buoys?"

"I'm not a complainer."

"There *is* a reason why they're not sunk, isn't there?"

James nodded curtly.

"Well, for the love of heaven, man, don't keep that mouth clamped shut! You've been the toast of St. Simons. The people are proud of the lighthouse, proud of you."

"So it seems."

"Talk to me," Couper pleaded, dropping down on the lantern platform. "Give me your side of the story."

James remained standing. "You've asked too late."

"Too late to have spared you this unfortunate humiliation, yes. I accept blame for that, although my request for a delay was voted down. But it is not too late to vindicate you. James, I beg of you, don't spoil the good feeling of neighborliness you've enjoyed on our Island while there's still a chance to preserve it. We've had enough trouble over the church. It's a disgrace to us all that even the vestry can't act together in harmony. That the rector has been forced to sue us for his unpaid salary."

"That's no affair of mine."

"Yes, it is. We desperately need—unity. Further misunderstanding over your position cannot but add to the evil already upon us. You were treated unjustly, but for your sake, for the sake of us all, I plead with you to give me a chance to make it right. On my word, there's nothing I want more than to vindicate you with both the Grand Jury and our neighbors. Believe me, I didn't vote against you."

James rubbed a smudge from the inside of the window pane with his jacket sleeve. He was silent for a long time. "I believe you."

"I'm thankful for that much anyway!"

"I have to believe you. All night long, I told myself—if Jock hadn't accused me, too, it wouldn't be so bad, but I want to know every man who did."

"All the others on the Grand Jury." Couper said wearily.

The hard lines of James' mouth drew into a cynical half smile. "Page, both Demeres, the Armstrongs, Roswell King, Dr. Grant. No matter what I say now, the damage is done. I'm an outsider."

"We're almost all outsiders, if you look at it that way! Few of us have been here long. Only the Demeres and the Wrights came with Oglethorpe." Couper held out his hands pleadingly. "Why weren't the buoys sunk, James? Did Turner know? Wasn't it your duty to tell someone *why?* Isn't it your duty now?"

James didn't answer.

"A man doesn't need to talk as much as I in order to—give himself, but a word helps now and then. In a small place like St. Simons, a man *has* to give himself a little."

James' voice was hard. "There were reasons why the buoys were not sunk and I was not to blame. No one can say I haven't given my best to the building and keeping of this light—unless he lies!"

Couper sighed. "James, James. You force me to say this. For some reason known perhaps only to the Almighty, it is not enough for a man to give his best to a piece of work. He must give himself to people, too. We're a human society, however faulty; put here to help one another. If you were having insurmountable problems with those buoys, you owed it to us to let it be known. I don't see that as complaining. I see it as a fair giving of ourselves to one another."

Watching him closely, Couper saw an abrupt frown crease his friend's forehead—almost a frown of surprise. Had this overly conscientious man never seen himself as being unfair in his proud, stubborn silence? "Sometimes I wonder if you realize how you affect others?" Couper went on. "Now, don't flare up until I've finished. It will do no harm to hear me out. The Bible tells us we are to know ourselves. 'Know thyself' or some such phrase. Do you feel you—know yourself, James?"

"As well as anyone, I guess."

"I don't agree. We cannot know ourselves as long as we prevent others from knowing us. You live in a shell. Your arm is raised in a figurative gesture of defense against every person on earth except your wife!"

"Janie has nothing to do with any of this."

"I think she has. She's your hope. Whatever you do, never withdraw from her, too."

James turned his back.

"I share your humiliation, believe me," Couper said. "We've done you a great injustice by accusing you without your testimony, but maybe out of it you'll find yourself. Find yourself free of your protective shell, able to admit when you've made a mistake. Free to let us know you and respect you for *more* than your fine work. Free to admit your need of God—the rest of the human race. He created. If ever a man needed a woman, you need Miss Janie, but you need to make room inside for more than just you and your wife and children. For their sakes as much as your own." Couper stood up. "I know you've done what few men ever do—made a dream come true. You've built your lighthouse, but I've known for a long time that would not be enough for you. You grumble about the crowded little cottage. Even if you lived in a mansion, James, I believe you'd still feel crowded—in your soul." He paused for a moment. "When you're quite ready, I want to hear your explanation for the fact that those buoys are rusting on the beach. I want to clear your name. I mean to, if you'll let me. But far more important, I want to hear you say, or at least begin to act as though, you're tired . . . of being too full of yourself."

James whirled to face him. "You've already said I'm ungrateful. Are you calling me selfish now?"

"Not without enormous effort on my part. Not without deep understanding of how hard it must be for you to see yourself—otherwise a generous, responsible man—as too centered on the success of James Gould. On the infallibility, the excellence of James Gould's work. Pride and humility cannot dwell at ease within the same heart. Pride exhausts a man. Humility liberates." John Couper took a deep breath. "Now, I'll ride back. But—I'll pray every mile of the way that you'll take the first step toward freeing yourself—of yourself. In your case, that step could well be simply to explain to me about those buoys. . . . Only the Almighty can do all things perfectly. You can't, James. Neither can I. I'm learning that the hard way a bit more each day I live."

James heard the slow clump of his friend's boots echo down the lighthouse steps; stood gripping the window frame to keep from shouting after him. He thought, if I don't tell him now, I may never ... I may never....

In a moment, the tower door closed. Couper was gone. He looked toward Jekyl Island; past it to the open water. Perhaps he should have told Couper long ago why the buoys had not been sunk, but for the life of him, he could not see what his failure to complain had to do with selfishness. "John Couper's Almighty knows how hard I've worked to reach my goal," he said aloud. "I know the reason people have trusted me—Budge, Captain Barry, McQueen. Even Mama. They trusted me because I was willing to work like a slave and knew my business! You bet I've built my lighthouse, John Couper!" He stomped the solid floor of the lantern room. "And it's a damn good lighthouse. Why should I go groveling to a bunch of men who know nothing whatever about either building or keeping a light?"

Couper had left the trap door open. He slammed it. "Let them find out the truth for themselves. They could have asked Turner. Let them ask him now. If they decide to put a lesser man in my place, what do I care? Any Negro I own can learn to scrape salt and trim wicks and fill oil vats. *I* am a builder."

For the first time, the thought did not lift his spirit. He felt afraid. Of what? Of being dismissed as keeper of the St. Simons Light at a paltry fee of four hundred dollars a year? He had received more than that from the warring vestry at Christ Church for ten thousand square feet of lumber. He laughed drily. They might not pay their preacher, but they paid James Gould. He'd already made a respectable fortune in timber; he would be a wealthy man now except for the Florida Creeks. The final payment for the lighthouse was safely in his Savannah bank, added to what was already there. He had not been poor a day since he walked away from Granville. Why be afraid now?

One boot tapped the floor nervously. He felt caged in the tiny lantern room, caged in the one place where he had always escaped to regain perspective. Not today! Thanks to John Couper.

He stepped to the window which faced the cottage. At the foot of the garden path, Janie stood looking up at Couper, mounted, ready to ride back to Cannon's Point. In a moment, he saw the Scotsman reach his hand to her, saw Janie cling to it . . . go on clinging, as though she too were afraid.

He pulled up the trap door and ran down the stair.

Bursting into the cottage, he demanded, "You didn't tell him why the buoys had not been sunk, did you?" He gripped her shoulders, unable to soften his voice, furious with himself that he was only making her feel more threatened. "I ran down here when I saw you talking to him because I don't want you upset—but on the way down I got to thinking you might have told him."

"No, I didn't. I still don't understand why you've kept the truth about the missing chains and sinkers to yourself, but I'm sure you must have a reason."

He loosened his grip on her shoulders. "They'll find out in due time. I get on my knees to no man. And I want you to forget about the whole thing, do you hear?"

When she spoke at last, her voice was strangely flat. "Of course, I won't forget about it. I'm human. I love you. You're tearing yourself apart over a misunderstanding you could so easily remedy. Can you expect me to forget a thing like that?"

He stepped back. "You—you *want* me to explain to Couper?"

"Yes." Her arms went around him. "Oh, James, you're too good to suffer like this!"

"Couper says I'm selfish."

She pulled his face down, held his cheeks to hers. "You're the most generous person I've ever known," she said at last, "with everyone but yourself. James, I pray every day that God will find a way to help you begin to be fair to yourself. Even your dear friend, John Couper, could not persuade you to—"

"To—defend myself when I've done nothing wrong?" He pulled away.

"No. To be honest. Simply to tell the whole story."

"Janie, my letters to Washington are on file there. Five times I've written about those missing chains and sinkers. Three letters for funds to hire men to help sink the buoys. Let the Grand Jury check the Government files!"

She made him look at her. "James, James, how is it that a man of your intelligence can be so—"

"Pigheaded?"

"No. Blind. I trust your heart. I believe if you could only see that for some reason you've barred and closed yourself to people, you'd want to change."

"I don't need anyone but you."

"Yes, you do! Sharing yourself with our neighbors, confiding in Mr. Couper—none of this would lessen what you are or what we have together. Oh, of all women, I'm blessed. You've given yourself to me—wholly. But, my dearest, what if—what if something happened to me?"

"I doubt I'd try to go on living."

"That's what frightens me! I'm fine, I'm still young. But people do die. What would you do? How long would it take you to learn to find solace in other people if I died? In God? The longer you wait to begin opening your heart to someone besides me, the tighter the door sticks, James."

He sat down across the room. "I've not known I—was so cantankerous. Until this unjust Presentment, I seemed well enough liked."

"You will be again when it's all out in the open, but you're the one who has to unlatch the door. From the inside."

"Never was one to defend myself."

"Sometimes that's a virtue. Sometimes it's just plain stubborn. Especially when you're asked merely to explain, not defend."

Toward the middle of December, James looked up from the boxwood hedge he was planting around Janie's new flower bed to see John Couper striding up the beach from the Gould dock, waving a newspaper in the air.

"Have you seen the *Republican,* James?" he called. "It's all here—you're exonerated! On my way to Brunswick, but I had to stop to be certain you'd seen this. Will you shake my hand today, friend?"

"All right, Jock." James took the paper, read to himself the Notice which Couper had marked:

TO THE PUBLIC

10 December, 1811

In answer to the Presentment of the Grand Jury of Glynn County, published in the *Savannah Advertiser* of the 18th inst., the Collector of the Port of Brunswick begs leave to make a few remarks. The Presentment cast severe reflections on the Collector and the Keeper of the St. Simons Lighthouse, therefore, . . . I call attention to the fact that buoys for the use of St. Simons bar were sent from Philadelphia in the summer of 1810, but by some mistake, were unaccompanied by sinkers or chains and could not be placed on the bar. No time was lost, however, in sending for these appendages by Mr. James Gould, Keeper of the Light. To this date, the chains and anchors have not been shipped. During the time of their expected arrival, Mr. James Gould sent several proposals to the Government for funds needed to seat all buoys and was rejected or his proposals overlooked. I further wish to plead that the Grand Jury did not correctly ascertain that the occasional dimness of the light was owing to neglect, since the light is oftentimes and unavoidably obscured by fogs. The Collector, therefore, takes the liberty of considering both himself and Mr. Gould exempt from blame.

Joseph Turner.

James folded the paper, handed it back to Couper. "I'd decided, the first time I had a chance, to tell you the truth of it, anyway," he said, "but I'm much relieved. Turner's Public Notice will help more than any story of mine."

"It will right everything, James! Especially when I publish an apology from the Grand Jury."

"You may have trouble getting them to back you on that, Jock."

"I anticipate no trouble at all. The men will all be happy your good name has been cleared."

"Some will, I have no doubt," James said. "Others will prefer to believe that where there was smoke, there was also fire. I'm sorry about—my part in it, Jock. The way I turned on you. I was wrong not to tell you about the buoys. I aim to overcome the accusation entirely—or leave the Island. Will you come in for a cup of hot tea before you start across to Brunswick?"

Couper considered a moment. "Thanks, I'd better let the men get started while the tide's right. But, James, no talk about leaving St. Simons, do you hear?"

"I can't promise that."

"It's bound to take time to forget all this, but you've been cleared, man—cleared." He thumped the paper, then said slyly, "You could resign as keeper any time now with a clear conscience and buy that Sinclair-Graham land. Will we see you and Miss Janie at church? You've stayed away three Sundays."

"I expect I'll bring her."

"The Almighty can boost your spirit too, you know. He's partial even to old rams like us."

James stood watching his friend hurry back to the dock. Couper turned to wave before climbing into his plantation boat. The Cannon's Point oarsmen waved too.

His heart lifted. Maybe there's a chance I *can* pick

up my life here, he mused. Jock is right. I can stay on as keeper now, until *I* decide to go. No leaving in disgrace. I can make my own choice.

He looked at his tower. Could I build the kind of house Janie really deserves on part of the Sinclair-Graham land and still keep charge of my lighthouse by setting two of my people to tend it? Say, Abraham and Bozey or Tapo?

Back at work on the boxwood hedge, his mind seemed to clear at least about his next step. "I'll take Janie and the children to Savannah for Christmas," he planned aloud, tamping the earth around each root. "While they visit, I can look over the building prospects, perhaps invest in that house for the Bunches and Mother Harris. Once I'm sure I can make a good living by building in Savannah, I'll be free to decide—on my own—to stay here."

He dropped the shovel and hurried up the path to the house, feeling ashamed for having just that minute realized he owed it to Janie to tell her that her husband was no longer accused of grossly neglecting the public welfare.

Chapter 36

From the moment they arrived in Savannah, nine-year-old Caroline Harris took charge of Jimmy and baby Mary. Slim, dark-eyed Caroline appealed to James. He thought her not unlike the way he had been at her age—willing to assume responsibilities beyond her years, somewhat shy, but confident that she could finish whatever she started.

Decorating the fragrant cedar tree which he and Stephen set up in the bay window of the dilapidated old Harris home had been a festive occasion, only shadowed by the absence of Father Harris and John Mackay and Charles. James felt he was discovering at last that Christmas is a personal time, for families especially. A time when everyone feels free, even eager to show affection. Until this year, he had been an onlooker, amused by Janie's delight in the season. Pleased that he had been asked to occupy John Hartley Harris' place at the head of the table at Christmas dinner, he made a warm effort to be as responsive as he remembered Harris to have been.

Christmas afternoon, when he would rather have gone off alone to read the newspapers, James remained instead in the big, cluttered parlor, trying to ignore the noise and talk and laughter as he caught up on the latest news from Washington. The United States had, rightly or wrongly, already claimed West Florida in the Louisiana Purchase. Now it looked as though Clay and Calhoun and the other war hawks in Washington were determined to make a conquest of Canada and East Florida as well.

He intended to stay in Savannah through January, not only to assure himself that he could make a good living as a builder, but to sound out Samuel Bunch on available town houses. Another month in town would also give him an opportunity to discuss the threat of war with his banker and other leading Savannah business friends.

He tossed his newspaper aside. Janie had begun to play carols on her mother's old harpsichord. Stephen and Caroline and Mother Harris were singing. Three-year-old Mary was having a nap on a blanket in the big worn leather chair where he had sat the first afternoon he visited the Harris home. He went to look at the child, already so like Janie, then got down on the floor with Jimmy to build houses with new Christmas blocks.

"I worry some about your mother living in that decaying old place," James said early in the year, as he drove Janie home from a shopping trip in their new carriage.

"Mums is sturdy. Don't worry. You've been so generous with her, dear James, buying those new warm clothes—" She laughed. "I can see her, wrapped regally in the long padded velvet cape, admiring herself in her chilly parlor on a winter day. Mums has humor, you know. She'd entertain at tea in her new cape and think nothing of it, if the house seemed a bit chillier than usual"

They drove in silence for a few minutes, James pleased to be riding beside her—his wife, the most beautiful woman in town, sitting proudly in their new green and gilt carriage, buttoned to the chin in a fashionable plum-colored redingote. He chuckled.

"What's so funny?"

"Just thinking about this carriage, our new clothes—and the keeper's cottage. But don't worry," he added quickly, "I'm not going to grump."

"Good!" After a moment, she asked, "Has Samuel tried to borrow money from you this visit?"

"No. I think he has a little, right now, from one or two pieces of real estate he's sold."

"I hope he doesn't owe it all."

"He might make a decent living if he'd only stick to selling real estate. He's learned Savannah property; he's a good talker. In fact, before we go home, I intend to have him show me a house or two from his listings."

She stiffened. "James, you're not still thinking of buying a house for my family, are you?"

"If Samuel can find one I consider a good investment, yes."

"Please don't! I'd be so—humiliated to think you felt you had to spend your hard-earned money to make Mums comfortable. Especially when you long so for a larger home yourself"

"That will come. I'm not buying anything until we know more about all this talk of war with England."

"Are there more threats?"

He shrugged. "The trouble with Napoleon may simmer down any day now. Britain would be free to fight us."

"I don't understand any of it!"

"I doubt that even President Madison understands the whole picture. I only know I don't intend to make a move of any kind as long as there's a chance of a naval war."

She slipped her arm through his. "I just want to cling to every happy moment of—right now."

He waited to tell her his big news until they had almost reached the South Common. "I've also satisfied myself that I could earn a fine living building houses here in Savannah, Janie. I've had the offer of three sizable contracts."

"Do—do you mean to move us here?"

"No," he laughed. "I have no plans to move us to Savannah. I just needed to be sure I could do well in the city, that's all. Don't you understand that?"

"Yes. Yes, I understand why you needed to be sure. But, now that you are sure, could we just do what I keep feeling we ought to do? Cling to every lovely moment? Never permit even one to slip by unnoticed? Unappreciated? Can you be content with that—for now?"

He drew up in front of the Harris house, turned to look at her tenderly. "I do cherish every moment, Janie."

"I know you do," she smiled, suddenly cheerful again. "Of course, one must look ahead sometimes.

For instance, there is a definite reason why this summer of eighteen twelve will be important."

He helped her from the carriage. "Is it a secret?"

"Not from you. But I do want to stay in our cottage by the tower at least until after August, James. If I do well—and oh, I pray I do—I hope to give you another son then. I *very much* want a son born beside his father's lighthouse. Am I silly?"

On the afternoon of August 12, soon after war had been declared, in the midst of a wind and hail storm so severe it dislodged their porch roof and broke a window in the lighthouse tower, Janie's second son was born, as easily as an apple falling off a tree.

"A very good thing he was so willing to join us," she said as James knelt beside her bed. "I don't believe poor Larney could have held out much longer."

"Larney's baby isn't due 'til next month, is it?"

"No, and she's ashamed to be feeling so poorly a whole month ahead of time. I'm glad our new son was considerate of her. He caused very little trouble for either of us. Do you like him, James?"

He looked at the golden-haired child tucked against her breast. "Yes," he said softly. "Yes, I like him fine. The little fellow looks like a Massachusetts buttercup." He grinned. "Am I going to be consulted on his name?"

"I'll consult with you, but I already have a very strong conviction."

He stroked her cheek. "You didn't think I really expected I'd have anything to say about it, did you? What are we going to call him?"

"You never mention your brother, and I don't need to know why you've been estranged. But, might it help you if we named our new son—Horace?"

"Horace?"

"Horace Bunch Gould. Does that—displease you?"

He looked at the child, then at Janie. "No. No, it just surprised me. I'd like that name fine. Elizabeth and Samuel will be pleased, and—it'll take a load off my mind. My brother's mind, too, I expect."

Chapter 37

Larney was opening the bed when John bumped wide their cabin door, his arms loaded with firewood.

"You gonna' hab our front do' lookin' lak eber other niggah's do' bangin' it wif dem oak logs," she grumbled.

He dumped the wood on the floor and began to build up the fire. "Go look. Dey ain' a mark on it!"

"You tote plenty ob wood to Mausa Gould?"

He straightened up from the fire, grinning. "Co'se ah did. Effen ah don' keep dat new baby boy warm up, ah gonna hear from *you.* Ah never see nobody carry on 'bout no white baby de way you do 'bout dat un."

"Dat li'l Horace be *Larney's* boy—jis lak her own gonna be." Tears began to stream down her cheeks. She went toward him, her arms out. "John, what make me cry lak dis?"

He held her for a long time. "All de folks, dey 'pends on Larney fo' dis and 'pends on Larney fo' dat, 'til you got yo'sef b'lievin' you made outa pig iron. You ain't, sweet woman. You made outa warm, brown flesh an' good red blood. An' you's carryin' our fus' baby!"

He led her to the bed, gently pushed her down, plumped the pillows and began to take off her shoes. "Ah needs to make my wife a new pair ob shoes. You wear this'n plumb through."

She pulled him down to her. "John gonna hab to make a pair ob mighty li'l shoes 'fore long."

"When yo' reckon?"

"Three weeks, I spect. Miss Janie, she gonna hep me."

"Kin dat li'l thing hep wif a birthin'?"

"Sho' she kin! While dat li'l Horace was a comin' into dis worl', Miss Janie, she pay 'tention to what ah do. Me an' her, we got it all plan. She gonna come ober here to our cabin—Mausa Gould gonna look after de other chillurn—an' you gonna git Miss Janie what she need, den behave!"

"Reckon will Miss Janie feel dat strong by den, Larney? Mausa Gould, he kin git Rhina from Cannon Point. Rhina be good at birthin'."

"Me an' Miss Janie don' want *no*body. We ain' had nobody wif her—we don't want nobody wif me."

John patted her swollen abdomen. "We gonna hab us a *big*, fat baby."

"A big, strong son."

"How you so sho'?"

"Larney be de sebenth daughter ob a sebenth daughter, don' forgit."

She moved over so he could stretch out beside her.

"What we gonna call our boy?" he asked, his head on her shoulder.

"July."

"July? When he be born in September?"

"We git married in July, John! July be de bes' month ob all to me, long as ah lib. We call 'im July."

"Where you s'pose our son gonna grow up? By de water an' Mausa Gould's lighthouse? Or some other place?"

Larney sighed. "Dat good man got thunder in his min' dese days. He don' talk no more'n he eber did, but he don' hab no peace in his heart eber since dat Gram Jury do 'im so wrong. Seems lak he tryin' harder den eber, but ah kin hear de thunder in his min'. He might could do mos' anything."

"We done set de buoys now. Ain' no more to accuse. You know what ah thinks, Larney? Ah thinks Mausa Gould ain' gonna res' 'til he build Miss Janie a fine, big house. He be a proud man."

She didn't answer for a long time. "What come to me is he tendin' to buy lotsa lan', build Angel Miss a big house—an' plant cotton."

"But las' year he tol' all his fiel' hans we might would be movin' to S'vannah to hep 'im build houses."

"Mm-mm. Ah don' care what he tell 'em las' year, Miss Janie, she wanna lib on S'n Simons. An effen

Miss Janie wanna lib here, here's where we gonna lib."

John sat up. "Effen you sho' Miss Janie wanna stay here, den why don' he buy lan'?"

"You kin be so dumb to be so smart! He ain' ready. Be thirteen niggahs enough to farm a big piece ob lan'? Who be de blacksmif? Who be de groom? Who be de carpenter? What black woman Mausa James got but me to bear 'im mo' hans?"

"You know what ah heerd de las' time ah rode to Cannon Point? Margin, he tol' me long time ago he hear Mausa Gould say he don' b'lieve in ownin' slaves."

"Hm. Be de bes' thing effen he own all de po' niggahs. Ah ain't neber think he 'tended to buy me in S'vannah dat day. He buy Larney to save her from—" She broke off. "*Dis* baby gonna be mine—to keep! Mine and yo's, John; ah gits to keep our son."

"An dat's why"—John leaned down to kiss her—"it don' make no diffurnce where he grow up. He gonna hab bof' a mama an' a papa. Mausa Gould, he tell me he neber sell one ob us away."

"Sing holy unto de Lawd!" she whispered.

"Yeh. Sing holy unto de Lawd."

Just before suppertime on September 19, Janie laid a wriggling little bundle on the bed beside Larney.

"You all right, Miss Janie?"

"Yes," she whispered. "He's a beautiful boy! I'll get John. Try to rest."

On the cabin porch, John jumped to his feet.

"Larney's prophecy was right," Janie said. "You have a son, John. You may go in to her now."

Without another word, she hurried down the steps and across the yard to the lighthouse cottage. When James opened the door, she fell into his arms, weeping.

"Janie, what's wrong? Larney's all right, isn't she? And the baby?"

"Yes," she sobbed. "They're both—fine."

"Then what is it? What's happened?"

She reached in her apron pocket. There was a

letter from Elizabeth. "Mums—is dead, too. I didn't tell you because I was afraid you wouldn't let me—help Larney."

As soon as Larney was able again to look after Janie and the children, James left for Savannah. At Old Town, before he boarded the schooner, he posted a letter for John Couper with George Abbott, the new Frederica postmaster. In it, James had tried to express his gratitude for the loyalty and patience Couper had shown him. He had waited months to write the letter, thinking as clearly as possible, as he gained the perspective of time, about his own behavior over the Presentment.

> I swear to you, Jock, I did not realize I was being unfair. After having lived all these years believing I would succeed only if my work was perfect, I am finding it hard to learn that is not enough. As a boy, my mother's approval seemed only to come—if indeed it did come—after I had performed some piece of work well. Except for Miss Janie, I have always felt I was liked according to the quality of my work. I am a proud man. Too proud. I may die that way, but as I look back, I begin to see that perhaps you were partial to me for myself. I have tried to be generous with the Harris family, and am now on my way to Savannah to do what I can in their most recent bereavement—hoping to follow some of your advice about sharing myself as well as my means with them. I must have seemed like a testy school boy whose sum had been questioned. Be sure, I am still giving thought to all you said to me.
>
> Your friend,
> James Gould.

Hour after hour as the schooner plied the inland waterway to Savannah, he thought about his letter. *I doubt I made myself clear, but ever since I likened myself to Mama and how shut out she always made me feel, I've understood a little about what Jock meant. Janie, too.* He remembered a Proverb Lemuel Haynes used to quote: "Wisdom resteth in the heart of him who hath understanding."

"I've come to do what I can to help," he said, when he called a family conference in the Harris home. The circle of faces around him seemed pitifully small—only Elizabeth and Samuel, Caroline and Stephen were left. "Whatever indebtedness remained from your father's estate, Elizabeth, I mean to clear up. The same for your mother's estate. Stephen is fifteen and needs further schooling. Do you still want to be a schoolmaster, Stephen?"

The tall, serious boy looked at James with a worshipful expression. "Oh, yes, sir! More than anything, I want to teach. Do you mean you might help me? I'd gladly pay you back every dollar!"

"I don't like loans. I'll pay your school fees, buy your books and needed clothing, but you must earn your board and keep. We'll discuss suitable masters for you later." Without giving Stephen a chance to thank him, he turned to Caroline. "Young lady, how old are you now?"

"I'm ten."

"Would you like to teach, too?"

"I—I don't think so." She looked at Elizabeth. "I just want to be of help to—whoever needs me in the family."

"I need you, Caroline dear," Elizabeth said quickly. "Caroline will always have a home with me, James. I'll tutor her. She'll be a splendid homemaker some day. The child is more unselfish than any I've ever known."

James looked at Caroline for a long moment. "That's the nicest compliment anyone could receive," he said quietly. "Even hard-working, helpful children are often selfish. Some never get over it. You're fortunate, Caroline."

The girl's face reddened. "I didn't know I was unselfish," she said shyly.

"Maybe that's best." James smiled at her.

"Thank you ever so much, anyway, but I don't believe I need anything at all."

Samuel Bunch laughed. "Just imagine not needing anything at all! Seriously, dear brother, you're more than generous, but I do want you to know that—well, in a matter of just a few months from now, I'll be able to handle all the family financial matters myself."

James and Elizabeth exchanged glances.

"I'm quite sure neither of you believes me," Samuel went on pleasantly. "But this time it's true. I'm earning a manager's salary at the hotel and selling real estate on the side, when there's time. One more decent commission and I'll put a down payment on the hotel. I mean to own it myself very soon."

"I wish you success," James said, "and perhaps, in case you're still in need of a commission when I'm ready to buy, I can find the property I want through you, Samuel. I'm still considering buying a well-built house here in Savannah. Only. . . ."

Bunch jumped to his feet. "How extraordinary that you should be looking for the very property which came on the market yesterday!"

"Not now, Samuel," Elizabeth said. "I believe James was still talking."

Samuel smiled. "Terribly sorry, old man."

"I was merely saying that I regret not buying a good house before the War—before Mother Harris died. She needed a warm place to live. As soon as I can see my way, I want to do all I can from now on, to protect Janie against any more grief."

Tears stood in Elizabeth's eyes, but Samuel was striding up and down the room, proclaiming the excellent value of a well-built house on Bryan Street.

"Part of the Hampton Lillibridge estate, James. In all Savannah there's no bargain to compare with the Lillibridge house! Not only has it been kept in excellent repair, his widow has now remarried a Mr. Joseph Grant, who, in order to turn a quick sale, recently repapered and repainted the entire edifice. Its very design should please you as a New Englander. Most unique architecture for Savannah. Mr. Lillibridge came from Rhode Island, you know. Gave his Savannah town house a typically Rhode Island gambrel roof. Not an old dwelling, either. Built in seventeen ninety-seven—just fifteen years ago. Located in a fine neighborhood."

"I'm hard to fool on houses, Samuel, but when the time comes, I'll consider your advice. I mean to leave money with you, Elizabeth, to shore up this one until we see which way the war clouds blow."

"James, I don't know what to say."

"Neither do I, dear Elizabeth," Bunch agreed. "You are most generous, sir. But surely, since you're in Savannah, there can be no harm in our having a look at the Lillibridge house today?"

"None at all. I intend to."

That afternoon, James walked from room to room of the four-storied house on Bryan Street, ignoring most of Samuel's enthusiastic remarks, making quick sketches of all four floors to show Janie; taking particular note of the brick flooring in the basement—a good way to keep dampness from the rooms above. The cellar rafters and joists passed his inspection, as did the good floorboards, well laid with wooden pegs. He liked the 32-inch dado on all the first-floor walls, approved the simple woodwork and the design of the wooden mantels. Even the windows appeared to be in good condition. All except the attic dormers were six over nine double-hung sash.

Back on the street, he sketched the exterior, a handsome, tall, wide clapboard house, two rooms deep. Samuel Bunch was right. At twenty-five hundred dollars, the Hampton Lillibridge house was an excellent buy.

"What do you think?" Bunch wanted to know, as they walked back toward the Harris home.

"I hope it's still on the market next year. If so, I'll buy it."

"But, James"—his brother-in-law made one last attempt—"the price could be far higher by next year!"

"Not if the War goes on. The blockade will dry up port cities like Savannah. I'll wait."

The War seesawed with victories on the seas for both sides. The Frigate *Constitution* defeated the *Guerrière,* but the following year 1813, the British *Shannon* was victorious over the *U.S. Chesapeake.*

On the Georgia coast the action seemed remote except for the money squeeze from the blockade, but there were signs. Elizabeth wrote that Fort Wayne in Savannah had been strengthened; a regiment known as the First Regiment of Georgia Militia, made up of the Savannah Volunteer Guards and the Republican Blues, had been organized and was always on duty in the city. Still, most of the fighting was taking place at the North, and because he was convinced Savannah was not a special object of British ill will, James began to agree with Couper, James Hamilton, and his other neighbors that the South would see little or no action, but would feel only temporary economic effects.

On a sunny May afternoon, James and Janie walked along the beach, discussing the purchase of the Savannah house, while Jimmy and four year-old Mary scampered ahead with their new puppy.

"I need to confess something, James," Janie said, after assuring him once more that she did like the sketches of the Lillibridge house, that she did think it a good buy. "I've had trouble talking about it with the excitement you feel, because I've been considering only my own shame that my family needs charity—even from you." She linked her arm in his. "Now, wait—let me finish. I've stopped feeling ashamed. I've come to see that perhaps owning the Lillibridge house would have great meaning for you, as well as providing my family with a lovely place to live. Is that true, James? Do you need to own the house?"

"Yes. Yes, I would like to own it."

"Then, by all means buy it!"

He was smiling slyly. "Even you have to admit our family is getting too large for the cottage, Janie." He stopped walking, turned her toward him, a big grin on his face now. "Shall I buy part of the Sinclair-Graham tract too?"

"Are we that rich?"

"I can afford the Savannah house and at least eight hundred acres of the Sinclair-Graham tract. Later on,

I'll add to it, after I've built the kind of house you deserve."

She said quietly, "What about leaving the lighthouse, my dearest? Can you give it up without too much heartache?"

He nodded. "That's all settled in my mind. Turner says Bozey and Abraham can tend the light if I inspect it three or four times a week. I'm convinced I can trust them both. John's calling Abraham 'Old Lamp Black' already!"

"Will you—buy more people to plant all that land?"

He scuffed a broken sand dollar with the toe of his boot. "I'll have to, I guess. But not for a while. John Couper says he'll rent fifty field hands."

They walked on. "If everything is perfectly clear in your mind," Janie said, "about the Savannah house, about the land, then I must confess something else. Oh, nothing bad. I've tried not to influence you, but I'm so happy I could cry—that you don't want to leave St. Simons Island!"

Early the next week, leaving Horace with Larney, James and Janie and the two older children set out happily for Savannah, by land this time, in their carriage, floated by flatboat to the mainland.

While Janie and Elizabeth and Caroline packed for the move from the old Harris place on the South Common, James, with Samuel in tow, bought the Hampton Lillibridge house for twenty-five hundred dollars. From his bank, which held title, for two thousand dollars, he bought eight hundred acres of the Sinclair-Graham tract. Both deeds were drawn June 1, 1813. He paid the total amount of forty-five hundred in cash, and for the first time since he left Bangor, felt in complete charge of his life.

Mary had been reminding him in every letter that she still didn't know the new baby's name. He had waited until he had his own affairs arranged exactly as he wanted them. With Janie the center of his world, it had been years since he had suffered any bitterness over his brother's marriage to Jessie. Something far deeper had kept him silent.

Now, the silence could end. Horace still worked at the mills, still lived in the house which James had built and paid for. He had no children. James Gould was the father of two sons and a daughter, held title to a large tract of rich cotton land and a valuable piece of Savannah property; he was in the exhilarating process of designing a home for Janie. And he had built his lighthouse.

Next month, when he sent Mary's money, he would write to Horace.

Chapter 38

Bangor, Massachusetts
12 August, 1813.

Dear James,

Since I'm not much of a letter writer, this will be short on words, but long on gratitude. Old brother, you have made me a happy man, although none of us can guess why you kept your secret so long. I am writing this, as you can see, on the first birthday of my namesake, Horace Bunch Gould. I guess the Bunch comes from your wife's family, but I forgive you for that, since his first name comes from me. Just be sure you know that, as you said in your letter, a big old load has rolled off my shoulders, too. I felt bad about our estrangement, but I didn't know what to do except to just keep plugging along. We are all three fine, except that those Britishers are soon likely to cause us a mite of bother. They say we're sitting on a powder keg these days.

You sure have been successful, and I'd say it's a good thing one Gould boy turned out so well. We all knew it would be you, but I'm still the good-looking one. No doubt your son Horace is also handsome, intelligent and charming. He'd have to be with my name. Good luck and joking aside, if you happen to go to church, pray for us up here—for a few months anyway.

Your Brother,
Horace Gould.

The year 1814 brought a smoldering stalemate in the fighting along the Canadian border, and James' anxiety over his family in Bangor increased, in spite of his absorption with the plans for his new house. Through the years, because of his bitterness toward Horace, he had simply closed his mind to worry even about Mary. He could no longer do that. Raids by the Royal Navy would surely begin again with the spring thaws up there, and with greater intensity. Napoleon had fallen. The British were free to hammer at the United States Navy and the coastal cities.

James thought a lot about both men and war. "In war," John Couper had said, "feelings replace logic. You'll see, James. I honestly doubt old Wellington wants an American campaign. His cold, military mind would see the futility of it. This country is too vast. But British civilians feel otherwise. I'll wager they tighten the blockade, perhaps invade New York by way of Canada, perhaps even move down to attack New Orleans from the sea."

Yet in spite of dire predictions, on St. Simons Island there was no hint of war, and James could sense Janie's growing involvement in the design of their new house. Night after night, when the lamps had been tended for the early part of the evening, the children put to bed, they dreamed and planned. James filled the parlor floor with drawings of the front elevation, to face Frederica Road, and of the rear, with a wide veranda, to face the expanse of marsh and the Black Banks River. He was going to build a Georgian-style, two-storied house, of brick and tabby, the roof line simple and steep. Because bricks were more plentiful, there was no longer any need for a one-chimney house. His house would have two, built entirely inside, into the longitudinal walls.

"How will our chimneys look from the outside, James?"

"Like this." He sketched the roof line, the chimneys standing along its ridge several feet from the gables. "I don't know exactly how many feet, yet," he explained. "That will depend upon the size of our rooms. Let me show you what I mean." He sketched an interior, showing how each chimney would provide two fireplaces back to back on the main floor, then two more back to back upstairs, allowing a fireplace in each of the second-floor bedrooms. "Do you think eight rooms and a kitchen built off to one side—connected to the big house by a pass-through—will be large enough, Janie?"

"Oh, yes! A mansion. Just be sure Larney's kitchen wing is spacious and airy. I've felt so sorry for her here with that fire heating up our little low-ceilinged kitchen in July and August."

"Don't worry about Larney's kitchen. The exterior of the house will be in better proportion, anyway, if I give her a twelve- or even a thirteen-foot ceiling."

She sat on the floor beside him, fascinated, as room by room, their house began to take form. Together, they decided on a spare bedchamber instead of an extra sitting room at the right rear of the wide central hall on the first floor. Janie sat up very straight trying to picture it. "Now let me think—we'll have four bedrooms upstairs, a wide downstairs central hall with a spare chamber on one side at the rear and our dining room across from it. Do I have that right?"

He nodded. "And to the front, downstairs, on either side of the hall, the parlor and drawing room."

One eyebrow arched, doubtful. "Do you think we really need a drawing room, James?"

"Every fine house has one."

"But wouldn't you like to call it a library—so for once in your life you can find your books—and sit in there for long talks with your men friends? The way Mr. Couper does?"

He looked at her face in the firelight. "Except for Couper now and then, Janie, I'll always prefer just to be with you."

On Christmas Eve, as he came out of the woods, his arms loaded with cassina and cedar, James saw young Jones ride up to the cottage with the mail. "Evening, Lewis."

"Evenin', Mr. Gould. Seems like you're gettin' ready for Christmas. I brought a letter from way up in Massachusetts this time! From your family, I guess. I hear they're feelin' the War up there."

James dropped his evergreens, took the letters and papers, thanked Lewis, called "Merry Christmas" as the boy rode off, then stood looking at the letter from Mary. He suspected bad news. If so, he would rather read it alone. He started for the lighthouse, then stopped. To do that didn't fit with his new resolve, his sincere effort to change the part of his nature which always withdrew in a crisis. He picked up Janie's Christmas greenery and headed for the cottage.

After admiring his selection of berried cassina boughs, Janie asked, "Is something wrong, James?"

"I don't know yet. Where are the children?"

"I told them they could stay on the beach a little longer, since it's Christmas Eve. After all the rain we've had, they've been like wild bucks in the sun today."

He took the mail from his pocket. "We have a letter from Mary. I'd like us to read it together. Before the children come in."

Beside her on the sofa, he broke the seal and began to read aloud. " 'My dear James and Janie, We have no idea when you will receive this, but we pray God has kept your hearts from too much anxiety over our well-being.' " He stopped. "Janie, Mary wrote this on the fifth of September! It's been held up almost four months. We still won't know they're all right now."

She pressed his arm. "Read it, dear. At least, we'll have some idea of what's happening."

" 'We have not been harmed, but Horace, along with the other one hundred and ninety-one men of Bangor, had to sign a document admitting themselves to be prisoners of war to the British Advanced Military and Naval Forces in the Penobscot, and pledging themselves not to take up arms against Great Britain during the present hostilities. By signing this document, the men are admitted to a parole of honor, so that, except for the dreadful suspense because Horace is liable at any time for British military duty against his own country, he works as usual at Budge's Mills.' " James sighed. "What a crazy war this is! Poor Horace."

"Shall I finish it for you?"

"No. There's not much more. 'It is a strange and frightening time, but the three of us thank God that we are safe so far. I'm sure I haven't made it clear yet, James, how happy you have made Horace by naming your second son for him. He talks about you all the time now and seems so proud of his brother's success. Horace jokes about being a prisoner of war, but I know he needs our prayers. Please let us hear if the War has disrupted your lives. Horace said to tell you he would have written another letter just to give you the shock of your life, but he is not permitted to communicate with anyone. You both have the love and concern of all three of us, Horace, Jessie and Your loving Sister, Mary Gould.' "

"Oh, James, I somehow feel they're going to be safe."

"I hope so. Guess Horace is right. Might as well joke about it."

"But, aren't both sides talking over a settlement now somewhere in Belgium?"

"Ghent. I'm afraid the British are in no hurry to settle. We didn't stand by them against Napoleon. It must still rankle. Neither side can win. It's a futile war, any way you look at it." He began to pace the small room. "Americans are rankled too, with Cockburn and Ross burning the Capitol and half of Washington just last month."

"James?"

He came back to sit beside her, trying to smile. "Do you have an opinion about this senseless war, Mrs. Gould?"

She kissed his nose. "No, sir, I have none—except that all wars are senseless. But it's Christmas Eve. I think we can believe, since there's been no fresh news of fighting up there, that your family is still unharmed. Besides, we're going to trim a Christmas tree for our children tonight."

"That's right, we are."

"What will we call our new plantation? Have you thought about that?"

He grinned. "I wonder if any man ever got the skillful handling I get!"

"I'm serious, James. We'll have to give it a name."

He thought a minute. "Well, the land may have belonged originally to an old Englishman named St.

Clair or Sinclair. Knowing how you British pronounce Saint as Sin, I think his name was St. Clair. Anyway, I purchased part of what's known as the old St. Clair holdings. Why don't we call it New St. Clair?"

"That's perfect! And do you know why?"

"No, why?"

"Because living there will be a whole new beginning for us." She jumped up. "Now, will you run out to the beach and find our offspring? It'll be dark in no time. I'm sure Larney has their supper ready."

"Guess I'd better check the lamps too, before we eat." He lighted his lantern at the fireplace and started for the door.

"Mr. Gould of New St. Clair—before you do any of that, would you please hold me close for a minute?"

In January, on the afternoon of the fifth rainy day in a row, they watched from the front window as John Couper galloped up to the Gould stable, turned his horse over to Abraham, and headed through the downpour to the cottage.

"Get Jock a change of my clothes, Janie," James said, as he hurried to the porch. "Come inside out of this weather, Jock! Miss Janie's laying out dry clothes. What brings you down the road on a day like this?"

The men shook hands, but for once, John Couper was not smiling, as he stomped sand from his boots. "I'd welcome dry garments, James—and a hot cup of tea. Then we must talk."

Janie served the men tea and left them alone before the fire.

"I'm going to get right to some disturbing news, James," Couper said. "There's trouble. How far it will go, no one knows. I took my family and young Miss Ann Page to Cumberland for a house party the Shaws and Nightingales gave last week. While the young people danced, there was a knock. Shaw opened the door of Dungeness to—Rear Admiral Sir George Cockburn and a host of Royal Naval officers and men!"

James frowned. "They'd just landed on Cumberland?"

"According to their boasts, immediately after having taken St. Marys by force. We were held prisoners two days at Dungeness—for what earthly reason, I cannot say—then released to return here under guard."

"Are the British on St. Simons now?"

"At least the men who convoyed us back in our own boats. James, I don't want to be pessimistic, but I expect an invasion—right out there." He pointed to the Sound. "Perhaps not a bombardment. They know we're unarmed. One of the handsomer Royal officers, a Lieutenant John Fraser, who took an immediate fancy to my daughter, assured her they had no intention of harming us."

"Just hold us captive, eh? Much the way my brother is being held up North in Bangor."

"Yes. I look for them to occupy St. Simons, destroy what property they choose, steal our horses and cattle, and entice away as many of our Negroes as possible."

James got up, stood with his back to the fire. "And, as with my brother, there's nothing we can do."

"Nothing beyond attempting to convince our Negroes that the flamboyant promises of wealth and freedom cannot be taken seriously. James, may I stay here for a day or so? From your vantage point—both here and surely from the tower—we can see the British approach the outer bar. I'd have time to ride home before they could make a landing. I want that margin of warning."

"You're more than welcome, Jock. Make my trips to the tower with me tonight. I doubt they'd try to land in the rain, but from up there, we can see them if they do."

By midnight a west wind had begun to blow the rain clouds out to sea. James and Couper stood inside the lantern house scanning the dark waters of the St. Simons Sound.

"Quite a difference from the last time I was up here with you, eh, James?"

"That was a bad night for me. Worse than this one, in many ways."

"I still treasure your letter. And you're to be congratulated for the way you weathered that Grand Jury storm. Proof of how much confidence both Turner and the Treasury Department have in you, that they now prefer you to retain your commission as keeper even after you're living up the Island some five miles from the lighthouse."

"I'm glad to keep control of the light. It means a lot to me."

Couper chuckled. "No one could doubt that who watched just once, as I did tonight, the way you handle those lamps."

James was silent for a while. "Jock, do you suppose the British will try to—damage my tower?"

"I don't want to cause undue concern, but if they've a mind to destroy—"

"They'll have to bombard it from the sea," James said grimly. "I'll guard it with my own gun."

"Well, now, we could be borrowing trouble. They took such a trouncing at New Orleans several days ago, it's quite possible we'll suffer merely boastful occupation. Enough to make Cockburn's reports look better. Our charming spy, my daughter, felt that Lieutenant Fraser rather looked forward to his 'visit' to our Island. Indeed, Ann is so smitten with him, I think she anticipates their coming."

"Jock, look!"

A bloom of flame burst into the darkness above Jekyl Island.

"That's duBignon's place! They're burning it down. We can expect them here tomorrow."

John Couper rode home at first light next morning, but the anxious residents of St. Simons waited through twelve interminable days before two British ships of the line, seven frigates, and a number of smaller vessels dropped anchor off the outer bar.

James spent almost every waking moment in his tower, his long glass trained on the enemy ships, but still another three days passed before he saw the British begin to lower the boats. He and Couper had decided that nothing would be gained by James' attempting to misdirect the landing party. "Our Island roads are well cared for," Couper had said, "and we're too small for them not to locate the larger plantations sooner or later."

When nearly three hundred officers and sailors poured onto the beach, James stood by his lighthouse, his gun leaning inside the door just out of sight.

"You've a splendid tower here," an officer called, as he strolled in the direction of the lighthouse.

"We think so."

"Are you the keeper?" he asked pleasantly.

"I am."

"I had an uncle once who kept a light—important work. I wonder, sir, if you'd be so kind as to tell us how to find a plantation owned by a Mr. John Couper? Also, the plantation of a Mr. James Hamilton."

James gave them the directions they wanted, watched them march west, along the wooded bridle path toward Hamilton's place.

"They're aiming to steal Hamilton's horses, I'm sure," he told Janie. "Horses and Negroes and wagons. After all, they need a way to get up to Cannon's Point. I'd give my right arm if I could let Couper know they're coming, but I suppose he's hidden everything he can hide, anyway."

"Will they come back here to harm us, James?"

"Hard to say. Funniest invasion I ever heard of! The officer who spoke to me seemed more like a man on a holiday."

In spite of his efforts to conceal them, John Couper lost eighty Negroes, James learned later. Pierce Butler lost more than a hundred. The Demeres and Wyllys lost people too, but the three weeks of occupation were strangely uneventful, almost pleasant. The

Islanders were permitted to go about their affairs without hindrance. Some of them—the Coupers, at Ann's insistence—and the Hamiltons even extended hospitality to the invaders.

No move was made toward damaging his lighthouse, and when in mid-February James stood on the beach with Jimmy and watched the British forces weigh anchor and sail away, he had suffered no loss whatever.

"Is the reason they didn't bother us because you're so much smarter than anybody else, Papa?"

James grinned down at the eight-year-old. "No. There wasn't much the British could do to a piece of overgrown land up on Frederica Road. That's all we've got here, so far. Your guess is as good as mine why they left the lighthouse alone."

"They were terrible mean men, weren't they?"

"Well, that's a puzzler too. Funny kind of invaders. Seemed to have a good time here, mostly. I guess Mr. Couper's daughter aims to marry one of them when the whole thing blows over."

Word had finally reached St. Simons Island late in February that the Treaty of Ghent had been signed with Britain on Christmas Eve of the preceding year. The Battle of New Orleans had been fought for nothing. The British had no cause to occupy St. Simons, to rob Couper or Butler or Wylly of their Negroes—no reason to invade Cumberland or St. Marys or to burn part of duBignon's buildings on Jekyl.

Where, James wondered, were the stolen slaves now? Poor devils. In spite of his losses, John Couper had kept his promise to rent fifty men to help clear the New St. Clair land. Even with the added help, it would take two years to prepare the entire tract for crops. James would have to plant as he cleared. After the new house was paid for, his available money would be running low.

Well, he was not going to worry this time, he decided, as he climbed the tower on his forty-eighth birthday. The War was over. His family in Bangor was safe. He had Janie and the children—and a new project ahead. Now that it was spring, he could survey the timber and begin clearing his land.

Chapter 39

Alone at the New St. Clair house site, James studied the results of his day's work. In the upper right-hand corner of the sheet on which he had drawn the front elevation were the words: *Staked out by J. Gould, Builder, 20 November, 1816.* Some day his children would look at the plans and know that on this date their father had himself driven the stakes and stretched the lengths of cord that marked the shape of his second dream—the house where he would live out the remaining years of his life with Janie.

He could hear John's shouted instructions to the Negroes who had spent the day clearing out undergrowth, and he knew John was attending to the collection of hoes, shovels and scythes before allowing the people to quit. Larney's John would make a superb driver for the new plantation. The big man had supervised all the clearing done so far—almost two hundred of the eight hundred acres, including the house site; had followed James' timber survey to the letter. Today, John had been his choice to help with staking out the Big House. John understood him, shared his excitement. Together, they had also selected the site for what John called "Larney's cabin," down a winding lane just north of the Gould house. They had even laid out the lane, John chuckling: "Gotta git dis road nice an' smooth. Larney, she gonna be makin' tracks up it runnin' to Miss Janie an' de chillurn."

By spring, he and John expected to be able to plant at least three hundred acres. Drainage was a problem anywhere on St. Simons. The Island's highest point rose only eighteen feet above sea level, but New St. Clair was naturally better drained than most plantations. They could work out a system of drainage ditches once the house was actually under way.

James looked up into the soft, cheering color of the

scarlet tupelos and sweet gums standing around the area where he would erect a white picket fence. For the sheer joy of it, he stepped off once more the distance between the fair-sized oaks and pines, the one enormous magnolia left standing—not too close to the roof for limb damage when hurricanes struck—spaced to let in enough sunlight for the garden of imported trees and shrubs and roses he meant to plant for Janie. With the specimens of native plants Couper had promised, she would have a garden at New St. Clair so rare, so beautiful, she would never again miss her walled garden at Mills Ferry. He could see it all in his mind's eye: the house, the picket fence, the garden, the whitewashed tabby quarters barely visible down the shady lane, a large barn and blacksmith shop set back by the cotton gin, the fields of pink-white cotton in bloom.

Within three years, he predicted, New St. Clair would be producing enough long-staple cotton to assure that neither Janie nor the children would ever want for anything. Unlike Elizabeth, his wife would be free of worry and debt, even after he was gone.

He swung into the saddle for the ride down Frederica Road to his lighthouse. There would be barely enough time to pick up their mail from Postmaster George Abbott's place just across the way fom New St. Clair, and still reach the tower before dark. He had worked too late, but he would be able to tell Janie that their house was, at last, staked out.

Near the entrance to the tower, suspecting that James would be late, Janie had built a small fire. From this he could take a flame on the candle in his tin lantern and carry it directly up to the waiting lamps.

From the parlor window a few minutes later, she saw him hand his horse over to Jimmy and stride across the sand with the easy swing of a young man. I've never seen him so happy, she thought, so full of purpose. She watched him until he closed the tower door behind him. Somehow I must keep him convinced that our new home means as much to me as it means to him. It does, really, because building it makes him happy; still . . . the peculiar rush of anxiety swept over her just when she had determined it must never come back. A sense of uneasiness, for no reason that she could discover, about James himself. Larney thought the feeling stemmed only from having to "tear up dis li'l place" and move again. Janie didn't agree.

Four-year-old Horace startled her as he ran into the shadowy parlor, and threw his arms around her.

"It's dark in here, Mama!"

She returned his hug. "Mama thought you were in the kitchen with Larney having your supper."

"I come to find you."

"*Came*, dear," she corrected him gently.

The boy clung to her. He had been behaving in this odd way for days, as though he too felt anxious.

"We'll light our candles just as soon as we see Papa's first lamp go on. Let's watch together, shall we?"

She held back the curtain so he could see out the window. "Now . . . any minute now, you'll see Papa's light; then, before he can come all the way down those stairs and across our yard, you and I will have our house blazing with light too—for Papa."

One by one, the lamps began to glow at the top of the lighthouse, the lantern to turn slowly red, white and blue.

"Do you want Mama to tell you something, Horace?"

"What?"

"I've been proud every night I've seen Papa light those lamps. I'll never, never forget the night—long before you were born—when Larney and John and Mary and Jimmy and I stood out there and watched them come on for the very first time."

The boy was quiet a minute, then he said, "Mama, it's dark in here!"

She kissed him and hurried to light every candle. Horace clapped his hands, his blue eyes shining.

"In just a year or so, we'll be moving into our fine new home Papa's building for us and then we'll have even more candles to light!"

The boy's face clouded. "I wanna stay here! I'll be afraid of the woods."

"Of course you won't be afraid. Papa's going to buy a pony, there'll be the Black Banks River, you can go fishing—and climb big, tall trees. Why, those are going to be the happiest years of our lives, Horace!"

A letter from Elizabeth was in the mail James brought, but Janie waited to open it until after tea—until after he had told her all about staking out their new home. She had never known him to talk so much or so excitedly. With one ear, she listened to Mary and Jimmy arguing out in Larney's kitchen, but could also hear Larney singing to Horace; so the fuss must not be serious.

"I've sent off the first lumber order," James was saying, his face alive with the same interest she had adored when he was building the lighthouse. He seemed still stronger now—mature, successful, sure of his future. With the building of this dream, no little Port Collector would be breathing down his neck; he would have no faceless officials in Washington to please.

"George Abbott said my lumber order would be posted tomorrow, when a schooner for Darien stops at Frederica to pick up the last of Couper's cotton. The cotton market's opened up again. I tell you, Janie, I was smart not to buy that land and try to farm it during the War. The blockade would have cost me hundreds, maybe thousands of dollars. Forgot to tell you—I've decided to retain Lively and Buffton as my Savannah factors. Made that decision riding home tonight."

She refilled his teacup. "It all sounds terribly exciting, James."

"By the way, we must make a trip to Savannah just as soon as I have the framework up on the new house."

"Good! Any special reason?"

"To begin buying our furniture. You're going to be the mistress of the most graciously furnished house on St. Simons Island!"

"Shouldn't we buy just what we'll need at first,

though, until you've planted another crop of cotton?"

He smiled at her. "We'll buy whatever you want. My girl's lived like a cracker long enough." He looked into the fire, his smile gone. "Janie, Janie, I don't think you know, even after all these years, that I live for one reason—to make you happy."

The elusive anxiety crept over her again. "But I do know, dear James. I wonder sometimes if *you* know that my happiness depends upon being certain—down deep inside—that you're all right. Are you?"

"We're together, aren't we?"

"Yes. For always, we're together." She paused. "But, as excited as I am over our new home, I love you so much I could live the rest of my years right here in this cottage—because you're here, too."

He leaned back, sighed. "You've been so patient about this place. But just wait. Just wait 'til you see the new one."

She knew he was in no mood for serious talk; still, the words tumbled out: "James, please be glad that I'd love you even if you'd failed at everything you ever tried—like Samuel!"

"I don't see how that's possible. I wouldn't be me if I settled for failure."

He hadn't flared up, as she feared, but his answer didn't reassure her. "Try, please, James, just for a minute, to put yourself in my place. I'd never known material security until I married you. I never dreamed of living in a fine house, of wearing fashionable gowns, of having servants. I dreamed only of finding one man to love. I found him." She was sitting very straight. "None of this makes sense to you, does it?"

"Are you worried about something?"

"I don't know. Help me, James! I—I need to be sure you're *all right.*"

He looked at her with a puzzled half smile. "Janie, I've never been better in my life. What is it you're trying to say?"

She had gone too far to back down now. "I hadn't meant even to let it show, least of all to tell you. But, for quite some time, I've—I've felt—uneasy about you."

"What on earth for?"

She took a deep breath. "James, I'm afraid you don't have enough faith—in God. And it frightens me."

He stared at her with a look that drew her to him painfully, as she had been drawn to Horace just an hour or so ago. A look of vulnerability which she longed to wipe out. James must never be vulnerable, never be exposed to any more pain or suffering. She would have to think of some way to give him back the joy and exuberance of this day. Instead she heard herself say: "God has helped me through every loss and heartache I've ever had. Since I was a little girl, I've felt close to Him. I've never had to hunt wildly to find Him when a blow struck. I already knew He was there." She wanted to take his hand, but didn't. "I need desperately to know that if something happened to your new dream, our house, your success as a planter—one of the children, even to me—you'd know where to turn for help."

After a long time, he said very quietly, "I'll think that through, Janie. I promise. But you must promise me to stop worrying. I imagine God's nearby in the good times, too. Like now." He moved a table with a lighted candelabra near the sofa where she sat and picked up Elizabeth's letter. "Here, you haven't read your mail yet."

She forced a smile, opened the letter and began to read aloud:

17 November, 1816

My dear Sister and Brother,

After only five days of searing pain in his head, Samuel lost consciousness and on 16 November, he left me. We buried him today. Of course, he left more debts than assets.

Except for his military uniform and equipment, valued at $50, and four young Negroes, Dick, Tom, Fanny and Louisa, nothing. Nothing and yet everything. For all the years of our life together, I loved Samuel and he returned my love. My legacy is a large and welcome one. Do not ask me to visit you because I must increase my tutoring now and begin at once to learn to live in this house without him. Stephen is teaching and will help all he can. Caroline is my comfort in every way. We send you deepest love and I will write more soon.

Your sister, Elizabeth Bunch.

Janie threw herself in his arms and sobbed, "Oh, James, this is what I mean. Still another death! I—need help—from God, don't you?"

She felt his arms tighten about her. "Yes, Janie. Yes, I do." They clung together for a moment, then he said, "I'll buy Samuel's Negroes. Perhaps pay off the indebtedness, if it isn't too much."

"No." Janie pulled back until their eyes met. "No. Buy the Negroes if you need them, but give my sister the chance to preserve—her dignity."

"Whatever you say. I only meant to help."

Chapter 40

In a little under two years, the house was finished. The cedar and oak paneling had been rubbed and polished, the garden planted, even most of the furniture was in place, when James and Janie said good-by to the keeper's cottage and moved up Frederica Road to New St. Clair.

Janie had asked John and Larney to follow with the children because James had set his heart on carrying her over their threshold—with no one present, not even the children.

When he set her down in the wide central hall, they stood for a long time holding hands. . . . Finally, he whispered, "We're here, Janie. We're here."

Tears brimmed in her eyes. "Now, don't scold because I might cry, James. After all, this moment is the beginning of all the rest of our lives!"

She let him lead her from room to room, knew he was watching her. Asking, "Do you like it, Janie? Do you really like it?"

Side by side on the spacious, columned veranda overlooking the marshes and the Black Banks River, she felt his arm slip around her waist, heard him whisper, "I'm going to love you even more in the years ahead, Janie. I don't see how I can, but I know I will." He hesitated. "I—don't know how to say this, but I want you to know, I think I *do* have faith, now."

Their first dinner guests were the Coupers. James was impressed that during the years at the cottage, Larney had forgotten nothing about proper serving. Her baked fish, prepared with what she called Gould dressing and adorned with sprigs of fresh dill, and the crusty roast lamb were excellent. Somehow she managed to go back and forth between her steaming kitchen and the table looking neat and dignified.

After dinner, James led Couper into the high-ceilinged parlor, leaving Janie and Rebecca sipping coffee and talking at the table.

"I hope Miss Janie doesn't forget and jump up to help Larney," James joked. "She's been so used to helping."

"You'll simply have to buy a few more people," Couper said, still in the doorway, obviously appreciating his first glimpse of the room.

James watched, as his friend's admiring glance took in the soft blue wood-block wallpaper which Janie had selected to go above the oak wainscot, the full-length shuttered windows. Neither spoke while Couper bent down to touch the thick nap of the bird-and-rose-patterned carpet, then moved slowly from one piece of furniture to another, running his hand over the tapestry-covered easy chairs, feeling the patina of James' brass-bound, mahogany travel desk and that of the cherry table on which it rested.

"James Gould, a man could not ask for a finer house!"

Offering a chair, James went to the lacquered corner cabinet just brought from the Frederica dock yesterday, opened the arched glass doors, took out a bottle of port and two glasses. "I've waited for this moment, Jock. First time in the twenty-odd years we've known each other I've had a presentable place to welcome you."

Couper sniffed the bouquet of the wine, nodded approvingly, then lifted his glass: "To the master and mistress of a splendid new estate! May their years together be long, filled with joy and happy bairns!"

"I'm obliged to you." James sat down. "Seems as good a time as any to tell you our fourth child will be along at the end of this year. Miss Janie informed me last week."

Couper leaned back. "I congratulate you on the birth of still another child, but my wishes go far beyond the end of this year of our Lord, eighteen eighteen. You've made your second dream come true—your second big dream—and you're only fifty-one." His eyes twinkled. "Let me tell you a secret. The sixties are even better than the fifties. Mark my word when you reach them. Your children will be finding their places in the world, your house and Miss Janie will grow more beautiful with the years—and you more content. God has blessed you."

"It's been a long time coming," James said.

He felt Couper studying him intently. "You've matured with every struggle, James. I've watched you. Watched you come out of your protective shell a wee bit more with every joy and every knock." He sipped the port. "You're still not a communicant of our church. Have you thought any more about it?"

"No, but I expect Miss Janie does. More than she lets on."

"We've had a time of unrest in Christ Church, as you know."

"My sister, Mary, writes from Bangor that the church there is like a battlefield, too. Doesn't make sense to me. Always seems as though a man should find peace in a church."

"You're an idealist, James Gould. Churches are made up of faulty human beings."

"Must make the Lord wonder."

"I'm sure it does. But I don't see that this lessens my duty to do what I can as a peacemaker. You have to admit we've a fine rector in Dr. Matthews now."

"I like to hear him preach, but I'm no judge."

Couper set down his glass. "James, we need you. I have a dream of my own and you're part of it. I know that if we had our own little church building, the way we planned it before money got so tight and all the trouble took place over the rector's lawsuit, the people would rally round it."

"Sounds plausible. I remember two Sundays we've gone to the wrong parishioner's house. You change around so."

"Exactly. The cotton market's good again; I feel the time is right to begin taking subscriptions once more and build that church up there under those big trees at Frederica."

James nodded. "Make a lot of folks happy, I expect."

"But you're still talking like an outsider. My dream is for James Gould to design and build it!"

"I've never built a church, Jock."

"You'd never built a lighthouse, either."

James grinned. "If you're trying to get me in the church by rousing my interest in another building project, you're wasting your time. When and if I become one of you, it will be because I feel I've enough faith. Am a good enough man."

"Ah, but you'll never be good enough, my friend. Not a man on our vestry is good enough. If man had natural goodness, the young God on His cross would have been wasting His time!"

James stared at the fire. "I—I hadn't thought of it that way."

"I don't know that I ever thought about it like that, either, until this minute. But it seems to me all our trouble at Christ Church sprang from some of us believing we *were* good—knew it all—down to the last jot and tittle of Holy Writ! It just might be that the kind of man God needs is an openhearted, *helpless* man. Not one who has all his life under control, the reins securely in his own hands."

"I've been helpless," James said. "I don't feel I am now."

"Neither do I, at the moment. I suspect I would be if tragedy struck my life in some way. Meantime, I go to the church on Sundays, do what I can. I doubt that many people feel much need of God when all's right for them. That may be one reason for going regularly to God's house. A man grows familiar with Him by those regular visits while life is good. He's acquainted with the Lord then, when the heart breaks. Knows the Almighty's at hand. To be counted on."

James threw a small log on the fire, stood watching it catch, his back to Couper. "I remember hearing my wife say something like that. Sounds sensible."

"Yes, it does. If you hadn't spent so much time with me at my house, you wouldn't be so sure of my friendship."

James nodded. "You're not ready to build a church any time soon, are you, Jock?"

"Dr. Matthews has set a goal for eighteen twenty."

"That's a long time off. In the meanwhile, don't tell Miss Janie you asked me to build it. I don't want to get her hopes up. I just want us both free to enjoy New St. Clair—and each other."

The birth of their fourth child, a girl, whom James insisted upon naming Jane, was so easy, Janie felt well enough to help Larney when *her* daughter, Ca, came just a month later.

"Look lak Angel Miss an' me's runnin' a race," Larney laughed, the afternoon James took Horace to play with July, a week or so after Ca's birth. "Me an' her's had two boys, Horace an' July, an' now two girls be born—all jis' a month apart! Don' mah lil Ca be beautiful, Mausa Gould?"

"She certainly is, Larney. I hope she grows up to be half the woman her mama is."

"Ah thanks ya. But be dem new little niggahs you done bought in S'vannah takin' proper care ob Miss Janie an' her baby?"

"They're doing fine. If Horace gets in the way today, just send him home."

"Effen you thinks Larney's boy eber git in her way, you jis' don' know how him an' me gits on!"

The four Negroes bought from the Samuel Bunch estate seemed genuinely happy to be living in the country. Larney's John was his driver, leaving James free to keep the accounts, to handle in person the sale of the timber from his cleared land. With John in charge of the field hands, he could go to Savannah to confer with his factor; to Darien, where he now transacted part of his business at the newly opened bank there. So far, even his twenty new field hands appeared satisfied. He had been saddened at the news, in Mary's letter, of Lemuel Haynes' illness, but James no longer wondered if his friend would condemn him for owning slaves. There was no other way to grow cotton.

He and Janie had become communicants of Christ Church Frederica, and she had thanked him so sincerely and so often for going into the church with her, he felt a twinge of guilt that he hadn't done it before. His life was too good, though, he was too content, too busy, to feel guilty for long about anything. They had lived almost one year at New St. Clair, and it had been the happiest, most rewarding year of his life.

One evening not long after they became a part of the fellowship of Christ Church, Janie insisted that he hear the children's prayers for a change. "You don't know what you're missing, dear, by not hearing your own children ask God to bless their papa and keep him from harm."

"All right, ma'am." He laid aside his newspaper. "But you wait for me right there in that chair. I suspect a trick, anyway," he teased. "Think you might get your old husband to say a word of prayer too?"

It took no time at all for Jimmy to finish, and Horace did a fairly swift job of spieling off the names of all the people he wanted God to bless. But when it was Mary's turn, she jumped up from her knees, threw her arms around her father and whispered, "Oh, Papa, before I pray for you I just want you to know that I ask God to look after you because—because I love you more than anybody in the whole world!"

Back in the parlor, he breathed deeply of the gardenia-scented June breeze stirring the curtains at the open windows and looked across the room at Janie. She had fallen asleep, her head resting against her chair, her book slipped to one side in her lap. Maybe she was just all tuckered out, he mused. Maybe that's the reason she wanted me to hear the children's prayers. I'll carry her upstairs in a few minutes. I haven't done that in a long time. But first, I'll enjoy her. Will I ever get to look at Janie all I want to? Her straight, perfect nose she had given to Mary. Lucky little girl. Mary appeared also to have her mother's long, graceful neck and dignified bearing. Dignified without being haughty. Her mother's naturalness, too, which through the years had helped him ease gradually out of his shell.

Janie stirred slightly, still half asleep, and clutched at her book. He looked closely at her hand, slipping again from the page. Janie had strong, square little hands, but this one was badly swollen. He looked at the other hand. Swollen too! Had she put on weight since Jane's birth? Her face did look more rounded; even her normally slim throat bulged unnaturally.

He took a step toward her. She opened her eyes and smiled up at him—and when she smiled, he knew something was wrong. Her cheeks contorted with the smile like a child with mumps!

"I must have dozed off," she said. "I haven't felt quite well today."

His heart caught. "How, Janie? Tell me how you feel—does anything hurt?"

"My head aches, for one thing. It's ached a little for several weeks. But more today."

He lifted her in his arms. "I'll take you up to bed."

"Thank you, I'd like that. Only please don't sound so worried."

"When you're ill, I worry!" His voice was almost cross.

"But it's only a headache and a little puffiness in my face."

She clung to him as he climbed the stair.

"Your ankles are swollen, too—and your hands."

In their large front bedroom, he laid her tenderly on the bed Larney had turned down and began to undress her. She lay against the pillows, barely lifting her feet for him to take off the buckled slippers.

"I'll feel fine soon, dear James, I promise."

"Should I get Larney tonight?"

"Take her away from that adorable little Ca when I've only a headache and swollen ankles? Mums' ankles always puffed when she sat a long time without moving about. It's nothing, James. Kiss me, then get undressed and come to bed. I want to sleep on your shoulder."

Before he left for the summer, Dr. Grant had bled Janie twice and prescribed complete rest. "I'm not a woman's doctor, Gould. I just don't know. I frankly don't know. I refuse to give you either hope or cause for alarm."

Janie was willing to obey Dr. Grant's orders to rest. During the steaming days of July and August, she stayed still while Larney tried to keep her comfortable by waving a palm-leaf fan. When Larney had to leave her for other duties, which now included nursing both Ca and little Jane, Louisa, the older of the two Bunch girls James had bought from the estate, took her place. Louisa, on strict orders from James, never spoke unless asked a direct question.

One day Janie said, "Louisa, don't you feel free to talk to me?"

"Mausa Gould he say not to talk none."

"Oh, that man!" Janie laughed. "Is he making life miserable for you and the others because I'm in bed for a while?"

Louisa nodded yes, then shook her head, no.

"Mr. Gould doesn't mean to be cross, if he is."

"Maum Larney say he be a good man."

Janie smiled at her. "He's the best man on earth," she said. "Louisa, would you like to go to Savannah with me? Mr. Gould wants me to be under a doctor's regular care so I can get well faster. And Larney can't be spared here."

Louisa's face broke into a smile, and her white teeth—too big for her tiny face—popped. "Yes, um. Ah don' wanna be *no* place but wif you, Miss Janie."

"I feel like taking a ride in our carriage, James," Janie announced the day before they were to leave by schooner for Savannah.

"You feel up to that?" He studied her face, almost afraid to hope. "Why, Janie, except to sit on the veranda a few times, you haven't been out of bed for over two months! Do you think it's safe to—take a *carriage ride?*"

She held out her arms to him. "Are you refusing to take me, Mr. Gould?"

"You know better. Anything you want. Anything!"

"All right," she said almost pertly. "With all my heart, I want to see our—your lighthouse again."

She hadn't seemed so bright in such a long time; he was caught between hope and fear. "That's a long trip, Janie. Can't you just take my word for it that Abraham and Bozey are doing fine with the light? Why, since you've been sick, I haven't had to ride down more than twice a week."

"I'm not worried about the maintenance of the light," she said firmly. "I want to see—your tower. If we go now, I can watch you light the lamps again, yourself. I need that—buoyancy I always felt every time I saw my husband light the lamps in his lighthouse."

The expression on her face was itself a radiance. "All right, Janie, just as soon as Louisa can get you dressed, we'll go."

Larney sat by John on the front seat of the carriage. Behind them, Janie, dressed by her own choosing in the old high-waisted yellow muslin she wore when they lived in the keeper's cottage, lay back in the curve of James' arm.

The five-mile journey down Frederica Road had never seemed so long to him, but Janie enjoyed every mile. Now and then she sighed deeply and rubbed one swollen ankle against the other—in pain, he knew—but she chatted off and on all the way; mentioned how the woods had changed since she saw them last; noticed every molting nonpareil and cardinal, every mass of bindweed entwining its full lavender bloom in the palmetto and scrub oaks. Still, not once did she let go of his hand.

When they rolled down the old lane, in full view of the lighthouse, Janie ordered the carriage drawn up close beside the narrow front porch of the cottage.

"I'll watch from here," she said, smiling, as he climbed out. "I'm a little weak to stand. But, wait"—she handed him his old tin lantern from the floor of the carriage. "You'll need this to light your lamps, and the stair is always dark this time of evening."

He kissed her and walked toward the tower, signaling Bozey and Abraham not to follow.

After lighting the lantern from the small fire kept burning at the door, he began numbly to climb the familiar spiral stair. With every step, rejecting the fear that hammered at his mind. . . . *No, Janie! No! No!*

His strength had drained away by the time he reached the trap door. He was relieved to find it open. From habit, he set his lantern up ahead of him on the floor, and hoisted himself into the little room. From habit, also, he began to check the oil supply, to trim wicks. Then, although it wasn't quite dark, one at a time the lamps flared.

When they were regulated to suit him, he opened a window and stepped out onto the railed gallery.

The sea was smooth, dark, at low tide; the afterglow blood red, unmarked by a single cloud. Strange to find a plain sky in August. He could see far out to the deep water beyond Jekyl Island. Not a shred of mist anywhere.

Clear. A wholly clear sky.

"Oh, God," he breathed, gripping the railing with both hands. "Oh, God, let this be a sign that she'll get well!"

He must go back to her, but not for this one moment—one moment in which to ask help for himself . . . courage to go on living if he lost her.

The gray beach below was spattered with little pink pools, reflecting the afterglow; tracked back and forth by gull and term and willet and piper. For more nights than he could remember, he had stood like this on the gallery looking out from his tower . . . looking until he could bear it no longer without sight of Janie . . . and then had climbed inside, to run down, round and round to the ground, to the cottage where Janie waited.

This night, if only God would give him the courage he lacked himself, he would run down his spiral stair to be—whatever she needed him to be.

His gaze moved painfully up the beach, to the dark cottage where their carriage waited.

Slowly he relaxed his grip on the railing. He stood straight. He could go to her now.

The afterglow touched her yellow muslin dress, her uplifted face. She waved to him triumphantly.

He waved back.

Afterword

In the issue of the Savannah newspaper, *The Daily Georgian,* dated January 21, 1820, there appeared this Notice:

> The Friends and acquaintances of Mr. James Gould and those of the kindred family of his late consort, Jane Harris Gould, are requested to attend her funeral from the Bryan Street residence of Mrs. Elizabeth Bunch this afternoon at 4 o'clock.

Janie did not die of the illness for which James had placed her under the Savannah doctor's care. She improved and was ready to come home when the great Savannah fire broke out on January 11. When she and her family were forced to flee the Lillibridge house and take refuge at the home of a neighbor, she contracted pneumonia, died and was buried in the Colonial Cemetery before James could reach her. I have heard that on the completion of the Christ Church building later that year, his plans to move her body back to the St. Simons churchyard were thwarted by a hurricane. Janie's now unmarked grave must be near those of other members of the Harris and Bunch families whose names are cut into one flat granite slab in the old Colonial Cemetery; but most of the other main characters in *Lighthouse,* as in *New Moon Rising* and *The Beloved Invader,* are buried in the churchyard at Frederica on St. Simons. The Lillibridge house has now been moved to St. Julian Street in Savannah and fully restored.

Since the novels which comprise the St. Simons trilogy were written and published backward in time, perhaps a brief explanation is in order. The reason is simple: I found the material in that sequence. What began as a single novel, *The Beloved Invader,* grew, at the suggestion of my editor, into three books based on the story of the descendants of James Gould.

Lighthouse, although written last, is chronologically the first in the trilogy. This has presented a difficult and often confusing task covering a decade of work so absorbing, so a part of my life, that I shall be bereft without my "people."

Still, through the ten years, I have been rewarded with enduring friendships among the descendants of James and Janie—Colonel James Dunn Gould, Jr., who owns James' old travel desk; Mr. Potter F. Gould; Commander Horace Bunch Gould II; Mrs. Deborah Diggs; Mrs. Jeff Powell; Miss Clara Marie Gould and her cousin, Mrs. Barbara Whitlock, who found valuable family documents for me in the Glynn County Courthouse; Mrs. J. H. Bruce; Mr. David Gould; Mr. Joseph Gould; Mrs. Eustace Shelfer, and Mr. and Mrs. James Dunn Gould III, who have permitted me to keep James' old tin lantern beside me as I worked. James' great-granddaughters, Mrs. L. W. Everett and Mrs. Douglas Taylor (my late, dear friends) now lie in Christ Churchyard, but to me, they are not dead; from the beginning, Mary Everett and Berta Taylor were my mainstays, and my memories of them go on cheering me. I have received only encouragement and enthusiasm from every member of the Gould family, and the expression of my gratitude to them and the real story of the writing of all three novels will have to wait for a future book, now being planned to share the entire experience of finding the Island and the people who have so influenced my life.

I must here thank at least some of the many other persons who have helped in concrete ways through the writing of *Lighthouse*: Mr. Bernard Berg of Ocmulgee National Monument, Macon, Georgia, and his son, Mr. Andy Berg; Mr. and Mrs. Paul C. Nobbs, Sr., of Granville, Massachusetts; Mr. and Mrs. Charles Morton of St. Simons; Miss Frances Pitts of Duluth, Minnesota; Miss Kathy Roach of Bangor, Maine; Mr. G. M. Strader of Lyons, Georgia; Miss Easter Straker, Lima, Ohio, Mrs. R. W. Hayden of Blandford, Massachusetts; the Misses Sarah and Mary Plemmons and their mother, Mrs. Lorah H. Plemmons; Mrs. Emwyn Fendig, Mr. Marvin Long, and Mr. and Mrs. Johnnie Wilson of St. Simons Island.

Miss Nancy Goshorn of Charleston, West Virginia, not only handled much of my early research but has been in hourly involvement with me from the first page of the story of James Gould, along with her aunt, Miss Mary Jane Goshorn, and her next-door neighbor—my mother, Anna S. Price.

As with the writing of *New Moon Rising,* Mrs. Burnette Vanstory, author of *Georgia's Land of the Golden Isles,* again helped with factual research in furnishings, wearing apparel, and, especially through the Archives in Washington, D.C., in securing specifications, letters, and other documents related to the lighthouse itself. I am most grateful to her and to Mr. Richard A. Everett, widely known historian at The Cloister, Sea Island, Georgia, for careful reading and minute criticism of the manuscript. I also thank them both for their understanding that novelists, unlike historians, must be permitted some latitude in both data and dates. I acknowledge help also from Mrs. Lilla M. Hawes, Director of the Georgia Historical Society of Savannah, and from her assistant, Miss Marian Brown; from Miss Bessie Lewis, historian of Pine Harbor, Townsend, Georgia; Mrs. Mary M. Dickenson, Granville, Massachusetts, Public Library; Mrs. Esther Bartlett of the Bangor, Maine, Chamber of Commerce; Miss Helen C. Haydon of the Utica, New York, Public Library, and prompt, courteous, year-long cooperation and assistance from Mrs. Dorothea Q. Flagg of the Bangor Public Library. I again was able to count on Mrs. Fraser Ledbetter and Mrs. Lillian Knight of the St. Simons Public Library; and there is no adequate means here to thank or commend the personnel and facilities of the Brunswick, Georgia, Public Library, not only for personal interest and efficiency, but for the superb source material they were able to find for me. In particular, I am grateful to the director, Miss Theo Hotch, to Mrs. Harriette Hammond, and Mrs. Virginia Shields. Part of the Spanish East Florida material was obtained for me by Miss Dena Snodgrass of Jacksonville, and Mr.

B. I. Pennington and Captain Alfred A. Brockinton of St. Simons offered graphic, firsthand information on lumbering and the handling of the frigate sequence. Mr. Alfonza Ramsey and Mr. Monroe Wilson educated me in the art of roasting a pig over an outdoor pit, and I am especially indebted to my cooperative "nautical expert," Harbor Pilot Lawrence Gray. Mr. Alfred L. Hartridge, now of St. Simons, supplied a description of the only known portrait of James Gould and a copy of Janie's silhouette, along with other family letters and documents. Mrs. Gladys Fendig, author of *Native Flora of the Golden Isles,* again graciously answered my many questions concerning trees and wild flowers. At the Georgia Department of Archives and History in Atlanta, I am indebted to Mrs. Pat Bryant, Miss Beatrice Fairchild Lang, Mrs. Mary Reeves and, in particular, to Mr. Marion Hemperley. Again, I had ready access to the remarkable resources of the Margaret Davis Cate Memorial Library at Fort Frederica National Monument, where I especially thank Mr. Lawrence D. Roush, the Superintendent.

In spite of emergency surgery and a heavy writing schedule of her own, my dearest friend, Joyce Blackburn, not only has given me minute-by-minute encouragement but has created, in our home in the woods at Frederica, the best possible atmosphere for writing and managed somehow to give me more hours of careful, critical assistance than on any other book I have written. I must add that her two biographies, *James Edward Oglethorpe* and *John Adams,* were invaluable for clarification of the historical and political background against which James Gould lived his life. Joyce's mother, Mrs. Leroy Blackburn of Mt. Vernon, Indiana, helped with hard-to-find details and a steady flow of inner strength and confidence.

Lighthouse is dedicated to the gentleman who, without my realizing it until we met late in 1969, is responsible in a very real way for the entire trilogy. Mr. Walter C. Hartridge of Savannah, one of the South's leading historians, is the grandnephew of the late Agnes C. Hartridge, whose unpublished manuscript aroused my initial interest, and it was Walter Hartridge who, as a boy, urged his Aunt Agnes to write *The History of the Goulds of New St. Clair and Black Banks.* Beyond that, for countless weeks, he worked without letup, searching out valuable materials on the Bunch, Harris, and Gould families—motivated only by his sheer interest and involvement in history and in what I have attempted to do with their story. I could not have written *Lighthouse* without him, and the meaningful plus is the gift of a cherished friendship with Susan and Walter Hartridge and the lovable members of their Savannah household, including young Walter, Miss Gloria Green, and their dog, Elizabeth.

When I endeavor to communicate my gratitude to Miss Tay Hohoff, my editor, words grow stubborn. I can only say again "Thank you" and wonder if she will ever recognize the extent of her creative influence on me as we have worked together through all three books of the St. Simons trilogy. I speak for Tay Hohoff, too, I'm certain, when I thank our careful and caring copy editor, Mrs. Peggy Cronlund, for another piece of beautiful work and Elsie Goodwillie for still another expertly done typescript. In view of some unavoidable obstacles in my path, the deadline might not have been met without Elsie Goodwillie and my long-time friend, Miss Lorrie Carlson of Chicago, who so obligingly and skillfully helps with my mail.

The remainder of James Gould's life is told in *New Moon Rising;* a still later chapter in the altogether colorful history of St. Simons Island and the center of its culture, Christ Church Frederica, in *The Beloved Invader.* An author doesn't thank her characters as a rule, but I must thank mine. With few exceptions, these were real people who lived and suffered and loved and died on the enchanted little coastal island where I hope to live out the remainder of my life. James Gould, his children, his grandchildren, their "people," Larney, John, Ca, July, Adam, Bozey, Abraham—his friends, the Coupers, the Pages, the

Kings, the Wrights, the Hazzards, the Abbotts, the Wyllys, the Caters, the Demeres, Anson and Ellen Dodge and James' granddaughter, Anna Gould Dodge, are all my friends too. In their separate ways, each has added dimension to my life. And St. Simons Island, off the coast of Georgia—even in the midst of encroaching 20th-century technology—still holds and welcomes us all.

Eugenia Price

St. Simons Island, Georgia
March, 1971

ABOUT THE AUTHOR

EUGENIA PRICE has won a devoted readership of millions who find pleasure and comfort in her deeply religious, inspirational nonfiction. Her novels, too, have achieved bestselling stature, and she is truly at home in the delightfully mixed combination of novels based on historic truth, such as *New Moon Rising* and *LIGHTHOUSE.* Miss Price was born in Charleston, West Virginia, and was educated at Ohio and Northwestern universities. In 1960, she and a friend discovered St. Simons Island, the true setting of the story of the Gould family. Researching the history of Christ Church Frederica on the island, the author discovered an unpublished manuscript, written years ago by one of Horace Gould's granddaughters. From this manuscript, Miss Price wove the brilliant and colorful saga of the Goulds. The author now lives on St. Simons Island.

Her previous books include *Beloved Invader, A Woman's Choice, Learning to Live from the Gospels* and *Just As I Am.*